William Whiting Crane, John Hawkswell

Autobiography And Miscellaneous Writings of Elder W.W. Crane

William Whiting Crane, John Hawkswell

Autobiography And Miscellaneous Writings of Elder W.W. Crane

ISBN/EAN: 9783337029593

Printed in Europe, USA, Canada, Australia, Japan

Cover: Foto ©Raphael Reischuk / pixelio.de

More available books at **www.hansebooks.com**

AUTOBIOGRAPHY

AND

MISCELLANEOUS WRITINGS

OF

ELDER W. W. CRANE.

COMPILED AND PUBLISHED

BY

JOHN HAWKSWELL.

SYRACUSE, N. Y.
A. W. HALL.
1891.

PREFACE.

This volume, comprising the autobiography and selected articles from the pen of Rev. W. W. Crane, which appeared at various times, and for several years, in the *American Wesleyan*, has been prepared with the hope that it may be one means of inciting to the love and practice of righteousness and truth; to the yielding of becoming at one with Him who was meek and lowly in heart, and went about doing good; to honor and love all men, and be compassionate toward domestic animals.

It would have seemed well had the work been issued years ago, but in regard to the compiler, untoward circumstances prevented. Had he not done it now, or made arrangement for it to be done, he would have dreaded to pass through the Valley and Shadow of Death, and to appear before the Judgment Seat of Christ.

In a letter received from the author five months before his departure, he said: "I feel little interest in any thing earthly; yet I will try, by divine help, to do something for the moral improvement of the world; but I must work as one out of the world while in it. I expect to feel about the same interest in the affairs of this world, when I am in another world, that I feel now. ·

"Some things I cannot do there. I cannot there finish my history. I must do that here or never do it. I earnestly desire to leave a world's history, which will give a proper view of the sinfulness of war. It will require nearly a hundred more chapters to complete this work. Hundreds, perhaps thousands, of errors, typographical, in the *Wesleyan*, I wish to correct; then complete my chart, and leave the whole for somebody to publish. If God should spare me to finish all, and find a publisher, and correct or read proof, I then should lie down quietly in death."

That the reader may possess, in more or less degree, the humble, kind and reverential spirit of the author, and have, before departure, the consolation, through faith in the Redeemer, that he had, and have part in the resurrection of the just, is the prayer of

THE COMPILER.

Wesleyan Methodist Publishing House,
    Syracuse N. Y., Feb. 13, 1891.

INTRODUCTION.

It affords me great pleasure to certify to the superior merit of the volume containing the autobiography and selections from the writings of Rev. W. W. Crane. One who perused the able productions of the subject and author of these pages as they appeared in the *American Wesleyan* cannot fail to entertain a high estimate of their superior worth. For some years he was one of its corresponding editors, and enriched its columns from week to week with articles from his able pen. The writer became early and deeply interested in those communications, and read them with much pleasure and profit, never allowing one to pass without careful perusal. There was an affectionate tenderness breathed in their spirit which never failed to carry the irresistible impression that their author was a fervent lover of God and humanity. The good of men and the glory of God was his supreme aim.

From such articles from such an author an uninteresting and unprofitable volume could not be compiled. It is an occasion of gratitude on the part of our people, and al lovers of pure and soul-inspiring truth, that high personal esteem and true Christian friendship has inspired the mind of the compiler to give to the public a volume of such peculiar interest and intrinsic value. The obligation of appreciation is heightened from the fact that, of the proceeds of sale, one-third is to be devoted to the mission work of the Wesleyan Methodist Connection, one-third to the surviving son, Mr. Wm. M. Crane, and one third to the son-in-law, B. N. Huff. On the death of the son, one-half is to be devoted to missions, and one-half to the son-in-law, to be equally divided on his decease between the granddaughters.

On the part of the compiler, it is a work of benevolence, as he asks and receives nothing for the outlay of money and labor in giving this valuable book to the reading public.

N. WARDNER,
Editor of Wesleyan Methodist.

CONTENTS.

AUTOBIOGRAPHY.

MISCELLANEOUS WRITINGS.

AUTOBIOGRAPHY.

CHAPTER I.

WILLIAM WHITING CRANE was born April 23, 1805, in the town of Nelson, Madison county, New York. He knows little of his paternal ancestry. His grandfather, William Crane, was left an orphan in his infancy, and the subject of this memoir was born fatherless, his father, William Crane, having died two months before, in his twenty-sixth year, leaving one brother, Whiting Crane, and four sisters, all younger than himself. Three of the sisters died in their youth of consumption. Whiting Crane died young, of the same disease, leaving two children, Albert and Eveline.

In 1836 the subject of this memoir was visited in Spring Arbor, Mich., by Sally Crane, a maiden lady, his father's youngest sister.

Albert and his sister, who had married a man by the name of Chauncy, resided in Broome county, N. Y. Mr. Crane had no brother by his name. He had one sister, Harriet Crane, who was never married. She was feeble from childhood, and died in Eaton county, Mich., in 1846.

From the time of the visit of his Aunt Sally, in 1836, Mr. Crane has had no intelligence from her, or from his cousins, and notwithstanding the most diligent inquiry he has no

certain evidence that he has, out of his family, a relative
bearing his name.   It is, however, highly probable that this
nearly extinct family descended from a Welsh family, which,
on coming to America at an early day, separated into three
branches;   one locating in Massachusetts, one in Connecticut, another in New Jersey.   It is also probable that from
this Welsh family have sprung nearly all bearing the name
of Crane in this country.

When the subject of this memoir was three years old, his
mother married her second husband, David Dunham, by
whom she has had two daughters and seven sons, five of
whom are yet living.

On the maternal side Mr. Crane has numerous relatives,
and is able to trace his ancestry back in several lines from
150 to 200 years.

Anthony De Zozier, a French gentleman of some rank,
went to Lisbon to visit his sister Rosanna, the inmate of a
nunnery.   Being denied admittance, he with a friend whose
sister was also there, broke into this church fortress.   Officers of the Inquisition were directly on their heels, and
they fled for refuge on board a British ship, which at once
set sail for North America, and landed in New Haven·
They left large estates, which they never recovered.

In New Haven De Zozier, who subsequently spelled his
name Sizer, married Sarah Tryon.   Their oldest son, Abel
Sizer, married Sarah Mitchel.   They were the parents of
five daughters, who were extraordinary women in virtue and
intelligence.

The first-born of these daughters was grandmother to the
late Lydia Jane Pierson, and the second daughter, Sarah,
who married Joseph Pierson, was grandmother to the subject of this memoir.   It was from these extraordinary wom-
en, with four of whom Mr. Crane was intimately acquainted in his childhood and youth, that he obtained most of

his information in regard to genealogy. They were never weary talking of their paternal grandfather, the French nobleman. They were equally fond of tracing their maternal pedigree to their great-grandfather, William Howe, whom they represented as belonging to the family of the ancestors of Admiral Howe, and General Howe, of Revolutionary celebrity. He came from England to America, and married Elizabeth Stuart, a Scotch lady, who was claimed to be of royal blood. Lydia Howe, their daughter, married Jonathan Mitchel, and Sarah Mitchel became the mother of these five sisters.

The remarkable longevity of these people gave them great opportunities for correct tradition. Mr. C.'s Grandmother Pierson lived to the age of about ninety years, and the youngest of the five sisters was very lately living, and probably is now living. The Piersons were as remarkable for long life. About the time that Mr. C.'s mother, Sarah Pierson, was born, her father's great-grandmother died, aged ninety-seven years. Mr. C.'s mother is yet living (1862) in her eighty-first year. Her life united to that of her great-grandmother Pierson, who died on the year she was born, amounts to 177 years, and reaches to the ninth generation.

Ten or twelve years ago there appeared in a New Haven paper an account of the death of an aged maiden lady, by the name of Pierson, in Derby, Conn. The writer states that more than two hundred years ago, Thomas Pierson made a purchase of land of the Indians, in Derby, and that the deceased is the last of the race of Pierson. Mr. C., on reading this account, remarked that he could inform the writer that his grandfather, Joseph Pierson, who left Derby about 1790, had a numerous posterity, of more than 150 souls, scattered through New York, Ohio and Michigan.

CHAPTER II.

We have already mentioned the birth of William W. Crane, in Nelson, N. Y. His parents had been married in Alfred, Mass., about four years before, and emigrated to the West in 1804. William was born on what was known for more than half a century as the Pierson farm, three miles east of Cazenovia. He has a distinct recollection of some things which happened there when he was but three years of age. After his mother's second marriage she lived on an adjoining farm, and William spent much of his time with his Grandmother Pierson.

When four years old he was sent to school at Jackson's Corners, a half mile east. Each morning, as he journeyed alone to school, he thought the sensible horizon was the end of the world, and wondered if anybody had been there and looked off. The most that he learned was to dread the school-house, and tremble at the voice of the teacher, who was a stern man. The next summer he was sent to the same place, where he was under another equally stern male teacher, whose voice and countenance always terrified him. The boys were generally older than himself, and their rough habits, running, jumping and yelling, annoyed him much, as he was in danger of being run over and trampled down. He kept away from them, and while alone, he fell in with a little colored boy who was equally solitary. This boy, though very meek and innocent, was so taunted, on account of his color, that he went into the brook and tried to wash off the black, and while his tears fell like rain drops on the water, he pushed his hand to the bottom and brought the sand and tried to scour off the black. William and black Jerry became very intimate friends and passed much of their time together.

Jerry's father had been a soldier in the Revolutionary

War, and Washington's cook. He received his name,
Plymouth Freeman, from General Washington, and a discharge in Washington's hand-writing, which secured him a
pension for life. He was a native of Guinea, and a slave
until the beginning of the war.

William received his first religious impressions from a
little girl, when he was four or five years old. She told
him that when people died their souls still lived in a most
delightful country, if they had been good, but in a lake of
fire if they had been wicked. These impressions never left
him, and he was often in great distress in view of his sins.
He was greatly perplexed to know how the soul could live
in the body. He thought there was an open space in the
body, in which the soul lived until the body died.

A theme of frequent conversation with the children was
the hanging of Hitchcock, a merchant of Cazenovia, for
poisoning his wife. The idea of a man hanging by the
neck, and dying, filled them with indescribable horror.

William, on returning from school, was passing the house
of Mr. Alger, a near neighbor, whose boys had a great
variety of little sleds. A very small one stood in the road.
He stopped and looked at it, saying to himself, "I wish I
had a sled. I cannot make one, and no one will make one
for me. Mr. Alger's boys have a great many. This is a
little one, made of two shingles or little pieces of board. I
found it in the road. Anybody has a right to what he
finds in the road." He took hold of the string and was
drawing it home, when a young man met him and said,
"You have stolen a sled, and you will have to be hung."
He was filled with the utmost terror, saying to himself,
"Oh, I am a thief! What shall I do?" He hid the sled
beneath some logs, near his mother's house, and such was
his painful sense of guilt that he never touched it or even
saw it again, although he passed by it every day. As long

as he lived in that country he was in fear of being hung for stealing. This incident made so deep an impression on his mind that time could never remove it; and few men have had so deep a sense of the sacredness of property.

Many have read Grace Greenwood's narrative of "Crazy Lucy." This unfortunate woman attracted the pity of all. The cruel circumstances which led to her insanity moved every heart.

Lucy Dutton, on her wedding day, waited with much anxiety for the arrival of the bridegroom. At a late hour he arrived, but only to inform her that he was already married, and married to her own sister. Lucy went out and disappeared, and for many days could not be found. It was thought that she was dead, as some of her clothes had been found on the shore of Cazenovia Lake. When found she was so totally demented that she had no knowledge of passing events, and it seems that she never had one ray of reason until she was dying in the almshouse more than forty years afterwards, when her reason returned, and she thought it her wedding-day, until she saw with surprise the wrinkles on her hands.

Crazy Lucy used to call, in her endless wanderings, on William's mother, and the impression made on his infant mind was such that through life he has had very great pity for the insane.

CHAPTER III.

In the summer of 1810 Mr Dunham and several others went on a landhunter's expedition to the Far West. They came to the Genesee River, where Rochester now is, and found no bridge. They were in an extensive wilderness, low, swampy, and without inhabitants, except two families, one at the Falls, and the other one mile above. Land,

where the heart of the city now is, the price of which would
nearly cover it with banknotes, could then be bought for
five or six dollars per acre.   Mr. Dunham remarked:
"Here is a great water-power, but it must long remain useless in this wilderness   It will be a place of great business,
but not in my day.   [He is yet living.]   I do not want a
farm amidst these swamps, infested with rattle-snakes and
fever and ague."   He went from this gloomy place and
bought a farm in what is now the town of Henrietta.

  The removal to this wilderness home in the spring of
1811 was an affair of interest to William and the other children—his sister Harriet and the two children of Mr. Dunham, Maranda and Albert.   The year of 1811 had the
earliest spring that has been known in this country.   On
the 15th of March the face of the earth was green with herbage, and on the 15th of April the forest was dark with
leaves.   Corn planted in March and corn planted in June
matured.

  During this delightful spring news came that a minister
had come to the neighborhood, who would preach on the
coming Sabbath.   The family went to meeting, crossing the
woods without a road.   William was in great glee at the
thought of this excursion. ' It was the first meeting that he
remembered to have attended.   He went to the chamber
to dress for meeting, when suddenly he thought of what the
little girl said: that the wicked would dwell forever in a lake
of fire.   He knew that he was wicked, and was therefore
without hope.   He wept in the most bitter agony of soul.
As he was going down the rude ladder, the thought came
that God was reconciled to him, because he was sorry for
his sins.   This was his first idea that sin could be pardoned.
He had never heard of such a thing.

  This was doubtless regeneration; although he did not
reckon it to be anything.   He had no idea of regeneration,

or conversion; no idea of pardon, or justification. He simply felt that God had ceased to be angry, because he was sorry. It would have been well if he could have fallen upon this simple experience in after years, when he reason-ed on the nature of faith, on eternal decrees, predestination and election, until he was lost in the fierce tornadoes and wild whirlwinds of despair.

> " As the red comet by Saturnius sent
> To fright the nations with a dire portent."—HOMER.

The comet of 1811 was not only an object of great in-terest to men of science, but also of painful interest to com-mon people, who regarded the "Blazing Star" as the awful sign of coming war. William used in the silent night hours to stand gazing with indescribable solemnity at the star, set on fire by the hand of God, and wonder how soon the terrible savage war-whoop would be heard around his mother's house.

The war soon came on and kept the western settlements in alarms for three years. Buffalo was burned; the British repeatedly tried to land at the mouth of Genesee River; many inhabiting the country west of the Genesee fled to the East, and of those who remained most of the men able to carry a gun were often obliged to leave their families and meet the enemy.

William and Albert, the stepfather's son, soon threw off their fear, and jumped and shouted with joy when they heard the cannon roar. Nothing pleased them more than to see men at midnight melting lead and running bullets, and women cooking and filling knapsacks with food for a short campaign. They caught the martial spirit, and wish-ed to be men, to go to the war. This spirit increased with their years, and when they began to study military history, their ambition to become soldiers became a raging passion.

Almost every young man in the neighborhood had been

in the army, and had brought home with him the vices of the camp. At town-meetings, trainings, logging-bees, and in the harvest field, these men from the army were almost constantly describing their vices with great pleasure, using the most obscene language. Even church members would join in describing the most revolting scenes of debauchery, with loud bursts of laughter. Such were the influences under which little boys were growing up, learning these lessons of vice from men whom everybody honored because they had been in the glorious war.

There were many old men in the neighborhood who had served in the Revolutionary War; and although more than half of them would be drunk at every public gathering, yet they received so much honor that their vices seemed sanctified, by the fact that they had learned to drink, and swear, and commit fornication in the glorious war. This was a dark age, when drinking whisky was universal, and when deacons and the most prominent men in the churches would keep boys laughing by telling most obscene stories.

CHAPTER IV.

The year 1816 was so cold through the summer months that a gloomy apprehension of coming famine rested on the minds of the people. The sun shone dimly and frosts appeared every month.

Elder Tenney, the pastor of the Baptist Church in Henrietta, began to prophecy the end of the world, which produced great seriousness; sixty or seventy professed conversion, including William. He was truly sincere, though poorly instructed in regard to conversion, having never heard anything but Calvinism. He prayed sincerely every day for nearly a year, when, nearly all the younger converts having fallen away, he was carried away by the multitude. He was soon deeply engaged in reading martial history, and visions of military glory absorbed his mind by night and day. Everything grand and romantic in nature or art fanned this flame ; every strain of music, even raging storms, lightning and thunder, were witnessed with great delight ; so much like the grand battle-scenes of Thymbria and Borodino. This all-absorbing ambition excluded all religious seriousness, blunted his moral sensibilities, and plunged him into many vices. Military drills and parades wrought in him the highest enthusiasm. Plumes, epaulettes, grand horses and roaring guns enchanted him.

The fore part of the nineteenth century was the age of camp-meetings. These meetings began in the West, on the frontier, among a hardy, bold, independent, and yet coarse and unpolished people. Camp meetings were peculiarly adapted to the backwoods manners of these people, and most perfectly suited to their taste. Loud shouting, clapping of hands and jumping were no reproach, but rather an honor, in the estimation of the religious. Many of these rude people possessed a strong relish for the sublime, which was gratified by an encampment in a dark wilderness. the sound of the trumpet calling to worship, the voices of thousands in sacred song, echoing among the trees, joined to a deep sense of the divine presence. The age of camp-meetings is past. They are no longer adapted to the habits or tastes of mankind. They no longer rise spontaneous. Camp-meetings now are but puerile mimicry of a past age, where a few tents are erected by great effort, frequently in a small patch of woods, almost in the open field ; comparing with the olden time camp-meetings as the child's play-house compares with her mother's mansion.

It was said that ten thousand people were at the camp-meeting on the Honeoye, below Norton's Mills, in Mendon,

in 1816.   Two years later another camp-meeting was held
on the same ground.   William obtained liberty to attend.
He started on Saturday afternoon with several others ; they
did not arrive until evening   Passing a long way into the
wilderness, the distant sound of prayer and praise arose upon their ears, and gradually became more loud and clear.
This was very solemn, but when they began to behold the
glowing fires and white tents of the great encampment, the
scene became awfully grand.   They crowded through the
multitude which thronged the way and all the ground, and
came unexpectedly upon an altar, filled with most deeply
devout people.   Oh, what a scene to William's mind ! He
stood as near as the enclosing fence would allow, gazing
with astonishment on faces which glowed with unearthly
light, and listening to brief sentences of prayer and praise,
uttered in mild, subdued tones, until his emotions overcame
his strength.   He seized the pole before him, and held firmly, to avoid falling, reflecting on his sins, on the pride with
which he had come to despise and mock this people.
Bleeding at the nose had sometimes endangered his life,
and now, having an awful sense of the divine presence and
overwhelmed with a sense of guilt, the blood began to flow
from his nostrils, and death seemed to be at hand.   Finally, recovering a little, he walked a few steps and sat down
by a tree, and long remained silent, having no relish for the
company of his companions, who were rude and trifling.

    The scene in that altar could never be forgotten.   Its
mighty impression moulded his religious taste, and fixed his
ecclesiastical destiny.   Even down to old age it was to him
an ever-present vision.   It was to him a model prayer-
meeting.   Whatever he has witnessed through life which
most resembled that prayer-meeting, came nearest to perfection.

CHAPTER V.

William read Homer when he was fifteen years old, and although it expanded his mind and quickened its energies, yet it was a moral damage, inflaming his martial ambition, already his ruling passion. Homer's giant heroes and mighty gods were grand models for his admiration. The following are his views of Homer, now in old age:

MORAL INFLUENCE OF THE HOMERIC LITERATURE.

The controversy regarding the identity of Homer, and the existence of Troy, has probably ceased. It was an idle controversy. He must have a greedy relish for skepticism who doubts that Troy or Ilion existed, or doubts that one man—call him Homer or what you will—wrote, or composed, the Iliad and Odyssey, a few ages after the destruction of Troy.

Besides his compositions, we know little of Homer. We know not where he was born, or where he died. We know not even when he lived, and least of all do we know whether his blindness was a fact, or the whim of the fancy of succeeding poets. We know not whether he wrote his compositions, or whether he recited them to younger bards, who handed them down to the literary age of Greece. We know that in that age they were written, re-written, and carried everywhere; that they influenced all people and kindled a flame of martial ferocity which burns to this day.

It would be vain to attempt to depreciate Homer. There are glaring faults in the Iliad. Some of his comparisons are puerile—comparing mighty armies to flies around the shepherd's milking-pails, and the noise of battle to the bleating of lambs and sheep at milking-time. His long lists of single combats are monotonous. Some will plead that the monotony is relieved by the variety in the manner of deaths.

This indeed is a poor relief, when we read one has his bowels torn out, another his face split through with a javelin, another's brains bestrew the ground, and another has his bosom crushed by a rock from Ajax's hand. The pleasure with which Homer describes the most revolting scenes of tiger-like murder, proves him to have been of a tiger's barbarity.

No criticism was ever able to check the influence of Homer. He formed the martial character of Greece, and of nearly all the ancient world. Succeeding poets, orators and historians copied after Homer; inflaming all men, until the martial spirit ran so high that the sword fell on the neck of poet, orator, historian and artist, the battle-ax fell on statuary, and the fire-brand of war was thrown into the library and gallery of paintings; until ancient empire died under a thousand sword wounds, and the sun of ancient civilization went down in blood. We see the influence of Homeric literature in the awful ruins of ancient cities and ancient empires; in the degradation of Chaldea and Egypt, of Persia and of Syria, of Greece and Rome. This high-wrought martial spirit was a sure element of ruin in the ancient literature; and it has fulfilled its destiny. If in the general destruction every volume of Homer had perished, it would have been no damage to the morals of modern nations.

Homer is revived in all modern tongues; his influence is everywhere seen; and it may continue through all coming ages. The moral character of the Homeric literature will not bear Christian criticism. Homer's gods and goddesses are murderers, liars, adulterers and fornicators. I will concede that we are doomed to be disgusted by this character of the gods in all ancient literature. Homer is not an exception. His great fault is his martial spirit, in which pride, malice and wrath are glorified and deified; while meekness and forbearance are held in the utmost contempt. The meek are everywhere called cowards, wretches and dastards. Forgiving injuries is unknown among his heroes. There is nothing amiable or morally good in the reconciliation of Agamemnon and Achilles; it is all sordid selfishness. If there was any redeeming feature in the Iliad, it would be some case of friendship, but these are nearly all tarnished by some base passion. Thetis mourns with her mortal son and weeps over his wrongs; over the fact that the great king had snatched away one of her son's beautiful mistresses from his bed of fornication. The friendship between Achilles and Patroclus was great, but not amiable; it was the friendship of two ferocious giants, who walked together like two Bengal tigers. Achilles mourns deeply for his friend, and we should be touched if we could separate his mourning from his wrath. While he drives his chariot with Hector's dead body dragging behind, every day around the tomb of Patroclus, or while he burns twelve noble sons of Troy on the funeral pile, humanity has no tear to mingle with his grief.

That the Homeric literature is at variance with the spirit of Christ none can deny. Homer honors the strong however vicious; Christ honors the virtuous, however weak. Homer admires a proud and haughty spirit, a high sense of honor, that resents and retaliates every supposed injury. Christ loves the meek, the forbearing, the forgiving, the poor in spirit, the gentle and compassionate.

The Homeric literature deserves much of the credit for the martial spirit which at this time pervades civilized nations; covering the seas with ships of war, and bristling every coast with military works. It is conceded that we sprang from ancestors who were as bloodthirsty as tigers before they heard of Homer, or of Grecian literature. The transition, however, of our ancestors from pagan barbarism to Christian civilization might have removed this brute-like ferocity, if the Christian schools had not everywhere set the pagan classics above the mild teachings of Christ ; and if modern *literati* had not made the Greeks their models in history, oratory and poetry.   Alexander said, " The reading of Homer made me a conqueror"; and Charles XII of Sweden said, " Reading the life of Alexander made me a conqueror."   After eighteen hundred years Christ's teaching of forbearance and love to enemies is not allowed to have any real meaning ; and our Christian literature teems with the praise of resentment and retaliation.

CHAPTER VI.

In 1821 William, having a great anxiety to see the world, left home without the consent of his mother, with the purpose of going to sea.   His sorrow for her, however, caused him to abandon his purpose, and he returned home, after an absence of three months.

This was a time of most deep and solemn reflection, of repentance and prayer.   He became fully resolved to lead a new life.   A circumstance occurred, however, on his return which overthrew all of his pious resolutions.   He visited his Grandfather Pierson, in Nelson.   While there his uncle, the late General Spencer, of Canastota, then brigade inspector, called and passed the night with him.   This visit with his uncle, and the excitement of general training the next day at Cazenovia, aroused his former ruling passion— military ambition.   He struggled with this enemy several weeks, and was at last overcome, concluding to wear a sword and epaulettes, even on the road to eternal death.

He now became more indifferent to the interests of his soul than he had ever been, and the year that followed was the most wicked of his life.   His great object now was to study law and military science ; and he was perplexed with deep anxiety to know how to meet the expense of his legal and military education.

The 8th of September, 1822, is an era in the life of William W. Crane.   On that day he attended a husking-bee in the south part of Henrietta, and continued with a multitude of men and boys until a late hour, the night being light and the weather delightfully warm.   On his return homeward with many others, a plan was laid to surprise some thieves in a large orchard.   W. W. C. and one comrade were placed as silent sentinels under the fence, while the others reconnoitered.   He, always confiding, kept his post, while his fellows played him a trick, and went on their way.   He soon overtook them, to meet their merciless ridicule.   This slight circumstance was the turning-point in his life.   An immense tract of flood-wood may commence by the lodgment of a straw.   He had yet two miles to walk, and in that time he reflected on the unsatisfactory nature of earthly things, and especially on the treacherous character of human friendship.   He formed a solemn resolution to seek the favor of God, which has never been broken.   He began to read the Bible with attention, he shunned the company of the wicked, and went seriously to religious meetings at every opportunity.

The deep impression made on his mind at the camp-meeting, four years before, had not left him, and now, as he was deeply in earnest in seeking the way of salvation, he went five or six miles to find a Methodist meeting.   The first that he attended was a quarterly-meeting in Pittsford.   Goodwin Stoddard was presiding elder.   Cyrus Story and Andrew Prindle were the preachers on Bloomfield circuit then including all of Monroe county east of the Genesee River and parts of Livingston and Ontario counties.   He

now found the place of regular service where these venerable ministers preached.   They were old men.

The principal denomination in Henrietta was the regular
Baptist.   This church was in a very bad state.   The church
clerk ran a distillery, making whisky for his brethren;   the
minister was becoming a drunkard;   many members were
hard drinkers;   the church was divided into two hostile
parties, biting and devouring one another; and their enmity
had become so great that they met in separate congregations.

The Methodists in Pittsford were much more spiritual,
yet they had not their usual prosperity.   They had strife
among themselves, and the secession under Oren Miller
caused an unhappy excitement through all that country;
both parties feeling a bitter and unchristian temper.

W. W. C. had often resolved to lead a new life, but not
committing himself when strong temptation came, his resolution had failed.   He now resolved to commit himself
strongly as possible.   He accordingly promised the Lord
that he would on the next Sabbath go to meeting in Pittsford and stay in class-meeting.   Sabbath came and he was
at meeting according to promise;   but when the congregation was dispersing, he was going with it, and near the door
he thought of his promise to stay in class-meeting.   He did
not dare to break his promise, and accordingly sat down,
trembling with embarrassment.   Nothing but a solemn
promise would have held him there.   He was among strangers.   Father Prindle said to him, " Do you enjoy religion?"
He answered, "No, but I desire to."   He was now committed, and the whole class was interested in him.   This
was one of the most important steps of his life.

In that congregation he became acquainted with David
True, a young man of deep piety.   An intimate friendship
arose between them, which was broken off by the removal

of D. T. to Indiana.   For nearly forty years W. W. C. has
hoped once more to meet this dear friend, but tidings now
come that D. T. is dead.

CHAPTER VII.

The popular doctrine in Henrietta was Calvinism ; and
although they who hold this doctrine generally profess the
greatest disinterestedness and resignation, and although old
Elder Brown taught that to be acceptable to God we must
be willing to be eternally damned, yet it was evident from
the life and conversation of many of these people that they
were as selfish as others.   They gloried in the idea of their
own election, and sure perseverance, or, rather, sure salvation, whether they persevered or not.

They were taught from the pulpit that the elect sinned all
the while, in every thought, word and deed; sinned enough
in their best prayers to damn them forever, yet they were
comforted by the doctrine that their salvation had nothing
to do with their works, but was secure by their election.
Strange sights and sounds and wonderful visions often formed the ground of their hope.   When their doctrine was opposed by argument, they were irritated, seeming to feel and
say, like Laban, " What have I left ?"   They were told by
their minister that Arminians were fools, and they regarded
Methodists as low, ignorant and despicable.

Such had been the religious education of W. W. C.; and
now, deeply in earnest for the salvation of his soul, he began to investigate the doctrine of Calvinism.   If the doctrine of election proved false, salvation was in his reach ; if
it proved true, he had but little chance, perhaps one in ten,
to be saved.   But the subject soon assumed tremendous
importance, eclipsing every other interest.   Having always

heard the Scriptures read and quoted in a Calvinistic way, Calvinism seemed to be the plain reading of the Bible   The ninth of Romans seemed unanswerable.

Yet he struggled hard for life, for eternal life ; struggled mightily to find some passage of Scripture which would give him hope.   Every promise was snatched from him and given to the elect.   He would fain cry to God for help, but "The prayers of the wicked are an abomination to the Lord" sounded in his ear.   If he felt that his lot was hard, he heard in thunder tones, " Who art thou that repliest against God ? Shall the thing formed say to him that formed it, Why hast thou made me thus ? Hath not the potter power over the clay of the same lump, to make one vessel unto honor, and another unto dishonor ?"

He attended a Baptist Association in Pittsford, and when the letter from the church in Henrietta was read, it filled his soul with anguish, as it contained the doctrine of predestination and election, expressed in the most harsh and grating language.

A misfortune happened to W. W. C. about this time, which had an important bearing on his mental exercises, and indeed upon his health of body and mind through life. His spine was partly broken, in turning the screw of a cidermill.   He had been working extremely hard for many weeks, partly from excitement of mind, but more from necessity, as the whole work of the farm, except the labor of a small boy, fell upon him, his stepfather lying sick, unable to leave the house.   Day after day he was doing far more than would be required of the strongest man, sometimes doing two full days' work in one day.   On the day of his misfortune he had worked in a feverish frenzy, designing to finish cider-making and be ready on the morrow to attend to other important labor.   At evening he was screwing down for the last time, and having brought two levers

around to a certain degree, he tried the third, which stub-
bornly refused to move so far.   He resolved that it should
go, and planting his heels in the firm clay, he made a
mighty effort and brought it around; but a sword seemed
to go through his spine.   He got home in great pain, and,
strange to say, he was at work the next day, and continued
working, for it seemed that the produce of the farm must
be saved.   Inflammation set in, extending to the brain.
He was at this time but seventeen years old, was growing
fast, and working very hard.   The spinal and cerebral inflammation increased the intensity of his thoughts, and the
intensity of his thoughts increased the inflammation.

The doctrines of predestination and election soon occupied his whole attention, and as the inflammation of his
brain increased, he became a monomaniac.   The Bible
seemed to make unconditional election certain, and he felt
that he had infallible evidence that he was a reprobate.

It is evident that few who talk of reprobation and endless
punishment have any real sense of the same.   How can
they really feel that nine out of ten of their neighbors were
from eternity predestined to endless punishment, and yet
talk, and jest, and laugh with them as they do?   They
would shriek to see a man writhing in the flames of a burning house for ten minutes, and yet they talk of their reprobate neighbors writhing in the most intense burnings to all
eternity.   They talk of this with cool indifference.   Their
belief of this does not disturb their relish for food, or drink,
or sleep.

With W. W. C. these things were all reality—vivid reality—terrible reality; as real as though he were already in
the lake of fire; as real as though the Judgment was sitting,
and he was now hearing, " Depart, ye cursed."   He looked
into eternity as few look into it.   The stars stood each for
a million years, the drops of the ocean each stood for a mil-

lion years, and all the dust of the earth stood each particle for a million years; and when this awful length was gone, eternity was still the same He then counted each particle of dust or matter which forms the sun and all the stars as standing for a million years, and often exclaimed, "Oh! when all these millions of years are gone, eternity is still the same!" He felt willing and anxious, deeply anxious, to go to hell, on the condition that he should remain there as many thousand years as there are particles of dust in this whole earth, and then be saved. If this offer had been made to him he would have eagerly jumped into the lake of fire. He grieved deeply that he could not have even that chance of salvation. To pass a meeting-house where he had heard reprobation preached, caused him to shudder; when he met a minister who preached this doctrine, a chill went through him; he could not even take into his hand Watts's Psalms without horror, as this book always accompanied Calvinistic worship. Some days when the sun shone without a cloud, his anguish was so great that the air looked dark as midnight. He often went into the woods and sought the most gloomy valley, where he sat on a moss-covered log and listened to the winds which wailed through the leafless trees, anticipating his future endless misery.

CHAPTER VIII.

One evening, after hearing an aged minister preach reprobation in the most shocking language, W. W. C. returned in such mental agony that he lay awake the whole night, turning from side to side. A log fire was burning on the large hearth, and he felt that if he should put his foot into the fire and burn it off it could not increase his agony, but would rather diminish it, by diverting his attention.

He arose in the morning feeling that he did not wish to see the face of any living being, and went back on the farm, into a pit dug for watering cattle, and sat down, wishing in vain for annihilation.

During that dreadful winter he went a short time to school, and, strange to say, made good progress in science. As spring came on his distress increased, being aggravated by his periodical melancholy, which every year came upon him, from the time of his father's death in February, until the time of his own birth in April. No language can give the picture of his sufferings, as no language can describe despair—total, blank despair. He still worked hard, but worked by fits; for stopping to pray probably one hundred times in a day, he conscientiously worked hard enough in the intervals to make up for lost time, and also the time spent in attending the weekly prayer-meeting.

The spinal and cerebral inflammation was rapidly undermining his constitution ; his once perfect form was going ; his spine assuming a hideous bend, where it was injured in the cider-mill, and his head and shoulders falling down. Thus, one born for perfect symmetry, giant physical strength, and at least some mental power, was fast becoming a mere wreck, by one fatal pull at the cider-mill shaft, and yet more by the soul-freezing influence of a doctrine which seems to strip the Deity of justice, mercy and goodness, and to charge his government with the most shocking partiality. His groans, and sighs, and wild looks caused most people to shun him. Few were willing to own his acquaintance. Even his Methodist friends mostly drew off, unwilling to come near this frightful object. This neglect sometimes stung him keenly, but despair, which has a deadening influence on the finer sensibilities of the soul, commonly made him indifferent.

Why should a man without hope care for the neglect, or

even the frowns of men? Why should one who cared not what became of him, who cared not whether he was sent to prison or hanged—whether he was drowned in the sea, or crushed beneath a falling rock, or thrown into a volcano, care for being despised?

In June, 1823, W. W. C. went to camp-meeting in the town of Springwater. When he arrived at the encampment he was among strangers, twenty-five miles from home. He was glad to meet the presiding elder, walking off from the ground. He approached him with a momentary thrill of cheerfulness and spoke to him. The elder coldly gave him his hand, and said, " Where have I seen you?" This was like cold steel going through the heart. He had followed this elder from one quarterly-meeting to another, and heard him preach with eager attention, and now if he could receive no kind word from him, to whom should he look for spiritual advice? This was the first and last time that W. W. C. ever spoke to Elder S., although he admired his preaching above that of any other man. It is not strange that he was not benefited by this meeting; no one comprehended him; no one was able to sympathize with him. There were two ministers, however, who never forsook him, who were ever ready to give a word of kind counsel. These were Cyrus Story and Elisha House.

A new affliction now arose to W. W. C. His Uncle Pierson, who had been very kind and partial to him, and who had had extravagant hopes of what he might become, said to his mother: " William is lost, and all of our hopes of his future greatness are blasted." He advised severe measures to be taken with him, but his plan was abandoned.

In August news came that his Uncle Crocker, of Roches-ter, was dead. This was most melancholy news. In his infancy his mother's youngest sister, a beautiful and amiable woman, was married, at the age of seventeen, to Captain

Crocker, of Cazenovia, a young man of great promise.   His
business was lucrative, and military and civil office gave him
high popularity.   He was social, generous and urbane and
this noble nature proved his ruin.   Public business often
led him to drinking saloons, where he met his friends with
the warmest greeting, always ready to treat them and drink
with them.   Public opinion approved of it, even demanded
it ; and the church of which he was an acceptable member
did not condemn it.   While his drams increased and he
became jovial and noisy, he was still honored as the fine
gentleman and owned as an accomplished officer; all treated
him with flattering respect, and even the church was yet
proud of him ; but when at length he became too drunk to
walk erect and flourish his sword with grace—too drunk to
know the price of his goods or post his books correctly—
too drunk to arrest a criminal according to the forms of
law, he was kicked from all respectable society and crushed
to the dirt.   He was soon out of all office, expelled from
the church, out of business and bankrupt.   Thus, friendless
and in despair, he seemed to plunge for a while into all the
depths of degradation.

He soon, however, rallied and made a manly resolve to
break away from his dreadful associates, and reform.   He
accordingly removed to Henrietta, resolved never again to
be drunk.   This was in 1818.   W. W. C., now thirteen
years old, felt a strong attachment to this uncle, and a lively
interest in his efforts to reform.   On one occasion he heard
his uncle in a religious meeting, confess his faults in an
humble manner, and pathetically beg the congregation to
watch over him.   William's young heart melted with sympathy.   But what could his poor uncle do in such an age ?
The chief man in the church made whisky, and all his
brethren drank it.   It was kept in every house, and every

woman was proud to have the decanter and foot-glass in fair view on her cupboard.

He unfortunately rented a house of the distiller, within the stench of pig-styes and whisky ; both calculated to degrade both mind and body. They who had the deepest interest in his welfare would ask him to drink, to show friendship and encourage his reform. W. W. C. was walking on the road, when he beheld far ahead a man walking with a rough crooked stick, and reeling to and fro in a frightful manner. As he approached nearer, he found to his horror that it was his uncle ; his hat crushed in and his garments smeared with mud. Oh ! how the poor boy felt ! His uncle was lost !

Some time after this the uncle removed to Rochester, where he engaged in keeping a grocery-store more properly, a drinking-saloon. He was now hopelessly lost. For four months before his death he was never sober. and his last four days were spent in almost unbroken stupor. Thus he passsd away.

To W. W. C. the funeral was the most painful scene of a funeral kind which he had ever witnessed. This man, once so honored, was now so unknown, or rather, despised, that it seemed difficult to assemble citizens enough to decently bury him. Elder Tenney took for his text, ·' The day of one's death is better than the day of one's birth," and endeavored to console the mourners by saying : " If the deceased was ever a Christian, he is now in heaven." The minister seemed dull, dry and unfeeling, and was evidently glad when his task was finished.

The degraded man was not buried in the village cemetery, but carried away where strangers were buried, to a piece of ground surrounded on three sides by heavy forest. The sun far away in the west sent his beams through the waving trees, and streaks of light and shade slowly chased each other over the open grave.   Silence reigned until the rude sexton rolled some heavy lumps of dry clay on to the naked coffin, which sent forth an unearthly, hollow sound, loudly echoing from the surrounding woods.   Although the minister had to pass this wilderness burying-ground in going home, yet he did not stop.   The sexton, with great embarrassment, dismissed the little band, which seemed the only honest part of the funeral service.

When the widow, yet blooming with youthful beauty, and four lovely young daughters turned away from this dishonored grave, W. W. C. felt an indignation against all dealings in intoxicating drinks which has marked his course through life.   The pauper grave-yard has long been covered by streets and dwellings of the city of Rochester, and the grave is lost until the resurrection ; but there is one who can never forget that funeral scene.   It made too deep an impression for his health.

CHAPTER IX.

A few days after the funeral he was seized by a heavy chill, followed by fever.   His strength, which for some time had been kept alive by excitement, now gave way entirely ; the disease of his spine and brain having preyed upon his constitution nearly a year, now brought him near the grave. He was soon unable to rise from his bed without help.   His spine was so diseased that all muscular power in his back failed.   When on his feet his head and shoulders fell down to a horizontal position, and he walked a little with a very short stick for a staff.   When in his chair he bowed down in the same manner, having no power to sit erect.   One year had changed one of the best formed bodies in the town to this miserable wreck.

The mind was as much a wreck as the body. Despair, like the deep gloom of an Egyptian night, rested on him. Few, or none, expected his recovery; he was pronounced in the last stage of consumption, and expected soon to know the worst of his future destiny.

In October or November a very large abscess appeared on his back. When opened it discharged nearly a half gallon. This, instead of producing death, as all expected it would, was the harbinger of his recovery. He began slowly to mend, and by February was able to attend school. Soon, however, his season of periodical melancholy came on, and there was disease enough left to arouse to serious magnitude, when influenced by this unhappy season.

Conscience, or conscientiousness, was so diseased, that he condemned himself for nearly everything. He scarcely dared to speak or act, for fear of speaking or acting wrong. During this time he went on a journey alone and on foot. Falling in company with a stranger, he had some conversation with him, and after leaving him he was afraid that he had unintentionally given a wrong impression in regard to some important thing. Conscience bade him go back, but a sense of propriety forbade his going back. He went on, often stopping and turning back. The next morning he arose early; and conscience prevailing over a sense of propriety, he went back fifteen miles to correct this trifling error.

On returning home he tried to comprehend his mental state. If he had been acquainted with physiology he would have traced his mental state to a chronic inflammation of the brain, and would have known that his conscience was diseased. He knew that somehow conscience was leading him into many absurdities and follies, and therefore resolved that henceforth common sense should rule conscience. This resolution saved him.

He had doubtless experienced pardon nearly a year and

a half before, and had had many transient intervals of peace; but despair had always followed in a few hours or days.

During that dreadful year and a half, when he was tossed on a stormy ocean, under Egyptian darkness, he investigated the great points of Arminian and Calvinistic controversy in the most thorough manner, and brought from this dark period a fund of argument which has furnished him with the best thoughts he has had in doctrinal preaching through life. After the above-named resolution he gradually became more cheerful and happy, and although he was doomed for life to be humpbacked, yet he became strong, and performed more labor than common men.

In autumn the family removed to Mendon, an adjoining town, and W. W. C. attended the meetings at Norton's Mills. Having a very low opinion of his religious attainments, he joined the church as a seeker, which relation he had borne for some time in Henrietta. He had three miles to walk, but was rarely absent from meeting. The church was large, and in it some old men and women who were among the first settlers in Western New York.

Isaac Puffer was preacher in charge, and Thomas Wright his colleague. Matthew Ogden was class-leader. This was in 1824.

Nearly all who professed religion in the neighborhood of W. W. C. were Baptists and Congregationalists, and he attended many prayer-meetings among them. The Baptist Church which worshiped at East Mendon was large and in a prosperous state. Their prayer-meetings were regularly kept up during the winter. The Congregationalist Church was small. Rev. Mr. T. had brought with him from Connecticut a few choice families of intelligence and refinement, who formed the nucleus of a church in Mendon. Mr. T. was a man of great ability, but for some reason he exerted but little influence.

On one occasion W. W. C. was with Mr. T.'s congregation at the monthly prayer-meeting for foreign missions,
when the minister gravely called three or four to pray, and
among them Dr. W., a wicked man and a notorious drunkard. The doctor asked to be excused, when the minister
said that it was perfectly proper, at these prayer-meetings,.
for men to pray who did not profess religion. The minister,
who knew the doctor to be a very wicked man, wished him
to pray because he was a college graduate, while he would
have been filled with horror if the most intelligent and pious
woman had engaged in prayer.

CHAPTER X.

In this winter of 1824 W. W. C. was deeply affected by
the death of Mrs. Sophia Monroe. Sophia was born in the
same year and the same neighborhood with him, and as she
was half-sister to his stepfather, he and she were playmates
almost from the cradle. The two families moved to the
West, where he and Sophia were again playmates and
school-fellows, and through life he has reflected with great
pleasure on the evenings spent at Grandfather Dunham's in
company with Sophia and her intelligent mother. Her
father was then an old man of few words; but whenever he
spoke, the word of Deacon Dunham had great weight. He
sometimes enlivened the scene by an account of what he
had witnessed in the Revolutionary War.

Sophia was beautiful in form, feature and complexion.
She had extraordinary conversational powers, and a voice
of charming melody. Her disposition was mild, kind and
generous; and, possessing a quick and sprightly vivacity,
she was the life of every circle and the belle of her neighborhood. She had experienced religion in the revival of

1816, and united with the Baptist Church at eleven years of age. Not only her fond parents, but all of her relatives, felt a deep interest in her welfare, and no one felt a deeper interest than W. W. C.

The Baptist Church in East Henrietta had always been under the pastoral labors of old men; generally plain, coarse and old fashioned. Their manners were rough and backwoods like; their language ungrammatical, and their pronunciation the broad Yankee.

Memory at this distant day calls up old Elder Brown, in his coarse homespun, his long gray hair, the old jerk of his head, his "ah-hems" and his singing tones to fill up his pauses; his constant chewing of tobacco, and dropping his face into his right hand, about the time of "secondly," as though he had the tooth ache, but really to throw out his quid.

Elder Evans was still more uncouth. His snow-white hair, hanging carelessly dishevelled over his collar; his broad Welsh accent; his dropping his under lip and chin and pitching forward at the end of every sentence, live in the memory after forty-five years.

When Rev. Mr. Monroe came, fresh from college, it was deemed by some almost sacrilegious for a handsome young man in broadcloth to occupy the sacred pulpit. However, his polished manners, his intelligence and charming voice won for him the attentive hearing of crowded congregations. Among his enthusiastic admirers was W. W. C., who rejoiced in the improvement of pulpit elocution.

Deacon Dunham lived near the place of meeting; the new minister called on the family often, and his acquaintance with Sophia resulted in marriage in less than a year. She was sixteen years of age, had been petted by fond parents, her sisters and her brothers, and her wisest relatives deemed the marriage on her part premature; but most of her kindred were reconciled to her union with a man every way so noble.

Rev. Mr. M. soon manifested a great fondness for hunting; this brought him into improper company. His pride in sharpshooting led him to attend shooting matches, where he had for his companions swearers and drunkards. He was not very long in acquiring the habit of pretty smart drinking; but all ministers drank, everybody drank; and if the young minister drank smartly, he was only following the example of his venerable predecessors. W. W. C. was once present with his mother when Elder Evans came in, complaining of a pain in his heart. She offered him some oil of cedar; her foot-glass being broken, she took a tumbler and filled it with whisky, then dropping the oil of cedar into it, said, " Drink this, Elder; it will help you." She expected him to sip off the oil, but he brought up his under lip, which usually hung down, and drank the whole in a moment. William stood amazed. He knew that a tumblerful of whisky would make a wicked boy like him drunk as a fool, but he did not know but an old minister might stand it.

Mr. M.'s hunting frolics on Saturday began to disqualify him for Sabbath duties, and word was often sent on Sunday morning to the congregation that the minister was sick. Thus his preaching waned out, and he removed to Rochester and gave up to downright drunkenness, debauchery and blasphemy; and when his young innocent and amiable wife became fearful that he would kill her in a drunken fit, she went home to die of a broken heart in the embrace of her kind parents. Her death produced a very great sensation through an extensive circle of friends.

Three years had brought her from a fair young maiden, full of hope of a life of bliss, to a pale, wasted consumptive, dying of grief.

She sleeps in a neglected grave in a small cemetery in East Henrietta. When this noble woman had quietly slept there twenty-five years, the body of her unworthy husband was buried by her side. They will soon be forgotten, as no monument records their names.

CHAPTER XI.

While W. W. C. was suffering the horrors of despair, all thoughts of matrimony were banished; but during the few lucid hours which he experienced, he thought that if he was ever united in holy wedlock it would be with Phebe Griffin. She was a member of the little Methodist Church, or class, in Henrietta that he first joined; was about his age, and was deeply pious. She was a plain, modest girl, of Quaker training, and seemed to him the most proper person in the world for his companion. He was grave and rigidly chaste in his views and feelings on this subject, and was so fearful of improprieties that he seemed cold and unsocial in female company. He looked upon courtships in general as decidedly wicked. It was not until he had resided a year in Mendon that he felt the importance of making known his feelings to Miss Griffin. He found that during the year of their absence she had thrown off her Quaker simplicity. She had engaged in teaching, and felt the dignity of her station. She now felt contempt for his strange appearance while in despair, and treated him coldly; and when he made known the object of his visit, she bluntly denied his suit. This was a terrible shock to him; no less from the blasting of his connubial hopes, than from the conviction that he was despised by religious friends, for the gloom and anguish which he had lately passed through.

It was evening when the cold, blunt answer was given.

He was ten or twelve miles from home. He brought up his horse and rode away in the moonlight of a genial, autumnal evening, his mind laboring under mighty thoughts and form- ing weighty resolutions. He resolved to sever his attach- ment to Phebe Griffin at once and forever ; resolved never again to see her, and as far as possible to forget her. He never saw her again.

He reflected on the wreck which despair had made of him ; on the importance of recovering as far as possible what he had lost. He resolved to adopt a most rigid system of study, to arouse every energy of his mind and qualify himself for the widest field of usefulness which Providence might open for him. That evening was an epoch in his life. As he rode on, listening to the solemn notes of insects, singing in the orchard trees, laden with foliage and fruit, and cast a look over grain fields and meadows whitened by the soft moonlight, he seemed to be traveling into a new world, full of toil yet full of hope.

W. W. C. had been taken from school when six years old to hoe corn, and was never sent to school again in the sum- mer. He usually went to school a short time in the winter. Teachers had usually been poorly educated and unable to give him much aid. He had learned to rely upon himself, spending his evenings in study, and in a manner his days also, carrying his books to the field. He worked extra hard for an hour, then sat down and learned a short lesson ; and while working extra hard the next hour, he repeated his lesson thirty or forty times. Thus he continued through the day, and at evening he repeated all that he had learned during the day so many times that it was fastened upon his memory. On Saturday he reviewed all of the lessons of the week ; and all he had learned during a month was thoroughly reviewed during the last two or three days of each month.

He found this method so successful that there seemed no bounds to what might be learned, except the bounds of human life.   Ignorance seemed inexcusable in any man who could own a book and have the wide world for a school-room.   No man worked harder, and yet from morning till night, and day after day, his repetition of lessons kept time with the strokes of his ax or hoe, his scythe or sickle.

His Calvinistic education, the strange sights, sounds and wonderful circumstances commonly related in telling religious experience ; but most of all, his extreme caution, kept him much of the time in doubt whether he had been truly regenerated.   He still refused to be admitted into full membership in the church, choosing to remain on probation, as a seeker or catechumen.

Methodists placed as much confidence in excitement in religious experience, as the Baptists had in visions ; and as he neither had visions nor overwhelming emotions, he often doubted his conversion.   Loud shouting, jumping, and especially falling, were deemed sure evidences of holiness ; but W. W. C. was not called to or privileged with such exercises, and when he witnessed them in others, he sat down in sorrow, mourning over his unworthiness.

In October, 1825, he commenced school-teaching in Mendon, and after five months' teaching he attended an academical institution in Rochester, taught by Zenas Freeman, for three months.   This was the only opportunity which he ever had in any classical school.   This brief privilege was interrupted by four weeks' absence in harvest, and although he worked very hard, yet he continued his studies, so that on returning to Rochester he found that he had kept up with all of his classes.

CHAPTER XII.

While Mr. C. was at school in Rochester he was one morning called to the door by a gentleman, who informed him that Albert was dead. This news gave him indescribable sorrow. He started at once and walked to the house of mourning, fourteen miles distant, showering tears of anguish along the way, exclaiming within himself, " Oh, is he dead? gone forever? Can he no more look upon me? no more speak to me? no more hear my voice? or grasp my hand? Oh, what is death? what the boundaries of time, over which they pass to the unknown? Time will pass on; the sun will rise and set; the change of seasons come; and I grow old, infirm and gray; but Albert never returns—he is gone ! gone forever !" There lay the cold stiffened body, the eyes shut, never to open. Silence reigned, for no one felt like speaking.

Mr. C. retired to the woodland; crossing the garden and fields all blooming with flowers and fresh young green foliage; the fields and woods were vocal with songs of birds, but nothing cheered; sorrow filled the air with apparent darkness, seeming to becloud the light of the sun, and the song of birds seemed the funeral dirge of the world. Slow and solemn the mournful train moved six miles, and buried the dead where he had frolicked and played in early childhood.

Albert Dunham was the son of Mr. C.'s stepfather, near his own age. They were brought together when three years old, lodged in the same little bed, ate at the same table, dressed alike, and trudged together to school. They rambled together over the hills and valleys of their neighborhood. When fourteen years of age Albert was apprenticed to a tanner, so near home that the separation increased, rather than diminished, their friendship.   Few brothers ever loved each other so well.

They both began at an early age to read history.   They often met and talked of ancient nations, and scholars and heroes of antiquity.   When about fourteen years of age, they got hold of Pope's "Homer," and devoured it with a keener appetite than they had ever felt over the choicest food.   They had lived on the frontier during the war; had heard the roar of cannon with delight; had grown up among returned soldiers; had heard their stories of glorious deeds of war;   had listened with veneration to old men talking of Revolutionary times;   and were both seized with martial ambition, which grew to be a ruling passion.

William's conversion ended his martial aspirations and somewhat alienated Albert, but their friendship was too strong to be broken, even by death; for if friends recognize friends in that far-off, unknown, mysterious world, William and Albert will yet meet.   Albert had just entered in business for himself when his last and fatal sickness came on. He changed his under-garments from flannel to linen, and rode to his father's house, seven miles distant, on a damp winter day, and took cold, which brought on consumption. He was soon removed home, and as William was teaching school in the neighborhood, they were often together; and as the disease increased in malignity, William watched with him every night, lying on the floor near the bed of his poor brother, and springing up at every plaintive call, or cough, or groan, with the most yearning tenderness.

This continued for many weeks, until duty seemed to call him away; but after being in Rochester a few weeks, he returned home again and took his former position by the bed of the sick.   His presence gave Albert so much comfort that he could not bear the thought of ever leaving him; but the symptoms becoming more favorable and some hopes being entertained of his recovery, he again left him, though Albert's last kind, yearning, affectionate look on him is vivid to-day, and he only wants an artist's skill to paint that look just as it was thirty-seven years ago.

Mr. C. has never reflected on being absent at his death without painful emotions. The little rural grave-yard in Henrietta, N. Y., where Albert sleeps was visited by Mr. C. in the autumn of 1852, after an absence of a quarter of a century. It seemed to be filled with dead, unable to con-tain more, and therefore forsaken and left to solitude. The sun was going down, large and red, through the thick at-mosphere of an Indian summer evening, shedding its mel-low beams on the tall grass, which seemed not to have been trodden by human feet for years. No hour could have been more solemn. Here slept three of Mr. C.'s brothers, many other relatives, playfellows of his childhood, the almost adored Sophia, and many old neighbors of all ages. While this obscure spot, on an obscure road, scarcely traveled, seemed to be forsaken and forgotten, it was to Mr. C. full of interest, awakening more recollections than any other spot on earth.

Here, on this very spot, Albert and William had played in the wildwood when six years old. Here the gallant and accomplished John R. Bell was buried He had served in the army twenty years ; but failing in health, he left the garrison at Charleston, S. C., of which he had the command, and came north for recovery, but soon died ; and though his burial was attended by a grand martial parade, yet, after nearly thirty years, no monument, no marble slab, nor board, pointed to the place where he slept. His father and mother and sister were there, alike forgotten. If a distin-guished officer, a favorite of General Jackson, is so soon forgotten, what is fame but the passing wind ? How soon oblivion covers all !

Albert had experienced religion when eleven years of age, and continued faithful for some time. In the general apostacy of almost all the fruits of a great revival he was carried away with the flood, but he returned to the Lord in his last sickness, and died in peace.

Mr. C. returned to Rochester after Albert's burial, and in mid night often ardently desired and prayed that his departed brother might appear to him; but he never came.

To meet with the ghosts of dear ones gone has always been his desire, but they never come, and probably will not till the sea gives up its dead.

Although Mr. C. was at school in Rochester only twelve weeks, and although the school was but a low grade of academical institution, yet it was an era in his life. He studied rhetoric, chemistry and Latin, all of which laid the foundation for thought and study through life. He also spent some time in map-drawing, which he has always regarded as a childish waste of time.

In October Mr. C. commenced school-teaching in the town of Canandaigua, where he continued a year. While at Rochester he purposed to study law. This showed great ignorance of himself, for if he had become as learned in law as Blackstone, his timidity of countenance was such that he could never have competed with even an impudent blockhead at the bar. This timidity has embarrassed him in all the walks of life. His measures have often failed in conference, when truth and reason were most clearly on his side. He even dreaded to meet the most brutish Mormonite in debate. He never gave nor accepted a challenge for discussion.

Yet this timidity was physical, not moral; he never sought shelter under the wing of a great party, political or religious; he has generally been with the minority, and started in every reform in its earliest beginning; and when, more than twenty years ago, he aroused the wrath of men by trying to aid some colored people, the public indignation became so great that some anti-slavery friends forsook him and joined in his persecution; though his life was threatened, yet he was nerved to a stronger determination to persevere in opening his mouth for the dumb, everywhere, except in a face to face debate with an impudent disputant. He could have burned at Smithfield, but he could not have disputed with Bonner, nor with Bonner's hostler, if he had a face of brass and an overbearing temper.

CHAPTER XIII.

During the winter of 1826, Mr. C.'s old friend, Rev. Elisha House, was providentially brought into Canandaigua. Their meeting was a very happy one   Mr. C. began to exhort his scholars, and he had the happiness to see many of them converted.   In the spring he received license to exhort, and began regular appointments.   He had been seriously impressed with a sense of this duty from the time of his conversion, and now, as his labors had been blessed, he became settled in a sense of duty.

In the interval between the summer and winter terms of school he studied divinity with Rev. Seth Mattison, of Canandaigua, and on the 24th of May, 1827, he was married to Lydia A. Mattison.   She was deeply pious and an excellent scholar.   In October they removed to Manchester, where Mr. C. taught school five months.   It was to him a very laborious and unhappy winter, as he had one hundred scholars, rude in manners and uncultivated in morals, and encouraged to rebellion by a very immoral community; and Mrs. C. was sick most of the winter.

In the spring they removed to Mendon, where they lived

a few months, and in September removed to Batavia. Here Mr. C.'s opportunities were very much enlarged. He preached in several destitute neighborhoods, one of which, in Barre, north of the Tonawanda swamp, became subsequently one of the most favored parts of Zion.

In Batavia their first living child, Harriet C., was born, March 6, 1829. She was a beautiful and interesting child, and the happy parents were very thankful to the Lord for this precious gift; and though beginning with nothing, they both worked exceedingly hard, yet the remembrance of those days is very pleasant. They were the last years in which poor Mrs. C. had any health. They had buried their firstborn in Mendon, and now to have a living child so sprightly and interesting was constant sunlight on their way.

Those were times of the most violent anti-Masonic agitation, and Mr. C., having resided in Canandaigua during the twelvemonth following the abduction of Morgan, and subsequently residing in Batavia, the place of Morgan's first arrest, had a great opportunity to learn facts connected with that wicked affair, and was cured of all desire to be connected with that brotherhood.

Those were also times of great agitation in the Methodist Church, on account of the great secession, and organization of the Protestant Methodist Church. The names of the leaders of the secession were in the mouths of all, and nearly all were filled with horror at the hand that dared to write the "History and Mystery of Methodist Episcopacy," and found great relief in reading the "Defence of Our Fathers." Yet the confidence of thousands was incurably shaken in the sacredness of the episcopal office. The ordination of Dr. Coke has always suffered by exposure to the light, but by distance of country and distance of time it has grown sacred in America. The zeal which was displayed in putting down the Radicals, and blasting the reputation of their leaders, was worthy of a better cause.   Presiding elders published around their districts how all secessions had been failures, how the Lord had guarded, protected and blessed his own true church, and followed seceders with every mark of his displeasure.   Preachers followed suit, and threatened the divine indignation on all who should withdraw.   Exhorters learned and repeated the same lessons of denunciation, and class-leaders expected to be displeased if they showed Christian charity for seceders.

On one occasion Mr. C. had the pleasure to see a Protestant Methodist preacher, for whom he had much respect, invited on to the stand at a camp-meeting.   He was taken to be a Presbyterian, and as soon as the mistake was discovered, half the preachers began in audible whispers to debate what should be done, and agreed to treat him with total neglect

While Mr. C. resided in Batavia, he, with his family, attended a camp-meeting in Elba, where he met Lorenzo Dow.   His curiosity was great to see and hear the man who had made himself known to more men than any other man living, and who had attracted to his audience British lords and a British king.   Mr. C. thought his sermons rather extraordinary, developing much knowledge of the world and of human nature ; but men of equal knowledge and far better manner and elocution were often met with, who had but little reputation.   What than gave this man such wonderful popularity ?   This question is not easily answered.   His popularity always began with the low multitude, whose taste was coarse and unrefined, and when governors and lords and kings followed after him, they were carried by the vulgar tide.   His piercing eye never turned aside for the look of any man ; it looked through a man from the countenance to the soul.   This gave him great command of men ; and this, like every other exhibition of power, is pleasing to all men.   It is true a maniac, or a tiger, may look a king out of countenance, but when a man whose mental state approaches that of a maniac, but who still possesses wit, humor and reason, looks every man out of countenance, he never fails of popularity.   When one's popularity fills the world, he is henceforth popular, because he has been popular; every one wishes to see him, because he has heard his fame, and with many his commonplace remarks are wonderful.

Lorenzo Dow had great faults; his vulgar language offended all refined taste, his blackguardism approached the style of Billingsgate, and though he was called a very meek man, pride was his ruling passion.   He was too proud to regard public taste.   He would not stoop to conform to custom or taste in his dress or manners; hence pride made him a sloven and a clown.   What did he care who was pleased or disgusted with him?   Pride often made him unsocial, uncourteous and uncivil, haughty and overbearing. It is pride, rather than humility, commonly that makes a man coarse and blunt.   "I trample on the pride of Plato," said Diogenes, and he leaped in all his dirt upon Plato's sofa.   "Yes, Diogenes," said Plato, "but with still greater pride."

About this time Gray was hung in Batavia.   He, when drunk, had stabbed with a jack-knife a tavern keeper, who was attempting to put him out of his bar-room.   Mr. C. would not see the execution, believing it unchristian to break a man's neck; but he learned from his hired man, who stood near the gallows, that Gray was asked by a clergyman if he felt prepared to die.   He, all bathed in tears, answered no.   The rope was immediately put over his neck and his probation cut off.

"Whoso sheddeth man's blood, by man shall his blood be shed."   How often this passage is quoted, with all the assurance that it would be if the language was this : He that sheds man's blood shall be hung, by the sentence of a court. Why is it that this passage receives so much attention, while its counterpart in the New Testament : "All they that take the sword shall perish with the sword," is hardly noticed? Both passages evidently teach that human nature is such, that they that kill will be likely to be killed. There seems to be no more authority in the one passage than in the other for judicial execution. No one thinks of judicially arresting every soldier and putting him to death, although Christ has said, "All they that take the sword shall perish by the sword."

The advocates of capital punishment are advocates of war, and would deprive Christ's words of any meaning. They do not believe his word, that taking the sword brings the sword, brings destruction; but in opposition to his word, they believe that taking the sword and killing men brings liberty and peace. He that sheds man's blood was always in danger of having his life taken. Cain expected to be killed, but the Lord protected him.

Murderers in all ages and in all lands have been in danger of being slain by the friends of the murdered person. They have been hunted, pursued and waylaid, and often been slain in distant countries, long years after their crimes. As human nature is, killing calls for killing, violence wakes up violence, wrath kindles wrath, and taking the sword brings the sword. A kingdom spreads itself by conquest, but the conquered provinces, at the first opportunity, will bring back the sword and lay the conqueror in ruins. Forbearance and kindness only can give safety. All nations who have done violence are in danger.

About this time the great temperance movement began. Mr. C. went to hear the first lecturer who ever came near him, and signed the pledge, and began at once to preach

the doctrine of total abstinence.   Methodists were very
shy ;   it was called a Presbyterian movement for " Church
and State."   The *Christian Advocate* cautioned the people
against the movement, claiming that the Methodist Church
was the great pioneer temperance society for the world, that
Methodists deserved the honor of being the true reformers,
and scorning to go over to this Presbyterian organization.

Mr. C. had to contend with strong opposition from older
ministers one of whom called him a Presbyterian cat's-paw.
But while he found most of Methodist families using whisky,
most brethren drinking at raisings and all public gatherings,
all, with scarce an exception, furnishing whisky and rum for
harvestings, raisings, bees, butcherings and all jobs, and
found a decanter of bitters (so called) in every Methodist
house, the plea of Dr. Bangs that the Methodist Church
was a sufficient temperance society looked very ludicrous.

In 1829 Sam Patch made his fatal leap at Genesee Falls.
Mr. C. condemned severely the multitude who, for the
pleasure of excitement, would come together to see a poor
inebriate foolishly risk his life.   He never attended a circus,
a wire-dance or rope-walking ;   considered it wicked to encourage or countenance such life-risking and totally useless
feats.

CHAPTER XIV.

Shortly after Mr. C. removed to Batavia he called on a
very poor and deeply afflicted family, with whom he had
been acquainted in another land.   He found this worthy
family in the depths of poverty ; a group of little children
poorly clothed, and the father and mother both sick.   The
poor mother said to Mr. C., " 'Squire ———, one of your
Methodist brethren, threatens to take my husband to jail."

"Take him to jail for what?" "For a debt of one dollar; a dollar's worth of straw to feed our cow." Mr. C. looked on the pale face of the consumptive man and felt how cruel it would be to lock this poor coughing man up in jail for this debt; yet the laws of the State and the discipline of the church allowed it. This 'squire was a wealthy man, and received more respect from the pastor than any other member of the church. The pastor would pass by poor men with a slight greeting, apparently with some disgust, and hasten on to grasp the hand of the wealthy 'squire.

This is a great evil in all denominations. It is so different from the spirit and practice of Christ that it deserves the name of heathenism.

Mr. C. had occasion to take some stone from the ground for building purposes. In breaking the stone he found great numbers of horns of some beast now unknown in this country. They may have been the horns of buffaloes, but it is more likely they were the horns of some species now unknown. An extensive stratum of limestone crops out along the north line of Batavia where these horns are found in great numbers. Mr. C. found one of these horns in the loose earth, far from any rock, perfect in shape, even to a wrinkle. This was also perfect limestone.

In 1830 Mr. C. was employed by a presiding elder to travel Aurora Circuit, which was in the south part of Erie and Genesee counties, N. Y. He traveled once through the circuit in November, and returned to Batavia for his family. At the first quarterly-meeting the circuit was divided, and Mr. C. took the southeast part, a country new, poor, and exceedingly broken, being the highlands from which flow the Buffalo, the Tonawanda and the Cattaraugus Rivers.

He found the country so unimproved that no house could be found to shelter his wife and child, and after they had

rode with him to all of his appointments, over those mountain tops, during half of a severe winter, he, with a little
assistance, cleaned out a log pen, where he had kept his
horse at one appointment, and where hogs had slept, laid a
floor, made a roof of hollow logs split, laid a pile of stones
in one corner for a fireplace, and thus fitted up a mansion
twelve feet square, without chamber or cellar. Here he left
his patient wife and went on with his labors, having fourteen
appointments for every fourteen days. In the spring the
log roof was found to be so perforated with worms that it
leaked in every part and the place became absolutely unin-
habitable, and Mrs. C. and her child lived again on the road
until he closed his labors on the circuit. Her health was
now so poor, her constitution so broken, that Mr. C. abandoned the idea of traveling, and concluded not to offer himself
to conference.

Mr. C. had a hard year's labor, and felt that he had not
labored in vain. This field had been considered so far a
missionary field that ministers sent by conference to care
for those poor people had been, to a large extent, supported
by the couference treasury. Mr. C. had received so little
from the people that his claim upon the funds would have
been of considerable importance. Nine hundred and eighty
dollars was divided among the indigent, but Mr. C. was not
allowed to present a claim because he was a local preacher,
although the Discipline said, "When a local preacher fills
a traveling preacher's place, he shall receive a traveling
preacher's reward," and he had filled a traveling preacher's
place. No local preacher was allowed a seat in conference.
He sat with other local preachers in the gallery, with his
Discipline open at the clause; but it would have been out-
rageous for him to speak from the gallery, and no one below
speaking for him, he saw the whole business soon settled,
the money all divided, one hundred dollars going to the man

in whose place he had traveled, who had spent his time in book-peddling.

Mr. C. had become so poor in this year's toil that he had come to conference in a borrowed coat. He returned to his afflicted family, sold his only cow, and bought a coat, and went to work cutting and splitting rails, to clothe and feed his wife and child.

Mr. C. had found on coming to Aurora Circuit a deplorable want of temperance principle. A prominent member of the church was a rumseller, a class-leader was a hard drinker —kept whisky in his house and compelled his little child to drink it, and many who would shout and get very happy in meeting were hard drinkers, drinking everywhere, and some of them most violent opposers of the temperance cause.

This to him was a sore trial. In one of his largest classes more than half were hard drinkers; one was occasionally drunk and sometimes riotous, and yet sometimes very religious. This nest of drinkers he never succeeded in breaking up, although he did succeed in inducing many of their neighbors to become consistent temperance people. It was the inconsistent lives of this people that convinced Mr. C. of the danger of trusting emotion in religious experience. He had never found any Methodist equal to them in emotion, in getting happy and shouting. Their shouts sometimes mingled into one sound like the roar of a tempest, when no individual's voice could be distinguished. There were, however, many excellent men and women on this circuit, who were ready for every good work, who strengthened his hands in this arduous work of reform, and who were ornaments to the church and to human nature. A cause which has on its side humanity and truth, and marshals under its banner virtue and intelligence, cannot fail.

> " Truth crushed to earth will rise again,
>   The eternal years of God are hers."

Mr. C. finally saw the triumph of that cause in that country.

CHAPTER XV.

Mr. C. had removed his family to the town of Barre, Orleans county, where his son, William M., was born, November 16, 1831; and there he taught school during the winter.

At this time Worcester's great work on the evils of war fell into his hands. This he devoured with the most lively interest. Its peace doctrines agreed with his every sentiment. He was in raptures to find that so much was being done in this cause. From that time the power of kindness formed an important part of his preaching. He had been, when first connected with the church, to some extent a party man, while he enjoyed the pleasing dream that Methodism was immaculate; but he had been for some time awaking from that dream, and now felt that all Christians were his brethren, the world was his country, and all mankind his countrymen. He could never after this countenance the severe spirit of anathema on some called heretics, as before; he held no more close class-meetings, and refrained from expressions in doctrinal preaching calculated to wound the feelings of honest hearers. He applied these principles to school government, and nearly abandoned corporeal punishments.

In the spring of 1832 he removed to Java, Genesee county, and built a house, about half a mile from the log pen in which his family had dwelt when he was traveling Aurora Circuit. Here he commenced clearing a new farm, and preaching on Sundays to many congregations, going on foot over an extent of country larger than many circuits at

this day. The circuit preacher engaged him to fill his appointments for a short time, but charged him to expect no
pay, as local preachers were expected to preach for nothing.
He took this task upon him, traveling sometimes twenty
miles in a day, and preaching twice or three times. His
own appointments were nearly as far away. The people
were kind, but very poor. They wished to do something
for him, but he made no demand on them for anything.
However, after long enduring extreme poverty, at one time
confining himself to a diet of potatoes and milk for more
than a month, while working exceedingly hard, he offered
at length to labor for neighbors at their own prices, who
would supply his pressing necessities. A crisis finally came.
He was informed by his patient wife that all of their food
could last but a few days; he had no money, and could find
no man who would sell any grain or meat for work. He
said to his excellent companion, "The brethren at one of
my appointments, where I have preached on the Sabbath
for more than a year, invited me to go over with a wagon
and get some provisions. I will get a horse and wagon and
go to-day." He did go, and got eatables to the value of
two dollars and twenty-five cents; and for this he was called
to an account in quarterly-meeting conference, and kept
under catechism and rebuke for more than an hour; traveling ministers insisting that local preachers violated the Discipline in receiving anything for preaching anywhere on a
Methodist circuit.

During these trials he was invited to become permanent
pastor of the Methodist Church at Weathersfield Springs.
A liberal offer was made, which, if realized, would place
his family in circumstances of comfort. This appointment,
however, he could not receive except from the bishop, and
to receive it from him Mr. C. must unite with the conference of traveling preachers, and be liable to be removed at

the end of the year to any circuit within the Genesee Conference, or even within the nation. Mrs. C. dreaded an
itinerant life so much that she preferred to continue in
poverty.

Mr. C.'s lot seemed hard, and he sometimes almost concluded to withdraw and get loose from such embarrassments,
but the dread of seeming to vacillate, and the fact that none
got out of the church without a severe scathing, always induced him to remain and suffer these great inconveniences.

In the winters of 1832-33-34 he taught school in Java;
improving still more on the plan of governing by benevolence. While he resided there the meteoric shower occurred.
Millions of stars seemed to fall from every point in the
heavens, each spinning behind a small beautiful streak of
flame. It was witnessed over a vast extent of country.
That these were common meteors, no man of science
doubts; but why the atmosphere should be so largely charged with meteoric matter, perhaps none will ever know.

Not long after this Mr. C. saw a meteoric light about
three or four o'clock in the morning. A light much above
that of the stars, shining suddenly around him, he looked up
and saw a luminous body, nearly of the color of the moon,
a parallelogram in shape, perhaps ten feet in length and
three in width. It seemed fixed for a moment, and then
slowly spread, growing paler and thinner, and at the same
time longer and broader, until it faded out of view. The
night was cold, still and cloudless; the stars shining very
clearly. No sound attended it. The light which shone
from it to the earth faded as that faded, and disappeared as
that faded out. The whole scene may have lasted five
minutes.

This was the era of South Carolina revolt and Nullifica-
tion, and Mr. C. received from Washington the speeches in

full of Adams, Webster, Clay, Calhoun and Poindexter, delivered on that occasion.

This was the era of the first cholera in our country. A
fast was proclaimed, and Mr. C. preached to a very solemn
congregation.

This was also the era of the first anti-slavery movement
under Garrison and the Tappans.   This great movement
broke upon Mr. C. like an eruption of Etna.   He, with
several other ministers, attended by invitation a religious
mass-meeting, on the fourth of July, 1833, at Weathersfield
Springs.   Mr. C. was to be the speaker.   Mr. Blanchard,
the first speaker, delivered a speech, denouncing coloniza-
tion, and advocating immediate emancipation.   He then
informed us that there was a simultaneous movement of
this kind throughout the land on that day.   This was unex-
pected and startling to most of the congregation.

The Mormon apostles, who had for some time been going
to and fro in the earth, came to Java in 1833.   Mr. C.
thought this movement so absurd that he deemed opposition uncalled for ; but soon found his neighbors going out
like a flood after this imposture.   He then felt aroused to
action, attended a prayer meeting, mixed of all people, in
which Mormonites seemed to be carrying all before them.
Toward the close of the meeting he arose and warned the
people to beware of this moral pestilence, and gave a brief
account of the origin of the movement.   Many stood astonished ; some, perhaps, expected to see him fall down dead ;
for a strange and bewitching awe had come over them.   He
was too late, though this speech arrested the evil and saved
many who were wavering ; yet many others were so bound
in the bewitching web of this necromancy, that no warning
availed.   They sold their possessions at ruinous prices and
went to the promised land, which was then Kirtland, Ohio.

It may be proper here to give a brief account of the origin of Mormonism.

A family by the name of Smith lived near the township line between Manchester and Palmyra, N. Y. They were distinguished for nothing but ignorance and superstition, unless we add indolence and dishonesty. Joseph, their oldest son, was a stout, fearless, impudent fellow of very bad morals. The mother was a person of most extravagant wonder, always seeking for the news of some strange, marvelous and supernatural event ; while the father was weak-minded and very credulous. Their house was the resort of persons like themselves. Much of their conversation turned on money-digging, in which they were often engaged in their neighborhood.

Joseph had much more originality and energy of character than his parents, but partook of their superstition and indolence, and far surpassed them in dishonesty and falsehood. He procured a stone, somewhat irregular in appearance, found in digging a well, by which he pretended to see objects far under ground. His father and his money-digging comrades, now felt sure of success, with Joseph to lead them to buried treasures. He enjoyed the fun, as he richly loved to deceive, and as long as these night excursions gave him food by sheep-stealing, he liked this business better than honest labor by day.

They extended their money-digging down the Susquehanna, digging in various places, at one of which Joseph said he saw two bars of gold, large as a hogshead, crossing each other, at a certain distance below the surface. This worked the company to great enthusiasm, and in the excitement Joseph divided this vast treasure into shares and sold as many as he could, and then went on to Pennsylvania after more fortune. He there found the woman who became his wife by eloping with him. After the poor dolts who had bought his shares of the great gold bars had toiled long and hard, Joseph returned and advised them to stop digging, as he had seen the gold move off to parts unknown.

He made a journey to Ohio, where he probably met with Sydney Rigdon.

One evening was spent at Smith's—Joseph living with his father—in conversing about a gold bible, said to have been dug up in Canada. The next day Joseph was coming home. after a severe shower, when he saw some beautiful white sand, which he thought would be of service to the women for scouring. He took off his tow frock and putting a quantity of sand into it, swung it over his shoulder and went home. Coming to the open door, he was met by the women, who exclaimed, "Joe, what have you got?" "I happened to think," said he, "of the talk the night before about the gold bible, and I said, 'I've got the golden bible.' 'Let me see it! Let me see it!' they exclaimed. 'You may all see it,' I said; 'but the first one who sees it will die in a minute.' 'Oh!' they exclaimed and started back." Joseph saw that there was no danger of any of the affrighted family looking into the tow frock. It lay undisturbed while he went to a neighbor, who was a mechanic, and engaged him to make a nice small chest to hold the same, telling him the whole story, and saying he had made d—d fools of the family, and now intended to carry out the joke. The sand was locked up in the chest, and became the celebrated Plates of the Golden Bible.

Rigdon, pastor of a Campbellite Church at Kirtland, Ohio, asked leave of absence for a few weeks. He said he might go as far as Pittsburg. When he had been absent some months, the church learned that he was in Palmyra, closeted most of the time with Joseph Smith and Martin Harris in secret conclave.

Dr. Spaulding, a distiller in Conneaut, Ohio, failing in

business many years before these events, sat himself to writing a book in imitation of the Old Testament history. He was an atheist, and boasted that in a hundred years his book would be as highly esteemed as the Bible. Spaulding moved to Pittsburg, where he carried his manuscript to a printer, and tried to get it printed, but died without accomplishing it. Rigdon at that time was pastor of a Baptist Church in Pittsburg, was often in the printing-office, and doubtless saw the manuscript, and doubtless be purloined the manuscript from the office, where it had long lain unnoticed, and carried it to Palmyra; for when the chest of sand was translated, it proved to be a version of Dr. Spaulding's romance. This was proved by a neighbor who had heard Spaulding read the manuscript while writing it, and also by Widow Spaulding, who testified under oath that the Mormon book was the same in substance as her husband's manuscript

Martin Harris, a natural born fanatic, mortgaged his farm to secure the printer, and the book was put to press. Thus arose Mormonism, one of the strangest things in this century.

That so many have been carried away by so gross a deception seems incredible, but shows how many never reason, never think of proving what they believe.

Mormonites are now of two kinds: first, honest, sincere persons, who, in their ignorance and credulity, believe in Mormonism; second, political Mormonites, who, being infidels, unite with Mormonites for secular and political ends. These are doubtless numerous, and often exhibit the grossest depravity, the most ferocious tempers, and most debauched manners.

CHAPTER XVI.

Mr. C. attended a prayer-meeting in the summer of 1834 and gave an exhortation, at the close of which one arose for prayers; he then continued his appeal, and another came. From time to time another and another came until all the unconverted, eight in number, came, and all were converted before morning. the meeting continuing until daylight. One of these, a young girl fourteen years old, struggled long and nearly in despair for hours. The powers of darkness seemed determined to prevail. Mr. C. knelt by the child, and re-solved to continue there and neither sleep nor eat, or even rise to his feet, until victory came to Zion. The mother sat behind the child, supporting her in a kneeling posture. The most plaintive expressions of despair were often heard from her, moving every heart. The child had a father and mother, a grandfather and grandmother, uncles and aunts and cousins residing near, most or all of whom were there and most deeply concerned for the light of the divine coun-tenance to shine into her darkened mind. Towards the close of night her countenance changed; beams of glory were on her face, and she exclaimed, "Jesus is mine! Jesus is mine!"

At another prayer-meeting all of the unconverted, six in number were converted. Here Mr. C. was so exercised in silent or inarticulate prayer for some young persons who had shown no signs of awakening, that he continued kneeling more than an hour, and when he arose he found these per-sons most earnestly seeking salvation.

Mr. C.'s constitutional melancholy and the injury to his nerves by the partial breaking of his spine, have been named. He was often nearly in despair after his conversion, and often preached when he rather expected to be lost. At such times he preached with great zeal and pathos, feeling the value of

souls in the highest degree.   It gave him some relief to be
able to guide others to heaven, though he should go to hell.
His melancholy was much influenced by his health and by
the state of the atmosphere.   He attended a camp-meeting
in Sheldon while he resided in Java.   As others grew ani-
mated and joyful, he became sorrowful, seriously doubting
the genuineness of his conversion.   He could get no relief
while in the congregation, and went into the wilderness, far
away from the encampment, and wrestled long in prayer,
but returned without comfort.   He left again, and went still
farther into the wilderness, beyond the hearing of all men,
resolving never to go out of the woodland without a witness
of his acceptance with the Lord.   Hour after hour he
wrestled in prayer in the most earnest manner, and yet no
light came to his darkened mind.   He raised his head from
the ground, stood silently on his knees, and said within himself, " I may as well give up ; I can do no more ; I give
myself up entirely; I am willing to be anything, do anything
whatever, and yet I get no relief.   I am a reprobate ; there
can be no salvation for me.   Hell and destruction are behind, yet I cannot go forward."   As though a voice from
heaven had been heard, these words went through his mind,
Jesus tasted death for every man, and he said, " If Jesus
died for all, he died for me.   I would claim Jesus as my
Savior if I had faith ; but I have not faith, never had faith,
cannot get faith ; have sought faith for ten years, but cannot
obtain it, never shall obtain it.   What shall I do ?   Shall I
give up in despair ?   All is lost unless I go forward.   I
must claim an interest in Jesus or perish   I will claim it
now, without waiting for faith.   Jesus died for me.   I claim
an interest in his blood.   I hold him by a trembling hand,
but never will unloose my hold.   I cling to his bleeding
side, and never will let go."   A voice, as from beneath,
said, " Presumptuous wretch ! · to claim Jesus as your

Savior; so vile, so infamous, as you are." He trembled, but seeing nothing but destruction behind, he resolved to go forward, and again exclaimed, "I hold to his bleeding side, and never will let go." Involuntarily he had arisen and stood with countenance uplifted toward heaven, rejoicing with joy unspeakable. He had now found that faith was to venture on Christ, without waiting for faith. Before this he had regarded faith as a mysterious gift of God, something external to himself. He now found faith to be something in himself, a voluntary exercise of confidence in God. Many doubtless fix the foundation of their hope in strong feelings or emotions; some risk their salvation on their having seen a strange sight, or having heard a strange sound. All of these things are worthless. Simply trusting in God through Christ brings salvation. All else must fail.

Mr. C. had been educated to expect something in religious experience which he never could find. He never found those emotions which some have, and if these are essential to salvation, he must fail.

The temperance cause still flourished in Java, and Mr. C. took an active part and felt a lively interest in it. Before he left that country there were over four hundred members of temperance societies in his town.

A fellow-townsman, in 1834, a reformed inebriate, a man of much intelligence, made an invention, which for a time made a great noise. It was a propelling power, by gravitation. He had invented a regulator for the descent of large weights. This was an original invention, and very interesting. It was judged by men of science that it would make the descent of the largest weights perfectly regular in time. Thousands now concluded that steam was superseded on land and sea, for all saw that the descent of great stones would move the most ponderous wheels. A model was sent to Washington, and a patent applied for; the rights of

States were bargained for at four and five thousand dollars, and one man in cold, inhospitable Java was going to be rich.   The raising of the weights had been little thought of, the great inquiry having been, how to get them down. When the inventor was asked about raising the weights, he confidently answered, " Two men can raise the weights in six minutes, and they will be twelve hours descending." Michigan was offered to Mr. C. and he had serious thoughts of entering on this business, but first sat down to consider, and found that after the most complex contrivance of levers, pulleys and wheels, it must take same power to raise weights as to propel the machine.

December 6, 1833, there was born to Mrs. and Mr. C. their second daughter, Zelura D.   The health of Mrs. C. was every year declining.   Her husband, as far as possible, shared with her in the care of their children and in every kind of housework.   He was clearing a very heavy timbered farm at great inconvenience, as he had no team.   An un-lucky stroke of his ax inflicted a large and deep wound in his leg; but this did not stop his labor more than fifteen or twenty minutes—time enough to bind up the wound when he was again at work as hard as ever; and thus he con-tinued day after day and night after night, giving himself but short hours for eating and sleeping.   He moved large logs great distances with his handspike, and gathered all of his ashes without a team.   Lame as he was, he was obliged to work in rain storms, to save the little property on which he depended for the support of his feeble family.   His wound became badly inflamed, and barely escaped gangrene, and the diseased part was never afterward sound.

It would have been hard to take such land as a gift.   It was, however, bought at $3.50 per acre, each settler taking an article and paying generally a small part at the time. These articles were so drawn, that the failure of any one payment, or part of a payment, forfeited the settler's claim to anything even to his buildings. This was on the Holland Purchase. In 1834 agents were sent through all of that country, warning all who had thus forfeited their claims to be ready to leave their homes, even when men had paid at the land-office all of their income, and had made extensive improvements.

Mr. C., satisfied that he could not meet his payments and support his family, sold his claim for $100, and prepared to leave that country for the Western States. Some who had large improvements were waited on by men who informed them that they had been to the land-office and bought their farms from under them, ordering them to leave in so many days. The indignation of the people became very great. Land-offices were threatened; one was destroyed with all of its books, and the parent office at Batavia was guarded by armed men.

Men of legal wisdom investigated the history of the original purchase of this land by the Holland Company, and found it of such a nature, that if it had been an affair of yesterday, it would probably have been set aside by any honest court. Age alone had made it valid.

There is not much land on earth the original title to which has anything of justice or equality about it. Age alone has sanctified it. The titles to the large estates in England arose in the most wicked robbery. The land titles in Ireland nearly all arose in despotic tyranny; Cromwell, and after him William III, driving nearly all original land owners from their homes, and putting Englishmen and Scotchmen in possession, and the iron heel of their sons is at this day on the necks of the ignorant, degraded and starving descendants of the former Irish land-owners.

A case of hereditary insanity occurred in Java which deeply affected many. Rebecca ——— had come with her father's family from Vermont. Her mother had been insane from Rebecca's birth, and was left in Vermont. A worthy young man, who was to be married to Rebecca in 1832, died of cholera on Lake Erie, under circumstances painfully romantic and calculated to work with great power on her active imagination. Instead of the sympathy which she should have had from her father's family, she only received ridicule and soon became insane, took poison, and only escaped death by overdosing. Reaction saved her. After recovering she attended Mr. C.'s school. He felt a deep interest in her welfare, found her to be amiable, intelligent and pious, and labored faithfully to settle and establish her mind in perfect health.

He introduced to her a young man whom he highly esteemed, and this resulted in marriage. For years prosperity attended them, but insanity returned at intervals, and finally became permanent, when she procured cambric, and in a neat and tidy manner made four shrouds, for herself and three youngest children. This was done so secretly that no one knew that a shroud was made, and, strange to say, all deemed her sane, because she was capable of managing her house in proper order. The husband and father came in after a few hours' absence, and was informed that the mother had gone to the corn-field with the three little girls; one had got away. He found in the corn-field his wife and two children, with their throats cut, side by side, dead.

While Mr. C. was teaching in 1834, two boys came to school who had been despised and hooted out of school so often that they doubtless came with little courage. Their father was a most degraded drunkard, and their poor mother was so broken-hearted and discouraged that her house was kept in bad order, and the family was held in contempt. The boys felt no self-respect and expected no respect from others. Mr. C. bestowed marked attention on these boys, inspired them with confidence, hope and self-respect, and found them well-behaved and studious, promising scholars. He moved to Michigan in the spring. Sometime in the summer, Isaac, the oldest of the above-mentioned boys, about fourteen or fifteen years of age, said to his mother, "I am afraid father will kill me when he is drunk; he knocks me down with a handspike. Had I not better leave home?" "Where can you go, my poor boy?" "I will go to Mr. C., in Michigan." "Then I will help you off," she replied, and he left for Michigan; but passing through Ohio, weary and moneyless, he fell in with a boy about two years older than himself, one of the worst in the world, who had been his playfellow from infancy. Isaac, glad to find a familiar face after being so long among strangers, loitered a while with him, and was drawn into crime. Stolen goods were found with them, and though Isaac was probably only guilty of partaking of the stolen property, both were sent to the penitentiary for five years, and before the end of the time Isaac died.

CHAPTER XVII.

Mr. C. in his journey west stopped of necessity in Jackson county, Michigan, becoming too sick to journey farther. They settled in Spring Arbor, purchased eighty acres of land, a cow, and provisions for a few weeks, when their last dollar was paid out. Emigration was now setting in like a flood. Every house and hovel was filled with inhabitants. Mr. C. erected a hut and moved into it as soon as it was shingled, without floor, doors or windows.

As soon as his house was made comfortable he was obliged to work by the day for provisions, going from two to three miles to find inhabitants. He settled on burr-oak plains, far from any road, and the rank grass and weeds made walking very inconvenient.   Mrs. C. at one time did not see a woman in three months.   In July, a little before harvest, no grain could be bought.   Mr. C.'s family were reduced to one day's provision of food.   He arose on Sunday morning and went without eating to his appointments, and late in the afternoon, after preaching twice, he was invited to eat.   He carried home a little corn meal, which sustained his poor wife and children until he was able to get some flour, brought from a distance of fifteen miles.

He worked extremely hard, sometimes going before daylight, and returning after dark, not seeing his home by daylight for a week.   At such times he cut his firewood and did all other necessary chores in the night, then traveled two, three or four miles in season to commence a day's work ; often carrying home on his shoulder a bag of provisions.

Mr. C. was in health and very strong.   He was self-reliant and felt sure of supporting his almost helpless family, so long as his health continued, even if he did two days' work in every twenty-four hours.

He usually preached twice or thrice every Sabbath, traveling from eight to eighteen miles on foot, often traveling without roads, the whole land being open and smooth, the annual fires keeping down all underbrush.   These plains during summer were covered with innumerable flowers ; the few trees, which seemed like ornamental trees and orchard trees, were the resort of many birds of song, and the enormous sand-hill crane, which stood higher than a cow, sang shrill tenor, which at times was heard three miles.   These great birds were then very numerous about all moist lands.   Sometimes, in the heat of summer, they soared to the higher atmosphere, where they could scarcely be seen, and where their shrill notes sounded to earth like music from heaven.

Deer came along in droves of ten or fifteen, and when startled, raised their plumes and went off in beautiful style. Large flocks of turkeys often came along with lofty strides, and prairie hens were very numerous.

To Mr. C. the country was then far more interesting than since the hand of man has spoiled the beauties of nature. His little children were very happy, roaming over the plains after flowers, humming-bees and birds; but poor Mrs. C., sick and shut out from human society, felt lonesome and disconsolate.

Not long after their removal to their wild home Mrs. C. was taken violently and dangerously ill, and seemed about to die of hemorrhage. The oldest child could not find the way to the nearest neighbor. A family had just come in, a mile and a half from them. Mr. C. ran all the way to their house and back again, trembling with fear that he would find his wife dead. She, however, recovered from the very gates of death, to the great joy of her husband and children.

Those were days of the wildest speculation. All men seemed partially insane. Some made themselves rich in a day in land speculation, and therefore all hoped to do the same. Lands bought for $1.25 per acre were deemed worth $5.00 per acre the next day, for somebody had sold wild land at that price. Villages and cities had grown up like mushrooms in some places, and therefore a thousand other places were considered fit sites for cities. Surveyors were employed for weeks laying out a great city in Spring Arbor; a millwright was employed a long time; and a canal was dug, and attempt made to force a little sluggish stream to become a great and rapid river; but twenty years afterwards the main streets and public squares were yet a wilderness; the costly workmanship for the interior of the mill lay rotting under the wild brush, and the weeds grew rankly along the bed of the canal, and the little sluggish stream enjoyed its own channel through the marsh. On a small brook near where it fell into Grand River a city was laid out and named Columbia; a mill was built, and a little village of huts arose; but in a few years all turned back to wilderness again.

Branch, in Branch county, became a lively village, with splendid and costly buildings, but is now a wild desolation with scarce an inhabitant.

Methodists seemed to take the lead in pioneer religious enterprise. The itinerant preachers were more noble than those of Western New York. They treated the local preachers with respect, and did not complain for what they received of the people.

Mr. C. received some help, without which his feeble, helpless family must have suffered most extreme destitution at times. Mr. C. was on terms of friendship with the Indians, always treating them with kindness. If they had come on to his land to raise corn, he would not have disturbed them, believing that their title to lands was usually extinguished by coercion and oppression. He would have been safe in traveling among the most ferocious tribes, provided they understood his disposition. Such was not the spirit generally manifested towards them. Their cultivated fields were plowed up while they lingered around them, and one man in Spring Arbor tore down their wigwam to get the poles.

Spring Arbor felt sure for some years of being graced by a splendid Methodist college, because a city was to be there, and a city was to be there because a college was to be there; but neither city nor Methodist college arose, and though Spring Arbor is a very rich agricultural town, it seems doomed never to have a village.

When Mr. C. passed through Detroit on his journey west, a convention was in session, framing a State constitution.

It was some time, however, before Michigan was admitted into the Union, on account of a disputed State line between Michigan and Ohio. A boy was then governor of Michigan Territory, adventurous and energetic, but rash and indiscreet. He called out an army and marched to Toledo to defend Michigan's rights and drive the Buckeyes from the ground. This boyish movement—a mark of disgrace on the pages of Michigan's history—resulted in wanton depredations on the property of principal citizens and in foolish boastings of what we would do to the Buckeyes. It brought on us the just contempt of wise and sensible men everywhere, especially in Congress. The affair was compromised, and Michigan was admitted with the Upper Peninsula, instead of a few acres of swamp on our south line." The Boy," as our territorial governor was called, was popular with the adventurers of our country by his urbanity and bar-room sociability, and was elected governor of the State. The result has proved the folly of the people's choice. The effect of his wild, impracticable measures are seen to this day, in the gloomy ruins of abandoned public works, and felt in tax paying. The Upper Peninsula has proved of almost infinitely more importance than the port of Toledo. It opens a vast field of enterprise and wealth; has finally opened Lake Erie to navigation, and filled a once barren waste with a most stirring population. Toledo at the same time is important to Ohio and is destined to become one of the great cities of the West.

In 1835 Mr. C. was erecting a house at what was called Spring Arbor village, though no village was there. A debate was coming off on Emancipation, and Mr. C., wishing to open his mouth for the dumb, inquired at his boarding-place for some book or paper on the subject, and found nothing but an extremely small paper called *Human Rights*. From this he gathered his ammunition for the combat. A prominent Methodist preacher opposed him, pleading that emancipation would ruin the South, as white men and women could not work, and must therefore starve, if deprived of their slaves.

This committed Mr. C. as an abolitionist, but his constitutional caution made him for some time rather silent, as the Methodist Church held a rod of terror over the head of every agitator. He dreaded controversy and greatly desired the peace of the church; but when he read, in the *Christian Advocate*, an article from Nathan Bangs, apologizing for the murderers of Lovejoy, he laid the paper down and, silently musing, said within himself, " Which side does God take ?" The article was entitled, " Read Both Sides and then Judge." It was to him clear as demonstration that God was on the side of the oppressed and opposed to this wicked apology.

He was now determined to throw off all restraint, agitate this subject, and let the consequences be what they might. If the church was determined to join hands with the oppressor, he determined to cry aloud and spare not, though the church should be rent in twain, and though he might be a martyr to this hated cause.

In the spring of 1836 Mr. C. and his family sat in their rude hut around their fire one gloomy night, when a man called in whom Mr. C. had often seen—a man of proud and lofty mien, a prominent citizen and a leading politician. He had waded through water above his boots, and came in drenched in mud and water. They were greatly embarrassed to receive a call from a gentleman accustomed to the elegancies of life. What rendered their embarrassment greatest, they had brought into the house a poor sick calf, or yearling, and laid it by the fire. Their embarrassment was soon removed when the 'squire informed them that he had come to inquire the way of salvation.

The evening was passed in most interesting conversation and devotion. In the morning 'Squire —— requested Mr. C. to come and get provisions at his house, which he did to the amount of fourteen dollars. This was most certainly providential, for they were nearly on the point of starvation. A fortune of thousands falling to some families could not have made them so happy as this donation made the family of Mr. C. He felt to exclaim, "Surely goodness and mercy shall follow me all the days of my life."

How cheerfully they sang, how merrily the children played, now they had both bread and meat. Squire —— said Mr. C.'s hut was to him a palace, and surely he made it a palace to them, though it had in it but one chair, and a table made of a whitewood slab. Perhaps no donation ever blessed a family more.

On the 22d of June, 1836, their son, John Emory, was born. No physician, nor even any neighbor, was present. It was a time of deep trial, but the hand of the Lord was with them. Mrs. C. passed through her trials with less suffering than usual, and rejoiced in the possession of an interesting little son. ·

That was a very wet summer, and all of the lowlands were flowed with water. Mr. C., to meet the wants of his family, worked on the marshes seven weeks at haying, a large part of the time standing in the water, which filled all the spaces between the bogs. He often returned home after dark across an extensive marsh, wading sometimes in water two feet in depth. His feet and legs became inflamed, and doubtless these hardships hastened the scrofulous state which, in after years, afflicted him so severely.

In August Sally Crane, youngest sister to Mr. C.'s father, called on him, expecting to spend her life with him; but being naturally proud and having been accustomed to the best society in cities, she was disgusted with a new country,

and especially with Mr. C.'s Indian-like home, and returned
soon to the East, promising to write soon; but as he never
heard from her again, she probably died on her journey and
strangers took her money, which must have been considerable, as she had lately sold the homestead of the Crane
family in Great Barrington.

In the autumn of 1836 Mr. C. sold his land in Spring
Arbor, and in company with several men plunged into the
wilderness in search of a new home.   Night overtook them
in a swamp, which they attempted to cross.   They waded
through a slough of mud and water up to their knees, and
finding a small spot where the land was barely above water,
they started a fire with lucifer matches and prepared to pass
the night.   They erected two crotched sticks and laid a
pole across for a seat, as the ground was too wet to sit on.
As soon as they were all seated on the pole the crotches
sank in an instant their whole length in the ground, bringing
them suddenly down.   They managed, however, by standing
around the fire, to dry their clothes, which were wet to their
hips, and to eat their supper, while the water of the swamp
was freezing.

A young Vermonter, who was rather timid, said, "Somebody lives near.   I hear dogs howling."   His cousin, who
had spent some years in Michigan, replied, " I guess you
hear no dogs."   "What is it?" cried the Vermonter.
" Wolves," was the answer.   " Wolves!" cried the affrighted son of the Green Mountain State; "will they come
here ?"   Mr. C. and his Michigan neighbor smiled, being
more familiar with wolves than with sheep.

They assured their friend that the wolves would not come
there, but they had like to be mistaken, for they came so
near that all expected to see the glare of their eyes, constantly howling.   They, however, turned away as soon as
they had examined the encampment, and their shrill howl-

ing sounded farther and farther away until the sound died away in the distance, when it was near midnight.

When they had chosen their lands, which, for themselves and others, amounted to about forty lots—more than three thousand acres—they started across a very extensive wilderness to the land office at Ionia. Nothing of interest occurred on the way, except sleeping on the ground nights and wading through some swamps, until they came to Grand River, near Ionia. They found no way to cross, and called aloud and fired guns to bring some one to the ferry, but all in vain. They finally, with a small hatchet, cut grape vines and tied flood-wood together and made a raft. They found at the land office an amount of fraud surpassing all that Mr. C. had ever witnessed or imagined. The clerks were taking advantage of the crowd of applicants, and defrauding in every possible way. "We cannot attend to your business now," was said to scores of men; "you must wait your time," and while they waited and honestly slept, others bribed the clerks to open the office at midnight and supplanted them. If two applied at once for the same lands, they were put at auction, and all above $1.25 per acre the clerks took to themselves.

It was announced that they took only specie. A broker's office was opened across the street from the land-office where they demanded ten per cent. discount on the best eastern bills. Mr. C. and his company, fearing that they might wait till winter, being elbowed back by violence and fraud, paid one of the clerks forty dollars to induce him to do what he was employed by the government to do, and paid by government for doing, that is, to attend to their business as soon as convenient. He told them that they need not take their paper to the broker, as he would take it at five per cent. discount. Mr. C. did not then think that he was paying a bribe, but always afterwards regretted this transaction, and never again would hire a government officer to do his duty.   He was informed by the inhabitants of Ionia that the broker's office belonged to the clerks of the land-office, and that the government took bank notes for their lands, and knew nothing of the specie transaction at Ionia, and that the gold and silver was taken from the land-office every night and carried to the broker's office.   If so, these clerks must have amassed immense fortunes in a few weeks.   If public officers are commonly so corrupt, there must be great iniquity in their appointment and continuance.

Mr. C. was hurried away from Ionia without provisions, one of the company saying that he had engaged provisions at the last house on entering the wilderness.   They were there disappointed, a company of landhunters having eaten nearly all in the house.   Three men, including Mr. C., entered the wilderness with one-third ration.   On the second day they were waterbound by the Thornapple River.   They had crossed on flood-wood going down, but could not find it on their return.   They spent half a day in searching for the crossing in vain.   Mr. C., after turning over logs to find mice or frogs to eat, found none, and became so weak that he staggered while gathering wood, and said to the company, "I can bring no more wood.   If there is no room for me by the fire, I will stay away."   They took him at his word, and lay down entirely around the fire, and he sat down on a log.

A snow storm sat in, and Mr. C., while he sat faint and cold, could not refrain from smiling to see his comrades with heads and shoulders white with snow, while their feet were near to burning.   They were all wrapped in the soundest sleep, while he sat like a gloomy sentinel.

He heard a scream, which he took to be that of a panther, and felt encouraged, hoping to encounter the panther, to overcome him and roast and eat him.   If they had met, it would have been ludicrous; a hungry beast and a hungry man, each fighting more for his stomach than his life.

Mr. C. slept some before morning. At an early hour all agreed to go up the river until it could in some manner be crossed. About ten oclock they came to higher lands, where the current was swift and channel narrow, and here a tall tree had fallen across, on which they passed over. A very small biscuit for each had been sacredly kept, to be eaten on this side of the river. On the strength of this they traveled till four o'clock, when they came to a house about five miles northwest from where Eaton Rapids now is.

Mr. C. was very lame during this journey, one of his ankles being so swelled when he arrived at Ionia that every wrinkle in the boot-leg was filled with flesh; and the boot was cut open down to the sole to get it off. He arrived home in about the same state.

CHAPTER XVIII.

In December, 1837, Mr. C. removed with his family to what is now the town of Eaton Rapids. Mrs. C. was nearly blind with inflammation in the eyes, and otherways very ill. It was fifteen miles to any place where medicines or provisions could be obtained. The winter was terribly severe, the snow lying two feet deep with a hard crust. The wolves went in droves over the crusted snow, sometimes fifteen together, and came by night around every house. They made terrible havoc among the half-starved deer, as these poor timid animals, when frightened into running, broke through the crust and became an easy prey.

Mr. C.'s time was spent taking care of his sick family, drawing his hay twenty miles, going for food and medicine, and cutting logs for a house. Disappointments came from every side; he failed to build a house, and in the spring was already so much in debt to doctors and others, and so much in need of clothing and provisions that he was obliged to sell half of his land.   Flour delivered in Eaton county cost $18 per barrel, and clothing was very dear, and doctors were unmerciful in their charges.   Mr. C. was prompted by yearning attachment to his sick wife and feeble children to tax his energies beyond mercy, working with most driving force all day and part of the night, doing housework of every kind, cooking, washing, ironing, baking, nursing the sick, taking care of an infant child, and at the same time laboring more each day and night out of doors than he would have required of a hired man.

On the Sabbath he went in search of congregations, and established religious meetings in almost every settlement, crossing the wilderness without a track, and sometimes wading through Grand River, and sometimes going twelve miles from home on foot, and returning before he slept, to assist his family.

In the spring of 1837 a town was organized, including four geographical townships, and named Eaton. Mr. C. was elected supervisor, also school inspector, which involved him in unpleasant cares and some censure, and led him to resolve never again to hold civil office. He was nominated for the next year, but declined.

Those were the times of "Wildcat Banks."   A general banking law was among the wild features of a boy's administration.   It was no doubt honestly passed, with a design to benefit the people, but it left an opportunity for most extensive swindling; and it was astonishing how many prominent citizens were ready to act the knave. Hundreds of thousands of dollars were quickly in circulation, most of which was nearly worthless in a few months. How unequally are the penalties of law distributed, when the notorious scoundrels who issued their worthless paper, and thereby sent misery to ten thousand persons, were never punished; but many of them were promoted to important places of honor and trust, while a poor ignorant man was sent to the penitentiary for offering a five dollar bill which proved to be counterfeit! It is an argument for a final judgment that justice is so unequal on earth. How many, after committing great crimes according to law, are elected to Legislatures, to make more laws with loopholes for their future iniquities! How many become judges, to pander justice, and take a reward against the innocent! And how many in the possession of ill-gotten wealth make their "money power" an engine of oppression!

Mrs. C., on recovering from inflammation in the eyes, was attacked with a violent disease of the lungs, which never left her through her life. Her sufferings with asthma were too terrible for description. She often seemed to be dying for want of breath, and dying in the most horrid agony. For some years various physicians were applied to, and many different medicines procured, but all in vain. During the most violent convulsions and spasms she obtained some temporary relief from narcotics, saltpetre, lobelia, tobacco or opium, which relaxed the inflamed and tightened muscles of her lungs and kept her from suffocation. Being exceedingly industrious and anxious to make her family comfortable, she sat in her bed and did the knitting and sewing necessary for their clothing.

Those were the darkest days that this suffering family were ever called to pass through. Mr. C. had hardly begun to cultivate his land when the demands of physicians, the cost of medicines, and the stern wants of his family obliged him to sell his oxen. He then worked for his neighbors for the use of teams to cultivate a few acres, and became so reduced that he found it nearly impossible to clothe his

family.   He cut up his portmanteau and made shoes, and
once said to Mrs. C., " I would be glad of the rags which
many throw away into their back-yards.   We could sew
them together and clothe our poor children."   He was
then working as few men ever worked, not sparing himself
by night or day.

He had appointments every Sabbath, preaching much of
the time to the poor, in the newest settlements where no
other minister would go.   One of these congregations, eleven
miles from his home, to which he walked every month for
more than two years, was large, but never paid him more
than two or three dollars a year, and this came from one or
two men.   Being the first minister who settled in that part
of Michigan, he was called on to attend most of the funerals
in an area of more than fifty miles in circumference, sometimes leaving his work three days in a week, and going to
weep with the bereaved.   Nothing ever kept him from a
funeral when called on.   In 1842 he estimated that he had
attended about four hundred and fifty funerals in Michigan.

His zeal in the temperance and anti-slavery causes gave
him enemies.   He delivered a discourse from Isaiah, fifty-
eighth chapter, in an obscure place, on the Sabbath.   Two
brothers, of giant strength and iron will, started for home
across the woodlands, both aroused to great heat by the
sermon, one for and the other against slavery.   From words
they came to blows.   Both were men of influence, and this
scene started an excitement and agitation which has never
subsided.

Mr. C. was now doomed to many curses from the profane, which he bore with fortitude ; but the opposition of
the brethren in the church cut him to the heart and brought
him into deep sorrow.   He sometimes felt himself bewildered
when he viewed himself standing against the voice of the
bishops and the judgment of nearly the whole church ; but

revelation, reason, humanity and conscience rallied around
and sustained him.   His presiding elder became cold in his
manner towards him, and he saw that he was marked for
neglect, and set aside with a few whose influence was to be
broken down.

In all of the western country the subject of lost children
has engaged the public attention.   Many have perished by
wild beasts, by starvation and cold.   The bones of some
have been found, the bodies of others, where they perished,
and others have never been heard of.   About twenty miles
from the residence of Mr. C. a little boy was with his father
where he was splitting rails, out of sight of their house, when,
about sundown, the father said, "You hear the cow-bell
just out there in the woods; go and drive the cows here
and we will go home."   The little boy went, but never
returned.   The few inhabitants of the wilderness joined the
afflicted family in making the most diligent search, and a
week from the time he was lost he was found dead.   He
was mired to his knees in a swamp, and stood leaning
against a tree, where he perished with hunger and cold.

About six miles southeast of Jackson a little boy, the son
of a Mr. Filley, accompanied a servant girl into a swamp
for huckleberries.   He became weary and wished to go
home, when the young woman led him to a path from which
he could see the house, and left him to go alone.   He was
seen no more.   Search was made for three weeks by a great
number of men, some going twenty miles to aid in the benevolent movement.   The search was easy, as the country
consisted mostly of open plains thinly timbered and without
underbrush, and this led to the conclusion that he was either
murdered by some citizen and his body buried or sunk in a
lake, or that he was carried away by Indians.   The latter
conclusion was their only relief ; it was at best a sad relief
and brought no rest to the poor mother, who lingered a while

in unendurable anxiety and died.   Some years had passed
when Mr. F. heard of a boy in New England taken from a
wandering tribe of Indians, who had come from the West.
As hope clings to straws, he went to see the child, and
found a mark or scar which convinced him of the identity
of his long lost son, and overwhelmed him with joy.   All
sighed to think the poor mother could not have lived to
embrace her child.   He was but five years old when lost,
and it was thought to be reasonable that he should have
forgotten his father and home.   He had a confused and
dim recollection of being with white people before he was
with the Indians.   Scarce anything ever happened in Michigan awaking more romantic emotion among all classes.   All
the romance, however, passed away when doubts in Mr.
F.'s family about the identity of the boy arose and increased
until they had no comfort in him.

Mr. C. was called on in the summer of 1837 by a boy,
who informed him that his little brother was dead;   that he
lived ten miles off in the wilderness, and that he wished him
to attend the funeral.   He stayed over night, and in the
morning piloted Mr. C. to his wild home.   The mourners
were all Dutch, and held around the coffin a long lamentation in the German language.   There stood leaning on his
staff an old man, patriarch of the family, who had been a
Hessian soldier in the Revolutionary War.

The next March Mr. C. was informed, just after a severe
snow-storm, that three of the children of that Dutch family
were lost, and had been out two days in the storm.   He
started in haste to hunt for them, but soon learned that they
were found.

Two girls who were twins, aged eleven years, and a boy,
aged seven, were left in the woods, boiling sap.   They were
barefooted and very thinly clad.   Being hungry, they wandered away, searching for leeks, late in the afternoon of a

cloudy and dark day and became lost.   When night set in,
despairing of finding their way home, they nested down in
some dry weeds in a swamp.   Soon it began to snow, and
knowing that they must perish where they were, they went
to a hollow log, and gathering some chunks of rotten wood,
they crawled in, and, drawing in the broken timber, stopped
the entrance to keep out the wolves.

There was quite a heavy fall of snow, and the next day
was very cold.   Men were all through the woods, calling
and shouting, but the children thought they were Indians
and dared not to look out.   At night, however, when they
heard no more voices they looked out and saw a stub on
fire, into which a man had discharged his gun.   They
crawled out and went to the fire and sat around it all night.
The weather now changed; the sun arose warm, and the
children started for home barefooted through the snow,
when they were met by men.

Mr. C. passed by this place some years after and found
the Dutchman a justice of the peace, owning fine buildings
and a valuable farm.

A very remarkable instance of a lost child occurred in
Lenawee county.   Mr. C. has often passed the place where
once stood a cottage in the wilderness, solitary in immense
forests.   Mr. ——— was chopping some distance from his
house.   Near sundown a fine little boy five years old ob·
tained leave of his mother to go to his father and come
home with him.   The father came in about dark with Mr.
T., a neighbor, who had been working for him.   They had
not seen the boy, having gone to another part of the woods
before he went out.   They ran to the chopping, but the
child was not there.   They found his tracks in a light sift-
ing of snow, and Mr. T. stood by the track while Mr.———,
the father, went for a lantern and some neighbors.   They
came and found Mr. T. surrounded by wolves and driven

up a tree. The wolves fled at the approach of men with a light, but howled near them for hours. The men followed the track as far as they could, but finally lost it for want of snow. They still went on in the same direction until midnight, when all but the father refused to go any farther, declaring it impossible that the boy could be so far from home. On this announcement the father became frantic, and Mr. T., to pacify him, went on with him, all others staying behind. Both finally agreed that it was useless to go farther, and were turning back in despair, when Mr. T. thought best to call. He called aloud but got no answer. He called again, but got no answer. He felt that calling was of no use, yet to call once more would only cost a breath ; he therefore called with all his might, and hoped he heard an answer. He now kept calling, and soon got a distinct answer. The child was found and carried home, where they arrived at the dawn of day. He was a school-boy when Mr. C. traveled in that part of Michigan. The latter afterward heard that he was at college, and finally that he was practicing law.

CHAPTER XIX.

As Mr. C. was one of the first settlers in that country, he had a school district organized for his neighborhood, a school-house built and religious meetings established, so near that Mrs. C., in her poor health, could attend. But others who came in afterwards were determined to have the best accommodations, and broke up religious meetings, and finally the school in Mr. C.'s neighborhood. They formed other school districts, centering from two to three miles from him on every side, and his family were out of any district ever after, as long as they remained in that country.

Mrs. C. was overwhelmed with sorrow when she saw the school-house torn down, and predicted that her religious privileges were now at an end.

The Indians who remained in Michigan were generally honest, quiet and peaceable. Mr. C. was always on terms of friendship with them ; but the selfishness of white hunters called for their removal. A company of United States soldiers prowled through the woodlands, hiring hunters to assist them in finding these poor injured creatures, who were driven before the bayonet out of the land and beyond the Mississippi, late in the season and near winter. There, without means and unacquainted with the hunting-grounds, they passed a dismal winter, and great numbers died. One returned to Mr. C.'s neighborhood the next spring, and said that nearly all who went from there were dead. "All they who take the sword shall perish with sword." The few Indian children who survived that awful winter are now bringing down the sword on their oppressors.

The anti-slavery agitation raged with great zeal, and opposition arose like a howling tempest. Presses were destroyed, lecturers mobbed, a publisher was murdered, and another led through the streets of a Puritan city with a rope about his neck. The high priests of all denominations gave their influence in favor of the oppressor, and lifted the hand of ecclesiastical power over the heads of all who opened their mouths for the dumb. Five young preachers were brought to trial before the New York Conference for disobedience to the bishops, who had forbidden all agitation of the slavery question. In the Michigan Conference of 1839, Bishop Soule made his celebrated statement, that he had advised a slaveholder to keep his slaves, when he came to the bishop in tears, ready to emancipate them and settle them in a Free State.

At the same conference two local deacons, venerable for

age and usefulness, were rejected from elder's orders on account of their anti-slavery sentiments. In October of the same year Mr. C. attended an anti-slavery Methodist convention, in Sharon, Michigan, consisting of a few warm-hearted and zealous abolitionists from different parts of the State. This was to him a very interesting time. He had long labored almost alone in this cause, buffeted by the world and opposed by the church ; and now to mingle with those intelligent and pious men, whose hearts agreed with his own, gave him great joy. He returned to his wilderness home encouraged and strengthened, to go forward in his labors with cheerfulness, let the consequences be what they might.

Mr. C. became satisfied in 1840 that secession must be the eventual history of anti-slavery Methodists. When freedom of speech was denied to independent men, they must either break the rules of the church and incur a trial for disobedience, as in the case of the fine young men in the New York Conference, or peacefully withdraw. Mr. C. chose the latter course, and withdrew, when he was in peace and fellowship with his brethren. His Methodist abolition friends disapproved of his course, and stood aloof from him. He now stood on dangerous ground, like one on the summit of some lofty mountain, where nothing can be seen but the glossy surface of everlasting snow, and where no observation can be made to determine whether all is level, or whether some awful descent exists which would hurl him into instant death ; or like one out at sea, left alone to cross the ocean.

The tyranny of ecclesiastical rulers nearly destroyed his confidence in church organization. In the labyrinths of investigation and innovation he sometimes felt bewildered, as the foundations of ancient doctrines sometimes gave way. While well-fed conservatives walked softly in the midst of flattery, insured by interest against change, Mr. C. was wending his way across the forests, in patched garments, to preach to the poor, praying the Lord to keep him from error; as all the doctrines and usages which had been sacred with him were in review before him and liable to be rejected. Episcopacy first claimed his attention.

He had read in 1829 Emory's "Defense of the Fathers," and this work, designed to uphold episcopacy, had nearly destroyed his confidence in it. From that time he had never approved of the office of bishop, only on the ground of expediency, and now it seemed no longer expedient. Deacons, he had long thought, were not preachers by virtue of their office.

For a time he was in doubt in regard to the imposition of hands, without the gift of the Holy Ghost. The doctrine of the Trinity was reviewed, and for sometime he felt be-wildered, but finally became settled more quietly than ever in the belief of the Trinity, by firmly embracing the doctrine of "Eternal Sonship of Christ."

He gave close attention to the change of the Sabbath, and became satisfied the ground of the Sabbatarians was untenable. He had for some years thought immersion the scriptural mode of baptism, and finally believing that the Greek word *bapto*, or *baptizo*, signified Dip or Plunge, as fully as immergo in the Latin, or dip in English, he was immersed shortly after his withdrawal from the Methodist Episcopal Church. All manner of reports were in circula-tion about him, but he felt thankful to the Lord that no inquisition was allowed in this land. Untrammeled and free to read what he pleased, he became an admirer of Gar-rison, Phillips, Green, Myrick, Smith, and Goodel, and entered with all his heart into their humane, benevolent and anti-sectarian spirit. He learned from the *Union Herald* that there was an extensive movement to unite Christians, in which many men of intelligence and piety were zealously

engaged, and that they met annually in association.   In this
movement Mr. C. felt the most lively interest.

In the spring of 1841 he organized a church near his
residence in accordance with the Christian Union movement.   This church was organized with the following
peculiarities :

  1. Freedom of speech and private judgment.

  2. The right of all to membership who are acknowledged
to be Christians and in favor with God.

  3. The most perfect local church independence.

  4. Total abstinence from intoxicating drinks.

  5. Anti-slavery.

It was called the Church of God.

While it was quietly moving on, laboring for the moral
welfare of mankind, it encountered violent opposition, mocking, ridicule and contempt.   Mr. C. was set apart by a vote
of the church as an elder and pastor, without imposition of
hands.   He then supposed the union movement was to be
permanent and lasting, and designed to attend the annual
associations as soon as convenient.

In 1842 he organized another church on the same principles, in an adjoining neighborhood, and felt disposed to
spend his life in promoting Christian union and brotherly
love.

In the summer of 1843 the Union Association met and
adjourned *sine die ;* the *Union Herald* was suspended, after
having been published twelve years, and Mr. C. felt dismayed and discouraged.   As leading men in the movement
began to return to the several denominations which had
been their former homes, the union enterprise seemed to be
a failure.   He, however, advised his brethren to wait and
see what might be done at the convention at Syracuse, to
be held late in the year 1843, for the reorganization of the
union movement, before determining what course to take.

At the Syracuse Convention four leaders, William Goodel, Gerrit Smith, Beriah Green, and David Plumb each presented a plan differing from all the others, and each seemed not to yield but to stand upon his plan when the convention broke up.

Mr. C. now advised the disorganization of the churches which he had assisted in organizing, as the general movement was abandoned and the small churches, standing alone, would not only receive the opposition of the several denominations, but every discouragement from union men themselves who had given up the enterprise and gone to their old homes.   This was one of the most painful duties of his life.   It wounded the feelings of some who had been under his pastoral care, and gave a rich opportunity to his unscrupulous persecutors to say that he was ever changing and as unstable as water.

This step was, however, taken after long and laborious thought and much prayer, and was never regretted by him. Those noble and worthy advocates of union—Goodel and Smith, never agreed on a plan of church organization, but each went forward in his own way.

Mr. C. has ever regarded sectarianism as low and mean, degrading to Christianity and dishonoring to God ; blunting our best sensibilities and stifling that Christian benevolence which should extend its charities to all mankind.   Under the influence of religious bigotry man becomes more wicked than under the influence of atheism ; and Christian bigotry has shown as great cruelty and violence as Mahometan, or Jewish, or pagan bigotry.

The year 1843 will ever be remembered as the time fixed by William Miller for the end of the world.   The excitement, which began in 1842, increased continually, and by February, 1843, became so intense that in many instances chools were stopped, ordinary business suspended, and religious meetings were held night and day.   It seemed to many to be a time of most glorious revivals through all the land.

Men whose marvelousness and wonder was large loved the excitement and seemed anxious to see the world on fire; being persuaded in their own minds that they were prepared to come to Judgment; while others, who felt unprepared to die, and who had no relish for the sublimity of the approaching awful scene, were overwhelmed with fear and dismay. Many ministers, finding the doctrine of Miller a convenient instrument of revival, went on holding up the prospect of the immediate end of the world, without taking time to weigh the arguments used to support this doctrine.   Mr. C. said but little about it, because he knew but little.   When, however, the excitement became universal and swept over all the land as a flood, he sat down and devoted his time to the investigation of this subject, and found that Miller in his superstructure reasoned well and made his arguments plain to the reader and easy to be understood.   He then looked for the foundation, where everything should be proved to demonstration or moral certainty.   No superstructure should ever be built on a hypothesis, on anything assumed or taken for granted.

Here he found that Miller's fine arguments were a castle in the air, as he had assumed the three main pillars in his structure.   If the two thousand and three hundred days mentioned in Daniel viii. 14, began when the seventy weeks began, Daniel ix. 24; and, secondly, if the twenty-three hundred days signified years; and, thirdly, if the cleansing of the sanctuary meant the end of the world, then the world must end in 1843; but neither of these points was proved.

The first and third are highly improbable, and the second is only probable.   Few disputed that he had found the true year when the commandment went forth to restore and build Jerusalem, the commencement of the seventy weeks.

Strange as it may seem, few ever looked beyond this point for the foundation of his theory; never looking for his reasons for supposing that the 2,300 days began at the same time of the seventy weeks, and signified years, and ended with the end of the world.

When to Mr. C. the foundations of Millerism failed, he cautiously tried to check the excitement, believing that revivals built wholly on fear would prove a curse rather than a blessing; that men professing conversion under the influence of fear alone would be more sinful than before as soon as the danger was passed. This proved to be the case.

That was an awful winter, beside the excitement. The winter was so severe that nearly half of the domestic animals in Michigan died. March was one of the coldest months ever known; the snow remained two feet deep until March 31.

Mr. C was never a politician. He studied the history and constitution of his country at an early age; but party spirit, political policy, political intrigues and office seeking he abhorred. Few men have spent so little time in bar-rooms, shops and stores, or at the corners of the streets, where men resort to caucus. He was a democrat from the very instincts of his nature; a sense of human equality seemed born with him; his sympathies were ever with laboring men; he loathed the man who lives by speculation, and held in detestation the pride and pomp of aristocracy. When, however, he had arrived at mature age, he found the Democratic party very corrupt. They had started largely imbued with French infidelity, and their equality was little less than moral equality; that is, they despised no man for his sins. In their political circles clergymen could walk arm in arm with the most debauched men. They had thus swept into their ranks most of the moral dregs, and scurf, and pollution of the land. Atheists, blasphemers, Sabbath-breakers, drunkards and brothel-haunters flocked to this party, because here in all political circles and political movements they were treated as nobility.

Mr. C. could not enter into the spirit of this party, and therefore stood aloof from the polls for several years. The first vote which he ever gave for president was for William Wirt. From that time he occasionally voted with the Whigs, when any good to mankind seemed likely to be gained by their success. He disliked their cardinal doctrine, protective tariff. Free trade agreed with his views of Christian benevolence and universal brotherhood. The world was his country, and all mankind his countrymen. He felt no sympathy with starving foreign operatives to enrich our American manufacturers.

In 1840, when Harrison and Van Buren were before the people, he abandoned the Whig party, from anti-slavery principle and from disgust at the low buffoonry of log cabins, coon skins, hard cider and vulgar songs used by the Whigs to win to their aid the moral dregs, which had usually gone with the Democrats; and he voted no more until the "Third Party" seemed likely to make its mark for the welfare of mankind. He labored zealously in this party, and while town, county and State anti-slavery meetings began with prayer and were conducted with harmony and decorum and in the fear of God, he felt encouraged in the prospect of taking politics from the devil and bringing it into the service of the Lord.

He repeatedly introduced the following in anti-slavery meetings: "Resolved, that it is the duty of all Christians who vote to endeavor to establish a righteous party, and to vote only for men whom they believe will be just, ruling in the fear of God." Although this resolution was supported by many noble anti-slavery men, yet he rarely got a majority to vote for it.

Riding in company with Dr. H., he was accosted thus: "We are to have a debate in our lyceum on bringing anti-slavery into politics." "Why," said Mr. C., "should not anti-slavery be brought into politics?" "Because," said Dr. H., "politics is of the devil, and no moral question should be politically discussed; it would ruin it." "Then," said Mr. C., "I ought never to vote." "By all means," rejoined the doctor, "good men above all others should vote."

In the organization of our government our fathers had a just abhorrence of "Church and State," or government under ecclesiastical rule, as was then seen in most of the kingdoms of the Old World. Those governments under church rule were very different from righteous governments. They were sectarian, and persecutors of the truly pious. The ecclesiastical rulers were often the most unrighteous men, serving one sect at the expense of all others. A righteous government would be constituted of just men, ruling in the fear of God. They might be of one denomination or another, or of no denomination.

It is evident that French infidelity obtained a large influence in this country by the close of the Revolutionary War. Thomas Paine, a refugee from justice in his native land, alternated between France and America. His political influence in this country was almost boundless, and this gave him the most ample opportunity to sow the seeds of infidelity. France was prepared to decide by the vote of her representatives that "There is no God," and thousands in America desired that there should be no God in politics; no moral questions in the affairs of government; that Christians should divest themselves of Christianity on election days and enter the political arena as atheists, not as Chris-

tians.   This has been the prevailing sentiment of this country, especially from the campaign of 1800, when the cry of
"No religion in politics," prevailed.

A doctrine kindred to this has been embraced by the
American clergy, in the language of one of the most distinguished of their number: "It is the duty of Christians to
vote for the best of two devils, when one is to be elected."

It is no wonder that with such principles our country
should come to its present calamity.   In the earlier years of
the anti slavery movement mass-meetings and conventions
were marked by intelligence, sobriety and religious devotion.
They were far more Christianlike than religious worship in
general, and are remembered by Mr. C. as the most interesting season of his life.

At one time, Dr. C., an infidel, said in convention: "The
anti slavery movement has not yet become of sufficient importance to enlist politicians."   Mr. C. replied, "We do
not want them."   Not long, however, after this politicians
came in; devotion and trust in the Lord gradually died
away, and a sufficient amount of vulgar wit, comic song and
buffoonry was introduced to gratify the most corrupt and
vicious taste.   Ministers of the gospel had with great propriety preached politics, when the Third Party aimed to restore human government to righteousness; but now to see
them become the tools of unprincipled office-seekers was
painful.   It was degrading the sacred office, dishonoring
God, and reproaching Christianity; and most shocking,
when they turned buffoons, as some did, and played every
antic of a comedian.

In like manner the very soul had been taken out of the
temperance cause by low buffoonry in the Washingtonian
movement.   The Republican party is called the Anti-slavery
party enlarged and consummated; but how different from
that righteous party which the noble pioneers in anti-slavery

expected! When we behold in our armies so many officers notoriously licentious, drunken and profane, how can we call them the hosts of the Lord?

CHAPTER XX.

In the town of Salem, Washtenaw county, Mich., about half a mile west of Lapham's Conners, lies a confused heap of stones, where a school-house stood, in which several Methodist ministers met in 1841, and formed the Wesleyan Methodist Church.

Mr. C. heard with some interest of this movement. It looked like a step in the way of improvement, at least a drop in the bucket of the great and glorious work which was to emancipate and enfranchise mankind. The men who had thus united were strangers to him; he was far from them, could not easily become acquainted with them, and had no idea that their Discipline would suit him. Local church independence, the right of all Christians to church membership, and to freedom of speech and private judgment, were principles woven inseparably into the web of his nature and could not be removed.

In June, 1843, the convention met at Utica, N. Y., which organized a church on a larger scale, adopting the name and much of the Discipline of the Michigan Conference. Mr. C., as before, heard of this with much interest, but felt determined never to surrender his judgment to the power of a conference. Some months after this, being at the house of a Wesleyan friend, he casually picked up a copy of the *True Wesleyan*, containing the Discipline framed at Utica.

He was surprised at the liberality of the elementary principles, and thought, if the whole Discipline was to be explained by these that he could not object to it. He was, however, suspicious of conference power, and gave no encouragement of uniting.

The Union Association had now held its last meeting, adjourned without date, and abandoned the enterprise; and the *Union Herald* was closed. But Mr. C. looked forward with hope for a reorganization at Syracuse. When this failed, he felt very lonely, and painfully constrained to advise the disorganization of the little churches under his care.

He now gave his attention to the Wesleyan Discipline; conversed with some of the most intelligent brethren of that denomination in regard to conference power, and felt encouraged that explanations would be made, which afterwards were made at the General Conference held in the city of New York, granting independence to local churches. The Discipline seemed indefinite on the ordination of elders. His advisers thought it meant Congregational ordination, and it seemed so to him. Arrangements were therefore made for his ordination.

He had been ordained deacon according to the usages of the Methodist Episcopal Church, by Bishop Hedding, in 1834 He had also been ordained elder by the unanimous vote of the church of which he was pastor, without the imposition of hands, in 1841. This was in accordance with the usages of several respectable denominations. He had long been in doubt in regard to the imposition of hands, without the gift of the Holy Ghost; but regarding the imposition of hands as innocent in itself, and hoping to receive a divine baptism, he submitted to ordination according to Wesleyan usage.

He was ordained at a quarterly-meeting in Columbia, Jackson county, Mich., in February, 1844, Rev. A. W. Curtis presiding. His enemies, paying no regard to the fact that the union enterprise was given up, seized this opportunity to report him the most unstable of men, ever changing and never to be relied on. They added that he had be-longed to the regular Baptists, the Freewill Baptists, and the Christians, although he had never had any connection with either of these denominations. Doubtless many in the Methodist Episcopal Church believe these reports to this day, although a little candid inquiry would have corrected their error. The validity of his ordination was called in question by the advocates of strong conference power; in-volving, also, the ordination of Samuel T. Rice, who was or-dained at the same time. This led to an unpleasant discus-sion in the next conference, some contending that the word President used in the ordination service signified President of an Annual Conference; while others supposed it only meant president of an ordination service, after the manner of the Congregationalists. The conference decided in Mr. C.'s favor. The advocates of conference power carried the question into the first General Conference, held in October, 1844, where the question was settled; and from that time an election to orders by the vote of an Annual Conference has been essential. It is not, however, essential for the president of a conference to preside, as he often invites some other minister to preside in the ordination service in his stead.

In the spring of 1844, Rev. Jason Steele left Leslie Cir-cuit, and Mr. C. took his place, and filled the appointments until conference. This brought him into a pleasant ac-quaintance with Wesleyan brethren and sisters, who were meek and devoted Christians, and were in love and fellow-ship with one another.

The third session of the Michigan Conference, the first after the Utica Convention, was held in September, 1844, in Adams, Hillsdale county. Here Mr. C. met most of the members of Michigan Conference for the first time. It was to him a most interesting season.   Forming acquaintance with so many meek, humble and devout men, whose views and aims were mainly like his own, and becoming united with them in strong bonds of brotherhood, filled him with great consolation.   Marcus Swift was re-elected president, and A. W. Curtis secretary.   On the Sabbath I. W. Andrews and ———— ———— were ordained.   Conference closed in great harmony, and all seemed to go to their work with cheerful zeal.

Mr. C. recollects the conference at Adams as among the most pleasant scenes of his life.   He was appointed to Leslie Circuit with Silas Pomeroy.   This circuit was very convenient, as it included his home.   He worked at farming much of his time, as he received but a small salary, and part of that in work.

The Millerite excitement was then subsiding into infidelity.   Many who had been terrified, now returned to their former sins with greediness; and teachers who had said, "The Bible is false if the world does not end in 1843," now sow the fruits of their rashness in a general apostacy.

The fifth son of Mr. and Mrs. Crane was born October 25, 1844.   For strength of constitution, beauty and everything promising, this was a very remarkable child.   He was named Floridon Melancthon, and seemed worthy of the name, for his beauty was like the floral field, and he seemed destined in mind to equal the great reformer.   But the pleasant hopes of his fond parents were to be of short continuance.

Mr. C. had spent the winters of 1842 and 1843 in teaching school not far from home.   He had long been painfully sensible of the very imperfect manner of teaching geography. He had often found scholars who had spent years in this study and worn out their books, who were yet ignorant of the causes of the change of seasons, and the variation of the

length of days, and even ignorant of the spherical form of
the earth. They seemed almost destitute of any ideas, and
the little thinking they had done had only given them vague
ideas of the earth, as an extensive level in two great circles,
like the two hemispheres on their maps. They had no ideas
of the relative positions of the various parts of the earth.
Teachers for years had held the book in hand and read the
questions to the class, and read the answers as the class
answered. In this way teachers and scholars might go on
for ages and know little or nothing. Mr. C. had never had
one hour's instruction in this science. Without teachers
and with most meager books and maps, he worked through
alone by dint of thinking, while engaged in hard labor,
plowing, chopping or threshing.

In 1833 he had constructed an apparatus in which a can-
dle served for the sun, around which a globe passed through
an orbit, performing at the same time its diurnal motion.
The north pole was elevated twenty-three degrees and
twenty-eight minutes above the plane of the orbit. He was
now able to explain with ease the changes of the seasons,
and all the variations of the rising and setting of the sun to
all places. In 1842 he, by the help of his half-brother,
Orson D. Dunham, who was a good philospher and mechanic, constructed an apparatus, which was managed with
ease by turning a crank, performing the daily and yearly
revolutions with perfection. An intelligent child twelve
years old could, by this apparatus, construct a table showing
when the sun would rise and set every day in the year, at
any place on the earth.

Mr. C. had found similar defects in the teaching of other
sciences, where teachers had only heard recitations and
never explained by lecture. He found some students able
to recite everything in a grammar book, and yet unable to

tell the meaning of the word grammar, and unable to apply grammar to any possible use.

He has often thought Aristotle's method of teaching by lecture, while walking with his scholars through a grove or woodland, the best method ever used ; and word for word recitations from books the very worst method posslble.

In the summer of 1845 Mr. C., in company with Rev. S. Pomeroy, attended a camp-meeting in Lenawee county. An amusing incident occurred in this journey. They were to go on horseback, but Mr. Pomeroy insisted on going with a wagon as far as Jackson, to carry some wheat to market to get spending money for the journey. Mr. C., who hardly ever had any money, said, "I never provide money for going to religious meetings." Mr. P. replied, " I never go without money; but the wheat must be cleaned." "Come on, then ; let us be abont it," said Mr. C., who was always in a hurry. He commenced turning the fanning-mill with too much force ond broke the crank. "Never mind," said Mr. P., "it was old and worthless." "Then," said Mr. C., "I am glad the crank is broken, for now you will have to trust Providence on your journey." They started very late, and long before night they found it impossible to tell what course to pursue, for the notice in the *Wesleyan* was altogether indefinite. It was advertised to be at Wolf Creek; but the creek bore that name for ten or fifteen miles, and no one could tell them at what point in all that distance the camp-meeting was to be held. Traveling at random, near the close of the day, Mr. Pomeroy said, "What are we to do for money ?" Mr. C. answered, "I do not know; but I am glad the crank was broken." Still later they inquired of a lady who stood at her gate. She answered, "There is no camp-meeting to be held in this county. If there was I should know it." Mr. C., taking her to be an Episcopal Methodist, said to her, " It is a Wesleyan camp-meeting." "Oh, Wesleyan!" she replied; "I know nothing about it." They moved on as the sun was setting, still going at random, when Mr. C. said again, "I am glad the crank was broken." In an obscure place they found two fine bundles of oats in the road, which they gave to their horses. Riding after dark, in a.land of strangers, thinly settled, they began to think of taking lodging on the ground, as no one invited them to lodge; but at a late hour, when most people were asleep, they were by the fireside of a most hospitable Wesleyan family, who knew all about the camp-meeting.

They now found that they were passing the place of meeting, leaving it ten or twelve miles on the left; all for the want of a definite advertisement. They arrived the next day in season for the earliest exercises. This meeting was highly interesting, and much good was done. Rev. Orin Doolittle was the venerable patriarch around whom all the preachers clustered for instruction. There was much harmony and brotherhood among all Wesleyans then; probably increased by the persecutions which they bore.

Long will Mr. C. remember the sacred spot, where, for many days and nights was heard the voice of praise and prayer. The Wolf Creek Circuit was then in great prosperity, but has since greatly declined; and it must be confessed that through the Michigan Conference there is not the beautiful harmony and brotherhood that existed twenty years ago.

The Michigan Conference for 1845 was held in Ann Arbor. Here Mr. C. saw Orange Scott. He did not at first view look to him like the great man of whom he had heard and read so much. So meek and unpretending was he, that Mr. C., whose perception was always slow, could not see in him the mighty man who, at Cincinnati, had stood alone against the whole power of the Methodist Episcopal

Church, and prevailed; but before the conference closed Mr. C. formed a more exalted opinion of Orange Scott than he had before, and to this day he believes that the anti-slavery cause is more indebted to him than to any other man.

The conference was not wholly harmonious, yet it was to Mr. C. very interesting. He there received an appointment to Adams Circuit, and soon removed his family to the town of Adams, Hillsdale county.

Poor Mrs. C. was hardly able to endure the journey, but felt pleased when it was over, to be so near a place of worship as to be able to attend. Her children now had good school privileges, and she had the society of the kindest neighbors. It was on the whole a favorable change for her though her constitution was so broken and her health so poor, that there remained little comfort for her in any situation.

Mr. C. entered on his labor with much cheerfulness, though with some discouragements. There had been two years before a great revival under Millerite excitement, which had swept the land like a mighty flood, carrying all in its course, and the churches had been dangerously augmented in their membership. During the year 1844-5 there had been the same falling away that everywhere succeeded those excitements. Many of these dead weights still hung on the churches, and in some instances there was not vitality enough to exercise discipline. At one appointment he went into the school-house on Sunday morning at the time for preaching and found no fire. The snow had been blown in and covered every seat and every desk. Two women came in, and Mr. C., brushing the snow from a desk, read and sang a hymn, prayed and preached a short sermon, during which time three or four persons, including a little girl, came in from a distance of four or five miles, to the

shame of the thickly-settled neighborhood around the school-
house.   They were a family of English Independents, who
went to meeting from principle.   They had come on foot
and broken their way through a wilderness with a considerable depth of snow.   At Mr. C.'s next appointment there,
he carried fire half a mile and gathered an armful of wood
on the way to meeting.   His colleague, Rev. Elisha Bibbins, he found to be a young man of deep piety, much reading and profound thought.

They concluded, in the depth of winter, to hold a protracted
meeting in Florida, now Jefferson, where there was neither
school-house nor meeting-house.   A large log house, all in
one room, open and cold, was offered them for meetings,
provided they would furnish wood for fires.   As it was occupied by a small family, it was thankfully accepted, and the
two backwoods ministers borrowed axes and went into the
forest to prepare wood for meeting, on one of the coldest
days, and there Mr. C. froze one of his feet where, from his
youth, he had suffered from a broken joint.   This foot gave
him great pain the remainder of that winter and every winter
afterwards; and about the 1st of June, 1861, erysipelas set
in, followed by gangrene about the joint.   The flesh, sinews,
cartilages and bones about the joint decayed, and the disease
extended through a great part of the foot.   He has never
walked since, and probably never will.

These meetings resulted in a very gracious revival,
though not in the conversion of the family in whose house
the meetings where held.   The venerable Father Doolittle
was present during a part of the time of these meetings, and
labored efficiently.

In the spring there was a gracious revival in Adams, Rev.
William M. Sullivan assisting.   The summer was exceeding-
ly dry and hot, resulting in terrible mortality.   In July,
August and September dysentery and bloody-flux carried

off hundreds of people in the south counties of Michigan. In Mr. C.'s neighborhood death came to nearly every house ; his family did not escape, and as one after another was prostrated, he did not have but one night's lodging in seven weeks. Alphonzo, next to the youngest child, lay at the point of death, a mere skeleton, for a long time. Finally the youngest, the beautiful Floridon, was attacked. His constitution was so strong that his parents hoped he might recover ; but his attack was violent, and the air seemed to be all contagion. No night brought any cool, refreshing air; at midnight one would pant for breath in the open field, and when no cloud appeared the stars shone dimly through a mysterious haze, which seemed like a pall spread on the sky over the doomed children of men. On the morning of the tenth day of the child's sickness, which was August 31, 1846, he seemed better, and as the family were expressing their joy, he was turned over, and, behold! mortification had commenced on his back. Their hopes, so suddenly blasted, were followed by anguish which cannot be told. Oh! what a day! How father and mother, sisters and brothers, stood around the dear little sufferer, until about nine o'clock at night life ceased!

Poor Mrs. C.! This was terrible to one who suffered so much from her own diseases. As she came back from the grave she fell into the arms of her husband, overcome with sorrow. She never fully recovered from this shock.

This singular pestilence seemed to move from west to east about a mile in a day, passing from one township to another in a week. It will be remembered through this generation by the inhabitants of Southern Michigan and the adjoining counties of Indiana and Ohio.

The health of Harriet, the eldest daughter, began from that time to fail. She had been apparently of a vigorous constitution until the time of this pestilence, but was never afterwards perfectly well.

The Michigan Conference for 1845 convened at Wolf Creek, Lenawee county. Rev. Schuyler Hoes was present for the interest of the Book Concern. His visit was a great favor, in his wise counsels and eloquent discourses. Here Mr. C. prepared a resolution against horse trading as a speculation, which received so little favor and so much contempt that he was staggered to know what to do. He had seen this great evil in the Methodist Episcopal ministry, had mourned over it and labored in vain for its removal. To see a vice so great, so hurtful to society, and so universal, encouraged by ministers of the gospel filled him with horror. After his withdrawal from the church he had a long conversation on this subject with a presiding elder, who justified the practice, approved of this kind of gambling, justified a man—even a minister—in using his superior shrewdness to buy of one less shrewd as low as possible, and sell to one less shrewd as high as possible, and thus to enrich himself. Mr. C. was shocked, and as he lay awake musing on the subject to a late hour in the night, he felt that membership in a church holding such principles could be no privilege to him. He felt that such speculations were equally wicked in all property, but were more apt to be practiced in horse dealing, because the value of horses, like cards in gambling, was little understood by most of men. He felt that he had no more right to take his neighbor's property by superior shrewdness, than by superior physical strength, and that it was no excuse that civil law would punish for one deed and not for the other. Such speculations, in his view, could not be practiced in accordance with loving our neighbor as ourselves, or doing as we would be done by. It is difficult to tell the depth of sorrow which Mr. C. felt on hearing these speculations upheld by a Wesleyan

Conference, on finding that ,in this respect he had gained nothing by leaving the M. E. Church.

At this conference he drew up a standard of education for candidates for ordination.   The standard was by many deemed too high, and was strongly opposed, but it finally received the support of the majority ; and year after year it continued to be sustained in form, though it must be confessed that not much regard was paid to it in electing to orders.

Mr. C. was again appointed to Adams Circuit alone, and filled fourteen appointments in two weeks through most of the year.   A camp-meeting was held in Adams in August, which was blessed to the conversion of nearly thirty.   The death of Orange Scott occurred during this meeting.

Poor Mrs. C., who was converted at a camp-meeting, and who was enthusiastically in favor of these meetings, was able to attend this, as it was near her home.   This was a great blessing to her, and the last of the kind she ever had.

It was about this time that Mr. C. began to write for the press.   He had been seized with great ambition to write when about twenty years of age, and wrote with considerable self-complacency for several years, but offered nothing for publication but once, and then failing, his extremely sensitive nature shrank into discouragement, and he offered nothing more for publication for nearly twenty years.   Perhaps those twenty years were the best part of his life for writing, if he had been encouraged.   The mould of his mind fitted him best for parable, but the indiscriminate condemnation which Methodists bestow on all romance or fiction prevented his ever cultivating this talent.   Next to this he would have succeeded in history, having had from childhood a great relish for historical reading, and for reflections on the spirit, manners and customs of all ages of men in every land ; but history finds but few readers, and historical essays will hardly pay in newspapers.   He has therefore been confined to a narrow field as a writer—a few general essays. He has so little talent for verse that he has often wished that nearly every piece of his rhyme had been burned before it was published.

If he could have traveled, it would have suited his taste to describe every variety of scene, all landscapes, climates, animals, storms, earthquakes and volcanoes; everything in geology, and everything in the manner of men.   He deeply regrets that he has done so little with his pen, now that he is nearly unable to write.

Conference for 1847 convened at Allen's Prairie, and here for the first time Mr. C. met with Cyrus Prindle, who has done more for the Wesleyan Methodist Church than any other man living or dead.

The conference was quite harmonious and spiritual, and doubtless a rich blessing to the neighborhood in which it was held.   Mr. C. was appointed to Leslie Circuit, and removed his family to his former home in Eaton county, among his relatives and former neighbors, which was very pleasant. As he had traveled this circuit before, he was acquainted with the people and joyfully met them and entered with pleasure on his labors.   The year passed with much harmony between him and his brethren.

There were two unstationed ministers on this circuit, Daniel Smith and Samuel T. Rice, who with Mr. C. always took sweet counsel.   Silas Pomeroy also resided on this circuit, and when not traveling a circuit abroad, he was to Mr. C. as David was to Jonathan, a most constant and confident friend.

Conference for 1848 convened in the town of Nankin, Wayne county.   C. Prindle was again present, and exerted a most excellent influence.   Here Mr. C., contrary to his most sincere wishes, was elected president.   Nothing ever

threw him into deeper embarrassment.   He plead with tears
to be released from this responsibility, after his election was
declared, but was in a manner compelled by his brethren to
take the chair.   He was so deeply affected by his election
that he carefully concealed it from his family and neighbors
as long as possible, thinking the knowledge of it must degrade
the conference in their estimation.

He had received an appointment to travel at large through
the conference, to attend quarterly-meetings, and to superin-
tend missions.   No provision was made for his support, and
he was dependent on the voluntary gifts of the people.

The health of Mrs. C. had changed but little in several
years.   She was, however, now too far from meetings to
ever attend any more.   She read a great deal, and though
able to sit up but little, she did most of the sewing and
knitting for her family.   As the rest of the family now enjoyed comfortable health, the time of their extreme poverty
had passed ; they had plenty of grain, meat, and excellent
fruit.   This time may be fixed upon as the happiest in their
family history.   Harriet was now nineteen years of age, tall
and dignified in her appearance, very fair, with red hair and
expressive blue eyes.   She was an excellent scholar, a great
reader, very poetic in her fancy, an admirer of the sublime,
and a great lover of astronomy.   She wrote beautifully in
prose, and very well in verse, more easy and natural than
her father.   He sent to New York for a copy of Ossian for
her, which she devoured with uncommon avidity.   She
was, however, diffident and retiring, and therefore her intellectual worth was little known.   She had long borne the
responsibilities of a mother in the family, and it is to be
feared that extreme cares and hard labor were breaking her
constitution.

William was in his seventeenth year.   He was rather
small, feeble and melancholy.   He was very timid and

bashful, and was extremely shy of his father, who had been too stern in his manner towards him.   Mr. C. in his old age greatly regrets his sternness and severity towards his family, and sighs with deep sorrow when he thinks of any harsh word that he ever used.

Zelura was in her fifteenth year, a playful, happy-tempered child, very active and industrious, and a good scholar considering her opportunities.   She was extremely fond of the younger children, and always anxious to please them.   She had taken great care of the dear little Floridon while he lived.   When her brother Alphonzo began to go to school he was a very sickly child.   She led him to the school-house, nearly two miles, and though she was then a little girl, she often carried him a part of the way in her arms.

Emory, afterwards called John Emory, was twelve years old.   He was open, frank and honest, and less timid than the other children.   His active nature often developed itself in indiscretions and imprudences, which gave his parents much uneasiness and sorrow.   His associates were bad boys, and his frank, honest, confiding nature gave them great influence over him.   Emory, however, from his ever-cheerful disposition, added much to the happiness of the family.   He subsequently became one of the most sober, studious and noble young men in the world, eminent for everything manly and good, an honor to his family and to mankind.

Alphonzo, the youngest then living, was nine years old, a sickly little fellow, of a gentle, pleasant nature, very kind to everybody and everything, always kind to his afflicted mother, and ready to do everything for her comfort.   All of the family were very tender towards him on account of his innocence and tender age, and his sickly habit.

He and his brother William narrowly escaped death. They lodged in the heat of summer on a basement barn floor, near a heavy stone wall eight feet high.   Mr. C. led his horse into an adjoining stable, one dark night, and hearing the boys getting into bed, just under the wall, he said to them, " Move your bed to the middle of the floor; that wall may fall."   They moved it, and the next night it fell with great force, being thrown from its foundation by the lateral pressure of water from the roof in a violent storm. Mr. C. turned pale as he beheld stones which would weigh three hundred pounds lying on the very spot where the bed had been, and these stones piled three feet deep where the bodies of his boys would have been if the bed had not been moved.

This farm was in the southeast part of Eaton county, in the town of Eaton Rapids.   The house was on rising ground, about eighteen rods from the road.   A grove of one hundred trees was between the house and road, and a garden below the grove next to the road.   A small lake was west of the house, joining the farm, and a beautiful orchard between the house and the lake.   From the house, a few rods' walk over a beautiful grass lawn brought them to the upper floor of the barn.   This grass plat, always dry and always green, was a fine playground for the children. They also rambled over the fields, caring for the nests and young broods of numerous fowls, for lambs and calves, and young birds, of which they were all very tender.   Going to the swamp was a favorite diversion; and also boat-riding on the lake and catching fish.   In midsummer picking huckleberries was fine amusement.   In autumn the little boys with oxen and cart carried peaches and plums to market, and sometimes apples, and bought boots, shoes and clothes for winter, and groceries for the family.   In winter the boys had many fine excursions skating.

Mr. C. bought an accordion for Mrs. C., who, with great labor, learned to play it, and the children also learned·

Those were the happy days of this family. Ossian says, "Music is like the memory of the past, mournful and pleasing to the soul." Mr. C. delights in the pleasing melancholy of recollecting the few years when his children and their mother sat around his table and fireside; when his beautiful garden and orchard produced so many comforts; when the jocund voices of his children mingled with the songs of birds and clack of hens in his grove and the shrill notes of the loon on the lake; but he cannot escape the painful remembrance of the terrible work which death has since made with the once happy group.

One sleeps near their old home, one in Leoni, and one a thousand miles away where the ocean winds sweep the barren waste. The mother's counsels have ceased, and one who long divided her mother's cares, speaks no more; and one whose ever-cheerful countenance was sunshine to the family smiles no more on mortals; but, poor boy, languished into death in a foreign land, and sleeps with the thousands of the dead, all strangers to him.

Surely, all is vanity!

CHAPTER XXI.

Conference for 1849 convened at Leoni. Mr. C. reluctantly accepted a re-election as president. Here he first met L. C. Matlack, and also Edward Smith. The harmony of this conference was disturbed by a resolution pronouncing the action of the General Conference of 1848, on the subject of the employing of pastors by the churches, unconstitutional, and that part of Discipline null and void. This subject made much trouble for four years in every session of the Michigan Conference.

Mr. C. received an appointment to travel at large, as

during the year before.   It was during this conference that
he was attacked with fever.   He had spent fourteen years
in Michigan without an attack of fever, or ague, or any
serious illness.   His vigorous health had been proverbial;
but now he broke down for life, as he was never again
perfectly well.

He came to conference with great pain in his left ankle,
which had been injured in 1833, and had for several years
been in a very bad state.   From the inflammation in this
ankle the fever seized upon his whole system.   He remained
many days in Leoni, unable to get home.

While in a distant part of the State, in his religious labors,
his friends, without his knowledge, had nominated him for
representative in the State Legislature; and during his
sickness election came on, and a certificate of election was
sent him.   As the election was close, he expected his seat
would be contested.   He had made no effort, while his
opponent had scoured the county with all unprincipled
. lecturers, or stump-speakers.   On the day of election, as
the day was unpleasant, many of his friends stayed at home,
thinking him safe without their aid; but his opponent kept
his team going the whole day, bringing to the polls his sick
or lazy friends.   The number of votes was nearly equal, and
Mr. C., after occupying his seat a short time, very cheerfully left it in favor of his opponent by a decision of the
House.

Being unable from poor health and the increasing illness
of Mrs. C. to travel at large, he labored through the conference year on Jackson Circuit with Alvan Cassidy.   It was
a very prosperous year.   More than 150 professed conversion, or to be reclaimed from a backslidden state.

Mr. C. remained feeble during the year and went in poor
health to conference for 1850, held in Flowerfield, St. Joseph's county.   It was a time of great sickness, and the

people being unable to entertain the conference, they sat nearly the whole time night and day, until their business was done.   Mr. C. was again elected president and appointed to travel at large, but his health failing still more, and Herschel Foster falling in health and leaving Jackson Circuit, Mr. C. took his place, and traveled with E. Bibbins and John Wesley Brooks (colored).   This was also a prosperous year.

An amusing incident occurred on returning from the conference at Flowerfield, which showed Mr. C. how old he looked to strangers.   Sickness having come to nearly every house, he and his fellow travelers rode some miles after dark before they could find lodging.   They were at last entertained by a very kind family on Goguack Prairie.   When it was time to retire the kind lady said, "The old gentleman will lodge below," meaning Mr. C., "and the others will go upstairs."   Silas Pomeroy, who was more than thirteen years older than Mr. C., went upstairs, ready to burst with mirth, as he was a very merry man.

Mr. C., in company with S. A. Baker, went to Lansing, in February, to solicit a charter for the college at Leoni. He there learned much of the unprincipled character of legislators.

Harriet had attended school at Leoni during the summer of 1850 in very poor health.   In the following autumn she, with Emory, returned to Leoni and attended the winter term.   They unfortunately occupied a very cold house. Her health continued to fail all winter, and when her father went after her in the spring, he was filled with alarm at the sight of her pale face.   Her journey home, although in April, happened to be a ride of thirty miles in a violent and very cold wind.   She was quite overcome by the journey, and never went out of doors after arriving at home.

Her parents were flattered by physicians that she would

recover, but she slowly failed for three months, and died on
the 6th of July, 1851, aged twenty-two years.   It is too
painful to attempt to describe this scene.   Her life had
been so worthy; she had been so faithful in her duties in
the family, bearing the responsibilities of a mother from ten
years of age ; her morals had been so correct, her piety so
deep, her mind so intelligent, and her habits of study so
praiseworthy, that no pen can do justice to her history or
memory.   How patiently she bore her sufferings, how amiable her spirit, how kindly she spoke to all who approached
her !   The hearts of her parents were crushed when the day
came that all knew must be her last.   Oh, what a day ! No
day had ever been like it !   The light of the sun was strange
—strange clouds followed each other along the sky, and
night came with unknown gloom ; Harriet was dying ! Her
father, who had watched by her bed every night, stood over
her, watching all her struggles.   She said to him, " Father,
I am choking."   He attempted to turn her on her side to
remove the phlegm, turning her from him, but her eyes
kept fixed on him till the life of light went out.   Oh ! who
can describe it !   Harriet was dead !

In 1851 the conference met at Lapham's Corners, in
Salem, Washtenaw county.   The new Wesleyan meeting-
house was dedicated by a sermon from Edward Smith, deeply interesting throughout, though three hours and ten minutes long.   The subject of the power of churches to employ
their ministers was again agitated with great warmth and
some bitterness.

Mr. C. was in poor health during this conference, and returned to his afflicted family with no prospect of ever being
well.   He however traveled Jackson Circuit with E. Bibbins, filling nearly all of his appointments, although most of
his time in chill fever.   Sometimes he was so weak as to be
in danger of falling when he got off from his horse.   On

one occasion he preached in Rives in the forenoon, and then, having two other appointments, one in Leslie and one in Onondaga, he started in a fever and rode eight miles to Leslie, growing weaker all the way. He dropped his bridle reins and grasped the saddle, fearing every moment that he would fall from his horse. Coming into a lumber yard, he crawled from his horse on to a high pile of boards and let his horse go. There he lay, unable to walk or stand until a man happened to pass by, who procured help and got him into a house. In two or three days he was out again, having a nervous horror of disappointing a congregation. Thus the year passed away, the most melancholy year of his labors in the ministry.

Conference for 1852 met in Spring Arbor, in Jackson county, and on Jackson Circuit. E. Smith and L. C. Matlack were both present. Mr. C. was again elected president, appointed to travel at large, and elected a delegate to General Conference. He, in company with A. W. Curtis, went to Syracuse, where he had the satisfaction of seeing Wesleyan brethren from all the conferences, and most of the northern and eastern States.

This was to him most deeply interesting. He was there near his birthplace, which he left when five years of age. He was in a land of hills and dales, differing widely from the monotonous level of the West. He soon climbed the highest hill and looked with rapture on the city below him, the lake and the villages around it, the winding turnpike along which his mother carried him to the western wilderness more than forty years before, and the distant highlands scarcely distinguishable from the horizon sky. The power of churches to choose their pastors was here settled and agitation ended. The Book Concern was removed from New York to Syracuse.

Mr. C. on his return visited the land of his boyhood,

Henrietta, near Rochester.   This was of thrilling interest
to him.   In the city where he had spent some part of his
youth, the mischievous hand of art had spoiled everything.
The grand old river they had divided and carried away, as
woodsmen divide a log, and now children could play where
once the mighty waters flowed.   His own prospect hill
where, alone in the wild forest he used to stand and view
the falls, was now inclosed and locked up ; and the grand
falls which the Creator had made, audacious men had torn
down to get building materials.   This was worse than mu-
tilating the Egyptian Pyramids.   He looked for the place
where he had chopped firewood in his youth, so far off in
the forest that he carried his dinner in the depth of winter,
and lo ! it was now nearly in the center of the city.

Mount Hope grave-yard soon claimed his attention.
This had been nice playground for boys when he was a
child, and fortunately had been left in its native wilderness.
The hills and dales, trees and vines, were about the same
as forty years before, or perhaps a thousand years before.
It was autumn, and the leaves were falling, yellow and red,
upon the tombs and graves, and gravel walks, which me-
andered from hill to dale, and from dale to hill among the
sacred trees, passing here a magnificent tomb, dimly seen
in a solemn cloudy day through the vines, and there an
humble grave with no memorial, half covered with fallen
leaves.   All down the sidehill the marble slabs told where
the dead were sleeping, amidst trees and shrubs and vines
that hid from view the depth of the valley.   On the rising
ground beyond the vale the marble, looking out from thick-
ets brown, green and red, seemed to say, " Here we are
sleeping."   In a quiet little vale were, side by side, four
graves, evidently of the poor.   The survivors, too poor to
erect any monument, made the little spot a tiny garden with
green mosses and flowers.

Mr. C. felt that this was the most favored spot in this cemetery, visited so often by dear friends. As he wandered over and through these sacred groves, he reflected on the vanity of all sublunary things. Here sleeps the proud man of wealth who held in disdain the poor, whom he daily robbed by his extortions; and here the ambitious man of policy, who sacrificed all principle for promotion and power; here the gay, who once moved in flaunting robes at balls, operas and masquerades, at last are food for worms. These costly tombs may affect the living, but cannot reach the dead. They are brought to a level with the poor, with servants and paupers, all are here alike.

As he returned to the city and saw the banker and merchant at their desks, persons of wealth and ease, lolling in their parlors or riding in magnificence, sharp speculators on the alert for their prey, fops, coxcombs and spendthrifts promenading and vulgar loafers blaspheming, he said, "How soon all will be in Mount Hope!"

> "How shocking must thy summons be, O death,
> To him that is at ease in his possessions!
> Who, counting on long years of pleasure here,
> Is quite unfurnished for the world to come.
> In that dread moment how the frantic soul
> Raves 'round the walls of her clay tenement,
> And shrieks for help; but shrieks in vain!"

Mr. C. left the city where nothing interested him, and seating himself on the outside of the stage, rode to Henrietta, the land of his boyhood, viewing everything on the way with the most lively interest. Here is the place where I used to leave the road in my boyish glee to cross the wilderness to Chestnut Ridge, where showers of nuts, like a storm of hail, came down when the roaring wind played through the forest; when oh! such shouts from a score of little folks, running and leaping for the best picking, raking the bright red and yellow leaves to and fro to get the nice fruit.

There is where old Mr. Eaton year after year smoked his pipe and made potash; and lo! now, as sure as you are a living man, there is a nice white house on the little mountain of ashes which the old man threw out nearly forty years ago.   Forests and swamps have become grain-fields and meadows, gardens and orchards; and this road, where wagon-hubs used to roll below the surface of the mud, is now so smooth that this stage carries ten men on deck, and the baggage of ten more.

Over the meadows yonder on the other road is where, when six years old, I went to school to be scolded and whipped and turned out of a dirty log pen, noons and nights, to chase bumble-bees and beetles along the woods, and to forget the little learned as soon as possible.

Lo! we are coming to the old training ground, where, forty years ago, I stood barefooted, bareheaded, and clad in tow, my white locks waving in the breeze, looking with astonishment at Captain Bancroft, in his regimentals, who was then to me greater than Wellington has since been.   Ambition for martial glory seized my little soul as I ran along after the drum and fife.

Hurrah! here is a school-house where the old school-house stood, in which I used to bite my pencils in two over hard examples in Daboll; where I used to try my skill at composition and speaking; where Mr. Chamberlayne trained the youth to sing, and old-fashioned ministers used to pray forty minutes with their hands in their pockets, and sing through their sermons with their mouths filled with tobacco.

There the beautiful Sophia lived with her aged parents, and there she died of grief.   Here my tiny feet used to pad through the river; great river it was to me, though all of the water now might go through a two-inch pipe.

Here I come to the grave-yard where my little brothers, Alanson and Joseph, were buried, one in 1814, the other in

1816, each aged two years.   Here, too, is Albert and Sophia, and a multitude who are now forgotten by most of the
living.   The sun is setting just as it used to go down over
the western forests when Albert and I used to play here in
the wildwood, more than forty years ago.

There was our house, and there our barn, and those
apple-trees I helped set out in 1811.   Down yonder in that
meadow below the spring is the spot most cursed of all ;
for there stood the abominable distillery which flooded this
neighborhood with whisky, made of wheat, rye, corn, peaches
and pumpkins, and which made deacons and ministers red-
faced and surly.

Ah! here is where old Mr. Phillips lived, who used to
drink so much whisky, and who used to pray so loud in
secret that he was heard a hundred rods distant.

Thus Mr. C. went on musing, and came at twilight where,
when seventeen years old, he resolved to turn to the Lord.
Thirty years had passed since he, in walking over this very
ground, formed that resolution.   Passing still on he came
near the swamp where, when a little child, he was lost in
the woods in the night, forty years before ; and there ran
the brook where he and Albert had raised a pond, and were
making a canoe of a rotten log, when every now and then
they heard the British cannon, and shouted in sheer childish-
ness and wished the war would come where they were.

How recollections swelled his breast, as every step was
on ground that he had trod a thousand times before ; and
how a thousand memories crowded upon him ; his follies
and sins, his hours of repentance, his church hours, school
hours, few play hours, and weary days of hard toil; his
lessons of instruction from the minister, the teacher, and his
mother, most sacred of all.

Mr. C. on his return visited a school-mate, Seneca Dunham, near Albion, and thence proceeded to Niagara Falls,

where he had agreed to meet his traveling companion, A. W. Curtis. Failing to meet him, he crossed the river below the falls and went on foot with his baggage to Chippewa, though sick and lame, intending to take a steamer for Buffalo, where he was that evening to take boat for Detroit. He arrived at Chippewa just as the boat left its moorings— a shocking sight, as no boat would go until that hour the next day. He sat down, so exhausted that it seemed impossible to walk another rod; but recollecting that a train of cars would leave the falls for Buffalo about sundown, he sprang up, by mere power of will, and said, "I will see Buffalo to-night," and though the sun was almost down, he went back with his heavy baggage, and saw from the high bank the last omnibus going the zigzag road down to the last boat, and arrived in season to jump to the boat just starting, and was seated in the cars not five minutes before their time to start. He arrived in Buffalo, took the through boat and was in Detroit the next morning.

On his arrival home he found his daughter just recovering from a very dangerous illness.

CHAPTER XXII.

Mr. C., while he lay sick with a fever in the spring of 1853, was elected supervisor of the town of Eaton Rapids. When able to leave home he tried to get released from this responsibility; but finding every competent man unwilling to perform the duties of supervisor under the new tax law, then just passed, he commenced, while yet in a fever, this arduous work. The law then required him to go twice through his town, and as it was six miles by twelve and contained about four hundred taxable men, the task was great. It was nearly impossible to do these duties in so large a town in the time limited by law.

In order to see all of the land and judge of its value, he waded through swamps and rivers, while he was all of the time in chill fever. His anxiety to perfect the assessment and do justice to every man became so intense as to increase his illness. Party spirit ran so high that there was a determination to embarrass him and render his work as arduous as possible; and when these perplexing duties were done, most malicious falsehoods and misrepresentations were circulated concerning the assessment, and finally published in the *Eaton Democrat*. This cruel ingratitude and malicious party hatred so deeply affected Mr. C. as to seriously impair his health for several months, and was doubtless one reason for his removing from his old home in Eaton couuty.

Perhaps there is no place where Mr. C. has more friends than in Eaton county; but political party spirit is more cruel than the grave, uncourteous, unmerciful, unjust, envious, malicious, full of lies and hypocrisy. In every age and country this spirit has been the relentless destroyer of peace and friendship.

It was a great relief when he left home and entered into the spirit of love and devotion which prevailed at quarterly-meetings.

Conference for 1853 met at Sylvania, in Lucas county, Ohio. E. Smith and L. C. Matlack were again present. Mr. C. was again elected president, and appointed to Leoni, and soon after removed to that place. Mrs. C. hoped now to be able to attend religious meetings, but so failed in health as never to go but once, and then she was carried by her husband in his arms. The children were pleased with the privileges of school and religious meetings. Mr. C. entered on his labors with cheerfulness, preaching every Sabbath, teaching moral science and delivering historical lectures.   There was a gracious revival during the winter in which about forty were converted.

In the spring Mr. C. engaged in building a house, which too much engrossed his attention and injured his usefulness as a pastor, and much impaired his health.   He had for many years wished to write a brief universal history, consistent with the gospel, giving a truthful picture of war and its consequences.   He had an arrangement with S. A. Baker to publish such a work in the *Western Evangelist*, but this journal was swallowed up in the *Free Democrat*.   He, however, thought if he could lecture on history at Leoni two or three years, he could finish this work.

Pursuant to this plan, he sold his farm in Eaton county and invested all at Leoni, which proved an almost ruinous exchange.   He saw, long before the close of the year, that he could not be reappointed to Leoni.   Besides his unpopularity, there were other reasons which induced him as well as others to desire a change.   The college needed an additional teacher of high literary attainments, but was unable to pay his full salary; they must therefore unite the two offices of pastor and professor.   This plan Mr. C. recommended, but found to his deep mortification that arrangements had already been made for his removal, without his knowledge.

His long-cherished object of publishing a universal history must now be abandoned.   This was a heavy disappointment. but it did not so cut him to the heart as the coldness with which some began to treat him.   The office of president he had always found painful to bear, on account of his constitutional timidity.   He had accepted the office most reluctantly, and had borne it reluctantly five years out of six, and though eligible to re-election, he ardently hoped to be excused for throwing off a burden which he thought some other men ought to bear; but the manner of his removal from this office could not fail to painfully affect him.

Conference for 1854 convened at Leoni. He opened and organized the conference with a heavy heart; for in addition to his other griefs there was great sickness in his family. He went to dinner, and being delayed by the care of the sick, he found on his return that the election had taken place. No one had counseled with him, and no one took the trouble to step to his house, not more than ten rods distant, to inform him that this important business was being transacted.

The next morning Mr. C. came into conference, and being one of the committee on orders, he offered a motion, in substance, to extend the attention of the committee to some candidates for orders who had just arrived from distant parts of the State. This motion was called for by justice to these brethren, by every idea of courtesy and Christian kindness, and probably would have received unanimous support at any former conference; but a change had come. It was immediately opposed by a violent speech, after which the president left his chair to oppose it; finally a speech was made by a visiting minister against it, and the vote being then called, it was lost by every voice except that of the mover.

This was an era in the life of Mr. C. He had spent more than ten years with his Wesleyan brethren in the most beautiful harmony; but now, for reasons unknown to him, his influence was at an end. He has in every conference since been more a spectator than an actor.

Mr. C. received an appointment to Jackson Circuit, and though very feeble and often nearly chilled to death riding in the winter, yet he filled his appointments and witnessed the conversion of a considerable number. As the circuit was small (Onondaga Circuit having been set off from it), and unable to support his family, he worked at farming a part of his time, as he had done during nearly all the years of his ministry.   His health continued to decline, and in August he was prostrated by fever, and for several weeks was so really at the point of death that every hour was liable to be his last.   Most of the time he was deranged, sometimes preaching long discourses, and then apparently dying.

During this time he had enrapturing spiritual visions of heaven; feeling that he was just along the line of that blessed world, but not yet permitted to step over.   When he began to recover he felt that he was receding from that delightful country, and hoped to be able, if he ever preached again, to relate what he had seen of heaven; but as he recovered he receded from that beautiful land so far that both the view and the remembrance faded away.

All of his family were sick at the same time, and his son, John Emory, came so near death that his pulse ceased, and the family were informed by the physician that he must die. He, however, in answer to prayer, recovered, but was never after entirely well.   Mr. C. was confined to his chamber about two months, during which time he could never see the setting sun.

Conference again met at Leoni for 1855, but Mr. C. scarcely knew anything of its action, except by inquiry. Having been commissioned lecturing agent for Michigan by the American Peace Society, he received his appointment from conference accordingly.

As he so far recovered as to be able to leave his house, he was only able to walk with crutches, having nearly lost one of his legs during sickness by extreme ulceration.   Numerous cares were crowded upon him, and as he dragged himself about in torturing pain, he lost that sweet serenity which he had enjoyed and became melancholy and irritable. His boys were all sick, Mrs. C. was confined to her bed his daughter scarce able to be about, and he, by overdoing, was often prostrated by chills and fever.   During this long and terrible sickness Dr. I. S. Watts bestowed most faithful attention on this afflicted family, and generously gave his services.

One day when all were prostrated, the cold autumnal rain fell hour after hour in torrents ; they had no wood, the fire went out, and poor Mrs. C., becoming much chilled, they looked upon one another in despair.   At length Alphonzo, overcome by anxiety for his mother, staggered out into the tempest, at the risk of his life, and gathered scattered bits of timber and prepared wood for the dismal night which followed.

Mr. C. was invited to ride out about twenty miles for his health.   His friend was hindered, and it was not until the evening of the third day that Mr. C. returned home.   Mrs. C. had been failing alarmingly since he left.   She revived a little just as he came in, but soon became partially delirious, and her tongue became paralyzed so that she tried in vain to speak.   She continued in this state through the night, but having been in the same condition some years before, the family hoped that she would recover from it, and that she might not be near death.   She, however, never spoke again, though she often tried to.   She seemed to be in the exercise of her reason during the forenoon.   About noon, October 30, 1855, she waved her hand, evidently to show that she was going, and ceased to breathe fifteen minutes past twelve o'clock.

Mr. C. was now cut off from the society of the wife of his youth and mother of his children, under circumstances calculated to inflict the deepest possible pain and anguish. The grave was not far away, yet only one of the children was able to walk there ; the others rode   She is buried in Leoni, on the left hand of the cemetery gate.

Mr. C. continued almost all of the time in fever; his lame leg shockingly swelled, yet he worked hard gathering the produce of his ground—what had not been destroyed. He finally was prostrated on his bed, from which he crawled, got to the cars, crept in on his hands and knees, and started for his mother's, one hundred miles distant in Allegan county. On arriving in Kalamazoo he crawled into an omnibus on his hands and knees and went to a stage-house. There he sat in a high fever, in a crowded bar-room, so weak as to be in danger of falling whenever he attempted to walk, and so sick as to be in danger of fainting. Proud men, of lofty look and haughty tread, stalked around him, who seemed to him so cold, ungenerous and unfeeling that he could hardly endure to remain among them. He spoke for a passage in the stage, but was informed that he could have no seat except with the driver, and with great difficulty he climbed to that seat, in a winter night, so sick that there was danger of his falling to the ground. His sick children were entertained among his relatives in the neighborhood of his mother, except Emory, who, poor boy! was teaching in order to meet his coming expenses at college, although sick during the whole winter.

Mr. C. commenced his labors for the American Peace Society about the first of January, though lame and much of the time in chill fever. He sold books, distributed tracts and lectured every Sabbath, and nearly every evening through the week. He had long felt a deep interest in this cause, had read much on the subject, had written some, and had made it the theme of many sermons. No field of action could suit him better than lecturing on this subject, but for selling books and soliciting funds he had little inclination or talent. To go from house to house with books for sale was necessary, but exceedingly crossing. He met with all manner of treatment from the people, from rough ill-treatment to great kindness; but the subject was not pungent or exciting, and few cared to buy books or hear lectures. Some ministers met him in a friendly manner, while others treated him and his subject very coldly.

Mr. C. regarded the cause of Peace the most important of all causes, not excepting Christianity; for Christianity without peace is powerless for the reformation of mankind. He had been an attentive reader of ancient history, a careful observer of the religion and politics, the morals, manners and customs of the Chaldeans, Egyptians, Persians, Lydians, Greeks and Romans; had traced their progress to civilization, to eminent refinement of manners and the highest literary attainments; had viewed the perfection of the arts among them, the perfection of the science of government, their profound philosophy and wonderful genius in poetry and oratory. He had then inquired for the causes of the decline and fall of the ancient empires; the decay or total ruin of the most renowned cities; the loss of the arts and sciences, and the return of mankind to barbarism.

He had looked in vain for an answer in Gibbon's "Decline and Fall." That great work, important as it is to the student in history, throws little light on this subject. It rather insinuates that Christianity itself is the instrument of the overthrow of ancient empire, civilization and literature. Nothing is more untrue. Christianity brings light, not darkness. The ancient civilization contained the elements of its own dissolution. It cultivated the intellectual man only, leaving the moral man wholly unimproved. The religion of the ancients was corrupting to morals: their gods were represented as practicing the most flagrant vices, and possessing the most violent passions.

In the zenith of Greek and Roman civilization vice was as rampant as with savage barbarians. Plato informs us that in his day he had seen all Athens drunk at once during

the Bacchanalian feast.   The spirit of War was the great
element of dissolution to the ancient civilization, literatnre
and empire.   Physical power was admired in men when exercised in violence on their fellows.   It was deemed glorious for man to overcome his fellowman by superior physical
strength.   Forbearance was held in contempt, as mean and
cowardly; while retaliation was regarded as noble, manlike
and godlike.   Violence was recokoned as man's proper and
only defence against his fellowman, the only defence of tribe
against tribe, or nation against nation;   the only power to
bring liberty and freedom;   while patience, forbearance,
kindness and love toward enemies was held in supreme contempt.   Individuals, tribes and nations received the highest
honor when they adjudged to themselves their own rights,
claimed them, determined to maintain them, to fight for
them, and to conquer or die.

    Homer, whose genius has dazzled the world for three
thousand years, exalted and deified these heathen principles,
attributed them to the gods, and made demi-gods of men
who had distinguished themselves in tearing out the bowels
or hearts of men, or sinking war-clubs in their brains.
Homer surrounded these beastly acts with such glory as to
make martial ambition universal.   Succeeding poets, orators, painters, sculptors and historians made Homer their
model, and the ancients became mad in martial enthusiasm.
Nothing was honorable but the profession of arms, and as all
who were not soldiers were despised, whole nations—Sparta
especially—were from age to age soldiers, voluntarily, every
man devoted to war and sustained by the slave labor of conquered nations, of prisoners taken in battle.

    When the ancient literature had raised the martial en-
thusiasm to this height, the sword fell on poet, orator and
historian themselves;   the firebrand of war was thrown into
the gallery of painting, and sculpture was broken beneath

the battle-ax.   Thus ancient empire died of sword wounds, and the sun of ancient civilization went down in blood. The only wonder is that anything escaped, for the martial spirit, so much praised in song, tends to the destruction of all things and all men.

If it is noble in one man, or one nation, to say, "I am the judge of my rights; these are my rights; I will fight for them, and I will conquer or die," then the same is noble in all men; and if all men and all nations have this spirit and persevere in it, all mankind must be exterminated in a short time; if none yields, all must die.   Yet the ancient literature poured contempt on the yielding spirit, which saved men from extermination, and praised the unbending spirit, which would destroy all.

Mr. C. had traced the footprints of the warrior in all ruins; Thebes, Pellusium, Petra, Palmyra, Babylon, and Nineveh, all wholly gone, nothing left but frightful rocks, mounds, caverns and dismal swamps.   Amidst these gloomy haunts of owls, serpents and beasts of prey, no roaming savage pitches his tent.   Nearly equal are the desolations of Carthage, Memphis, Sidon. Tyre, Ephesus, Sardis, and Antioch; and what are Athens, Alexandria and Rome but villas built on awful heaps of ruins?

He traced the footprints of the warrior in the dismal ruins of ancient seaports, where once the ships of all nations were moored; in barren wastes where once grain-fields and vineyards abounded, and cities and millions of industrious people.   He also traced the hand of war in the tyranny that crushes to beastly degradation the descendants of Chaldeans, Persians, Assyrians, Lydians, Syrians, Egyptians, Phenicians and Carthaginians.   He has been astonished at the stubbornness of orators, poets and historians who tell us that war brings civilization and freedom, when the facts of history show that war has turned the whole ancient world

to barbarism, and has set up and upheld every tyrant that
has oppressed mankind.

He viewed the early Jewish wars as altogether unique,
and no more our example to follow than pestilence, earthquakes and volcanoes, or any other judgment of God.   He
considered that Christ came when the heathen doctrine
that violence is the power to bring freedom and prosperity
was proved an error by all facts of history, and when Jews,
left to themselves for hundreds of years without a prophet,
had been doing their part to destroy all things by war, and
had brought near the destruction of their temple, city and
nation.

Christ came to condemn the doctrines of Homer; to
strip physical power of its glory ; to exalt the weak and put
down the mighty ; to put away that false heathen doctrine
that force, or violence, is the power to overcome evil.   He
came to teach that patience, forbearance and kindness were
the power to overcome evil and subdue the hearts of evil
men.   Hence he taught " Resist not evil," " Turn the other
cheek," " Let him have thy cloak also," " Go with him
twain," " Love your enemies ; bless them that curse you ;
do good to them that hate you : and pray for them that
despitefully use you and persecute you " " Bless and curse
not," " Return blessing for cursing," " Overcome evil with
good."   Such were the teachings of Christ and his inspired
disciples.

Christ bade Peter " Put up thy sword," because it was
not the instrument to overcome evil, not the instrument to
subdue the hearts of bad men.   Violence only arouses violence, and taking the sword brings the sword upon him that
takes it ; hence " All they that take the sword shall perish
with the sword."

The question will be asked, " If forbearance subdues the
hearts of bad men, why did they crucify the Savior, who

was perfectly forbearing ?" He himself answers the question: "Father, forgive them for they know not what they do." If they had known him it is probable that his forbearance would have overcome them, so that they would not have crucified him. Many were lately come to the feast from distant parts and had scarcely heard of him until now; and having heard only false accounts of him, they were under ignorance and prejudice and knew not what they did. This accounts for martyrdom in general. Christ's forbearance took effect on the hearts of men, but too late to save him from crucifixion; and the forbearance of the martyrs took effect, but too late to save their lives ; yet this effect was great, carrying conviction to thousands. It was the great instrument of the conversion of men. It is absurd and audacious to say Christ bade Peter to put up his sword because he and his disciples were too weak to defend themselves ; for he said he could summon twelve legions of angels, and these could slay all living men in an hour. It is equally absurd to say that he bade Peter to put up his sword because it was lifted against government, which a late writer has done, making Christ to say, "All that take the sword against government shall perish by the government;" that is, Peter was a rebel and liable to be slain as a rebel by the sword of government.

This writer must maintain that the mob which took Jesus was a proper police, under a heaven-appointed government, and that the arrest, trial and crucifixion of Christ was legal, and opposition to it a crime; and yet this advocate for war who goes so far out of his way to destroy the meaning of Christ's words to Peter, is a strong believer in the right of the rebellious under Cromwell and Washington. Mr. C., in the firm belief that Christ's words to Peter signified that the sword was inconsistent with the principles of his king-

dom, and that forbearance was the power to reform the
world, entered with cheerful hopes on his mission.

The signs of the times were encouraging.   Several peace
conventions had been held, attended by some of the most
intelligent and noble men from nearly every civilized nation.
The absurdity of appealing to the sword to settle differences
of interest and misunderstandings seemed too plain to all
the wise and good, and a call seemed to arise from the heart
of all Christendom to withdraw from the seas those immense
belligerent fleets, intended for mutual destruction, and the
immense armies trained for human butchery, and a call for
the appropriating for benevolent purposes the thousands of
millions wasted in war.

The religious press seemed to be hailing the dawn of a
better day, and Mr. C. found no difficulty in obtaining the
columns of the press for the most full expression of his principles.   He was certain from the nature of Christianity and
from the word of prophecy that peace principles must finally
prevail and wars must cease; and he sometimes thought
the time was near when all nations should flow together in
brotherhood, and civilization and righteousness should cover
the earth.   He almost saw the cars moving over Sahara
and the plains of Tartary; almost heard the church going
bells from every hill and valley of Asia and Africa, and
almost saw universities rising from Cape Town to Tripoli,
from Suez to Kamstschatka.   The wolf in man was about
to give place to the temper of the lamb, the ferocity of the
bear to the quiet and harmless temper of the cow; and
men as violent and proud as the leopard and the lion were
about to become so meek that a little child should lead
them, and none should any longer wear the serpent's sting.

Such were the cheering hopes of Mr. C. as he dragged
his feeble body along to preach peace through one of the
hardest winters ever known in Michigan, his feet too much

swelled to admit of his wearing boots or shoes, often among strangers and sometimes coldly treated and opposed.

The most formidable opposition was from sober, grave and pious Puritans who were ever eulogizing Cromwell and extolling revolutions. These men greedily entered into the schemes of Kossuth, and hailed with joy every revolution in Europe, always making every revolution a Godly war.

The war in Kansas was raging, and many were deaf to any appeal on the subject of peace; collections were being taken in churches for the purchase of Sharp's rifles to be furnished to Kansas emigrants. Pulpits and presses called to war.

Mr. C. pursued the even tenor of his way in the midst of all this tempest of excitement. Whenever the question was asked, "What shall be done in Kansas?" he answered, "Stay away from Kansas and let it alone, or go there without weapons, trusting in the Lord; make no land claim that will involve you in strife with any man, retaliate no injuries, return good for evil, and blessing for cursing."

If all Northern men had gone to Kansas in this spirit there probably would have been no trouble. "But," was asked, "would you not fight for the poor slave?" He answered, "No, I would not do evil that good might come. The Lord has said, 'Vengeance is mine; I will repay,' and more than this, the Free State movement is not an emancipation movement, but only a non-extension movement, and the party sustaining it often boasts that it is not a Negro party, but the white man's party, determined to maintain the Northern white man's interests in Kansas. For these interests they took the sword and perished with the sword. The Missourians were exceedingly wicked; they were the basest of men and many of them were too ignorant to understand the merits of the questions arising from the 'Kansas-Nebraska Bill.' They were much like

those for whom Christ prayed, 'Father, forgive them for
they know not what they do.'"

Such men can only be convinced, brought to terms and
reformed and saved by forbearance and kindness.   Every
violent act toward them shuts their ears against truth and
virtue, and arouses all their diabolical rage and pushes them
on in their blindness to commit every outrage.   There were
wrongs committed by Free State men; first, in urging unjust
land claims; secondly, in a general spirit of speculation;
thirdly, in violently retaliating injuries, especially in the
shocking Ossawatomie massacre; and though these wrongs
may not have been one-tenth or one-fiftieth as great as the
wrongs committed by the Missourians, yet they were calculated to arouse the demon in those depraved men and defeat
every hope of their reformation.

Mr. C. had attended a political mass-meeting in 1855
when the settlement of Kansas was first agitated.   An aged
clergyman arose, trembling on his staff, and said: "There
will be blood shed in Kansas.   I am going there, old as I
am, and if slavery comes in there, it will come over my dead
body."   Another clergyman arose and went to him, saying,
"I am three years older than you, and here is my hand to
go with you."   To this the assembly cheered as though they
would throw off the roof by their shouts.

Such was the spirit of Kansas emigration, even before
any settlements were made, and such was the omen of what
followed.

CHAPTER XXIII.

In October, 1856, Mr. C. visited the land of his boyhood,
and went to a pond in Mendon where the most interesting
scenes in childhood had passed.   It seemed to have dimin-

ished tenfold, and had it not been that the same hills and
marshes surrounded it, and the bold shore where he had
learned to swim remained the same, he would not have
believed that this diminutive pond could be the same as the
sublime lake where he used to play.

He visited at this time his Uncle Joseph Pierson, in Rush,
an aged man, older than Mr. C.'s mother.   He also visited
his mother's only surviving sister, Mrs. Spencer, at Canastota.   His uncle, General Spencer, a very aged man, was
in an asylum for the insane at Utica.   He had seen this
uncle thirty-five years before at general training, then in the
vigor of manhood, a splendid and proud officer, and he had
not seen him since.

On Sabbath morning, October 16, 1856, Mr. C. was married to Eunice B. Kirkland, in Ellisburg, Jefferson county,
N. Y.   After spending about ten days with her relatives,
viewing the interesting scenery of that country, they returned
to Leoni.   He soon resumed his labors in the cause of
peace, still holding his commission from the American Peace
Society, and received the same appointment from conference for 1856, convened at Kensington.   His income was
small and his family was brought to extremities to live.

August 11, 1857, a son was born to Mr. and Mrs. C.,
whom they named Edwin R.   He seemed at first a healthy
child, but soon a defect appeared in the action of his heart,
which kept him feeble until his death.

Conference for 1857 convened at Coldwater.   Mr. C.
was elected president, but declined and was excused.   He
was sick during the whole time of the conference, yet he was
usually in his seat in conference hours, but exerted very little influence.   He received an appointment to travel at
large, and soon entered on his labors, which were described
in " Reflections by the Way," published nearly every week
in the *Wesleyan.*   This was a year of great labor, and much

suffering to himself and his family, Mrs. C. being left with a very sick infant child.

He took much interest in a camp-meeting held in Lyon, Oakland county, which resulted in much good.   His commission still continued as agent for the American Peace Society, and much of his preaching was on the power of kindness and the spiritual nature of Christ's peaceful kingdom.   He felt that the war spirit, which was everywhere arising about Kansas, if not speedily checked, would soon bring on such a war as was never known on this continent. This he often predicted, but few heeded it.

Conference for 1858 assembled at Leoni.   He received at this conference a very liberal donation in money and subscription, which relieved him very much from his financial wants.   This to him was a pleasant year, except the great strife about the removal of the college, which became too great to admit of any prosperity to the church or harmony between neighbors.

This terrible commotion was somewhat abated by a very liberal subscription at the conference for 1859, which was also held at Leoni.   This subscription for the payment of college debts amounted to ten thousand !dollars.   Such liberality has seldom been exhibited.

Mr. C. chooses to pass over the painful subject of college removal, college agency and college debts, nearly in silence; yet, having been a trustee almost the whole time from the commencement of college enterprise, it is due to his memory to say, that if his counsel had been heeded, no debts would have been contracted; and a great part of the financial business was done without his knowledge.   Perhaps he erred in consenting to be a trustee under such circumstances, when he could not cordially act with the board. He was accused at last by innumerable complaints from the people, and felt that not only the trustees, but the Wesleyan denomination in Jackson county, were under deep reproach. The liberal subscription at the conference for the payment of college debts wholly removed this reproach from the Wesleyan Connection at large, and led the suffering creditors to form a high estimate of the justice and generosity of the denomination.

Mr C., in behalf of the creditors, and in deep sympathy with them, wrote an appeal to the Wesleyan brethren and all friends of education to come to the aid of the college at Leoni.   This appeal was written in the spring or early summer, before the premises were transferred to the United Brethren, when there was no prospect that any part of the debts would be paid if the college at Leoni failed, for such failure would render void a subscription of more than eight thousand dollars, which was all the hope the creditors had.

This appeal did not save the college at Leoni; it failed and was transferred to the United Brethren.   The creditors were now nearly in despair, and Mr. C., in his sympathy with them, moved in the conference of 1859 for an investigation of financial transactions, which brought down upon him a majority of the conference, and from some the most severe attacks that he had ever met.

Thanks be to God for the spirit which came to the conference before its close, when almost every heart overflowed with generosity, and a wonderful subscription seemed to almost remove all complaint.   Many creditors, after all, have suffered much.

Mr. C., at the conference of 1859, received an appointment to travel at large, and was soon on the way, first visiting the western and northwestern circuits.   Mrs. C. accompanied him, spending several weeks with his relatives in Allegan county and with hers in Grand Rapids.

It was in this tour, and while riding over the pine plains in Newaygo county, that the hour of John Brown's execu-

tion came.   He was deeply affected, and on arriving at
Brother Barton's wrote his reflections.   It was easy for him
to see that John Brown might be as justifiable as Cromwell
or Washington, and far more innocent than President
Buchanan or Governor Wise ; yet he did not believe these
violent massacres were calculated to benefit the slave or reform the slaveholder.   He looked upon the Harper's Ferry
raid as a part of the machinery which was soon to involve
our country in most terrible civil war.   He preached no
John Brown sermons, and threw no fuel into the fire which
was soon to flame forth to the destruction of all things.

Quarterly-meetings at Berrien, Grand River, Muskegon,
Ottawa and Kalamazoo were interesting seasons, and gave
encouragement of prosperity to Zion.

Mr. and Mrs. C. returned home after an absence of six
weeks, and felt encouraged that the health of their little boy
was benefited by the journey.   In February, Mrs. C., hoping to improve her health, which was failing, accompanied
her husband in another tour, but failed in health every day,
and was finally wholly prostrated for several weeks at the
house of Rev. Samuel Phillips, in Pittsfield.   She was
brought home the 1st of April, but lingered long in great
debility.

Mr. C. had a severe attack of fever in July and August,
and when conference for 1860 came on, which convened in
Adams, Mr. and Mrs. C. and their child were all sick ;   he
consequently did not attend.   He never before had been
absent from conference since he united with the Wesleyan
Connection in 1844   He received an appointment to Nankin and Salem, with G. A. Olmsted.   He was also elected
to General Conference, to be held at Fulton, N. Y., but
failed to go for want of funds.

September 30, 1860, his daughter Zelura D. was married
to B. N. Hoff, of Michigan Center.

Soon after conference Mr. C. was on his circuit, though in very poor health. He returned home the first week in November, intending to take his wife and child on to his circuit, but found his dear affectionate boy sick of scarlet fever, from which he did not recover. He died November 9, 1860, aged three years and three months. After his death the poor afflicted mother accompanied Mr. C. to his circuit, in very poor health, and was immediately prostrated and lay dangerously sick at the house of Rev. Marcus Swift, two or three weeks.

This year, considering Mr. C.'s health. was the hardest perhaps of his life. His anxiety to do all that he possibly could for the circuit prompted him to drag his feeble body along in great suffering. Much of the time during the winter and spring he was, with his excellent colleague, engaged in protracted meetings, laboring in meeting every afternoon and evening and spending the intervals in going from house to house, often in such pain in his feet that he could scarce keep from groaning at every step. He was often so worn out that he felt inclined to give over and lie down anywhere, even by the roadside. He visited on the circuit about two hundred families.

He sometimes rode in the midst of chills and fever, scarce able to get out of his buggy without falling. His poor health deprived him of that sprightly cheerfulness and lively vivacity so essential to popularity, and his congregations were small, and grew smaller as he drew near the close of his earthly labors.

The coming on of war helped to weigh him down and bring him to the verge of the grave. He had labored more than thirty years to show the power of kindness, and had hoped to see all nations in a bond of brotherhood; but the change of public sentiment for the few preceding years had painfully affected him, and now even his friends who had stood by him, carried away by the plea that this is not war, but only a police effort to put down riot to maintain government. Ministers who would have their pulpits popular made them teem with harangues for war, and the cars ran on the Sabbath carrying tens of thousands to our cities to hear popular ministers and lawyers declaim on fighting. The religious press, where Mr. C.'s peace communications had for long years been freely published, was now closed against him.

While he stood thus alone and sorrowful, his sorrow was increased almost beyond endurance by the news of the enlistment of his youngest son, Alphonzo. He visited this son at the encampment at Detroit and found him determined to serve only three months.

The war spirit then raged to such an extent that Mr. C. jocosely asked a lady who wished to ride with him to the encampment, "Suppose I write on my pocket-handkerchief 'Peace on earth and good will toward men,' and nail it to my carriage before I go?" "Oh," said she, "I would not dare to ride with you." She feared the carriage would be demolished. Such was the wild frenzy which some called "a baptism from on high," and which all denominated patriotism.

Mr. C., on his return from Detroit, was violently attacked with ague and fever, but still went on through his circuit, determined not to spare himself, not counting his life or his health dear. As almost every minister was making capital out of the excitement, delivering war sermons and mingling with the crowd in their mass meetings, some seeking the office of chaplain and some becoming captains, Mr. C. felt sensibly that his silence on the exciting subject was bringing him into neglect and contempt; but he recollected that the Christians of the first ages were held in contempt for the same reason, and sometimes put to death. A change was coming over his brethren ; the meek and quiet temper of the gospel was giving place to bravado, boasting and threatening.

He felt that his sky was darkening and his doom was to walk alone, neglected, cast off and despised, until this tempest of excitement was overpast; firmly assured that

> " Truth crushed to earth will rise again ;
> The eternal years of God are hers."

In May he visited his son again, then at Fort Wayne. He found him sick in his berth, in the cabin of the steamboat " Mississippi," where his company was quartered, surrounded by such scenes of swearing and gambling as he had never before witnessed.　This regiment, the Second, had the reputation of being one of the most moral in Michigan.　Wherever he moved about the fort, or encampment, he was in the midst of profaneness and blasphemy.　The soldiers were so obscene in the presence of ladies visiting the encampment as to call forth a severe rebuke from the Detroit press.　He went to the encampment again the next day, and finding his son improving in health, he carried him out through the city and into the country, and passed the day with him.　It would have been a very pleasant day but for the reflection that it was their last intercourse, at least for a long time, as the son had re-enlisted for three years.

This dear and affectionate son who abhorred and shunned the wickedness of the camp, walked with his father to the boundaries of the encampment, where they parted with great solemnity and deep emotion.　Mr. C. got into his carriage and started away, and in a few minutes encountered an overwhelming rain storm.　He rode till evening in wet clothes, which was bad for his declining health.

CHAPTER XXIV.

After spending a short time in Perrinville, repairing his carriage, he proceeded on his way around his circuit, a worn out man.   His feet had for some time been so inflamed that he had been unable to wear shoes; but now finding for sale at Plymouth a pair of No. 12's, he put his aching feet into them, and proceeded to Salem, where, in the quiet family of Brother Peckham, he wrote the following :

" I am alone in my views of the war.   The political world is against me, and even the Peace Society forsakes me and leaves me alone.   I think it is not pride that thus separates me.   I would be humble at this time.   I would sit in sackcloth and ashes, in fasting, in watching and prayer, while alone, against the world.   Is truth with me ? or is it with them ?   This is a solemn inquiry ; for it would be a sad thing to stand alone and truth not with me.   Is God on my side, or on theirs ?   How solemn this inquiry !   It would be terrible to stand alone without God !   Is not the doctrine that violence is the power to overcome evil an error—a heathen error ?   Had not the heathen proved this an error before Christ came—setting all nations at variance, laying a thousand cities in ashes, and destroying in every age the greatest part of the product of all industry ?   Had they not proved that violence arouses violence, wrath awakens wrath, and taking the sword invites the sword ?

" Hence Jesus bade Peter put up his sword, saying, ' All they that take the sword shall perish with the sword.'   Was not this said of taking the sword in defence ?   Certainly in defence, for in defence Peter had drawn the sword, and Jesus bade him sheath it, as such instruments arouse more strife and commonly in the end bring destruction.   Has not forbearance saved the human family from extermination ?   When there has been no yielding on either side, has not one nation always been exterminated? Paley says: 'The earth could not contain one generation of unyielding men,' and yet Paley says 'these unyielding men always command respect.' Why are these men honored? men who this great judge of human nature allows would kill all mankind, kill each other to the last man, if none yielded to them? Why are yielding men despised? men whose forbearance Paley allows has saved the world from extermination in every age? men whose gentle influence now holds the violent in check and saves the human race from extermination? Why are they followed by this withering hiss— Tame! Cowardly! Pusillanimous? Is there not infatuation in this, like the infatuation of those who worship the most ferocious beasts and venomous serpents?

" Here lies the foundation of war, in Christian as well as pagan nations: honor paid to the spirit that would destroy the world, and contempt shown to the spirit that would save the world. The moral courage of primitive Christians who threw up their commissions and refused to fight when converted, chose to be numbered with a despised sect and cheerfully submitted to an ignominious death, was almost infinitely above the brute courage of warriors; yet nearly all Christendom in the nineteenth century lavishes its praise on · heroes for brute courage, and brands as a fanatic the man who trusts to forbearance to overcome the violent. Will any dare to say that the Scriptures mean nothing when they say, 'Love your enemies, bless them that curse you,' 'Overcome evil with good,' 'Return not evil for evil,' 'If thine enemy hunger feed him,' 'Turn to him the other [cheek],' 'Let him have thy cloak also'?

" Macaulay, the defender of Puritan revolution, the eulogist of Cromwell and the Prince of Orange, seems satisfied with pouring contempt on the Quaker interpretation of these words of inspiration, without giving them any meaning himself. What meaning could he and kindred writers give ? None, I think, consistent with their political doctrines. Doubtless the above words of inspiration, and others like them, establish a general rule of conduct, to appeal to the mind of every man in the spirit of love and forbearance.

"Jesus, who knew all men, knew that this rule was applicable to mankind in general; that mankind in general would be brought to proper terms when perseveringly appealed to in this spirit. There were doubtless exceptions to this general law of human nature then. Some few were too deeply depraved to be reached by the most persevering kindness. Though civilization has greatly advanced in eighteen hundred years, yet there are some few who cannot be thus reached. For them we need the penalties of law, police authority, prisons and force to secure mischievous and dangerous men.

"Nothing is more in the mouths of men, moderate men, church members and peace men, than the declaration, *This is not war. It is a police movement on a great scale.* I have given a careful attention to a declaration made by so many great and good men, yet I am not convinced. There seems a wide discrepancy between this war movement and any police movement. A police attempts to put down one, or ten, or one hundred, or one thousand riotous persons who arise for riot or mischief; and I say, let them be put down, if it takes five regiments of men to do it. If they are depredating on the lives and fortunes of men, and cannot be brought to terms by reason and kindness, I would aid in putting them down by force. They are a select band of extremely depraved men, whose object is not to form a government, but simply to act as banditti to bring anarchy. The case is very different when many millions, occupying a vast territory, agree, first by individual States and then by a confederacy of States, to separate from a larger and form a smaller government.

"They are not a select band of desperadoes. They comprise the elements of a whole people, bad and good, wise and ignorant, and begin to seem a nation in the eyes of the world.

"'It makes no difference,' says my friend, 'whether they are a banditti of fifty desperate men, or a whole people of many millions, able to form a government. They are still rioters, and should be dealt with as such.'

"My dear friend, your argument is spoiled by the fact that our government has acknowledged the independence of so many governments which have separated by revolt from larger governments, and your argument is spoiled most perfectly by the fact that our government came into being by revolt, revolution and secession. Our government has joined most other governments in acknowledging the independence of every (white) people who have united and formed a government, if they have seemed able to maintain it, caring little why they revolted or how they conducted their rebellion. Our whole people, South and North, have been educated for four generations in the right of revolution and secession. On this question the present war and that of 1776 are the same in character, both revolutions for secession.

"With this view the plea that this is not war has no force with me. It is war. The South is wicked almost beyond parallel in enslaving and imbruting men. Her guilt is increased by coveting territory for the extension of this horrid institution, and clamoring for the return of panting men and women, and most increased by rebellion.

"When the South in insane frenzy was hacking at the tie which bound her filthy self to the nation it was a pitiful sight, as when an insane inebriate cuts his own flesh. Every

Christian heart might have said, If they will go, let them go; let them have their revenue and the forts on the coast, and let the nation, the States which remain united, cement their union more strongly, and give their attention to every noble enterprise for public and private well being, and at the same time do good and not evil, even to the South; and above all let our nation bow in humility before the Lord, and repent for our participation in our great national sins, the guilt of slavery especially, which attaches to almost every Northern man.   Instead of this we have plunged into war. The whole land is moved by vast arrangements for mutual destruction.

"A prominent paper of the Northwest advises to push the war to the last, to the thorough whipping of the South, if it cost one thousand millions and a quarter of million of lives. When all this sacrifice of life and treasure is made, and greater damage to life and treasure in the South is accomplished, this journal asks as a condition of peace—what? oh, that slavery shall not be carried into new territory— leaving the question of slavery where it is untouched.   The motive of the war, as expressed in all publications which come under my observation, would carry despair to the heart of the slave.

"That horrid instrument, the Fugitive Slave Act, that reeks with gore and is encircled by the shrieks of despair, was never more fully executed than during this excitement.

"Is God in this movement, as exhibited in Michigan, from the affair at Fort Sumter to this time?   Colleges have moved, pulpits have moved, eloquent divines have appealed to their congregations, noble professors have harangued their students, Ciceros have painted the enormity of slavery extension, and many a Demosthenes thundered over the sin of secession and rebellion, and called the people to arms. They have rallied to arms, and their praises are on all tongues, in the journals, and in oral speeches. Valiant young men, noble fellows, patriots—our country's glory are their titles. The Lord knows them without reading news-papers, or hearing speeches. No doubt some deserve all of the above titles, and in addition to them the titles of intelli-gent gentlemen and Christian philanthropists; but having been several times in camp, I shall carry to the end of life a painful recollection of coarse and profane and blasphe-mous language, which gave me too much pain to ever be for-gotten. WILLIAM W. CRANE.

"*Salem, June* 1, 1861."

After writing the above Mr. C. arose and went forth to talk to the people on the interests of their souls, feeling al-most guilty that he had rested, though with pen in hand, a whole day. When hobbling from house to house, a letter was handed him, informing him of the dangerous illness of his daughter at Michigan Center. He hastened with the utmost speed to her, a distance of fifty miles. He stayed several days, his right foot growing rapidly worse. When his daughter seemed out of danger, he started back to his circuit, though not really able to walk.

At Dexter, where he passed the night of June 7, when he took off his sock, the joint-water from the great toe joint ran out, spirting at first four or five feet. From that hour he has never been free from pain. Saturday, June 8, he rode to Dr. I. M. Swift's, in Northville, for advice. Sunday, June 9, in spite of the protest of Dr. S., he started for his three appointments, the first seven miles, the second eleven, and the third fourteen miles distant. When he arrived at the first appointment, which was in Novi, it seemed to him im-possible to walk one step, but he got into the house by moving in torture, and preached a short sermon from Psalm 23, and felt a very cheerful resignation. He then rode four miles to South Lyon, and, crawling into the meeting-house

on his hands and knees, preached a short sermon sitting.
Thus closed his ministerial labors, after thirty-five years.

CHAPTER XXV.

After the close of this, his last sermon, Mr. C. was conveyed to 'Squire Bradley's, near the meeting-house, where
he received the most kind attention.   Tuesday, June 11,
seeing signs of mortification, he returned to Northville, wishing, if amputation were necessary, to be under the treatment of his friend, Dr. Swift.   This was a terrible journey.
The weather was very hot, and he did not dare to get out
of his carriage, fearing he could not get in again, and he
therefore drove eleven miles without stopping, except to call
for water, which some citizen occasionally brought and
poured on his foot.

He passed the first night at Dr. Swift's without undress-
ing, in indescribable pain.   The second night, the pain still
increasing, he took off his clothes, and saw them no more
in more than six weeks, and during which time he was never
taken out of his bed.

He had not before this supposed that any man could live
a day in such extreme pain.   He therefore thought that he
had a more vivid sense of the sufferings of Christ than he
had ever had before.   He felt much serenity in committing
himself to God, felt resigned to suffer and to die, but sometimes felt too anxious to have death come speedily.   Typhoid
fever set in, and reduced him so low that for several weeks
he spoke by whispering.   The ligaments and cartilages and
much of the muscle about the great toe joint rotted away,
and the flesh came off, leaving the bone bare some distance
about the joint.   Painful abscesses formed about his shoulder, some of them quite large, and these continued for two

months, rendering him nearly helpless. Language is scarcely capable of describing the kindness of Dr. S. and his family.

Mrs. C. arrived on the 14th of June and remained until she accompanied him to Leoni, about the 20th of August, when he was lifted from the bed into a carriage and conveyed to Wayne, where, after resting a little, he was lifted into the cars, more helpless than an infant, and carried to Leoni, and laid upon his own bed. The journey overcame him, and he only put on his clothes once in six weeks after his return.

It is evident that the bones became diseased from the commencement of his sickness, for the first piece taken out, not long after his arrival home, was black and very rotten.

He was overjoyed soon after his return by a visit from his dear son Emory and his wife, from Hillsdale College, and soon after by a visit from his mother and step-father, who had come alone by private conveyance one hundred miles. His mother was eighty years old, and his step-father in his eighty-seventh year.

Soon again his sky was darkened by the news that Emory had enlisted into the army. His foot was now rapidly decaying, in spite of sulphate of zinc, which was injected every day for nearly three months, torturing him terribly.

By December he was able to walk a little on crutches, but passed a gloomy winter, being rarely able to leave his house. He thought and wrote a little, but the whole winter seems nearly a blank in his life. Many remedies were used, none of which did any good more than a few days or weeks. In the spring he was weak and discouraged. A new physician advised him to use ale and more strengthening food. This improved his spirits and strength, but no medicine improved his foot; the decay went on. About the 1st of June he began to hoe his garden, standing on one foot and leaning on his crutch, usually going out from a half hour to an hour at a time, two or three times a day. Sometime about the beginning of July he employed another physician, who was confident that he could cure him ; but after long continued treatment, seemed to do no good, except in bandaging, which much reduced the swelling. There was no increase of strength, and no healing of his foot.

On the 26th of June he was almost overcome by the arrival of his dear Emory, who came from Norfolk, Va., on a furlough for his health. He was pale and weak, but so pious, intelligent, cheerful and happy, that his visit was a great blessing to his father. Precious was every hour when Emory was in sight, or when he could hear his voice in another room.

On the 4th of July his pleasure was increased by the arrival of his true and long-tried friend, Rev. A. W. Curtis, a friend equally to him and to Emory. It is pleasant to reflect on the few bright days of a dark life. The bright days were soon gone. Emory, one of the most conscientious of all men, was to leave on the 22d of July, and though unable to carry his knapsack to the cars, was determined to report himself at Detroit, instead of sending in the affidavit of a physician, expecting justice from a country which he had so faithfully served. Sad was the morning of July 22, 1862, when Mr C. parted from his son, saying, "The Lord be with and bless you."

Oh, how cruel, how inconsistent, for this noble young man, nearly ready to graduate, a candidate for the university, to be subject to vulgar and brutish men, to be neglected at the barracks, wasted to a skeleton, and then when too weak to walk more than six or eight rods at a time, to be pronounced fit for duty by a drunken surgeon, and ordered to his regiment, a thousand miles distant by a drunken lieutenant ! How cruel to bruise a patient sick man by a speedy journey to Fortress Monroe, until his whole body was the seat of pain and mortal disease !

Shortly after he parted with his son, Mr. C. wrote the following dialogue :

"I am confused," said James Gordon, "by the indefinite position of American Christians on the subject of war."

"You should have said, by their having no position," said John Porter. "They have no position. They talk confusedly of the right of war, the wrong of war, the virtue of war, the vice of war, the glory of war, and the shame of war; they talk of meekness, and of noble pride; of forbearance, and resentment; of forgiveness, and retaliation, until all is confusion. Patriotism is an undefined term. True, it means love of one's country, that is, partiality to one's country; but how far may it go? how far may it blind a man to the faults of his country? how far may he go in seeking to benefit his country at the cost of another country ?"

"There seems to me," said James, "no consistency except in the doctrine of non-resistance ; or, on the other hand, in the doctrine that war is man's normal state ; for either the power to subdue men and bring them to proper terms consists of wrath and violence, or it consists of love and forbearance. I believe that it consists of wrath, and that 'war is man's normal state.' You believe it consists of love ; therefore there is a fair issue between us."

" I believe this power consists of love, of love alone, never mixed with wrath ; and yet it admits of penalty," said John.

"You must exclude penalty and confine yourself to love, if we debate," said James.

" I shall confine myself to love," John replied, "but shall not exclude penalty, nor need I, for penalty should never be mixed with any degree of wrath. Penalty, unmixed with wrath, will be necessary in the family, in the school, in the state ; but when mixed with wrath it always fails of its object ; it always restrains, never subdues or reforms."

"Do you admit force ?" James inquired.

"I do. Force will sometimes be necessary. To love our enemies, to bless them that curse us, to resist not evil, to turn the other cheek, will in general subdue men, or Christ would not have commanded us to do thus. He knew what men were, and knew the power of forbearance and did not blindly utter these commands ; but if there is one in a thousand whom forbearance cannot subdue when fully tried, he must meet the penalties of the laws which he breaks, and force may be necessary to inflict the penalty."

"How much force may be used?"

"All that the emergency requires. To arrest a banditti may require a strong force."

"May life be taken ?"

"Life may be risked. Police should only aim to disable and disarm a banditti, yet in doing this they will be liable to take life."

"Why should not an offending nation be treated the same as a banditti?"

"A banditti is always a select band of desperate men, each of whom is one of those extreme cases of depravity, one of a thousand, who cannot be brought to terms by kindness and forbearance, while a nation, a whole people, has a conscience and a heart and may always be brought to terms by a persevering appeal of kind forbearance, by national arbitration."

"You surely will make no distinction between a banditti and a rebellious province ?"

"Most certainly I shall. The difference is nearly as great as the difference between a banditti and a nation. A nation is a whole people, which has already become a government ;

a rebellious province is a whole people struggling to become a government; while a banditti is a select band of wicked men, condemned by the public sentiment of any whole people."

"Do you not believe in the divine right of governments?"

"In no other sense than this: God made the laws of our social being, and by these laws governments naturally arise."

"Is not government so sacred that no rebellious province can have the favor of the Lord, though it succeed and pretend to form a government? And secondly, is it not the duty of every government to put down rebellion, though it have to scourge the people to the last extremity?"

"In answer to your first question, it is doubtful whether there is a government on earth that has not arisen by rebellion and secession, not excepting our own. If no government formed by secession meets the divine approval, none is approved. As to the duty of government to subdue a rebellion by the most extreme measures, amounting nearly or quite to extermination, as embraced in your second question, 'Let him who is without sin cast the first stone.' Bad as the South is, great as their sins are, it is shocking to see a government, composed of erring men, take the responsibility of destroying three or four hundred thousand lives, and many thousand millions of property."

"Would not the rebels have destroyed our nation?"

"That is a hasty conjecture. It is probable that if left alone in their confederation they would never have done us a tenth part of the damage which we have already done to ourselves. There is mourning for the dead everywhere; joy and gladness can never return to this generation, and still this wholesale slaughter goes on. It is horrible! Ministers and laymen, who believe in the endless punishment of the wicked, rejoice as they read of thousands of the wicked enemy killed, at the cost of thousands of our own men, not

one in a hundred of whom was fit to die, and rejoice in
hope that another battle to-morrow may send thousands
more to hell, if it will give us a victory.   Can it be that
these men believe what they profess to believe, and feel the
deep concern which they profess to feel for the salvation of
men ?   WILLIAM W. CRANE.

"*Leoni, Aug.,* 1862."

Mr. C. was absorbed in anxiety about his son, and when
a letter came informing him that the son was at the point of
death, he was nearly overcome.   Arrangements were speedily made to hasten Harriet, Emory's wife, to her dying husband.   She found him alive and able to talk with her, and
her arrival was a great comfort to him; but seventeen days
after her arrival he died, Sabbath morning, September 21,
1862, aged twenty-six years.   He died in the Chesapeake
Hospital, or Ladies' Seminary, near Fortress Monroe, and
was buried on Monday, September 22, about half a mile
north of the hospital; the water of the bay, or Hampton
Roads, lying a few rods from his grave on the west.   A
small cedar bush was then standing at the head of his grave,
and also a board containing his name.

He had always been an affectionate son, and for four and
a half years he had been deeply pious, a member of the
Freewill Baptist Church at Hillsdale College, and candidate
for the ministry.   He found his regiment, the Second Michigan Infantry, very irreligious, and deeply mourned the loss
of Christian society, but maintained most exemplary deportment, which gave him the confidence and respect of all.
Being feeble, he was employed in doing the writing for his
company; but too close application, writing sometimes until midnight, injured his lungs, which were much diseased.
During his last sickness he spent most of his time in prayer,
and closed his life in great serenity.

The news of Emory's death nearly destroyed his father's remaining life. It was his only consolation to talk to the mourning widow, his daughter-in-law, about the sufferings which his dear son had escaped, and the bliss which he now enjoyed. They sometimes felt that his happy spirit was with them.

Alphonzo wrote consoling letters to them, and soon informed them that he had consecrated himself to the service of the Lord. This very much strengthened the father and kept him from sinking in sorrow.

He went a few times to meeting, and was able to hear a funeral sermon to Emory's memory, delivered by Elder Tompkins of the Freewill Baptist Church; but becoming more feeble, he passed all the Sabbaths of the winter at home, rarely going out anywhere.

This winter, like the winter before, seems a blank, excepting the writing of the most of this history.

It is now April, 1863. The weather is becoming mild, and he hopes to be able to hobble out and trim fruit trees an hour at a time, which may improve his health. He has been at meeting a few times. His health has not improved for ten months, and his foot is no better. It seems incurable.

This manuscript he leaves to his children. May they faithfully serve the Lord, and may all meet in heaven. The will of the Lord be done! WILLIAM W. CRANE.

Leoni, April 19, 1863.

Composed by the author when commencing
his itinerant labors in 1830.

Adieu ye smiling flow'ry hills,
Where often childhood's hour strayed;
Ye fountains clear, and flowing rills,
Ye mountains through the woodland shade.

Soft murmuring through the woodland shade.
Still bloom ye hills, ye streamlets flow;
Though I'm a wanderer far from you;
Yet often on fancy's wings I go,
Over my childhood's scenes anew,
Adieu Wm. Crane Nov, 1866

MISCELLANEOUS WRITINGS.

My dear Harriet loved the spring season. Reared amidst the wilds of Michigan, she had long hailed the warm south wind, the birds and flowers, with peculiar delight. The late spring found her feeble and in pain, yet she took her pen, and wrote her last address to the season, entitled

WILD FLOWERS OF SPRING.

Wild flowers of spring, we love their bloom,
    Scattered o'er hill and vale ;
Breathing all day their sweet perfume,
    Along the passing gale.

How smiling does the violet look,
    From out its mossy bed ;
And flag-flower by some lonely brook,
    Lifting its lovely head ;

And the wild red rose we love,
    Blooming 'mid shrub and brake,
Where wild birds in the trees above
    Their sweetest music make ;

And the white thornflower, how sweet
    Amid its clustering leaves,
Peering from some gay retreat
    Among the shadowy trees.

Again we hear the south wind blow
    To wake these early flowers;
Its sweet and gentle voice we know
    And hail the sunny hours.

The wild pink flower, see here and there
    In richest purple drest,
Where downward through the stilly air
    The sunbeams come to rest.

'Tis pleasant now abroad to walk,
    When earth is robed in flowers;
When gently murmurs past the brook
    Through fields, and wildwood bowers.

How pleasant is the wild bird's song,
    Among the waving trees,
When every breeze the boughs among
    Wake gladsome memories.

But though so beautiful the flowers,
    How soon they fade and die,
When coldly through their leafy bowers
    The winds of autumn sigh !

And sweet flowers we love in spring,
    Ere autumn hours have come,
Lie prostrate, pale, and withering,
    While flowers of summer bloom.

How sad and true a lesson
    The lovely spring imparts,
Though so pleasant is the season,
    How soon its bloom departs !

It teaches all things beautiful
    Soonest fade from earth away;

If we would know where all is peaceful,
'Tis beyond life's transient day.

HARRIET C. CRANE.

LYDIA A. CRANE.

Death has again entered my dwelling.   This day at twelve
o'clock, noon, my wife breathed her last.

Lydia A. Crane was the eldest daughter of the late Rev.
Seth Mattison, of the Methodist E. Church.   She was born
in Marcellus, Onondaga county, N. Y., March 14th, 1805.
She experienced religion at the age of fourteen, at a camp-
meeting in Oneida county, and ever after maintained a
truly evangelical faith, and life of devotion.   In early childhood she suffered more than a common share of the hardships of a traveling preacher's family.   Her naturally feeble
constitution broke down in her youth.   She was married to
the writer at the age of twenty-two.   She was then feeble and
subsequently gradually failed; and during the last eighteen
years has been constantly afflicted with asthma, and has suffered more than any person that I have ever known.   This
terrible disease terminated in consumption and death.

Her death came unexpectedly to me, as she had borne
her sickness so long, I was expecting that she would live to
an advanced age.   On my return from a short journey last
evening, I was only able to converse with her a few minutes,
when her speech failed; and, oh, who can ever know my
anguish, when she tried a hundred times to speak, but her
tongue was palsied, and she could not articulate.   I have
lost a counsellor, a helper and guide, whose value I am now
to appreciate by painful bereavement.   Few persons ever
read so many valuable volumes, and few have acquired so
much useful knowledge.   My loss is her infinite gain.

WILLIAM W. CRANE.

Leoni, Oct. 30, 1855.

—From the Am. Wesleyan of Nov. 7, 1855.

TO MY DEPARTED WIFE.

I took thee when the radiant bloom
  Of youth sat smiling on thy face;
And then thou left thy early home,
  Without a sigh, for my embrace.

Where the beauteous silver lake
  Kissed the blooming flow'ry shore,
Each the other vowed to take
  In troth to cherish evermore.

Thy home was like to Eden fair,
  With groves, and walks, and village green,
With smiling lawns, and gardens fair,
  And merry, jocund youthful scenes.

To the wild woodland, dark and drear,
  I bore thy willing heart away,
There saw I the unbidden tear
  Down thy saddened cheek to stray.

Thrice by pinching want compelled,
  I moved from happier walks of life,
And brought in lonely cot to dwell,
  In poverty, my patient wife.

Sick, and in pain, thy weary frame
  Was dragged around our humble cot,
And, oh, how rarely did'st thou blame
  The cruel hardness of thy lot!

Often did my unguarded tongue
  Become a sword to pierce thy heart;
Ah, then my careless heart was wrung
  By keen repentant anguish smart.

Each of thy babes, when nursed in pain,

The subject of a mother's prayers,
Has thoughtless on thy bosom lain,
  When bathed with thy maternal tears.

Oh, I would sail the ocean o'er,
  Or tread the desert's burning sand,
To pass with thee one hour more,
  To hold again thy precious hand.

To talk of all our wedlock years,
  On all my follies to reflect,
To shed in floods repentant tears,
  For all my thoughtless, cold neglect.

Whither, oh, whither hast thou fled?
  Where in immensity of space
Dwell the free'd spirits of thy dead?
  In what locality or place?

WILLIAM W. CRANE.

—From the American Wesleyan of Dec. 12, 1855.

DEATH OF REV. W. W. CRANE.

A note received this moment from Brother Bliss, of Hart, Michigan, brings the intelligence of the death of Rev. W. W. Crane, which solemn event occurred Wednesday, May 26. Of his peaceful departure, Brother Bliss says: "I was in to see him a few days before he died. Speaking of his probable departure, he said: 'All is clear now. Before to-morrow morning I expect to be with my Savior—my dear Savior.' A moment after, looking up to Mrs. Crane and myself, he said: 'Tell Brother Crooks I stand very near the city, and that I say, no denomination stands nearer my heart than the Wesleyan; and now as I look back I can say, I love their reformatory standard. I love their rules; and I love my old co-laborers.' And then turning to me he said:

'Tell sinners to fly to Jesus.   Be instant in season ; out of
season.   Preach, oh, preach Christ and him crucified.' "

We regret want of time and space to add comments.
But his life is comment sufficient on such a death.   May we
be also and always ready.   Again are we admonished, that
what we do for Christ and humanity must be done quickly.

Will not some one intimately acquainted with this Christian reformer and truly great historian, please favor us with
an extended notice of his life ?

—American Wesleyan, June 9, 1869.

LOVE SAYS HE CAN'T BE DEAD.

Love says he can't be dead,
    My darling boy.
They tell me how he sadly bled,
When shot through the heart and head;
There they left him when they fled,
    My darling boy.

A comrade heard a rebel tell
How he was buried where he fell,
And there was left without a knell,
    My darling boy.

This was confirmed—
Doubtless the body was the same,
A silver medal bore the name
    Of A. D. Crane.

Yet love says he is still alive,
Beyond his death wounds does survive,
And to my joy will soon arrive,
    My darling boy.

I listen at each stopping train,
And hope to here a shout amain,

Lo, here comes Alphonzo Crane,
       Reported dead!

No shout is heard, the train moves on,
I stand out waiting when 'tis gone
To meet my dear returning son,
       My darling boy.

He comes not—sore grief cannot weep,
My dry eyes are withheld from sleep,
While I nightly vigils keep,
       Waiting a train.

Lo, it comes, and from my bed,
Suddenly I raise my head,
Love still says he can't be dead,
       May be he's come.

Though darkness reigns, the hour is late,
My eyes and ear turn toward the gate,
And I in longing silence wait
       For my dear boy.

Was that the wind? or footsteps near?
Is it a footfall now I hear?
I trembling lie 'twixt hope and fear,
       Oh, has he come?

Silence again resumes her reign,
My troubled head lies down in pain,
Oh, sleeps my darling with the slain,
       All in his gore?

I listen to the morning cars,
What tidings bring they from the wars?
What from the bloody field of Mars?
       None from my son.

Though they tell me how he bled,
When shot through the heart and head,
Love still declares he can't be dead,
My darling boy.

WILLIAM W. CRANE.

Leoni, Sept. 10, 1863.

———

"HOPE THOU IN GOD."

BRO. PRINDLE: When, a few days since, I wrote a brief memoir of my son, I felt that I was writing my last; that I should never take up my pen again; but I find no relief in hobbling through the garden, or along the street; no relief in looking over the green landscape, or at the sky; all is dark as the pall of death. I lie down and cannot rest; I rise and meet no cheer. Reading crowds painful memories upon me, and thinking consumes me. Writing brings a little relief.

The death of my father, before my birth, marked me for sorrow. When seventeen years of age, while deeply concerned for my salvation, and painfully investigating the doctrines of predestination and election, my back was partially broken. This was followed by inflammation of the spine and brain, and by despair, which lasted eighteen months, and came on at intervals for many years; and indeed the consequences of this injury continue to this day. No language can describe my anguish while in despair. The remembrance of it, after forty years, fills me with horror; the effects of it cannot be prevented without a miracle. A miracle might straighten my spine; a like miracle might remove the scars from my mind.

Many deny me any hope; and, indeed, if a man of sorrows cannot be saved, I must be lost.

I buried my first-born when I was twenty-three years of age. This was terrible. In 1846 I buried my darling

Floridon, a child of great promise. My heart was crushed. Harriet died in 1851, a kind, pious, and very interesting daughter, twenty-two years old. The dear mother of my children, after twenty years' sickness, died in 1855. Edwin, the child of my old age, died in 1860. John Emory was a dear son, soon to graduate and enter the ministry; and, oh, I cannot tell again the sad story of his death, at Fortress Monroe, last September. My bereavements had now brought me nearly to the grave; but Alphonzo remained a noble, moral and most affectionate son. He sent me most kind and consoling letters after his brother's death, full of devotion to the Lord, and promising to hasten home when the war should end, to take care of his afflicted father. He was my last dependence, and the hope of spending a few years with this dear son kept me out of the grave. He was to be married to an amiable young woman, who has been dear to me from her infancy. His three years' service would end in April. I was counting the time with increasing hope, when, alas! a rash and unnecessary order was given so charge the enemy's works at Jackson, Miss., when his energy led him to spring upon the rebel works, the first man, and to shout to his comrades to follow. When within twenty feet of the enemy, he was shot through the heart, and was there left to be plundered and buried as a brute is buried. His impetuosity in this charge was constitutional; it could not have been a spirit of murderous hate, for he was one of the most kind and tender-hearted boys that I ever knew. He wrote me at one time that war was wholesale murder, and at another time, that his prayer was that he might never be under the necessity of killing anybody. Oh, my dear boy!

I have written a full account of my life for the gratification of my children. I had given some account of my ancestry, for two hundred years before my day. My dear son, who sleeps at Fortress Monroe, wished to publish this, with selections from my writings; but all is now changed; my family is nearly extinct; my family name is soon to be for-gotten. I can claim relationship to no man of my name on earth, except my invalid son.

Let oblivion cover all I have been, all I have done. Let no monument tell to future ages that I ever lived.* Let my grave be as unknown as the graves of my sons, who sleep in the awful South. I have come to the twilight of life, darkness gathers on my way, my day has departed, my trembling steps are along the river of death; all is night here, but "there is light on the other shore."

Leoni, Aug. 3, 1863.

————

REFLECTIONS ON DEAR DEPARTED FRIENDS.

I told my little blue-eyed Emory that the babe was his brother; we would call him Alphonzo, and in a short time he would walk and play with him. Carefully he watched around the cradle, as days and months passed away. It was a beautiful sight when they walked hand in hand among the young green herbage, and wild flowers, smiling and prattling of the songs of birds, of their nests and young ones. They followed me in the garden, and made my labor easy; cheering me by their smiles and pleasant voices. They were together on the lake, listening to the shrill notes of the loon, and making bouquets of water lilies. Side by side they walked to school, leaping and shouting in merry glee.

They cheered our evenings with tales of wonder, riddles and childish games, and often with questions, seeking useful

*When the compiler was at the author's grave in the autumn of 1888, there was no stone with any lettering on it. Would not some person or persons enhance their happiness by contributing to have a neat and moderate-priced monument placed there?

knowledge. As they came to manhood, they were alike ambitious for all that was noble and good, coming with joy to every fountain and the true wisdom. Like twins, their souls blended into one. They were alike moved by their country's call. Both left home, and dear friends, and pleasant associations, and cheerfully entered on the severe hardships of camp life.

After long separation a pass was granted, and they met, and went to Mount Vernon, to the farm and garden, the house and tomb of Washington. This to them was a great day, the greatest of their lives. There the greatest man of all ages had lived ; there he had meditated the measures which laid the foundation of an empire, the best, the happiest, and the greatest in the world. What emotions filled the bosoms of these brothers, as they trod this hallowed ground. Their young souls glowed with high enthusiasm, as they went back a hundred years, and traced the footprints of the great prince, the modern Alfred, along the path of his eventful life.

They were entranced, and looked back over all ages, to find the equal of our great hero and statesman, but found none. As they left this hallowed ground they felt the holiest patriotism, and were ready to do and suffer without limit for their country.

Full of these noble emotions, they made every effort for a speedy return to their encampments, but lost their way on the great meadows, and wandered for hours in darkness ; often wading in deep water, mingled with the fast falling snow.

They finally reached Alphonzo's camp and passed the remainder of the night together, sleeping side by side as in childhood. This precious visit was suddenly broken off. John Emory leaped from his bed, and hastened with speed that overcame him to the depot. He was five minutes too

late for the cars.   For this accident this noble soldier, one
of the bravest, most faithful and honest, was sentenced to
twenty-four hours' incessant picket duty.   This laid the
foundation of death to one who had been the religious light
and moral example of his company.   He was subsequently
killed by the blunders of a drunken surgeon and drunken
commandant pronouncing him well and ordering him to
join his regiment a thousand miles distant, when he was a
pale skeleton, scarce able to walk.   This brought his life
to an end.

He sleeps a half mile north of Chesapeake Hospital, near
the water; heeding no more the sound of war, the seabird's
scream, or the ocean's roar.   This noble, generous heart is
still; the music of his voice has ceased.   May angels guard
his grave, far away in that distant land; far from his mother's grave, and far from her who was dearer than his life.

Terrible was the shock on Alphonzo.   His stricken soul
could scarce stay this side the boundaries of time.   Learning to trust the Lord, his spirit revived.   He nerved himself
for his country's struggle, and served uncomplainingly in the
hardest duties.   He had enlisted among the first in the
nation, had been in six battles and more than two years'
service; had his furlough ready to be signed, had sixty
dollars in his pocket for his journey, and was to leave camp
in six days to visit home and friends.   His wedding was to
be consummated, so long delayed by the war.

His warm, generous, friendly heart beat high as he seemed
almost in the embrace of dear ones in his native land, so
long absent and far away; when a rash order sent him into
the jaws of death.   Shot at once through the head and
heart, all was over; and his dear, manly, noble body left
with enemies, to be plundered, stripped and buried only as
a beast is buried.   Alas, that he was too prompt to obey

that rash order; that he took the lead, and virtually led the charge on that eventful day!

In the land fanned by genial, almost tropic winds, bearing perfume from magnolia groves, he sleeps at Jackson, Mississippi, on the blood-stained earth.

"He has fought his last battle;
No sound shall awake him to glory again."

His heart bled for outraged humanity from childhood, but he hears no more the voice of the oppressor, nor the sound of the whip.

May angels guard his unburied body, and if his spirit ever comes to view the scenes of earth, may it find no whips or chains, no sighs or tears of the oppressed; but freedom through the land. Oh, have they gone to return no more, not even while suns wax old and fade away? "I shall go to them, but they will not return to me"

Nov. 28, 1863.

"I AM BEREAVED."

BRO. PRINDLE: My son, Alphonzo D. Crane, was shot through the heart, in attempting to storm the rebel works, at Jackson, Mississippi, July 11. He was of Company K, 2d Mich. He was born May 13, 1839, in Eaton Rapids, Mich. He was a very gentle, kind-hearted child, and though feeble and sickly, he was a great comfort to his parents, always like the genial sunlight around the bed of his sick mother. His grief at her death was extreme, and a few months after, he left his home in Leoni and went to Allegan Co., Mich., where most of his relatives lived, and resided principally there until he enlisted, in April, 1861. He was a very intelligent, noble-minded and moral young man, but made no open profession of religion until after the death of his brother, John E. Crane, who died at Fortress Monroe,

Sept. 21, 1862.   From that time Alphonzo became deeply
pious; but for some time past he had complained that his
religious enjoyment had diminished, for want of religious
companions and opportunities.

For several years past his health has been good, and his
one great object, paramount to all others, has been to take
care of his afflicted father.   This has been the theme of his
letters for two years.   His last letter to me contained most
tender, touching language on this subject.

Alas, he has gone ! my last dependence !   I have but
one son left, and he has been a permanent invalid for ten
years, and one daughter, a sickly woman.   This terrible
news came two hours ago, and I feel as though I was using
my pen for the last time.   Surely my gray hairs are coming
down with sorrow to the grave.

The body of my dear boy was left in the hands of the
enemy.   This is horrible.   No one knows where he sleeps !
Oh, my son ! my son !

Leoni, July 29, 1863.

COMPARISON OF ANCIENT AND MODERN BE-REAVEMENTS.

TO MISS E. D., OF ALLEGAN CO., MICH.

DEAR MADAM : I find the counterpart of my state in
Ossian.   My stricken soul melts into his pathetic reference
to the last of his race.   His lot is mine.   Malvina, betrothed to Oscar, Ossian's noble son, who was slain in Erin,
soothed him when old and blind and bereaved of all his
kindred, sang with her harp, and led him into the genial
sunlight.

"Weep on the rocks of roaring winds, thou maid of Inis-
tore.   Bend thy fair head over the waves, thou fairer than
the ghost of the hills when it comes on a sunbeam at noon,

over the silence of Morven." Though the above was addressed to the maids of the Orkneys, looking for Swaran's
sails, returning from Ireland, yet the idea may have been
suggested by Malvina's watchings for Oscar. This I judge
from the following passage, so often occurring.

"Come thou beam that art lonely, from watching in the
night." When led by Malvina, and seated in the warm
sunlight, he said, "The murmur of thy streams, O Lora!
brings back the memory of the past. The sound of thy
woods, Garmaller, is lovely in mine ear." Then after giving
"a tale of the times of old," he said, "I feel the sun, O
Malvina. Leave me to my rest." He then addressed the
sun, "O, thou that rollest above, round as the shield of my
fathers! Whence art thy beams, O sun! thy everlasting
light! Thou comest forth in thy awful beauty; the stars
hide themselves in the sky; the moon, cold and pale, sinks
in the western wave; but thou thyself movest alone. Who
can be a companion of thy course? The oaks of the mountains fall; the mountains themselves decay with years; the
ocean shrinks and grows again; the moon herself is lost in
heaven; but thou art forever the same, rejoicing in the
birthright of thy course. When the world is dark with tempests, when thunder rolls, and lightning flies, thou lookest in
thy beauty from the clouds, and laughest at the storm. But
to Ossian thou lookest in vain, for he beholds thy beams no
more. Whether thy yellow hair flows on the eastern clouds,
or thou tremblest at the gales of the west. But thou art,
perhaps, like me, for a season; thy years will have an end.
Thou shalt sleep in thy clouds, careless of the voice of the
morning."   *   *   *   *   *   *

Malvina led the aged Ossian to the plain,
From Morven's heights that overlooked the main;
There seated on a moss-grown hillock, green;
Warmed by the sun, by Ossian long unseen.

Lara's murmuring streams were heard around,
Garmaller's woods sent forth a pleasing sound.
As gentle winds came moaning through the pines,
Times of the past were crowding on his mind,
When in the pride of youth his speed outran
The agile stag that bounded o'er the plain,
When great Fingal lived, generous, brave, and strong,
For noble, manly deeds renowned in song.
Thus spake the aged bard :
Thy sounds, O Lara ! to my remembrance bring
The times when, in the hall of kings,
Were hung the warriors' shields along the wall.
The minstrel took the harp, and through the hall
The song went forth, that told the well-earned fame
Of Trathal, Compal, men of mighty name,
Of Fingal's glory, strength and power ; and then
She sung of Trenmor, most renowned of men.
Oscar in silence sat, my noble son ;
Silent, though proud of many victories won.
His manly, golden hair waved in the breeze,
As when the gentle winds slow meet the trees.
The song went on, and music's numbers rolled ;
My son's ambition swelled his generous soul ;
He sighed to give to coming times his name,
With Fingal's, Compal's, Trathal's, Trenmor's fame.
He looked on thee, Malvina, and admired
Thy modest maiden blush—thy face retired.
His bosom heaved a sigh for noble deeds,
Where the loyal struggle, and patriots bleed.

*   *   *   *   *   *   *   *   *

CHAPTER III.

Let me call E. D., Malvina—Ossian again
Mourns his Alphonzo, his Oscar slain,

'Whose bosom swelled with noble high desire,
To shield the hapless young, and aged sire.
Alas ! his noble form, deprived of life,
Soon lay beneath the awful tread of strife.
How bled thy heart, and how convulsed thy frame,
When from the cypress land the tidings came :
Alphonzo is no more.　　While sea-waves roll,
While stars or suns endure, his generous soul
Comes not again, but lingers far away,
Beyond the sun's long beams the light of day.
His fair Malvina says, " It cannot be !
He can't be dead ! but lives beyond the sea.
Some cruel, foul restraint detains him there ;
Relentless rebels never heed his prayer,
To send one kind message, one word, to tell
How life yet lingers in a dungeon cell.
Some ship will bring him bounding o'er the waves,
Released from bondage in a land of slaves.
The day may linger, yet the day will come,
Our weary eyes at last shall greet him home."
Oh, soul-sustaining, never-dying hope !
Blessed, blind angel ! thus to lift us up
From fell despair, when sorrow's wasting power
Would bring, untimely, the departing hour.
Hope against hope in each sad bosom springs;
Yet truth and stubborn fact will often bring
Our hope to end.　　Alphonzo sleeps in death !
Shot through the heart and head—at once his breath
And soul took flight.　　There sleeps the noble, brave,
And valiant Oscar, left without a grave,
Where magnolia's beauties grace the early spring,
And gentle winds with grateful perfumed wing,
Shall fan his dust until the angel's call,
The resurrection trumpet wakens all.
Dec. 28, 1863.

MEMORIES

Of " dear one's gone
Come on music's wings."

How soul-stirring these plaintive notes. My heart is
moved; my tears fall; and this care-worn bosom trembles
on my sighs, like a frail bark on the waves. I hear the
humming bees, as they leave the flowers on the wild plain,
when the lengthening shadows of the trees warn them of the
close of day. My little ones prattle around me, culling wild
flowers, and with merry shouts, chasing butterflies and bees
in their flight. The gentle wind is playing with the yellow
ringlets around the little faces, upturned to see the flight of
the pelican, whose shrill notes, "Lull-lo-o" are heard at
once by every ear for many miles. The sun is traveling
through the yellow sky to the gates of the west, when we
greet the mother at the door of the cottage in the wilderness.

I placed my six children in file, from the oldest to the
youngest. Little Floridon, the last in the row, looked up to
me with so sweet a smile, that memory can never forget it.
A thousand times has the image of that smilling face passed
before me. Harriet stood at the head, with her noble, generous face glancing a side look at the little one. They were
strikingly alike in complexion and spirit. Their mother,
dear woman, sat with pleasure gazing at these six children,
reared by her feeble arm. Oh, it was a beautiful sight to
me, as I stood before them, and felt the tie that bound each ·
one to my soul. Coarse was our fare, but blessed with each
other's society, we came with joy around the humble board.

Dreary and mournful days and nights had passed, when
the dreadful truth was certain, that Floridon was dying.
He spoke our names, looked pleasantly upon us, but soon

voice, sight, and hearing were lost in death. I saw him in his last play, running over the green lawn, with his playful kitten; and see his bright face at this hour.

On the last sad morning of Harriet's life I was at her bedside. She was looking out on the foliage and fruits of the trees, as I talked of the living green of Paradise. Oh, could the tie that bound us be broken? Oh, such a day! Was it one of the days of my life? Clouds passed over with solemn march, not as clouds ever moved before, but as in the end of the world. After noon the clouds were gone. The sun shone with dim and gloomy light, and the silence was oppressive. Evening came; and one object alone absorbed my whole soul. My Harriet was dying. Her last words, "Father I'm choking," drew me close to her, and in a moment she was dead, with her eyes fixed on my countenance.

The night was long and dreary. The night passed away, and the day came; but not as other days, since then the light of day is dim, the sky is dark; and gloomy are the beams of the sun. I planted a willow on Harriet's grave, but in grief it bowed its head and died. Sad and heavy was the mother's heart, and while her feeble hand touched the notes of her loved accordion, tears like the raindrops fell. We often talked of Harriet, and mingled our sorrows; we talked of Floridon, and of our first born that slept in a distant land.

Oh that day! When the mother tried in vain, a hundred times, to say something, I know not what; her tongue was dying and could not speak. In patience she gave up the effort. In silence she leaned her head on my bosom, till weary nature fast failing, she lay down and soon waved her hand, as a sign that the moment had come. Oh she is gone! The snow is on her grave. I call her name, but no answer will come, while the dim light of the sun is on the path of my pilgrimage.

"CAN'T YOU WAKE HER UP ANY MORE?"

A very large assembly convened, the solemn service began with music,
                "There is light in the window for thee,"
was conducted by Reverends Pratt, Darling, Fay, and Ney: and ended with music,
                "Sister, thou wast mild and lovely,"
sung while we took a last view of the dead.   Rev. Mr. Huff, from California, brother to my bereaved son-in-law, with his lady, were lifting little Rosetta, less than three years old.   "That is your mama" said her aunt.   "Is she dead?" she asked.   "Yes" her uncle replied.   She, looking him intently in the face, asked again, "Is she dead? can't you wake her up any more?"

May the dear little ones live to learn that God will wake their mother, and all the dead.   I could wish that time to come to-morrow, and bring back to me my first-born son, buried more than forty years ago, my golden-haired Floridon, buried in 1846, Harriet, in 1851, their mother in 1855, Edwin in 1860, John Emory in 1862, Alphonzo in 1863, and the dear one buried yesterday, the day that Christ was born, 1868 years ago.

We must patiently wait till the "Stone from the mountain"—the kingdom of Christ—"shall break in pieces and consume all these kingdoms" (all that is opposed to truth and holiness in the nations and kingdoms of this world,) "and shall become a great mountain, and shall fill the whole earth."

How long it will be, none can tell; what nations or cities

shall rise or fall, what discov eries and inventions shall be made.   I have looked with lively interest to coming years, ages, and centuries; and judged the future from the past of the world, political, civil, and literary, and especially religious; viewed the hundreds of millions in our country, the future greatness of Michigan, with its soil, timber, mines, and vast sea-board; the future of our country, our town, and our rapidly rising village.   My mind has then gone to the future of other lands; South America and South Europe, when free from popery; the great empire of North Europe, so rapidly advancing in civilization.   The coming ages of Asia have arisen in glory before me, when a civilization, vastly superior to the Saracenic, or the old Chaldean, shall brighten her mountains, plains, and golden shores.   I have heard, in coming ages, cars on the great desert of Sahara, and school-bells, and church-bells, calling Africa's children to science and to devotion.   Oh, a change has come over me in this bereavement! I am dead to the world.   I expect still to write and speak of the world's past history, and feel an interest in the future; yet it is the interest of a dead, rather than a living man: the same that I expect to feel when in another world.   I feel a live interest in the grave-yard, here on the banks of the Pentwater.   Here I expect to sleep when my tongue and pen are still.

———

A few weeks after the foregoing was published, a letter received from Elder Crane contained the following:

" I have, as you see, been writing again for the *Wesleyan*, but my last articles were so printed that I am discouraged. I sent three distinct articles, each on a separate sheet, and under its proper caption, and signed by my full name, and one of these was an obituary, and all are strangely crowded into one article, destroying the sense of all of them."

It is thought that the mangling referred to, was the work of the foreman, and not the editor.

———

PLAINWELL, ALLEGAN CO., MICH.

BRO. PRINDLE: Since the death of my sons, I have found it necessary, for the health of body and mind, to turn from my grief and engross my attention in anything which may honor God and do good to men.

This requires effort; for, left to my feelings, the world has no light or treasure for me. In compliance with an earnest invitation, I came to this place to deliver a series of historical lectures.

Here is my venerable step-father, in his ninetieth year, but who has but recently failed in body and mind; and here is my mother, younger in appearance than myself, though more than twenty-three years older. She is a beautiful woman, in her eighty-third year, straight as in childhood, walks with an elastic step, and not having failed in the least in judgment or memory, is a most agreeable companion of old or young. Here my noble boy, my Alphonzo (my Oscar), spent many years, on this Kalamazoo, most beautiful of rivers. Wherever I go I tread where he has trod a thousand times. Here also is my grief-stricken Malvina, dear to me as she would have been if my boy had lived a few days longer, when they would have been joined in wedlock. How sacred is this ground, this sparkling river, and the winds moaning through the trees.

Here for eighteen consecutive evenings I have lectured to a most intelligent audience, never satisfied until I had talked an hour and a half; so that in twenty-seven hours I have lived four thousand years, walking with emperors, and kings, senators, and field marshals. I have walked with historians, poets, orators, and artists; and have walked the walls of Nineveh and Babylon, climbed the towers, and hanging gardens, and stood at the summit of Belus, with the astronomers of Chaldea. I went into Belshazzar's feast, and saw the handwriting on the wall, hailed Cyrus as he entered the palace, talked with Daniel of coming ages, and helped Nehemiah rebuild the walls of Jerusalem. I helped Archimedes lift a Roman ship aloft, and sent it diving to the bottom of the sea, lifted hard at raising the enormous stones of the temple of Herod, and harder to raise those almost infinitely larger at Baalbec and Thebes. I drove the team of Romulus when he plowed the mark for the walls of Rome, laid Cæsar's robe over his mangled corpse, and shed a tear; told Constantine it only thundered, when he said that a voice from God bade him conquer by the cross, finally advised Rome's last emperor not to yield his crown. It was painful to see ancient empire dying, with its civilization, and literature, under the tread of barbarians; to listen to musings of Mahomet, planning the foundation of an empire of sin; and to see the rising hierarchy of Rome.

It was pleasant to see the rising morning in the fifteenth century, after a night of a thousand years; to see the church coming from the wilderness; to see the enlargement of Japheth, the barbarian Teutons, Celts, or Gauls, and Scandinavians, changing to the enlightened Germans, French, English, Scotch, Danes, Swedes, and Russians, and to see Christian faith and worship rising from the abominations of the age of the infamous Pope, Alexander VI, to its present evangelical state. Everywhere I see God in history; not as many seem to see him, dependent on evil to bring good, on wrath and violence to bring peace and love. Vengeance is his, and it is most audacious for man to step unbidden into the executive seat of the Almighty. Let no man assume to make Joshua his pattern without an immediate and an especial revelation. Man left free, pours forth the vile streams of sin in motive and action; God sits above, and opens channels for all of these streams, so that they may do the least injury, and when possible, may indirectly tend to good.

With Galileo and Copernicus, I traveled the heavens; with Columbus I crossed the ocean, and walked with simple natives their tropic groves. I stepped from the "Mayflower" on Plymouth Rock, and knelt with the pilgrims on the snow; paddled the canoes of Marquette and La Salle over the lakes, and down the rivers, from the mouth of the St. Lawrence to the mouth of the Mississippi, amidst millions of beasts, and birds, never before seen by civilized men.

Plunged in these themes to enthusiasm, I have lifted my head above the waters of grief, a short time. The clouds and the waters seem closing over me again, but God sustains me amidst the waves. The respect, love and sympathy of my dear audience at the close of my last lecture overwhelmed me, and almost led me for the moment to doubt human depravity. May the blessings of the Lord rest upon them. A great revival is in progress here. Prayer-meetings always before the lecture.

HISTORICAL CHAPTERS.

The readers of the *Wesleyan* will be delighted to know that Brother Crane, our senior Corresponding Editor, has recommenced his chapters on History. His former series was on ancient; the one now commenced will be on modern history. Of the clearness, sweetness and beauty of Brother Crane's style, as also the amplitude of his knowledge, we need say nothing. They are well known to our readers. We hesitate not to declare our conviction that those articles alone are worth more than the price of the paper. The esteem in which Brother Crane is justly held by competent judges as a lecturer on history, will appear from the following truly complimentary resolutions :

At a meeting of citizens, held at Plainwell, Michigan, on Wednesday, April 11, 1867, the following resolutions were unanimously adopted :

Whereas, It has been the privilege of our community to listen to a course of highly interesting and instructive historical lectures, by Rev. W. W. Crane, and,

Whereas, A formal expression of our esteem for Mr. Crane as a Christian gentleman, and our appreciation of his profound ability as a lecturer, is the least possible tribute we can render to his worth ; therefore,

Resolved, That in view of the extent and accuracy of his knowledge of the past and present of our world, we consider Mr. Crane one of the first historians of the age.

Resolved, That the high moral and religious tone that has characterized his lectures, their defense of revealed truth, and the spirit of true reform, so kindly and ably exhibited, especially commend him to the lovers of Christian truth and morality everywhere.

Resolved, That his manner of presenting history, by means of a chart invented by himself, and so arranged as to exhibit at a glance the relative political importance of the various nations at all periods of their history, so simple as to be comprehended by the young, adds greatly to the general interest of his lectures.

Rev. S. Osinga,
Pastor of Presbyterian Church,
Rev. J. Fletcher,
Pastor of Baptist Church,
Capt. D. E. Kenyon.

It cannot fail to give additional interest to those chapters to know how much of effort it costs Brother Crane to write them. In a private note accompanying six chapters, which he has sent as the first installment, Brother Crane says : "My health has been very poor for three months, and I lately came very near death.   My hand is so tremulous that I can hardly put my food to my mouth ; but I clench both hands on my pen and write as well as I can, and will try to furnish a chapter for every week."

Only think of it !   Letter after letter, syllable after syllable, word after word, sentence after sentence, paragraph after paragraph, and chapter after chapter written in the manner above described : and all to feed the minds of others with food convenient.   What patient effort must this require !   What heart can fail to pray Heaven's richest benedictions upon one who thus labors to instruct mankind, and whose benignant and intelligent Christian life is to go down as a rich legacy to coming generations ?

The foregoing is copied from the editorial columns of the *American Wesleyan* of Nov. 20, 1867, Adam Crooks, A. M., at that time, editor.

———

MOTHER IS DEAD.

BRO. CROOKS : I have this day followed to the grave one of the best mothers that ever blest a son.   While lecturing at Wayne, there came off from the telegraph wires three terrible words : "Mother is dead."

To-day about fifty relatives came around the coffin.   My dear good mother lay beautifully smiling, just as she has a thousand times, when speaking kindly to me.   How gently and sweetly she passed away,   I felt that I was by the waters of Jordan, and could almost speak to her on the other shore, and hear her calling me, and my dear father seemed to meet her there, and join in calling me.   My honored parents, I congratulate you on your joyful meeting, after you have been separated sixty years ; and soon I trust you will hail your aged son, "on that blest shore."

An excellent discourse was delivered by Rev. Mr. Osinga; after which that dear form was lain to rest in a beautiful cemetery, on Green Plains, Allegan Co., Mich., there to wait the resurrection of the just.

Jan. 22, 1865.

___

REFLECTIONS BY THE WAY, No. 12.

LIGHTS AND SHADOWS OF ITINERANT LIFE.

How many thrilling memories arise on the pathway of my life of thirty years of ministerial labor. Although I have met great diversity of taste and disposition, I have found great difference of human temperament, and have experienced almost every kind of fare, from affluence to indigence, from the palace to the wigwam; yet I have commonly found men and women kind, generous and hospitable, and this not only among Christians but even among infidels.

Feb. 19. Here I am after a day's ride in the most severe storm of this winter. Terrible is the voice of the tempest, howling without, but only the sound reaches me; for in this stately mansion all is safety and comfort.

The fire is beautifully glowing, and throwing out from the chimney walls the grateful warmth, and music's consoling sound comes from an adjoining room.

"Music is like the memory of the past, mournful and pleasing to the soul." How the scenes of the past are carried before me on music's silken wings! The future is the downhill of life, an approach to the tomb, my last work.

Faith looks beyond the dark valley, sees another shore, and listening, hears music in sweeter strains from the heavenly world. How pleasant to witness the full and free exercise of the domestic affections! The hand of God formed the tie that binds husband and wife, parent and child. In this model family every look, every word, and every gesture, is in confidence and kindness. Three dear children are in heaven, and if ever permitted to come and see their parents and sisters, it will please them to see such harmony.   Perhaps no house in Michigan has given shelter and comfort to more fugitive slaves, or fugitives from slavery, than this. This ample room, where the genius of music now dwells, has been filled with the weary, downtrodden bondmen. Here the poor mother has embraced her child and felt that it was hers; but she starts at every sound and fears the approach of the detested wretch who would drag her back to woe; but my noble friend has calmed all apprehension at last, when he led them from the boat on to the blessed shores of Canada.

As I sat and listened to my worthy friend, and heard the interesting history of fugitives, fed, clothed, and carried on their journey to freedom, I revered the holy work of breaking that detestable Act, called "the fugitive slave law;" I revered the "higher law."

The villainous fugitive Act, emanating from sordid selfishness, compromising with perdition, never looked more infernal.   Oh, the *higher* law; emanating from him who is from eternity to eternity, who filleth immensity, infinite in wisdom and power; written on the table of conscience, and of reason, and glowing on the pages of inspiration, how high it claims!

Man is born with the right to go where he pleases, dwell where he pleases, and do as he pleases, so long as he does not trespass on the rights of any other man.   These are his rights, be his color what it may, whether he be the grand Patagonian, or the dwarf of Greenland; whether he choose to range the ice-bound shores of the North, amid Arctic tempests, or dwell beneath the torrid sun, to inhabit the mountain or the plain, the land or sea; these are his *rights*.

No parliament or congress shall ever bind me to crush my emotions of humanity, to violate my conscience, to sin

against God.   How mean and contemptible are human en-
actments, contravening the laws of the Almighty; made
where votes are sold, conscience and principle sold; where
the sergeant-at-arms is sent to places not to be named to
bring members to their seats; where drunken members are
shaken by their party friends, arousing them to vote.

REFLECTIONS BY THE WAY.–No. 18.

AUTOBIOGRAPHICAL.

I do not design in this to write my autobiography; yet as
this is my birthday, and as I am weatherbound in the wilderness, in a snow storm, after rains which almost make traveling impossible, my thoughts are upon the past.

"The murmur of thy streams O Lord, remind me of the
past."   In my rambles for two weeks, over northwestern
Michigan, not only plants and trees, but even the horrid
roads, bring mournfully pleasant recollections of early life.
The birds that sing are true descendants of those that
charmed my childhood's rambles.

The solemn voice of the wind in the wilderness is the
same that I heard when I first thought of God.   The little
cot, surrounded for a few rods by fallen trees, and then by
nature's own grand wilderness; the merry shout of ruddy
children gathering flowers, their flaxen hair flying in the
breeze; the tinkling bell, the bounding deer, call up my
childhood, and produce emotions that none but Ossian
could tell.

Fifty-three years ago this day a widow, whose youthful
husband had been two months in the grave, looked upon the
face of her only son, not knowing that he was marked with
all her feelings around the deathbed, and around the tomb;
born to repeat all her sighs; to feel in every opening spring,
what she felt when the spring of 1805 opened on my father's

grave, three miles east of Cazenovia village, in Madison county, N. Y.

Among the hills and dales of Nelson I learned to think of nature and of God.   There I was drilled through my alphabet, at Jackson's Corners, while Jeremiah Freeman, an African boy, was my chosen playmate.   His father a native of Guinea, who had been cook for Gen. Washington nearly through the revolutionary war, used to pass the school-house, bent with years.   A son of this soldier of the revolution, this favorite of Washington, older than my playfellow, was decoyed south, and probably sold into slavery, as he was never more heard from.   There are some striking resemblances between our country and Algiers.

In the spring of 1811, our family having left my father's grave and gone to the Genesee country, we heard, on one Sunday morning, the strange intelligence that a minister had come to our wilderness, and would preach.   We crossed the woods, without road or path, and found the people assembling at a log house, near where East Henrietta now is, seven miles southeast of Rochester.   While dressing for meeting I felt overwhelming consciousness of sin, and as I had never heard of pardon, I was without hope and wept in the anguish of despair.   As I was descending the rude ladder of our new home I felt that God was reconciled, because I was sorry for my sins.   This was my first idea of pardon; and I cannot fix a better date of my conversion than that morning, forty-seven years ago, although I lived most of my time afterwards without hope until seventeen years of age.

The war coming on in 1812 greatly checked the progress of our new settlement, and nearly ruined all morals.   Nearly all my lessons of vice were learned from young men who had been in the army.   Such was my mode of study that I have never been able to abandon the whim, that the best of all universities is the field or woods, and the best way to learn is to be hard at work, with a book on a log or stump, seizing the book with greediness at intervals and devouring a little, than dashing on with work, digesting what we read, with incessant thought.   Such students do not read over their books, nor do they need to waste several hours each day, in playing ball, to avoid rickets, *ennui*, or dyspepsia.

The Genevan theology was not suited to my nature. There are men who do not only endure, but relish, a faith, which views a God more terrible than the Woden of the Scandinavians, darkly seated in awful sovereignty; from eternity purposing to bring into being nine-tenths of human beings, to glorify him by filling the measure of their sins and being damned; leading, inducing, and instigating them to sin, according to his eternal decree; mocking them by offers of salvation, which he has determined shall never be theirs.   These doctrines, committed to illiterate men, of course blunt natures, were dispensed to me from infancy to manhood, stripping religion of all that was lovely.

The world gave me little pleasure, but my choice lay between that little and the worship of an awful God, if indeed I might be one of the elect.   My chance was but one in ten, and when resolved to give up the world, saved or lost, a circumstance happened which added feed to the fire that was consuming me.

When, in the autumn of 1822, my step-father lay dangerously ill, I was performing twice the labor daily that any man ought to do; and closing my labor at night, after an unreasonable day's toil, my whole system in feverish excitement from the agony of my mind, I partially broke my spine. I was alone at a cider-mill, attempting to screw the press for the last time.   I had brought two levers around to my satisfaction; the third was more obstinate.   After trying two or three times, I exclaimed, " It shall go," and planting my heel in the firm clay, and throwing my whole weight back with great force, it did go, and my giant constitution went with it.   A sword seemed to go through my spine between my shoulder.   A spinal disease followed, greatly affecting my brain, and giving Calvin's horrid creed all the power over my wretched self that the tigress has over the lamb when she has brought it to her lair, and leaves it a short respite, to amuse her cubs; her eyes glaring, her red mouth open, her teeth bristling, the death signal growl being uttered.   This figure is feeble and inadequate to describe my state before a Being who was eternal to decree my destiny, omnipresent to cut off my escape and omnipotent to execute my doom.   My mind was brought into tremendous activity on this theme.   I was capable of throwing off my measuring line on the vast ocean of God's eternity, space, and power.   I longed for annihilation, longed to make agreement with the Almighty, to dwell in hell as many thousand years as there are particles of sand in the whole earth, and then be saved; and that with a power to comprehend this awful length, far surpassing the power of any mind in ordinary health or action.

The infernal charm is broken—God is my father—"Like as a father pitieth his children, so the Lord pitieth them that fear him; for he knoweth our frame, he remembereth that we are dust."   I love to work for him, and with him; to be in harmony with his moral universe.   I desire to do all I can for the moral improvement of the world, and the glory of God.

CHANGES IN FORTY YEARS.

The love-feast was spiritual.   Devout men and women arose in rapid succession and spoke earnestly of faith and love.   For a short time, with my eyes shut, I was back in my fancy forty-one years, in a love-feast in the old meeting-

house, at Victor, N. Y., with Goodwin Stoddard presiding;
Cyrus Story and Andrew Prindle sat by him, with grave
looks, in homespun of brown and gray. Their white hats
with low crowns and broadbrims were on the altar table,
where Father Calkins sat with his long raven locks covering
his shoulders, and there arose and spoke as a patriarch.

As I looked over the assembly, all bonnets were alike in
form and color; how plain and simple, and yet beautiful!
so natural and useful, nothing about them gay, and nothing
needless. How clear and earnest the singing, mingled with
shouting and weeping! Opening my eyes dispels the vision.
I find myself not in Victor, N. Y., in 1823, but in Jackson,
Michigan, in 1864. Father Stoddard, Story, Prindle and
Calkins are all dead, and that humble, holy, and devout assembly have passed away.

> "They praise him again,
> Having passed over Jordan,
> With palms in their hands,
> Having gained the blest shore."

With them all peculiarities of dress have passed away, and
I can distinguish no one as a Methodist by hat or bonnet,
by coat or shawl; and as all distinction has ceased, the door
stands open and all go in alike. I however hear nearly the
same expressions of faith, zeal, and love, as I heard forty
years ago.

Now the presiding elder gives his text. I am all attention, for he is a very eloquent man. The pastor has just
prayed that the sermon might come direct from the mouth
of God; and from my heart I said amen; but what was my
disappointment to find that it was not even to come direct
from the mouth of man, as every word lay written on the
desk. The theme was "The Witness of the Spirit," and
my soul panted for the outgushing of the speaker's soul,
from holy union with the Lord. Instead of that he read a

sermon, good as Wesley's but no better; and I felt that I might as well be at home, with a volume of Wesley in my hand. The sermon was able and the reading perfect, yet on every side through the large assembly dullness became apparent; several fell asleep and others seemed absorbed in thoughts of anything but the "Witness of the Spirit" and I felt to exclaim, Reading sermons will never convert the world.

MUSINGS.

I expect the ultimate triumphs of the cross, the conquest of the world by Christianity, the perfection of civilization. In this hope I renew my youth, and travel in the winter tempest, and see my little earthly substance wasting away. In this great work, the conquest of the world, I am enlisted at the risk of sacrificing all of earth, and falling at my post among strangers.   I often inquire, What instrumentalities are now in use to bring about this perfection of human progress?   And secondly, What instrumentalities are needed? It is too evident that there is much imperfection in existing instrumentalities; yet I rejoice in all the improvement made, however imperfect the means.

The Mosaic dispensation was imperfect in itself, and yet it was the best for that age and nation.   Some heathen customs continued under that dispensation, on account of the hardness of heart of that people—polygamy, retaliation, and servitude, which are condemned by the precepts of the gospel.   The Christian dispensation is perfect, but it is poorly understood.

How little understanding of the nature of the gospel have the Catholics, and yet I rejoice in all the good they do. The Greek Church is still better.   Of numerous sects of errorists some are absolutely pernicious, as the Mormons;

others so mix good and evil, light and darkness, that it is impossible to determine whether the world is made better or worse by their existence.

With the most orthodox denominations there is much to mingle sorrow with joy. Of two great and opposite evils, we are unable to determine which most retards human progress; the pomp and vain glory on the one hand, or a low, degrading, earthly spirit on the other.

The kingdom of Christ was from the beginning spiritual, designed to stand on its own merits, and to repudiate all proffered help from human policy, from pomp and vain show. The Prince, born to redeem, was not laid in a manger from accident, or necessity, but because this kingdom was always to stand aloof from the glory of this world.

In the nineteenth century we gain nothing, but lose all things, by departing from the manger. Yet, on the other hand, how mournful to see men and women, under the pretence of simplicity and humility, degrading devotion by a low, vulgar, groveling spirit; by low wit, and clownish jests. If we must have the stage, the theater, let us have the intelligent and sublime Shakspeare, in his own place, on the public stage; rather than turn the house of the Lord into a low, vulgar, degrading theater, as many revivalists do! If we must hear the language of abuse and blackguard, let us hear it in the bar-room, or the street, not from men intrenched in the sanctuary. If we must witness dancing, let it be gracefully done in its own place, rather than those wild fantastic imitations of the lower animals. Here I will make some exceptions. In all the above abuses of devotion there are some very honest and truly devout persons; but their example is bad; they do little for the elevation of man. We have got to learn over again the true character, nature, spirit, and genius of Christianity. Simplicity without degradation, and sublimity without pomp.

Two other extremes stand in the way of progress.   On the one hand, Christianity without humanity, on the other, humanity without Christianity.   Both must fail, while from the ashes of the two will yet arise one true power.   The warm heart of philanthropy will yet pulsate in the bosom where the head of Christian truth shall regulate its noble zeal.   Then, both the *New York Observer* and the *Liberator* will be obsolete.   Then shall it be acknowledged that benevolence is the power to reform, and that true benevolence is found only in the gospel.

FORBEARANCE.

In a world of fallen and erring men, where perfection of judgment is never found, how important is forbearance !

Without forbearance the earth would have been without inhabitants long ago ; and without forbearance the present generation would all be destroyed in a few years.   Without forbearance no religious denomination or local church could continue a year.   In the political world there have always been some willful, unyielding men, who proudly claim to be the judges of their rights, and then declare they will have these rights—they will fight for them—they will conquer or die.   So in the church there have always been some willful, unyielding men, who proudly claim to be judges of all things, of rights of doctrines, and ceremonies, of meats and drinks, and clothing, of customs and manners.

They will have their way, everything *shall* conform to their views of truth and propriety.   They demand that all who differ from them in things which they call essential, shall be expelled, or they will secede from the church.

Some passages of Scripture, precious in themselves, but odious when preverted, are ever in their mouths, such as " First pure, then peaceable ;" " Contend earnestly for the

faith ;" " Come out from among them, my people." If they
are found on the side of error and wrong, they are relentless
persecutors ; the spirit of the Inquisition is in them. If
they are right on the great question of reform, salvation by
faith in Christ, as opposed to the traditions and dogmas of
popery, they have their own dogmas, to which they adhere
with inflexible obstinacy, and go on, after separating from
the Church of Rome, dividing and subdividing, until half of
the funds of the Protestant Church are wasted. Ministers
of five denominations are following in each other's tracks
over one parish, each one preaching to one-tenth of the
number that might hear him. Ministers are jealous of each
other's designs, and envious at each other's success ; for
each one's honor with his own sect, depends on his success
in increasing the numbers and wealth of his congregation.

Something more than the motives of honor often affect
him ; his bread depends on his grabbing his share of the
patronage. From the calls of ambition and of hunger, the
minister of the gospel, the sacred legate of the skies, sinks
to the degrading trade of proselyting. Oh, how degrading!
How the contemptible work of proselyting destroys the dignity of the sacred office, and crushes the self-respect of every
man who has a noble soul !

In the present deplorable state of the divided and sub-
divided church, proselyting and supplanting is almost inevitable ; and what is worse, is almost essential to the success
of each sect. Motives to sectarian success are so strong as
to lead to great corruption. In revival meetings every effort
is made to get up a whirlwind of excitement ; and in its
midst to hurry men and women, youth, and even children,
to a profession of conversion, and to membership in the
sect. Although the ostensible motive is to secure a moral
influence over those caught in the sectarian net, yet it is
known to the Infinitely Wise that a large amount of motive

is to outdo other sects in numbers, to build a meeting-house sooner than others build, or larger than others build.

Traveling at large brings the evils of sectarianism almost constantly before me, and leads me to set a high value on a noble, liberal, catholic spirit. I find men generous, humane, disinterested and devout, whose creed differs widely from my own; and instead of denouncing them, I would rather be praying for as good a spirit as they possess. Some would increase the divisions; would even organize a new sect, anti to the eating of meat, or drinking tea; anti to some form of church-music, or to the fashion of garments.   While integrity should be inflexible, and adherence to what we know to be right, and truth should never waver, yet the key to all union is diffidence of our own judgment, and respect for the judgment of others.

We are sinful in rejecting from our fellowship any man, or body of men, for anything which would not exclude them from the kingdom of grace and glory.   If we are rejected by any denomination and disowned, or compelled to withdraw, by being deprived of liberty of conscience, we may be innocent; but otherwise we are bound to be in fellowship with all Christians.

How beautiful is forbearance! Its influence over the heart is very great.   It is the subduing power.

> "Convince a man against his will,
> He's of the same opinion still."

The will, as an armed man, guards error; and the censor loses his labor on the errorist.   The will, goaded by severe rebuke, brushes away all evidence; but forbearance melts the heart, disarms the will, and lays the whole man open to conviction, and makes truth lovely and inviting.

"Father forgive them for they know not what they do," said Jesus when about being nailed to the cross, as he looked upon that motley mob-like multitude, who crowded around

Calvary; the same who had filled every open space about Pilate's hall, who had poured the savage yell of "Crucify him, crucify him," upon the ears of Pilate—a yell rolling from the housetops, and from all the avenues, and all the streets, like the roar of the ocean's storm.   They were doubtless wicked, very wicked.   Yet Jesus was moved with compassion for their ignorance.   More knowledge of what Jesus was would have changed their purpose and conduct; and it is probable that some of these savage men repented, when they had more knowledge and became disciples.

We should be followers of Jesus in this spirit toward all men.   Convince savage Indians that white men are just and generous.   While they believe that all white men intend to rob and exterminate them, it shall be my prayer, "Father forgive them; even though they kill me in their ignorance." Oh, how my heart bleeds, to think forbearance is so little esteemed, and heathen retaliation is everywhere resorted to! No man can be more anti-slavery than I am.   Rights of man—equality of men—freedom and liberty are themes which swell my soul.   The sentiments advanced by Cushing, and a thousand others, on the subject of slavery are terribly wicked; yet we, anti-slavery men, might have robbed them of many of their arguments, and saved them from much of their wicked spirit if we had been duly forbearing.

Missourians and Buford men were terribly wicked in Kansas, yet many of them were half civilized men, grossly ignorant of what Abolitionists were, and what they had done, and aimed to do.   Allowing that these men were human dogs, and tigers, and hyenas, yet they were human, and the moral influence of gospel forbearance was not faithfully tried on them.   The murder of Sherman, and Wilkinson, and three others, as reported by Brother Amos Finch, stirred up these wicked men to the maddest fury.   They that take the

sword perish with the sword.   The sound of Sharp's rifles
will long echo in horrid discord, but forbearance will finally
save the world.

———

"BEARETH ALL THINGS."—1 Cor. xiii 7.

Paley, in his Moral Philosophy, speaks of one class of men
who will never yield, and says, "Earth could not contain one
generation of them." That is, if, at any time, all should be
of this temper, they would inevitably kill each other, until
the last man was left alone on earth.

The two Hammets, Sidi and Seid, had joint possession
of Capt. Riley, and were conveying him from the great desert to Mogadore, to receive his redemption price. Sidi was
intelligent and generous, but his brother was ignorant, sullen and malicious.

A dispute arose between them about their captives, when
their cimeters clashed over their heads, and the death of one
or both seemed inevitable. Sidi's generous nature prevailed. He threw his weapon on the earth, and parting his
garment, laid bare his bosom, saying, "If you would kill
your brother, strike." Seid up to this moment was trying
to kill his brother, but this generous act melted his sullen
heart and brought him to terms of amicable settlement.

Such is human nature, even with murderous Arabs. They
traveled along the western shore of Africa. At one place
their path was along the narrow edge of a rock, a frightful
perpendicular descent below, terminating in the depths of
the ocean; and perpendicular rocks above, up which none
could climb. It was frightful to see the eagle go to her nest
five hundred feet above their heads, and hear the ocean
waves howl in caverns five hundred feet beneath them;
while one false step would hurl man or beast down the precipice. Here, said Sidi Hammet, two caravans with loaded

camels once met; one of Jews, and one of Moors. No camel could turn around, and one camel could not pass another. Nothing but forbearance could save them. Nothing but slowly and patiently backing the camels of one party to a widening of the road could meet the emergency. But proud man scorns forbearance, and willful man never yields. The Moors cried, "Throw your camels off, and let us come along." This roused the wrath and will of the Jews, and they yelled, "Throw your camels down, or we will throw them down for you." One man alone brought the news to Mogadore, that every camel of both caravans and every man but himself, went headlong down that awful precipice on that morning.

Such would be the fate of all if there was no forbearance. How important is this grace in the family, for harmony, quiet and happiness. If the child offend, let not the parent hastily punish, but give time for reaction and repentance in the mind of the child. He may, by reflection and the influence of your forbearance, be so self-comdemned as to come to you with voluntary confession. If the parent be unreasonably severe, let not the child be sullen, but obedient, and gentle, and the parent's heart will melt into kindness soon. Is the wife ill-tempered and peevish when over-worked and careworn? Let the husband be careful not to irritate her more by words of censure, but rather speak kindly and lend her a helping hand. It will be like oil on the troubled water. When husbands are ill-tempered and morose, nothing will so effectually calm them as the gentle, sweet temper of their wives.

A dear friend, one of the most gentle of all men, when his two daughters were grown to women, said to me, "Friend Crane, I never knew either of my girls to speak an unkind word to the other since they were born." This was beautiful. The gentle spirit of the daughters was copied from that of their parents. Few families are so happy. In most families a brother or a sister sometimes offends, and, if met by anger, grows more violent, until a tempest of mutual rage destroys all harmony, and makes a whole family most wretched; but if met by forbearance, all is soon harmony again. It would be a pleasant thing to be infallible, but I cannot claim infallibility. I honestly hold certain doctrines, which seem true beyond doubt and some seem self-evident; yet a large part of Christians do not believe these doctrines. They have failed to convince me that I am in error, yet I must respect them. I cannot call them dishonest, while many of them are better than myself in Christian temper and spirit; nor can I call them ignorant, while many are far more learned than I am.

I must be careful in making a class of fundamental doctrines for which we are to "contend so earnestly," lest I anathematize some whom God owns, loves and blesses; and careful in fixing tests of Christian fellowship. I am aware that vitiated public taste does not admire forbearance. It relishes more pride of opinion, more self-conceit, a more positive character; but the spirit which it relishes has always been contentious; it established the Inquisition, and has shed the blood of the innocent in every age.

Without forbearance no Christian denomination, or even a local church, could exist. As in the political world, revolutions tend to destroy our sense of the sacredness of government, so in the church, secessions tend to destroy our respect for church organization.

Americans have been educated for four generations in the doctrines of the right of revolutions. The cry, " Resistance to tyrants is obedience to God," has sounded in every ear for eighty years, and, indeed, in the ears of our ancestors since the days of Cromwell. The fruits of their teaching are now being reaped by our uuhappy country.

We have been pretty largely educated in the doctrine of church secession. We have seen it in the divisions and subdivisions of the church for three hundred years; many have lost all respect for God's institution,—the church in an organized state. It is alarming to see on what slight grounds secession is threatened. If the fragments of God's church are like the fragments of a world, which fly through their eccentric orbits in the heavens, those who come out and stand alone are like meteoric stones.

If the church requires us to sin or forbids us to discharge our duty, we are compelled to secede; but while we have our full liberty and all of our rights, we cannot secede on the account of the wrong conduct of some individuals, or on account of some things which we deem wrong in what the church believes, upholds, or sustains, while it is, on the whole, evangelical and really a church of God. If we do, we set an example which, if generally followed, would destroy every church in the world.

Without a great deal of forbearance no two denominations, even the smallest, can be united.

SUPPORT OF THE MINISTRY.

AN APPEAL TO THE HEART AND CONSCIENCE.

There are a few ministers who are rendered effeminate and voluptuous by wealth; but there are far more who use the wealth that Providence has put into their hands for the glory of God and good of men, giving alms to the poor, setting an example to their brethren, giving liberally to every benevolent and religious enterprise, and at the same time keeping aloof from secular cares, and devoting all their energies to their holy calling. But alas ! the greatest part of the Christian ministry in all ages has been sorely embarrassed by poverty. Gigantic men of the most noble

moral and intellectual frame, called of God to the ministry,
have been so borne down by poverty, that their minds were
not yet half developed, when from the end of their pilgrimage they made their exit from time.   Has a minister a right
to be a husband and father?   In all Protestant Christendom this is unquestionable.   Is it not enough that he is
separated from them most of the time in his itinerate labors?
Must his heart be wrung to bleeding, by beholding the health
of his wife perishing beneath the leaky roof of the old house
of some wealthy brother, who has abandoned it as unfit for
him, and has gone into his splendid new mansion?   Must
he see her efforts to conceal the tears that flow when she
looks upon the worn shoes and clothes of her shivering
children, or when she looks upon the meager meal upon
her table, or upon the empty cask or tub?   Behold a minister of venerable age, who has served the Church a quarter
of a century, of fair natural talents, one who has gained
what knowledge he could, under the weight of poverty.
Poverty is now his portion in the twilight of life.   With an
old and infirm horse, saddle and portmanteau rotten with
age, and with threadbare garments, he goes forth in the
cause of his Master.   He is not insensible to the hissing of
the fastidious and vain as he passes along.   Of his brethren,
some satisfy themselves by rebuking him for his bad appearance, telling him that he brings reproach upon the cause of
Christ.   Others are content in wondering that somebody
does not clothe him better.   The minister has his full share
of sensibility; happy would it be for him often if he had
less.   The thought of bringing reproach upon the cause of
Christ, even by his misfortune, breaks up the fountain of his
grief.   Mortification raises a commotion about his heart and
throws the hot blood to his cheeks.   Self-respect (for a
minister has some self-respect) struggles against want, and
prompts him to starve rather than beg; for a beggar is an

outlaw in this cold world, against whom this cruel generation takes unbounded license. But the wan cheek of his sickly wife and the pleadings of his children arouse him, and he makes a mighty effort against himself, crushes his noble nature, and goes forth to beg, with what success a thousand aching hearts can tell. In whose name is the minister engaged? Whose servant is he? He is the servant of the most high God. He labors and suffers in the cause of him who has said the earth is his, and the fullness thereof. There is wealth enough spent in superfluity to supply the wants of all the ministers on the earth, and as many more as would be necessary to convert the world. Horses used for pleasure riding would supply the wants of every weary minister. The wealth bestowed upon the libraries of vain men, who never read them, would give substantial books to every indigent minister who pants for knowledge and is denied its resources. In this great valley of the West, this garden of the world, the eye of every traveler is pleased, and wearied in beholding luxuriant fields beyond fields, until vision is lost in the distance, where the horizon meets the yellow grain and green meadow.

Oh, tell it not in Constantinople! Publish it not in Catholic Rome! That in this land of plenty, hundreds of evangelical ministers spend most of their time in working the land of their wealthy brethren on shares!

THE TUNE "CHINA," AND ITS HYMN.

I am a lover of music, vocal and instrumental; although I was never inclined to mirth, and even in my giddy childhood I abhorred dancing. I know not who was the author of this tune, nor when it was composed. I should almost think that it came from heaven, that it was caught by listeners to celestial singers.

I know as little why it was called China, as why China is called the Celestial Empire.   China is the most oriental of all lands, where earliest morning rises from the bosom of the Pacific on silver wings, with borders tinged with silver and gray.   I love this tune for the deep, rich, mournful sounds, and because its every note is capable of reminding me of each of the ten thousand incidents and circumstances of funeral scenes, which I have witnessed in village church or country school-house, in the mansion of the rich or lowest cottage of the poor, where the weeping mother sits by the babe whose rosy cheek in one week has faded into death; or when the father, who had just erected his cottage in the wild, has seen his patient wife, a thousand miles from her native land and all her friends, sicken and die, and now he sits between his little son and daughter, with the innocent and unconscious babe upon his lap, by the coffin; or where the mourning group consists of parents and children around the open ;coffin of a maiden.   Peradventure she was the eldest born of the family, the counsellor and guide of younger children.   The ear that heard their inquiries, and the eyes that smiled upon them are closed; the hand that was ever busy for their comfort is pale and cold, and lies upon the bosom that will never again heave a sigh of sorrow; and the tongue whose kind words were music, is silent as the grave.   There we sung:

> " Why do we mourn for dying friends,
>   Or shake at death's alarms?
> 'Tis but the voice that Jesus sends,
>   To call them to his arms."

With these words the rich notes of this tune rolled beneath the arch of the church, or through the chinks of t he poor man's cottage, echoing along the woods. Oh, how sweet, in this age of Utopian philosophy, when men are taught disgust at the hollow cough of the consumptive, when sick-

ness is accounted a sin, and death, short of old age, is accounted suicide,* how sweet and how consoling the good
wholesome orthodoxy of the last century, of the days of Watts
and Wesley, contained in this line,

"'Tis but the voice that Jesus sends."

And at this day, when the present life seems to be in the
estimation of many the end of man, and the preservation
and the prolongation of life seems, in their estimation, the
whole duty of man, how cheering to read:

" Nor should we wish the hours more slow."

Such were the sentiments that warmed the breast of one
who slept in death before our grandfathers were born.

" Music is like the memory of the past, sweet and mournful to the soul."— *Ossian.*

It is not only like the memory of the past, but often
wakes the memory of the past, and also brings to mind
scenes and things of which we have read far back in the history of man.   More than one hundred years have passed
since this wonderful hymn was composed.   The age of
William and Mary and all its scenes are gone, and all who
lived then are dead.   We might travel from pole to pole,
visit every kingdom, and, if possible, visit every house, and
call, but in vain, for one man to tell us that he saw and
heard what passed in the age of Watts and Wesley, Pope,
Swift, and Addison ; oh, I would like to go back just for a
few days to that age ; but it cannot be.

In this hymn we have the daguerreotype of the heart of
an evangelical Christian of that day ; one who walked by
faith and not by sight, whose life was hid with Christ in
God.

While Swift prostituted a giant genius and delighted in

* As a general rule, sickness and early death are the results of
violated physical laws, either by the individuals, or their parents.
" Do thyself no harm," is a Scriptural doctrine.

piercing hearts with his spear of sarcasm, in transfixing his
opponent to the wall, and laughing while the pale and
quivering flesh writhed in the agony of death; and while
Pope, haughty as Cæsar, dipped his pen in gall and wrote
his "Dunciad," Watts, the modern David, with his soul "as
a weaned child," gloried in naught but Jesus crucified.
Long as the spirit and faith of the Puritans continue, the
stanzas of Watts will be as pinions to the devout, but above
all, "Why do we mourn?" On the Celestial notes of China
will roll sublimely, away over Jordan, and mingle with notes
of the heavenly choir.

THE RIGHT USE OF PROPERTY.

The Creator has furnished resources for property sufficient
for all the wants of mankind. To reach these resources,
First, for all men to be industrious.
Secondly, to be industrious in useful employment.
Thirdly, to make a right use of property gained.
To be idle is to sin against God, against society, and
against our own health and life. The idle man robs society
of what he eats and wears. The man who is not usefully
employed is equally guilty. They who spend their lives in
pleasure, in pastime and recreation, are guilty before God.
Their wealth will be no excuse in the great day of judgment.
To be employed in anything not calculated to benefit, but
rather to injure society, may be equally criminal. The
manufacture of articles, not poisonous or absolutely hurtful,
yet wholly useless, not tending in any way to human happiness, is of very doubtful morality.
The right use of property is the great question before us
in this essay. We have nothing to do with property dis-
honestly gained, but to demand in the name of justice and
in the name of God that it be returned to the rightful

owners.   The man who has gained property by theft or fraud, by deceiving, misrepresenting and overreaching, can-not heal his conscience and remove his guilt by professing conversion, nor by giving to religious and benevolent objects or enterprises, nor even by giving to the poor.

Although the name of these is legion, and although they go unpunished by earthly courts, and unrebuked by public opinion, yet they shall not go unpunished.   " *Vox populi*" is not "*vox Dei.*"   The voice of the people is not the voice of God   The injured and defrauded will bring their appeal to the "Great Assizes," to the day of the judgment of the Almighty.

When that day comes, " Who shall be able to stand?" We leave these, and make our appeal to men who have property honestly gained.   We do not inquire how they have gained it ; whether as agriculturists, mechanics, merchants, men of commerce, professional men, or public officers ; nor do we inquire whether they have gained it by industry, or inherited it from ancestors.   In the providence of God, they are in possession of property ; and, as stewards under the Creator and Governor of the world, they are under most sacred obligations to use it in such manner as will most benefit mankind, and most honor God.

We will give the most ample room for that stereotyped passage : Tim. v. 8 :   " But if any one provide not for his own, and especially for those of his own household, he hath denied the faith, and is worse than an infidel."   This an-athema falls on the idler, who " works not at all," on the glutton and drunkard, who spends his substance on his own appetite, and leaves his family to starve, and go naked ; and on the adulterer, who starves his own wife to deck his wick-ed mistress; but it does not fall on the industrious and kind husband and father, whose little cottage gives his family a shelter from the storm, whose table is furnished with plenty of plain, wholesome food; and who clothes his family for comfort and health, not for the pampering of pride or vanity.

No passage of Scripture is more abused. It is in the mouth of every grade of extravagance to "Miss Flimsey" herself. This abused Scripture and the modern maxim, "Charity begins at home," constitute the plea for the larger and more elegant house, more costly furniture, clothes, and carriages; for the expensive food, often at war with health, parent alike to dyspepsia and lust, the plea for spending enormous sums in dinner parties and masquerades. "I must provide for my own" is the excuse for adding farm to farm, and increasing herds and flocks, for putting money to usury, for exultingly counting interest, and adding it to the principal, or foreclosing a mortgage on the farm, the house and home of some unfortunate debtor.

Pagan sages, with only the light of nature, saw that the love of riches was the bane of society. While luxury was undermining the Persian empire, the Spartans were forbidden the use or possession of money by their laws. All luxury was punished. No man was allowed a costly house, or garment, or expensive food. Those were the ages of Spartan glory and power. The Greeks returned from the conquest of Persia, contaminated, bringing the luxuries of the East, under the influence of which their glory and strength departed.

Under the wise counsels of the Roman Senate, great diversity of fortune was prevented. No man was allowed more than seven acres of land. The most eminent Romans lived in houses more plain and cheap than the houses of farmers at this day. The house of Cato, the Censor, consisted of one small room below and one above. Regulus called on the Senate to make a small appropriation for his family, because he had received a letter from his wife, while he was at the head of the army in a distant country, informing him that the man employed to cultivate his little farm had gone off with the farming implements, and unless they could obtain help their fields must go uncultivated.

When none became rich, few became poor. These Roman virtues did not always continue. Conquest brought home the vices of the East, the love of riches crept in, great distinction of fortune and rank obtained, luxury bred effeminacy, and finally dissolved the foundations of the empire.

Christ came when Rome was in the zenith of her glory. Her territory was the wide world, and all men were subject to her sway. Yet this vast empire was then festering beneath her pomp and pageantry, from wounds received by luxury and the sword. The ancient literature was confined to the intellect; the moral man was not educated, hence the ancient civilization had no preserving element, and could not be perpetuated. It contained even the certain elements of its own dissolution. These were luxury and the sword.

Pride and selfishness, receiving no check, produced their baneful effects everywhere. The rich wasted millions, while the poor were left to starvation. Envy, jealousy, malice, and ill-will poisoned all the walks of social life. Then came the Prince of Peace with the gospel; the religion of disinterested benevolence. Pride and selfishness were to be removed. Man was to love his neighbor as himself Human industry and the fruits of the earth were henceforth to bless all mankind.

How beautiful the description of the first Christian Church, Acts iv. 32: "And the multitude of those who believed were of one heart and of one soul: neither said any of them that aught of the things which he possessed was his own; but they had all things common." Ananias was at liberty to keep his lands, and to keep his money, after he had received it for his lands, so far as law and commandment was concerned. They had all things common because they were of one heart. Each loved his neighbor as himself; hence, verse 34, "Neither was there any among them who lacked." The reason for this is not only given in what follows in the same verse, but also in the 33d, "And with great power the apostles gave testimony concerning the Lord Jesus: and great grace was upon them all." They remembered the words of Jesus, "Lay not up treasures on earth."

The young man inquiring for the way of salvation was commanded to sell all he had and give to the poor; and as he was going away sorrowful, Jesus uttered words which should spread alarm through Christendom. "Verily I say unto you, that a rich man shall hardly enter the kingdom of of heaven." "And again I say unto you, it is easier for a camel to go through the eye of a needle, than for a rich man to enter into the kingdom of God." The disciples were "exceedingly amazed," and said, "Who then can be saved?" That terrible language is true to-day, and falls with awful weight upon the rich, who are wasting the goods of earth in extravagance of any kind, in houses, carriages, furniture, clothes, in costly feasts, expensive rides, in the gratification of the pride and vanity of self. In vain they strive to excuse themselves; cover their guilt with cobweb gauze, and search for some commentator who will ease their conscience by taking off the edge of this flaming sword; but God's own angel of truth holds the sword over their devoted heads, saying as Nathan to David, "Thou art the man."

Oh, ye rich men, who are turning aside the goods of this world from the direction which God would give them, while you are wasting in extravagance, or hoarding up money, or expending it to increase your estate, the sword is pending over your heads, and a voice from heaven, from him who sees all things, bids you behold the wants of a world! The poor who must be fed or starve, sick, without medicine,* without nurses, without beds, and nearly without clothes! While they pass the winter nights in dark, fireless cellars or garrets, there is a hand, invisible, writing on the wall in the halls of festivity, the doom of men and women who live for self! Oh, the sin of living for self! It will appear in its magnitude at that great day when God shall judge the world; when he shall ask you, What you have done for the poor, what for homeless orphans, what to instruct the ignorant, and elevate the degraded; what to snatch men and women from paths of pollution as brands from the burning; what to build churches, parsonages, and various asylums; what for various benevolent enterprises, for the distribution of tracts, Bibles, religious books, journals, and magazines; and what have you done for a living gospel ministry, to Christianize and save a lost world? When in the presence of the Trinity and holy angels these questions shall be brought home to the soul like living fire, how many will be overwhelmed with shame, as they are forced to say, " I lived for self!" How mean, how contemptible, how wicked selfishness will look in that Great Day! Many who have gained riches, and have been honored on earth, will "rise to shame and everlasting contempt."

Many, who in sordid selfishness sought for riches and never succeeded, will be equally lost. Selfishness often comes stealthily, in a sacred garb, cloaked by religious ex-

---

*Elder Crane, with all his intelligence and wisdom, was not free from the prevalent delusion, that what will make a well person sick will make a sick person well. If people, when sick, instead of swallowing corrosive drugs, would rest, and bathe with pure water, and use fruit juice or fruit tea, they would be physically improved afterward, and not dead, or invalids for life, as many are. Dr. David Nelson (author of " Cause and Cure of Infidelity"), the year before he died, remarked to the complier, " Fasting and repose are my potent medicines."

perience.   Many, who are very self-complacent and appear
very devout, are nevertheless very selfish.   They are always
praying to be happy, striving to be happy, and getting happy, faithfully attending meeting, prompt to pray in public
and in private, prompt to speak in meeting, to sing, to talk
about religion to every one, regular in their lives, and fault-
less in their temper.   And yet they are nearly worthless;
are even a disgrace to Christianity, and fearfully unprepared
to render an account to God.   Their great aim is to be
happy on earth, and be saved! What is there in this worthy,
noble or God-like? They are still selfish, are not consecrated to God, do not work with and for God.   They are yet
to learn what it is to "seek not their own," to "love not
the world," to "lay not up treasures on earth."   In vain
they talk of being weaned from the world, while their hands
hold like a death grip to property.

In vain they pray for the poor, the degraded, for a lost
sinful world, for the spread of religious knowledge, for the
conversion of heathen lands.   They leave it for others to
meet the expense, or leave the hungry to starve, the naked
uucovered, the prisoner to fester and famish in his chains.

No contributions from them ever gladden any heart!

For all that they will do, the gospel would not go to the
heathen; darkness would cover all heathen lands forever.
No meeting-houses would ever be built; and every minister,
not able to maintain himself, would be compelled to leave
the work of the ministry.   The world left to these selfish
Christians would go back to pagan barbarism.   There would
soon be no place of worship, no academy or college, no
asylum for suffering humanity, no benevolent society, or
benevolent institutions!

They go to meeting in houses which could never have
been built by such stingy gifts as theirs; listen to preaching

which must have long ceased, if nobody had been more liberal than themselves.

Year after year these covetous Christians go on robbing
God, and robbing liberal men of privileges which they never
pay for. Excuses are made which the Allwise will pronounce falsehoods. They are always pleading that they are
not able, while neighbors not more able, often not *half as
able*, build churches for them to worship in, and pay preachers for preaching to them, and build colleges and other
schools for these covetous Christians to educate their children.

Sometimes these covetous men, goaded by rebuke, cry
out against education, against an educated ministry and
meeting-houses of any expense or convenience; and some
secede and join some denomination which stereotypes this
cry; and some even leave all church relation and stand
alone, to escape all calls for money! They then profess to
be very free from sectarianism, and like unruly beasts jump
into every pasture. In other words they attend church
promiscuously, and where they find free seats, attempting to
deceive men, to deceive God, and to deceive themselves, by
pretending that all this is for union, when the Lord knows
their object is to escape calls for money.

I ask in the name of humanity, of mercy, of justice, in
the name of religion, in the name of God, if these are not
worthless Christians? Are they not a dishonor to the cause
of Christ? They do not work with God and with good men
for the salvation of the world. What avails their getting
happy, their church-going, their hymns and prayers, and even
their sober lives, while it is certain that if all Christians were
like them, Christianity would soon be lost in pagan darkness!

Oh, my delinquent, my covetous, Christian brother, be
not offended with me for this plainness. You and I must

soon meet before God! Oh, let me be plain; let me speak
the truth. The cause of God bleeds on your account. The
wheels of salvation move slow and stagger. God calls you
to help, and you will not. You have a certain amount of
property, and boast that you will do with it as you please;
but take care, my brother; do not rashly claim any thing.
Your *life, your all is the Lord's.* Lay all upon His altar,
and come to the sacred and exalted bliss of entire consecration. Lose your will in the will of God.

> "Oh, give your carnal interest up,
> And make your God your all."

Come into a sacred union and agreement with the divine
mind, and work with and for God. Honor God with your
property, do all the good you can. Make every dollar tell
to the utmost in the great work of making the world holier,
and wiser, and happier, and you will rejoice in that day,
when farms, and merchandise, and gold and silver are con-
sumed.

POWER OF EARLY IMPRESSIONS.

While the phrenologist is searching in physical formation
for the cause of what is peculiar in the disposition and practice of man, and the atheist is expatiating on the influence
of circumstances, I will leave both in their labyrinth, and
call the attention of the reader to the power of early impressions.

Probably there is scarcely a man who has not some pecu-
liarity traceable to some early impression.

When I was thirteen years of age I was in the dawn of
intellectual development.

I had read some meager volumes of history, loaned from
the scanty libraries of our backwoods settlement, and had
caught an imperfect view of a few ancient statesmen and

warriors, temples, and cities. I had also some crude notions of human nature, of philosophy, of politics, and of religion.

On a beautiful day in June in 1818, I left home early in
the afternoon to attend a camp-meeting, then in progress on
the Honeoye River, near the township line, between Lima
and Mendon, N. Y. I fell in with one and another on my
way, generally older than myself, until our company consisted of about fifteen. We lost our way in the wilderness, and night came rolling down over the valley of the
Honeoye before our journey ended. We were passing
through a forest on an elevated plain, when my ear caught
the first sound of devotion, brought on the wings of evening
zephyrs, through the green foliage of the trees. Passing on
I soon beheld in the valley the extensive encampment.
Lights on numerous elevated stands produced a brilliant il-
lumination. Onward I moved, the sound of devotion swelling more and more on my ear, pressing on through the great
mass of human beings who thronged the way leading to the
encampment, till I stood all suddenly and unexpectedly
against the pole enclosing an altar of prayer. This altar
was filled with worshipers, engaged in such devotion as I had
never seen; such earnest expressions of faith, such sounds
of praise, such expressions of love, and such countenances
beaming with unearthly light were new to me. Before this
I had known but little more of Methodists than of Mahome-
dans. I had heard them ridiculed, and had started for this
meeting with a spirit of persecution, which was increased by
the wicked conversation of my company, but now my persecuting spirit fled away. I was awestruck and filled with
solemn reverence to God, and to this assembly; my sins
came terribly to my remembrance. Overcome by the power of my feelings, I was unable to stand without holding to
the pole that was before me. How easily I might have

been persuaded to kneel for prayer; but I was a bashful boy among strangers, I knew nobody save the boys of my company.   I sat down with them at the roots of a tree.   The night passed away, and on the day following we returned to our homes.   I remained unconverted, but the impression that I received standing at that altar marked my religious taste for life.   Thirty-two years have passed since that night, but if I was a great painter I could draw that vast circle of tents, the lofty trees reflecting back the light from their leaves, and the numerous faces beaming with heavenly light in that altar of prayer.

THE INFLUENCE OF LANGUAGE.

Language was designed by the Creator to bless man, to sooth and console him along the stormy path of his pilgrimage.   Suavity, when it does not descend to duplicity, or prevarication, is one of heaven's best gifts.   It is a balm for the grief-worn and sorrowing; lifting up the countenance that is cast down, and restoring cheerfulness to the despondent.   The Censor might have been important to the Roman Senate, but censors are little needed now; indeed, it is time the office was obsolete.

Censorious words are often daggers.   If they do not kill outright, they wound the vitals, and slow consumption follows and brings the grief-worn to the grave.   A friend, dear to me by the strongest ties, was engaged in school-teaching. A kinder heart to children never beat in human bosom. Filled with the most benevolent design, she toiled most assiduously for their good.   But censors felt it their duty, regardless of her ill-health, to rob her of the affections of the children, and to wound her to the heart.   It was a vital wound, and the wild flowers are blooming on her grave. Nearly thirty years ago Mrs. B., one of the most worthy

women in L——, was in great mental suffering, reason beginning to reel, when Mr. ——, a conscientious censor, came
in and said, "Mrs. B., you act like a fool, and your neighbors say so." This drove her to distraction, and suicide
immediately followed.

The censor is often as cowardly as cruel, letting alone the
real and willful offender, because his interest prompts him
to favor, or because he fears the brass of his face, while he
goes off like a wolf upon the track of the meek and conscientious, and tears and rends them, amidst their indefatigable labors for the public good. The cruel censor feasts on
the sight of the anguish which he causes, and as the most
culpable and dangerous of men are quite indifferent to his
attacks, he passes them, and lets his scorpion lash fall on
the back that will feel most keenly, and he has the gratify-
ing sight of many a one descending to an early grave from
the bursting of a generous heart.

The influence of language on the happiness of a family is
very great. Who does not reflect with sorrow, or even anguish on a wound inflicted by an unkind word upon a wife,
a sister, a child, or a parent? But oh, when death has closed
the eyes and ears of a dear friend, when "kindness and pity
are vain," when apologies are unavailing, how bitter the
tears we shed on the grave!

AN OVERWORKED GENERATION.

There is no doubt that civilization is a blessing to mankind up to certain bounds. These bounds have been passed in this country. Idlers living by "brain work" luxuriate
on the proceeds of the toil of working men, men of "hard
work," who, H. W. Beecher says, must rank below men of
"brain work." Shrewd speculators, planters, jobbers, and
the incumbents of lucrative offices, constitute an aristocracy,

and abounding in money, set the fashion of houses, furniture, jewelry, dress, food and carriages so high as to waste
a great part of the hard earned substance of the country;
and at the same time so look down upon the honest laboring
class, as to give them a painful anxiety to imitate their extravagance.

These working people work too hard, work in pain, often
break down in body and mind, become prematurely old, and
descend to an untimely grave. Weary, nervous and cor-
roded with care, they have little serenity, and though Christians by profession, and by honest motive, their temper is
often sour, gloomy, and irritable. Their children inherit
their temper, and react on the parent's spirit. Mrs. Alger
received notice on Monday evening that Mrs. Bliss would
visit her on Wednesday, and that her two daughters from
the city and a friend of theirs would accompany her. This
notice gave very little pleasure. It came when Mrs. A. was
extremely tired with her washing. She was giving attention
to a sick child four years of age, and carrying a tired and
crying infant in her arms, and at the same time preparing
supper for her husband, who had just come in from labor.
"It is hard," she said, "to maintain my standing with Mrs.
Bliss's circle of friends. She is quite aristocratic herself,
and I am frightened in view of a visit from her daughters
from the city, and a stranger with them; but I must try to
maintain my standing, though I am working myself to death."
"I hope," said Mr. A., "you will not have to purchase
much to-morrow, for my account at Baldwin's has already
run so high that he wants a mortgage on our lot." "I cannot get along without quite a bill," said Mrs. A. "We
must have groceries, and an addition to our table furniture,
and a little ready-made clothing, as I have no time to sew."
"I am working very hard," said Mr. A. "but at this rate,
I must, as you say, work myself to death." He went on

Tuesday morning, and made the purchases, and came home with a heavy heart.

The visitors came and went, whether to speak well or ill of Mrs. A. I cannot tell. She had done her best; had worn herself out, broken down her nerves, and was half insane all the night and morning before the visit. She forced on a serene countenance when they came, which was near leaving her when the sick child groaned, when the babe, which was teething, crept after her, crying and seizing her dress, and when Willie came in with his new clothes smeared with mud.

An Irish cabin, with an earth floor, without debt, might be the seat of happiness. It is alarming to see how many women in this conntry are broken down in their nerves, and often distracted, by struggling to keep up with *custom*. Is this right? Hospitality, which, in the days of simplicity was a rich blessing to both giver and receiver, is spoiled and poisoned by custom. A prominent minister said he chose to make his visits, not only where he could be comfortable, but where he might be the *most* comfortable. This cut his poor parishioners to the heart; and it was pitiable to see how they toiled in pain, and went beyond their means to make their homes attractive to him.

When quarterly-meeting approached at ——, Sister Green worked so hard every day that she fell upon her bed every night exhausted and miserable. "Why," said Bro. G., "are you killing yourself with work, Sarah?" "I tell you, Henry, I must put my house in order. I cannot have my name bandied over the circuit as a slut or untidy." She said this in ill-humor, for one so extremely weary is hardly sane : and Peter's elbows had pushed through his sleeves, Nellie was crying with a sore foot, and twin babies were asleep on the floor.

When the parlor was filled with social guests, or when the

table was surrounded with cheer, no one but an old itinerant
guessed what pains the feast had cost; and perhaps he
alone excused Sarah Green for missing the love-feast, and
coming into meeting after sermon began.   He had learned
in almost every instance of fashionable hospitality, to look
out for a care-worn face.

At the camp-meeting in S ——, two families united and
built a large tent which, with a large table, became very
attractive and was soon thronged.   The two sisters, who
gave a continued feast, had each a helpless babe and other
small children to look after, and almost constant cooking,
setting tables, removing dishes, and making beds.

A happy group sat talking and singing, who brought no
cares with them to meeting, when Sister G. said, "Breakfast
is ready."   At table Rev. I. D. said, "Sister G., our sister,
Nancy Page, experienced sanctification last night in a glorious prayer-meeting, in the tent joining yours."   To which
Nancy assented.   She was a maiden lady of twenty-eight,
and was here without labor or care.   Would Nancy's sanctification stand the test of the toils and cares of Sister G.,
who had worked so hard the day before that she could
scarcely walk, and after subdividing her beds lay down at
midnight, but could not sleep, for the loud singing and
shouting in the adjoining tent, which continued all night?

ITEMS.

SECTARIAN LOGIC.

I once heard a man boasting of victory over his opponent.   Said he: "The devil is called a wolf.   Christ is
called a lion, a lion is stronger than a wolf; therefore no
man can fall from grace.   Thus I put my opponent to
silence, he could say no more."

—Said a devout woman: "A garden inclosed is my sister, my spouse; a spring shut up; a fountain sealed. So saith the Scriptures; therefore our denomination ought not to commune with any other."

—Cromwell, on his death bed, said to his chaplain, "Can a man, once in grace, fail of salvation?" "His salvation is sure," said the chaplain; "nothing is more certain." Cromwell answered, "I know I was once in a state of grace," and lay calmly down to die.

—"We are the favored of the Lord," says one. "We leap, and shout, and fall; we lose our strength, lose our consciousness, lose our reason, therefore we are the holy people; we stop not with the form of godliness, we have the power."

—"It is wicked," said an honest Christian, "to plant ornamental trees, and shrubs, and flowers; for the Scripture saith, 'Why spend ye your money for that which is not bread?'"

—"Oh, my child is lost!" said a daughter of Charles Carrol of Carrolton, "my child is lost, for I could not get it baptized before it died."

—A very pious old lady ran out of meeting, when she heard the heathen growl of a bass viol.

—"The sword of the Lord and of Gideon," cried Cromwell, with his long face and nasal twang. *i. e.*, "I am a second Gideon, you are heathen, therefore I hew you down."

—A grave and solemn man, in Connecticut, passed the day of a great military muster, seventy years ago, with great pleasure, seeing how they killed men; but when, in the afternoon, a part of these brave soldiers put on Indian caps and blankets, for a sham fight, he sighed deeply, saying, "Alas, they are making heathen of the Lord's chosen people!"

—"St. Peter" said a Jesuit, "had the keys of heaven

and hell committed to him; therefore the Pope's excommunication sends a man to hell" Again he said, "Holy men often do more good than is their duty, and these works of supererogation may be applied to pardon other men's sins, and to release men from purgatory."

—"You should be baptized," said a Spanish priest to a South American Indian doomed to die, three hundred years ago. "Why should I be baptized?" said the Indian. "That you may go to heaven," said the priest: "you are about to die." "Are there any Spaniards in heaven?" said the Indian. "Spaniards all go to heaven," said the priest. "Then I will not be baptized," said the Indian, "I will not go to heaven, I will go to hell."

—Said a man in my hearing, "If I was not a church-member, I would join you in wrestling," addressing a profane rabble. He stood, however, and enjoyed their sport in spite of their blasphemies.

HONESTY.

"An honest man's the noblest work of God."—*Pope*.

Truth, Justice, and Right, as eternal and immutable principles, lie back of all law in the nature and fitness of things.

The whole universe should harmonize with these attributes of God; then each part would harmonize with all the other parts, and harmony would be universal.

The physical universe is truthful. Suns shine, and planets roll, through all ages, according to promise.

A comet leaves, promising to return in a given year; centuries pass, and when the appointed time comes, no living witness is left; generation after generation has passed away; the manners, customs, and even languages of half the world have changed; the world look at the record, in a language now obsolete, and then, by night look on the sky, and lo ! the expected comet comes.

Of myriad kinds in the vegetable kingdom, each produces its leaf, of peculiar and certain form, and hue, never varying through all ages.

Behold those small seeds; how nearly alike, and yet, that slight difference promises that this will produce an esculent root, that a mass of food upon a sturdy stalk, and the last will be a tall branching bush.

See those eggs in the tropic sand; how near alike, yet this slight mark shows that this will be the chubby tortoise, and that an alligator. Thus nature is everywhere truthful.

As man should be in agreement with his Maker, in harmony with the divine government, he should be as truthful as nature; there should be no variance between his motive or intention, and his words, or his voluntary countenance.

With the truly honest there is no deceit, no false coloring, no expression of the eye or lips misleads, no tone, accent, or emphasis of speech conveys the least false impression.

How beautiful is nature in her truthfulness! For six thousand years man and beast have trusted her not in vain, they are never deceived.

What ruin would come, if nature should become false! Winter's awful power in mid-summer burying the unharvested grain beneath the drifted snow.

Though this dire calamity has not come upon the physical world, it has come upon the moral world. Alas!

"Man is practiced in disguise,
He cheats the most discerning eyes."

Man is false, and mutual distrust spoils the beauty and harmony of our social state.

Confidence is lost, and cold suspicions, like the "Mists of Lano," poison the air. Oh, tell us not that there is an equal chance for all, that each may put himself upon offence and defence, and in the general scramble, will be as likely to win as lose; as likely to supplant as to be supplanted.

Alas, that these heathen consolations should be administered in this age! but such is the moral code of business circles.

For eighteen hundred years sacraments and doctrines have been defended, but the time is yet to come for a cry to go through the earth, Except your righteousness shall equal the righteousness of an honest man, ye cannot enter into the kingdom of heaven.

Without honesty, what can orthodoxy avail? what the most punctilious observance of every sacrament? every right? and all sanctuary service? All avail nothing.

It is not with liars that we are laboring. Public sentiment puts a mark on them.   It is with such men of art and dissimulation as are slightly rebuked, or even honored by public sentiment, men of influence and of eloquence; it is with men of shrewd business talent, sharp-eyed and smooth-tongued dealers, polished and polite talkers, with all who mislead, gloss, color and give false impressions.   These overturn the foundations of social happiness, and expose their victims to that terrible retribution which awaits those who trample on the great principles of righteousness which lie beneath all human well-being.

Oh, when shall sordid selfishness cease? When shall man love his neighbor as himself, and do as he would be done by? When shall men buy and sell as Christians, giving a true description of all things?

I have never failed to find, in every land, during more than thirty years in the ministry, men who neglect their salvation, because their confidence in religion is destroyed by the frauds, tricks, and misrepresentations of church members.

What can I say to them? They often point to the most

prominent men in the church, to ministers, to the most popular and influential. I see immortal souls on the verge of
everlasting death; I would snatch them away! But, oh, the
horrid example of business men, financial men, trading men,
is a wind and tide against my effort. Oh, brethren! brethren! immortal souls are perishing! cease your speculations;
bring such an example as will restore confidence; repent,
confess, restore! Oh, give up the "Love of money, the root
of all evil"! Souls immortal are perishing! thousands have
perished, stumbled over the example of speculating Christians.

You have gained wealth, or eagerly sought it; and they,
by your example, are sunk to hell.

You had better die a beggar at the rich man's gate, than
gain the whole world by speculations, and lose your soul.

You may call the caviler or critic on your ways, infidel,
atheist, scoffer, vagabond, and what you will; wipe your
lips, and declare your innocence, but the truth flashes along
the whole face of the earth. The want of brotherhood;
the selfishness, the frauds, and false colorings; the misrepresentations, and dissimulations, from the great sweeping
stream, which bears away the honor of Christ, all confidence
in religion, and drives the deceived and wronged to atheism
and death.

Item by W. W. C., *Wesleyan*, July 7, 1853.

I have this moment heard the result of this day's voting
in our town, Eighty-two majority. I feel like shouting.
The setting sun seems to smile on Michigan as it never did
before. Glory to God, joy shall return to ten thousand
desolate homes, the mother shall smile, and hungry children
shall be fed!

FUNERAL SCENES.

DEAR BRO. LEE: I yesterday attended a funeral under most melancholy circumstances. An affectionate and happy pair were engaged in childish mirth, when an old superannuated gun, which had not been in use for many years, but which had been most heavily loaded a few days ago, without the knowledge of the family, was seized by the young bride. Her hand was applied to the fatal lock—a deafening report broke the scene of their mirth—and the young husband fell mortally wounded. Scarcely in my life have I witnessed such mortal agony as at this funeral. Walking from the grave to my home last evening, I fell into the following meditations:

I have now resided in Michigan more than fifteen years. During that time I have attended nearly five hundred funerals. For many years, when a stranger has called at my house, I have expected to hear him say, " You are requested to attend a funeral." It may be ten or even fifteen or eighteen miles away. Sometimes I am called to the mansions of the rich, but more frequently to the cottage of the poor. At one time I find the dead in the thronged and thriving village—at another time I am piloted far into the dark wilderness, where a group of mourners utter their lamentations in a foreign tongue. Now the coffin is small, containing the child that smiled so enchantingly a few days ago; again, as the coffin lid is raised, it reveals the face, encircled with white locks, of the venerable patriarch of a family. Youth is cut down while fancy is painting the fairest pictures of coming life, and the strong man becomes the victim of death, when his rising family are left without a helm on the stormy sea of life. But the most touching of all is, the cold hand of the dark winged angel freezes to death the maternal bosom. What an office is that of a mother ! What magic in that word mother on the lips of the child borne upon her arm, or led by her side. And, oh, when I find the mother cold in her coffin, and reflect on the midnight when she bade her children farewell, and pressed her babe to her dying lips, my heart melts away and I become a weeping child. This hour is solemn. The lamentations of a thousand mourners are reiterated. They sound along the river—they come in the voice of the moaning winds. Fancy hears funeral dirges among these hills. Moonbeams parted by the waving branches of the towering oak, move along the glistening snow like mourners marching to the grave. The proud will call this effeminacy. Robert Blair was called weak because he wrote a poem on the grave, and poor Cowper is roughly handled because he was a man of sorrow. If it is manly to be void of human feeling, I spurn the dignity of manhood ; if it is childish to ask pity and to bestow it, let me be a child. I knew a boy who, at seventeen years of age, from a melancholy temperament and erroneous theology, fell into despair. He ardently desired to have it in his choice, to plunge into hell and there remain as many thousands of years as there were particles of sand in this globe on condition that he might afterwards be saved. Friend after friend forsook him, disgusted with his writhings, lamentations and tears. This alienation extended to the church, and even to the ministry. Without hope of heaven, and nearly friendless on earth, literally to him,

> "The midsummer sun shone but dim,
> The fields strove in vain to look gay."

When disease was twining his vitals, he attended a camp-meeting in Springwater, N. Y, in June, 1823. He entered the encampment a stranger, in a strange land. One man he met whom he knew well. This was the presiding elder. He approached the elder with all the animation that his

emaciated body possessed, and said, "How do you do Elder
S——?" He dropped a cold hand into his and said, "Where
have I seen you?" That unfortunate youth is now the writer of this.   That elder's answer was the most cruel dagger
that ever pierced my heart.   O Lord, forbid that I should
ever be disgusted with the writhings, lamentations and tears
of the mourner!   Let me go to the house of mourning,
rather than to the house of feasting, for there I learn how
frail I am;   there I am shorn of my pride.   When I stand
by the grave, surrounded by a group clad in symbols of sor-
sow, with eyes red with weeping, and hear on every hand
the half suppressed sigh, I learn the vast value and importance of friendship.   Let the day speedily come when under
Messiah's reign, violence and pride shall cease, and men
shall sing not of Nelsons and Wellingtons, but of Burritts
and Howards, but still more of the Prince of Peace.

A MODEL CONFERENCE.

The brethren came from more than forty different valleys,
over the mountains and along the gorges;   their devotions
increasing by the influence of thundering cataracts, ever-
green forests, and moaning winds.   They came in plain at-
tire, as was the custom in that age of Christian simplicity.
When they convened, they left all salutations and conversation before passing the threshold, and walked silently to
their seats;   and each sat in communion with the Lord until
business commenced.

When the organization was completed, the presiding
officer arose in a manner so unpretending that it was evident that he claimed no superiority over his brethren;   and
yet his meek gravity, his intelligent countenance, and the
wisdom of his words commanded the respect of all.   He
was 'familiar with parliamentary usage;   that is, with those

rules for the regulation of deliberative bodies which arise in the nature and fitness of things, and which have been nearly the same in every age and country.

To "stir up their pure minds by way of remembrance," he spoke of the solemnity of the occasion. "You have left your parishes and come, many of you, from distant countries, for the honor of God and the welfare of his church. Consider the weight of your responsibility. We are called to die to the world, to die to self, to live for God and humanity. I trust that no measure of party interest, or individual interest is to be here introduced. We all desire order, decorum, and the proper improvement of our time. In order to this, no one will speak without arising and addressing the chair. No conversation, no discussion, or speech, will be allowed, unless there is a motion, resolution, or report before us. Every motion will be distinctly made, and every resolution and report will be fully written and distinctly read. No speech will be allowed in the mover, to precede his motion or resolution. No speech will be allowed which is not relevant to the question before us. Unless these regulations are strictly observed, confusion will attend our proceeings."

As he spoke, it was evident that he spoke the language of every head and heart.

In the examination of character, the utmost scrutiny was joined with the greatest kindness. The questions, "Is he holy in life and conversation? An example to his flock? Is he sober, and yet not morose? Cheerful and not given to levity? Is he familiar, and yet prudent? Is his heart wholly in his work? Does he labor earnestly for the conversion and sanctification of every one in his parish, visiting and laboring with every one individually?" were pressed earnestly yet kindly, in every examination.

Each was urged to avoid secular speculations, which al-

ways bring reproach on the cause of Christ.   If he must buy
and sell, he should keep his business transactions free from
the least appearance of fraud or extortion.   If he was found
wanting, he was rebuked with so much love that he was
melted into contrition.

There was no pride of opinion to shut the eyes and ears
of any one against conviction, or to cause him to willfully
struggle to maintain an untenable position.   Every one felt
that to be convinced of error, was to receive the greatest
kindness.   Hence, no anger was ever shown in debate, and
no harsh or boisterous words were ever used.   They felt
that "One was their Master even Christ, and all they were
brethren."

Many young men had come to this conference as candidates for the sacred office.   The aged looked upon them
with yearning affection.   They were meek and holy young
men, not "puffed up" with vanity and conceit; ambitious
for nothing but to do good.   In their examination, practical
knowledge and talent were valued more highly than scholar-
ship.   Natural and acquired ability to do good was deemed
essential.   The presiding brother, who was an aged man,
addressed them in the following language :

"My sons, you see that many of us are near the close of
life.   During the few years or months of our stay, we need
your aid in our parishes ; and we expect you to fill our
places when we are no more.   Take care of the churches
which we have planted ; may the truth never suffer by your
neglect, even though the terrible persecutions which we suffered in our youth should return upon you.   Yours may be
an age of martyrdom ; are you prepared for it ? Whether
you meet a martyr's death or not, may you leave these
churches pure, and well disciplined to your successors."

Great solemnity prevailed during this speech.   The aged
reflected on the past, and looked forward to the perils of the

church in coming years.   The arm of their strength had
nearly lost its power, palsied by age.   Their eyes were dim.
In the feeble light they beheld the faces of their sons, and
invoked on them the baptism of the Holy Ghost.   The
young men received into most docile hearts the counsel of
the aged.   Highly favored of the Lord was the valley where
this conference was held.

Love ruled all of the proceedings, and the influence was
salutary on the spectators.   In every house where the servants of God were quartered, their Christian politeness,
their sobriety and evangelical conversation, and their kind
and faithful dealing with each member of the household,
brought nearly all into holy consecration.

For many ages the inhabitants of this favored valley felt
the heavenly influence of this conference, and fathers and
mothers talked of it to the fifth generation.

GENTLENESS.

" How beautiful," said Sarah Prior, "is this text, 'But
we were gentle among you, evan as a nurse cherisheth her
children,' Thes. ii 7. I have the care of the four little children of my deceased sister, who committed them to me
when dying, and this text is ever before me, and it has kept
me_from ever uttering a harsh word to them."   " I may differ with you," said Catherine Lane.   ' I am sure that severity and what you would call harshness, is necessary in my
family.   Your sainted sister may have left you peculiar children, patterned after her amiable self ; but mine must be
chastised and scolded."

" My sister was very amiable, but her children had a very
turbulent father, who has transmitted his temper to them ;
but while I have suppressed all pride and anger in myself,
their stubborn will has yielded to gentleness and love.   The

apostle must have had a gentle nurse in view, who not only subdued the temper by love, but also calmed the grief and soothed the sorrows of the children she cherished, and such he informs was his spirit, and that of the other apostles towards mankind."

To which Catherine replied: "Christ called the scribes and pharisees hypocrites and vipers, and said 'How can ye escape the damnation of hell?' Luther and Knox were often very harsh and severe, and I do not believe that this wicked world will ever be reformed by gentle means." "Christ," said Sarah, "is God, to whom vengeance belongeth, and is no more our pattern in this, than is sending fire on Sodom; and Luther and Knox were uninspired, erring men, and we should be careful that we do not copy their faults. Christ has taught us to love our enemies, to bless them that curse us, to do good to them that hate us, to pray for them that despitefully use us and persecute us, to be gentle to all men, to resist not evil."

"I think," said Catherine, "that these passages cannot have a literal meaning; they must have a mysterious, figurative meaning. As human nature is, they cannot be obeyed in a literal sense. Can I love Jane who has slandered me?"

"Yes, if your heart is right you can love her."

"No, Sarah, I cannot. My nature shrinks from it."

"My dear Catherine, pray for a change of nature."

"I think I am a Christian, and need no change."

"Dear Kate, do pray for a spirit to bless Jane."

"I do not desire such a spirit while she curses me."

"My errand here was to have you go with me to assist her; she is sick and in want. Will you go?"

"No, she deserves her sickness for injuring me, and it is my duty to show a proper resentment."

"Are you sure that yours is a Christian temper?"

" I am; I feel as David felt towards his enemies."

" We may not understand David; but Christ's words are plain."

" What do you think of the destruction of the Canaanites, the hewing of Agog and the feats of Gideon and Samson?"

" Whatever may be the meaning of those things, Christ has brought in a new dispensation, condemning ,polygamy and retaliation and violence."

Sarah Prior went alone to the sick room of Jane Watson, bearing necessary medicine and food. She went in the spirit of love, and Jane.was melted into deep repentance and meekly came to Christ. Here she met with a neighbor who had lost her husband and two sons in the army, and who was nearly insane with despair, having been just told by her minister that her deep sorrow was a proof that she was not in the divine favor. She wildly told her story: her husband killed at sea and committed to the waters, William torn all to pieces by a shell, and John, her last dear boy, hung by guerrillas and devoured by buzzards, and " Oh !" she exclaimed, " I must be lost ! my minister tells me no one so sorrowful can be a Christian." Sarah Prior took her in her arms as a kind mother takes an afflicted child, think- ing of her favorite text, " We were gentle among you, even as a nurse cherisheth her children." "Oh, blessed spirit of the apostles," she silently said; "may God endue me with this spirit."

The afflicted widow looked through her tears on the kind face of Sarah, who was also weeping over her, and pressing her to her kind bosom. "Mrs. Prior," she sobbingly ex- claimed, "I must be lost; for my sorrow denies me the divine favor, and my despair increases my sorrow."

" My dear, dear Mrs. Brown," said Sarah Prior, "you are not lost; God loves you, tenderly loves you, in your grief. 'Like as a father pities his children,' so the Lord pities you. The divine arms are around you, rest in them. Your grief is not sin."

The poor lone widow grew calm and serene. The re-membrance of her terrible bereavement was not lost, but the assurance that grief was not sin removed the wild look and smoothed her countenance. But for this timely meet-ing of Sarah Prior, Mrs. Brown might have become a maniac, and might have perished like John Barlow, who, grieving for the loss of his sons, was told that grief was sin, and that God disowned him. Oh, cruel counsel! it drove him in-sane, and day and night he called his sons, and told them that for his grief God had cast him off; till finally his poor body was taken from the river, cold in death. At the men-tion of John Barlow's suicide, Mrs. Brown uttered a shriek, her poor wretched mind shuddered, hope was departing and despair again taking her as in the jaws of a lion, her eyes rolling wildly. Thanks be to heaven that the dear angel, Sarah Prior, was with the afflicted widow at this time, when one harsh sentence would have dethroned reason. And thanks to heaven that her pastor was absent. He was a man whose great constitutional hope and iron nerve spoiled him for comprehending despondent persons, or for sympa-thizing with them. He was unsparingly harsh toward them, pronouncing all who doubted their acceptance with God, heirs of perdition. "Oh dear," the poor woman exclaimed, "is John Barlow in hell?"

"No, no, dear Mrs. Brown," said Sarah, laying her hand kindly on the fevered brow of the afflicted woman. "No, that good man is not lost. His blameless life assures us of that."

"Our minister told me to-day, that John Barlow was dead and damned; and that if I did not arise from my melan-choly, I would soon follow him;" and Catherine Lane re-peated his words after he left, and added that she had never doubted her own acceptance, and believed all who doubted were damned.

Sarah Prior sighed to think of her conversation with Catherine an hour before, and to think their well meaning and devout minister had, by his harsh manner, driven to despair the good John Barlow, by harshly striking his heart when it was bleeding for his lost sons; when it needed the soothing influence of sympathy.

"Oh," she mentally exclaimed, "that I may never

'Deal damnation round the land,
On each I judge thy foe.'"

"No, my dear sorrowing sister, God kindly cared for his servant John Barlow when reason was lost, and he leaped from the river's bank." Sarah Prior took Mrs. Brown to her own house and gently cherished her, as a nurse cherisheth her children, carefully keeping her from seeing the minister, until her nerves got strength.

THE VALUE OF VIRTUE.

Augustine, in opposing Pelagius, carried the doctrine of grace to the extreme of unconditional election and predestination. Luther went to the same extreme in opposing the doctrine of merit of works, as held by Papists, and D'Aubigne, in opposing German and French rationalism, carries the doctrine of grace to the same extreme; and being determined to abolish all middle ground between Pelagianism and Calvinism, he disturbs the ashes of the venerable Erasmus, to rank him with the rationalists. All this tends to disparage the virtues of honesty, benevolence and mercy. In the preaching of this day there is much said of morality and moralists; indiscriminately condemning them, sometimes giving the moralist the lowest place in hell. One pronounces benevolence and mercy mere appetites, another pronounces them mere impulses, consistent with the most wicked and depraved heart; while, at the same time, he considers some degree of avarice and selfishness consistent with a state of grace, and even cruelty and dishonesty lamentable infirmities of the elect, but not sufficient to exclude them from the divine favor.

Such teaching tends to destroy the confidence of sensible men in Christianity. They cannot appreciate a religion that is not to make men more honest, benevolent and merciful; to make them better citizens. They appreciate virtue wherever they find it in this sinful world, and they appreciate it far more where it rises spontaneously, call it appetite, or impulse, if you will, than where it arises by the restraint of fear. We say much of principle, against impulse. This is well, when not carried to the extreme. Certainly, there seems to be more virtue in one whose heart melts impulsively when he sees suffering humanity, and who impulsively gives liberally for relief when he sees want, and melts in mercy toward his penitent enemy, than in one who grudgingly does all under the restraint of fear of hell.

We ought to act from principle; to do all with an eye single to the glory of God; but the cold, calculating man who has no spontaneous outgushing humanity, we have reason to fear acts more from fear than from love. Here is the great stumbling-block, the great hindrance to the reformation of the world. I would treasure up all the virtue which I can find in this world of cold selfishness, injustice, cruelty, dishonesty, pride, envy, ill will and oppression. I thank God for the little light which beams through so many clouds. I would lose none of it by scrutinizing the creed or profession of any man. Oh, that we might hold up before all our congregations the model Christian who loves God with all his heart, and loves his neighbor as himself; who does to all as he would have them do to him; who always

feels the high and holy emotions of human brotherhood;
whose soul never feels the frost of avarice or sordid selfishness; kind, forbearing, gentle, meek, a peacemaker, a
soother of the afflicted.   Then would men give heed to the
preached gospel.

THE OLD OX.

The old ox lay by the rail-fence chewing
       His cud of straw;
The north wind roared and along was strewing
       The winter snow.

There close by his side the snow was drifting,
       His head was cold;
Deep in their sockets his eyes were sunken,
       For "Bright" was old.

He had long since seen old "Buck," his brother,
       All skinned and torn;
The hide was already tanned to leather,
       Made up, and worn.

Chew, chew, for the night of rest's declining,
       Man's voice I hear,
Chew, for ere the morning sun is shining,
       Oh, he'll appear.

And then on my back, all hard with scourging,
       The lash will fall,
And ere my straw I have half done gorging,
       Loud he will bawl,

Whoa, whoa haw there; quick, old Bright, come under,
       Confound you, move;
Come along, come along quick, and if you blunder,
       The lash you'll prove.

When in my calfhood I oft was playing
    About the lair,
Or away o'er the green meadows straying,
    The world was fair.

Oh, the pain I now feel in recalling
    The galling yoke ;
Goaded on at all manner of hauling,
    No word I spoke.

Mo, oo, oo, the cold north wind is piercing
    My aching heart,
Hush now, hush, the tyrant's whip is cracking,
    I feel the smart.

Don't, master, don't; all my bones are aching;
    I'm poor and old;
Spare me, oh, spare me, my flesh is shaking
    Now with the cold.

Thrice he tried, when he succeeded rising,
    So weak with age ;
All the while the master stood chastising,
    So filled with rage.

Lo, when again I passed the tyrant's dwelling,
    Old Bright was dead;
The hide was gone, hungry swine were trailing
    His bones and head.

OUR DUTY TO KNOW GOD IN HIS WORKS.

Pollok writes of one who thought the sensible horizon the boundary of the world, and thought the moon no larger than his father's shield, who lived happy and was saved.

This is very well. Every benevolent mind will rejoice in the thought that the poor idiot had a quiet life and was saved; but this touch of the poet's fancy may encourage mental ignorance, especially when followed by the description of one who "had all knowledge human and divine," who lived miserable and was damned.

The idiot's happiness was negative; too much like that of the shell-fish, which, fixed to the rock, has no care about labor or property, no care to know the nature or extent of the element in which he lies. We can know but little of that future state to which all are tending; but reason would teach, and revelation does not deny, that the salvation of the idiot is hardly positive enjoyment. That he enters heaven a mere infant in the knowledge of God, of his attributes, will, law or government. He may there advance from that state, and grow in knowledge forever. The idiot is not to blame. He has the compassion of man, and of his Creator; he could not be wise in his imperfect body· There is, however, no excuse for the ignorance of those who are born with ordinary faculties, and surrounded by every favorable circumstance for obtaining knowledge.

Mental ignorance must be regarded as sin against God, and against ourselves. It is our duty to know the works of God. It is our duty to avail ourselves of schools, if we can, and if we cannot, we may have books. And as to time, we may gain extensive knowledge in our resting moments, on the workbench, on the plow beam, or on the stump or log, where we are felling the forest trees. While laboring we can think. Can that man be acceptable to God who cares not to know whether the stars are buttons in a blue tent over his head or a universe so extensive that our earth, in comparison to it, becomes more insignificant than a grain of sand? Whether the most distant star is within the eagle's flight, or so far away that its light, though moving at the rate of two hundred thousand miles in a second, would be many thousands of years in coming to our world? Or whether the bright star, which, during a part of the year, ushers in the morning, is really as much smaller than the moon as its apparent size, or a globe as large as fourteen hundred worlds like ours?

Surely we should behold the Almighty Hand in the heavens, holding the sun in his place, and whirling on its axis that enormous globe, the dimensions of which surpass all human comprehension; moving through their orbits the planets, in such order that no jar or confusion ever happens; so that transits, conjunctions, and eclipses may be calculated to an hour and minute thousands of years beforehand; and holding the north pole of our earth a fixed number of degrees above the plane of its orbit, producing the perfect order of the seasons, and governing its diurnal motion, producing day and night.

Can he be a worshiper of God who, from year to year, plants his seed and reaps his harvest, and walks through his fields and forests without beholding the Creator's Hand in the laws which govern the vegetable kingdom? The swine eats acorns without knowing that they fall from the trees. Shall we in like manner eat and drink? How many are so regardless of the wisdom of God in the animal kingdom that they never learn the science of the circulation of the blood, the office of the stomach, bowels, kidneys, liver, spleen, heart, or lungs? They know not why they of necessity have brains and know not whether the nerves are solids or fluids. They see, hear, and feel, but they know not why. They rise and walk, but know not why, and if asked why they eat or breathe, they could give no rational answer. They know not why their bones move at the joints. They stupidly behold the burning of wood, but never think of the cause, and think it annihilated when gone.

PRIDE.

Few terms are more in use than pride, yet few are used more vaguely, or with more ambiguity. Some good writers make this term synonymous with self-esteem. If this be its standard meaning, pride is neither virtue nor vice, only as circumstances make it so. Webster defines pride, "inordinate self-esteem." This is its Scripture meaning. Self-esteem is not in its nature sin; without it man would be a bad citizen, and a bad Christian; but when self-esteem becomes inordinate, or excessive, it is sin and the parent of innumerable and manifold sins. Many confound pride with vanity; they should be kept distinct. Pride arises from love of approbation. Love of approbation is not in its nature sin, but when it becomes inordinate, or excessive, it is sin, and the parent of innumerable and manifold sins. When love of approbation prompts to superfluity and extravagant expense, in carriages, houses. furniture, or clothing, while half the human family is suffering from want, it is a great sin. Without love of approbation man would be a bad citizen and a bad Christian, yea, a candidate for crime, for prison, and the gallows. Self-esteem and love of approbation are given of God, and, properly regulated, are the foundation of much excellence in human character. Pride makes a man haughty and overbearing; vanity makes him fawning and flattering; pride makes him cold, forbidding and unsocial; vanity makes him smiling, courteous and social. Pride sometimes makes a man coarse in manners and dress, even a sloven, regardless of public taste; vanity generally makes him extravagantly refined, neat, courteous and polite, almost adoring taste.

Diogenes was one of the proudest sages of all antiquity. He once came into the mansion of Plato, and leaped upon the rich sofa exclaiming, "I trample on the pride of Plato." "Yes," said Plato "but with greater pride, Diogenes."

This was true.   Diogenes was the more proud, but Plato was more vain.   The vanity of Plato prompted him to build and furnish his mansion with great cost to please the taste of his guests ;   while the pride of Diogenes prompted him to hold public taste in contempt.   This proudest man in Athens went about in his filth, and often slept at night in a hollow log, or tub in the streets of the city.

The proud man courts popular favor, not from any love of friendship, but from a design to make the people his tools in accomplishing ambitious ends.   The vain man courts popular favor from love of friendship.   He smiles and shakes hands sincerely, while the proud man smiles and shakes hands hyprocritically.   The vain man is sometimes generous and philanthropic; the proud man is sordidly selfish.

Sometimes a haughty and overbearing man, conceited and unteachable, cold and forbidding in spirit, coarse and eccentric in dress, and rough and unpolished in manners, becomes a loud declaimer against pride.   Such a man has sometimes guarded the love-feast door, proudly tramping on the feelings of almost every woman who presented herself for admittance.   Nothing is more contrary to Christianity than pride.   It is the foundation of oppression and tyranny, and also of political bigotry.   Sectarianism or religious big-otry will be the bane of Christendom, until pride of opinion is removed.

Oh, may the day hasten when men will learn of the Prince of Peace who is meek and lowly, when humility will break down the walls where error is entrenched, and bring together in brotherly love the servants of God from all the jarring sects in Christendom !

HOLY WEDLOCK.

MR. EDITOR: I wish to record something on this subject before I go hence—before my pen falls from the hand palsied in death. The sanctity of the family relation is the basis of the order and happiness of human society. There is no analogy between the condition of brutes and the social state of man. They are sensual, but he is intellectual. The distance between men and brutes is almost infinite, and yet how like brutes the most of men have lived since the fall. Licentiousness has been the universal sin of pagan nations. It has been represented as common in the celestial regions among their gods, and has been practiced in the most revolting manner in their temples. The Mosaic dispensation came when all earth was enveloped in darkness, and arose a glorious light in the east. It was, however, like the morning star; the gospel, as the rising sun, has followed, and now its glorious light covers many nations. The morning star is lost in day, and in this glorious light how clearly we see the sacredness of the family relation! Woman's rights are seen, the Savior's golden rule drives polygamy from Christendom. The cruel tyranny of man over the physically feebler sex is broken where the gospel exerts its influence, and woman arises in all her potent loveliness and worth, as the chaste virgin, but still more as the discreet matron at the head of her household. Oh, the beastliness of man, who would remove her from her devoted and important position, thus breaking the chain of order! Woman is naturally chaste. Had this not been true, the art of seduction would never have been studied. That woman is naturally chaste, is disputed by a few men who see no beauty in chastity, but who would be glad to see the whole earth one far-spread harem of pollution. But what is their opinion when opposed to the opinion of all the virtuous in Christendom? Woman is naturally chaste; many female

slaves have committed suicide to avoid dishonor.   A female
slave, sold some years ago to a libertine of the far South,
broke away from her keepers in the thronged street, and ran
for her honor.   She attempted to cross a bridge, but saw
men before and behind and on all sides, preventing her escape.   She looked on the dark water, and then gave a last
look o'er the landscape, and o'er the city with its church-
spires pointing to heaven.   But, alas! there was no hope of
help from American Christians.   She leaped from the bridge
and went, unpolluted, beneath the dark waters.

But if woman is naturally chaste, why do some

"Fall like stars that set to rise no more"?

Because all human ingenuity is exercised to effect their
ruin.   Man besieges the strong fortress of pure intention,
and when the base wretch succeeds, and like a demon,
looks down upon his victim, fallen to rise no more, it then
becomes him to slander the whole female sex.   Among the
wrecks of woman, those living in infamy in our larger cities,
and dying often in the morning of life of infamy's own pestilence, almost unburied and unmourned, even whose end
gather such awful clouds of gloom, how few could be found
who came to this awful condition from choice! Standing by
the rudely-finished and obscure grave of one of these, it is
natural to ask, "Had she a mother's counsel?"   The
answer will often be "No."   Whose eye saw her simple and
unadorned beauty when she was rising unto youth, innocent
as the flowers of the plain?   Was it one whose Christian
soul admired her purity, one ready to aid her to rise to
woman's noble dignity in our social state?   No, it was one
who had no soul to admire female innocence and purity;
one who had no interest in her honor or happiness, in time
or eternity.   Oh, demon that he was, he looked on her with
unholy lust, and followed her with his plans, professing to
be her best friend.   His purpose gained, she was thrown

from his protection.   Now feeling that she was fallen to rise
no more, she only wishes to escape from pollution and go
into obscurity, and to live and die in repentance.   But, turn
which way she will, she is met by some arch fiend, some
adept in the art of seduction, and is hurried on, step by
step, the downward way, till she awakes in eternal fire.

I recently witnessed the conversion of a young lady, the
adopted daughter of a pious family in this western valley,
picked up by them from a hopeless condition when a child,
in an eastern city, and watched over these many years past
by the mother who adopted her with all of a mother's solici-
tude, with counsels and tears and prayers, until she saw her
adopted into the church militant.   Oh, what a worthy example! Would to God that there were thousands of such
mothers in Israel.   Holy wedlock is woman's defence, and
the guaranty of woman's power.   She thanks the gospel for
the influence she exerts over the rising generation.   How
beautiful is the sanctity of home! What an outrage is American slavery upon the rights of woman, and upon the sanctity
of home, and the family relation! Viewed in this light alone,
how can it fail to shock the moral sensibilities of every
Christian ?

There now lies before me the authentic account of the
lodgment in jail in the city of Alexandria of Emily Russel,
by one who has lately purchased her for speculation, and
now offers her for sale to any American Turk for his harem.
Her mother, a worthy citizen of N. Y. city, wishes to purchase and save her from pollution; but failing to raise
$1800, is obliged to abandon her daughter in despair, to go
to the embrace of the tyrant libertine, or to premature death
by suicide.   A mother obliged to purchase her own child,
and for want of means, must see her borne shrieking away
in the grasp of a human fiend!   And that in Christian
America! What baser act was ever perpetrated in Con-

stantinople? Could anything more detestable have happened under Tamerlane? By the institution of slavery, the
sanctity of the family relation, with three millions of people,
is trampled down as though there was not a God to see it.
What is national compromise, or what is national constitution with me, so far as they uphold universal concubinage
and rape? "Shall we obey our dead father or the living
God?" Holy wedlock is one of the achievements of Christianity. Infidelity has always hated the restraints of the
gospel. Not only the vulgar, but even the most refined infidels of the present century and the past, have hinted that
when their principles triumph, the marriage obligation will
cease, and men will be as free from restraint as brutes.
Such principles and such hopes are almost wholly confined
to the male sex, and we are ashamed for humanity and for
our country, to have to record in this dark catalogue the
name of one woman. We could wish, for the honor of her
sex, that oblivion would cover the memory of Frances
Wright. But oblivion cannot. Her great, though shockingly perverted, intellect has given to her notoriety, and her
hateful name will go down on the page of history, a dark
and filthy spot to future generations.

Public opinion needs reforming. It is unjust and partial.
A villainous wretch pursues his victim with untiring zeal,
with all the arts of seduction, hypocritical smiles, and vows
of perjury. His object gained, his victim is "Cast abandoned on the world's wide stage," an outcast from charity;
while he expects to be received into virtuous society, and
smiled upon by virtuous woman. Virtuous woman smile
upon an incarnate devil! The thought is shocking. If for
anything woman deserves unmeasured censure, it is for not
driving by her frowns such base wretches from all respectable society. Should we feed and pamper wolves about our
sheep folds?

The libertine's triumph will end, Christianity will reform public opinion, and deal equal justice to the male and female offender. The gospel will throw a bulwark around the sacred family relation, on which stands the order and happiness of human society.

SACRED MUSIC.

Do not be alarmed at this caption. I can now say what I said ten years ago, when the church at Leoni came near being destroyed by discord about music. "Brethren, be in harmony, and I will agree to anything; have a melodeon, or have none; put your best singers in that corner, where you have had them, or in another corner, or in all corners, or distribute them through the chapel, or be Quakers, and have no singing, and I will cheerfully submit."

What would have become of us if the gospel had only been adapted to such philosophers as Plato, Seneca, and Newton, and music only suited to critics, trained in the school of Handel? Geniuses come like comets, one in a century. So came Timotheus, Mozart, Handel, and Paganini; and common music teachers start after them, as a meteor, born of a little swamp, starts on the track of a comet.

Which are the real followers of the great masters,—they whose artificial and mechanical singing pleases one in fifty, or the simple, earnest singing which moves the multitude? Christian influences should be adapted to mankind as they are, and take effect at once.

Fifty years ago, when Calvinists abhorred camp-meetings, they conceded that the singing surpassed anything that they had heard. When all Methodists sang, simple, earnest, thousands were melted by this influence, and brought to Christian experience. Is such the effect of the singing by a hired choir in a Methodist congregation now? Every one must answer no. Every aged man sees that this great instrumentality of early Methodism is nearly lost. Let men study the science of music, hold their concerts, and gratify the few who are called men of taste; but after all, this will never reach the masses to whom we are sent to preach the gospel. At the camp-meeting the singing reminded me of Methodism in childhood. All the Indians sang; a man of eighty-six, a woman of ninety, and a child of four years joined their voices with the multitude, whose soft Indian voices made the woods vocal as the sound of many waters. There was sacred music which swayed the multitude of Indians, and even melted the few white people, who knew nothing of the Indian tongue. Of all these, few, if any, ever heard of a singing-master, or a singing-book. While I could have listened with delight to this sweet and soul-stirring music from the rising to the setting sun, I thought of hired choirs, where I had sometimes preached, a half dozen proud young men and women hired to do this part of the worship for hundreds of good Christians, who stand awkwardly gazing about in silence. These naughty singing girls, always seated directly before me, have sometimes severely annoyed me through the sermon, by giggling and hunching. One howled the alto, much like a small dog, that used to perch on his haunches in the middle of the church, and lifting his nose toward the stars, join in the singing ; yet I do not remember that we paid him anything, even a bone to gnaw.

Our congregational singing is often cold and powerless. Our chorister slowly fumbles for his hymn, wipes his spectacles and puts them on, to help him think what tune to use. " Well let me see, New Durham; yes, New Durham will do"; I stand impatiently waiting, having tried to read the hymn with some effect, and fearful the impression is wearing away, cooling off. Now he is slowly searching his note-

book for New Durham. There, he has found it; now he
strikes his tuning fork, holds it to his ear, then sounds a
mournful note a few times, and all begin, with one eye on
the notes and one on the hymn. By this time the Indians
would have sung us up above the stars.

Hart, Oceana Co., Mich., Aug. 28, 1866.

THE IMAGINATION.

Imagination is the gift of our benevolent Creator. Without imagination, human life would be dull, sordid, groveling
and brutish. Man would follow his animal instincts; only
adding to these a crude and limited knowledge of facts, and
the dry calculations of gain; below the bee and the beaver
in instinct, and scarcely surpassing them in knowledge.
Imagination is the parent of invention. Although accident
has often given the first hint to the great improvements in
art and science, yet it is imagination which has traversed
the vast fields of experiment, where suppositions are tried,
again and again, until truth is deduced. When Newton
measures the dimensions of worlds, Locke travels back to
the point where the first idea is written on the canvass of
the soul, and from it traces all the development of the mind;
Watts and Fulton make the wonderful application of steam,
and Morse unites human tongues with lightning around the
world.

Poetry next demands our attention; we mean the poetry
of the soul, which the Creator has given to all who will improve it. This may be expressed in measured verse, or in
prose, or even be never written; yet it exists in every willing mind, enabling toil-worn and weary man to recreate
himself in beautiful ideal fields. Here let the sick forget
their pains, the lame forget aching limbs, the poor forget
their wants, and the friendless walk awhile with the gentle

and good, amidst loving countenances, beaming with heavenly light; let poor, exiled man go back, at times, to Eden,
from the swamps, and bogs, and deserts of earth; let the
slave be free.

Some writers, both of the religious and secular press, are
very severe on the exercise of the imagination, depriving the
sorrowful, the weary, and the oppressed of these consolations.   They talk gravely of the enervating influence of
these wild fancies, and counsel us to keep them facts.
What are the facts to which they would keep us? Shall we
follow their

> Unpoetic, calculating scholars,
>
> In lust, and rum, and pork, and dollars?

Or shall we follow the wild fancies of the imaginative Watts
to "Jordan's stormy banks" to view the "Transporting,
rapturous scene?" Our matter-of-fact men in America and
in England are reconciled by long custom to sing this imaginative hymn, and travel where

> "Rocks and hills and brooks and vale
>
> With milk and honey flow,"

but many a grave Puritan in Scotland, hearing this song in
church, would take his hat and go home to his rum and
pork, ready on the morrow to recount his dollars, and would
feel very saintly in so doing.   Nearly all of the language of
Scripture is figurative.   Spiritual things are illustrated by
material things; all the imagery of the universe is used, the
sun, the moon, the stars, seas, rivers, mountains, plains, gulfs,
pits, fire and smoke, winds, clouds, snow and rain; all domestic beasts, serpents and dragons, and beasts of prey.
Woodlands and gardens are used, springs, wells and brooks
of water, thunder and lightning, whirlwinds and tempests,
earthquakes, marching armies and battle scenes, houses,
temples, cities, grain-fields, vineyards, lanes, gates, roads,
etc.

In these vast fields of imagery, the ancient writers took almost boundless license. The early ages were eminently the ages of poetry, when the imagination was untrameled, flying everywhere, free as the bounding roe or soaring eagle.

The original Scriptures are in the language of the ages in which they were written. Figures of speech are such as men used, such as they understood; and if we would understand the Scriptures, we must become acquainted with men who lived two, three, and four thousand years ago, and enter into their imaginative spirit.

The glowing fancy of the ancient Orientalists gave life to everything, gave everything a heart to beat, eyes to see, a tongue to speak, and feet or wings.

From the earliest ages, religion, morals, philosophy, and even science was taught by parable, or supposed narrative.

Our Saviour adapted his language to his hearers, speaking Hebrew when that language was best understood, and Greek when that tongue was spoken. He would quote the Septuagint where that was best understood. He spoke in parables, according to the universal custom of the East.

How childish to attempt to show the name of the Prodigal Son, or the name of his father, or the name of his country, or the name of the rich man!

This method of teaching has great advantages. Mrs. Stowe has accomplished more in writing "Uncle Tom's Cabin" than she could have accomplished in writing the literal narrative of five hundred persons. Following the Eastern custom, which Jesus sanctioned by his own example, Mrs. Stowe has drawn the picture of American slavery, and made an impression on the world more deep than any uninspired author ever made since the world began.

At the great mass-meeting at Jackson, when the Republican party was born, a light mulatto ascended ¦the stage, when a cry arose, " Who is that?" " A fugitive slave," said some one. "It is George Harris," said another. "I am a part of George Harris," said the speaker, "for six men at least, are represented in George Harris." If Mrs. Stowe has condensed the essence of the history of six men into one, she has done well; and if she has condensed six hundred into one, she has done better.

If she has drawn a true picture of human life in America, her book is as true as the archives of our nation—true as the life of John Wesley.

If the author of the "Prince of the House of David" has laboriously toiled through the great fields of Oriental literature, and has become one of a million in his knowledge of human nature and modes of thought eighteen hundred years ago, and has condensed this knowledge into a small volume which every man can read, drawing his picture faithful and true, he is a great benefactor.

It would be well if all who lift the cry of "Novel," "Romance," "Fiction," "Lie," against these works, were as truthful in their speech. We would not be too severe on those who condemn these works, although they, in their wholesale inquisitorial censorship, condemn the Saviour of men, and the Spirit of inspiration.

"Cry louder, for he is a God," "Rivers of waters run down mine eyes," "The world would not contain the books," "Then said the bramble," "The mountains skipped like rams," "A husbandman planted a vineyard," "A certain man had two sons." The censorship of our conscientious inquisitors would condemn these, and a thousand other passages of Scripture. They would shrink from calling so large a part of the Bible lies, yet their definition of lies includes all this.

We find no fault with censorship which discriminates. We only find fault with that indiscriminate censorship which condemns all free exercise of the imagination, condemns a method of teaching which is older than history, and sanctioned by the wisest sages of antiquity.

That this method of teaching has been abused, has been enlisted in the cause of evil, no one disputes. Knaves have written romance, embellishing and making attractive the vilest deeds of man. Licentious men and women have written romance covering sensual pollution with gilded gauze; attracting, enchanting and decoying the young to ruin. These polluting books, so covered with outward decency as to escape the censorship of civil law, meet the unwary everywhere, on all the thoroughfares, in hotels, reading rooms, and in nearly all book-stores. Another class of romance whose name is legion, which fills ten thousand volumes, and crowds on to front pages in nearly all secular monthlies and weeklies, semi-weeklies and dailies, while not directly poisonous, is yet a waste of ink and paper, a waste of time and brains. This class consists of love stories, mere love stories. We do not charge the writers with licentious fancies, or with any immoral design, nor do we join in the indiscriminate cry against sentimentality.

We condemn them because their sentimentality is trashy and simpering, because they teach nothing, they develop nothing in man's moral or intellectual nature. They do nothing to make the world wiser, holier, happier or better. They do nothing for human progress. While other writers, as moralists, philosophers, and men of science, toil like veterans to develop man in all that is noble and Godlike, these simpering sentimentalists are satisfied to see their readers standing still, doing nothing, absolutely nothing, for the honor of God or the welfare of man. Selfish drones, lounging and fawning life away, leaving not a mark on the path of life to show that the world is better for their having lived. Public sentiment may be lenient, but the judgment of the

Almighty cannot fail to be terrible on those who live for pleasure and ease.

We leave this trashy literature, simply adding, these love stories are cut from one pattern, up to one hundred thousand, which pattern is in substance expressed in the following stanza:

> They loved, and swooned, fell out and cried,
> Made up and married and the old folks died.

Let us not condemn the good with the bad. We should discriminate. The cry of Novel against such works as are named in the commencement of the essay, is only equaled by the cry of fiddle against all beautiful instrumental music; and there is analogy between declaring that all the instruments on which David bid us praise the Lord are different parts of the mouth and throat of singers, and declaring that our Saviour's parables are all narratives of facts which had literally occurred.

Wise men would bring every instrumentality which is good in itself into the service of the Lord, and use it for human progress. Music is good in itself, the parable is good in itself, the imagination is good in itself; and if all have been used, or rather abused, in the service of evil, let us spoil the enemy and bring all into the service of the Lord.

Children and youth are fond of pictures. This taste is a wise provision of the Creator, for here is a vast field of knowledge. Pictures sometimes teach more in a day than books could teach in a month. We should be very unwise to shut this vast field from our children, because many pictures are corrupting, some lead to licentiousness, and very many incite to the wicked spirit of war. Let us discriminate, and cast away corrupting pictures. Children, youth, and indeed all people, have a relish for written pictures of human nature.

Superstition may make war on this natural taste and kill

it in the bud, by indiscriminately committing to the flames every work of romance, and placing the veto-mark on every moral tale in our religious journals, and accomplish more than we intend. We may make dwarfs of the moral and intellectual natures of our children. Some children, from whose hands Mrs. Stowe's books would be snatched, and especially "Don Quixote," or "Robinson Crusoe," finally break from restraint and rush to ruin. Their promising ambition, being denied a healthy channel, finds its way into the channel of debauched literature, which leads to death.

An able religious journal, the *Christian Herald*, supposes that three-fourths of the Sabbath-school books of our country are religious romance. What sane Christian would commit these to the flames, including that wonderful production of the imagination, "The Shepherd of Salisbury Plain?"

LO, THE POOR INDIAN.

Seeing in the *Wesleyan* an account of the dedication of a meeting house among the Onondagas, I was led to solemn thoughts. I was born in 1805, between the Onondagas and the Oneidas. The first apples which I ate were from their hands, and their hands made the baskets from which my infant hands took the fruit.

In spite of my very bad education, I have always loved the Indians. Although frightened by stories of Indian barbarity, my mind would always come back to kind feelings and settle in the conclusion that Indians well treated would be trustworthy friends. All of my acquaintance with them for more than a quarter of a century in this western country confirms this belief. More than twenty years ago a detachment of U. S. soldiers came into the center of Michigan—where I than lived—to drive off my kind and honest Indian neighbors. It was in Autumn. The poor creatures tried to hide in the dark forests; but they were hunted down and driven away before the soldier's bayonets. Fifty were taken near my house. They were driven beyond the Mississippi, where winter soon came upon them, all unprepared and discouraged. One came back the next summer and told us that nearly all who went from my neighborhood were already dead.

This was a part of the great process of exterminating the Indians. They were promised the land to which they were driven as an everlasting inheritance; but long ago it was in the white man's market. The Indian is driven on again. The white man comes up from the east, north and south, and surrounds the Indian's last inheritance, a little territory south of Kansas; and white men are crowding into that; and we are informed that the Indians must be removed from the Indian Territory. Where can they go?

Men with long faces tell us that the Lord has removed the Indians to give place to the white man. Puritan historians tell us that they, the chosen people, exterminated the Canaanitish Indians and came in possession of their lands, in the name of the Lord. This, however, is all gratuitous; for the Lord never pronounced our Pilgrim Fathers his chosen people, nor has he pronounced the Indians Canaanites. The murder of the Pequods will, at the judgment day, bear too much resemblance to the massacre of St. Bartholomew's.

The grave Jesuit and the graver Puritan must answer for the extermination of twenty millions of American Indians.

DANGER OF TRUSTING EMOTION IN RELIGIOUS EXPERIENCE.

I touch this subject with a trembling hand; fearing that

I shall wound some truly and devout persons. Yet the the subject is so important, that a sense of duty constrains me to speak. Perhaps all deep religious experience is attended by pleasurable emotions. I thank God that it is so. But these emotions may arise from many other causes, having no relation to godliness, and may be mistaken for religious experience and evidences of regeneration and sanctification. Here is terrible danger; for these emotions may arise from the influence of food and drink; from opiates, and exhilarative medicines; from music; from a glowing imagination; from electricity; and most of all from mesmeric sympathy with the spirit of those around us.

I once thought all were holy who, in religious meetings, shouted, clapped their hands and leaped for joy; and I have often mourned in deep sorrow because I was not exercised in the same manner. An experience of forty years has shown that while many holy men and women are exercised in this manner, many others are exercised in the same manner who are guilty of extortion, dishonesty, fraud, falsehood, violent anger, and even licentious practices. So much credit is given to emotion by some religious teachers, that these wicked persons think themselves good Christians, and some even boast of sanctification.

Young people who love the theater will love religious meetings when they are conducted like the theater. At the theater they thought their pleasurable emotions wicked; but at meeting they take the same emotions to be evidence of piety.

I have known some who love horse-racing, and practiced it after they became members of the church, who, at the same time, loved to have a warm and earnest prayer-meeting, a shouting time, or, as they would call it, "a good time." We should find among slaveholders the most extremely and emotional Christians in the world.

A great part of conversions at this day are spurious. Thousands enter into church membership, who live and die in the same temper and spirit that they had before conversion. This is a momentous subject. We are hastening to the judgment, where nothing but true holiness can avail us; where he that has loved his neighbor as himself, and shown it by his life, will be accepted; but woe to him whose self-interest has ruled his life, and can only bring to the judgment the remembrance of his own personal good feelings.

It is absurd to call the most powerful feelings, or emotions, love to God. He that truely loves God loves him intelligently; loves his attributes, character, will, law, and government. He who does not love God worships he knows not what, whether Jehovah, Jupiter, or Woden.

Happy is that people whose pastor instructs them in what God is in their relation to him, the nature of devotion, their relation to man, and all the duties of our social state; who is a peacemaker between contending brethren; who searches out the poor, the sick, and the bereaved; who encourages charity and disinterestedness; and who labors to elevate his parishioners in all useful knowledge. Though his congregation never experiences a frenzied state of excitement, yet he proves himself a good and faithful servant.

CONSCIENCE IN CHRISTIAN EXPERIENCE.

There is a great difference in the natural conscience, or conscientiousness of men; and this has a great influence on religious experience. Some come very easily to the conclusion that they are regenerated, and even sanctified, while others linger longer at the altar, weeping in painful uncertainty about their conversion, and this uncertainty sometimes afflicts them through life.

The former class condemn the latter as feeble and almost

worthless Christians, and some pronounce them no Christians at all. They plead the high character given in the Scriptures, and the woe pronounced upon the fearful and unbelieving.

Perhaps it is almost the universal instinct of man to honor the bold, and contemn the fearful. Our instincts, however though universal, are often wrong and wicked.

The former class have sometimes a very dull conscience, practicing many things of doubtful morality without condemnation, and even those who feel that they are sanctified, are sometimes selfish. Their bold and confident natures include the idea of high personal rights. They are hard dealers, grinding the faces of the poor, and yet they seem to feel no condemnation. They are said to die in the triumphs of faith, and yet they have left a bad account with their neighbors.

The sorrowful and despondent are not all Christians, but among them are some of the most benevolent, and most innocent of the human family; so conscientious that the least wrong act fills them with the utmost pain. Every day they sigh over some wrong in their conduct, though the former class would do the same without any condemnation.

Sometimes this active conscience becomes morbid under physical disease, and then it is impossible for these unhappy people to see any good in anything they can do.

Writers of buoyant hope are often severe on these sighing ones, condemning them in harsh tones, quoting, " There is therefore now no condemnation to them which are in Christ Jesus," " For if our heart condemn us, God is greater than our heart, and knoweth all things." Pastors often bluntly pour these texts, without qualification, on these tender consciences, sometimes driving to despair the most innocent of their flock.

I come now to the most solemn of all things, the death-

bed scene.   They who die shouting are canonized, while
they who die expressing fears for their salvation are given
up as lost.   Is this just?   A death-bed is not always a de-
tecter of the heart.

Some have shouted when they thought they were dying,
and on recovering have shown a bad conscience and led a
very unworthy life.   Some again, who thought they were
dying, expressed fears that they should be lost, but on recovering led a very blameless life.

Faith is certainly essential to salvation; but faith is often
mixed with presumption, while fear is often blended with
meek and trembling reliance on the Saviour.

FANATICISM.

At first view, Luther seems unpardonably coarse and
abusive in saying to the Anabaptists, " I slap your spirit on
the snout," yet after three hundred years, we are unable to
put any better words in his mouth for that occasion.   Nothing more refined, delicate, or courteous would answer.

Those fanatics had abandoned reason as their guide, and
were following impressions which they attributed to the
Holy Spirit, but which Luther, who used reason, attributed
to the devil.   No man can tell, without the use of reason,
what spirit leads him; nor can he tell without the use of
reason, which is a revelation from God, the Bible, or the
Koran, or the Mormon book.   The patriarchs, prophets
and apostles were rational men; they had reason, full, clear,
and indisputable reason, to believe and to know that God
inspired them, spoke to them, spoke through them; while
fanatics take it for granted, without proof, that they are led
by the Holy Spirit; or if they talk of proof, it is not rational, it is merely whim, or fancy, mere feeling.

This is the rock on which Perfectionists were wrecked a

·quarter of a century ago, and some who have borne the name of Nazarite are going to wreck on the same rock of spiritual destruction.   Some of these were deeply pious, honest and conscientious ; but when reason is abandoned, conscience is no longer a safe guide ; for when impressions, or mere feelings, have the importance of inspiration, conscience yields to the greatest absurdities, and even gross immoralities.   Reason is absolutely necessary in secular business ; and in many things God has left us to follow our reason so really, that it might be mockery to ask God to direct us.   It is always proper to pray for wisdom, for a healthy mind and clear judgment, but absurd to ask the Lord whether we shall plow with No. 3 or No. 4, whether we shall feed our team barley or corn, or whether we shall plow in April or in June.   A. is a hundred miles from home in harvest time, enjoying himself in religious meetings.   He asks the Lord whether he is needed at home, when common sense says his grain is going to ruin.   B. asks whether the Lord would have him go home and plant, or stay away all planting-time trusting Providence for a good yield.   C. owes a debt which is due, but he asks the Lord whether he shall go and pay it or wait a month.

An apprentice boy might as well ask the Lord to show him how to make chains, or shoes, or clocks and watches, and save him six years of apprenticeship.   The less there is of such praying and such faith, the more God will be honored.   He has given us reason and common sense, and is honored when we use them, but dishonored when we turn away from them to any idle whim calling it an impression from the Lord.

NOTE.—The compiler heard Rev. Elias Bowen, D. D., in a funeral discourse, enunciate the following : " Religion is the law of reason, the law of love, the law of angels, the law of God."

PROVIDENCE.

" Surely the wrath of man shall praise thee : the remainder of wrath shalt thou restrain."   Psalms lxxvi. 10.

Some Arminians now write and speak of divine Providence in war, in language suited to Calvin's " Institutes." They pronounce not only the present war a necessity, but also the rebellion a necessity.   God is represented as dependent on the war for the overthrow of slavery, and dependent on the rebellion to bring on the war ; and then, of course, he is dependent on the evil tempers of Davis & Co. to bring on the rebellion.   It is now but one easy step to all that Calvin has said of God, " Inciting men to do evil," " Decreeing whatsoever comes to pass." ' This necessarian argument is used to allay the horror that we feel in viewing the battle scene, and the field where ten thousand lie dead and dying.   It is also used to calm the anguish of the bereaved ; but as a necessarian argument, it has no force, unless it goes the whole length of Calvinism, or even fatalism.

As a fatalist, I might view a chain of causes and effects, beginning at the hand of God, and continuing forever, and might see the necessity of the death of my sons.   I have sufficiently described their death ; it is too painful to be reiterated.   Fatalism cannot come to my aid, for it would deny the moral character of all human action, making God responsible for all things done.

There can be no necessity for sin, and God cannot be dependent on sin.   When men are in sinful wrath, it arises from their own motives ; they act freely on their own responsibility ; and if God opens a channel through which this wrath may flow, so that the wrath of man shall praise him, we have no right to excuse this wrath on that account, nor call it a necessity.   I am a firmbeliever in special providence over all men, at all times.   I also believe God brings all the good that can be brought out of all evil human actions; but woe to them who do these actions.

It is presumptuous to say that God could not bring slavery to an end without this rebellion, this war, the destruction of a million of our young men, and five thousand millions of treasure; without the vast ocean of ill-temper that swells and surges between the South and the North; without the great increase of vice from camp life. What would have been the consequence if a host of missionaries had gone to the South, with no question of tariff, no questions of who shall make the most money out of lands in the territories, Northern or Southern men; missionaries with no political questions, no sordid interests, appealing kindly to the heart and conscience of the slaveholder, in the spirit of forbearance and patience? The teaching of Christ, the examples of Christ and his apostles, give great encouragement of success in such an enterprise. There would have been martyrs, but how few compared to the number slain in a battle. The martyrs would have been holy men, fit for heaven, while most of those slain in battle are unholy, and go from the battle-field, where? to everlasting death! The thought is overwhelming to all who send their thoughts forward along the awful ages of eternity. Oh, how can orthodox Christians and Christian ministers talk and laugh over accounts of tens of thousands slain? most of whom have entered on a state of everlasting punishment? We must doubt either their humanity or their honest belief in their creed. The bereaved are told that the son slain might have proved a curse rather than a blessing. Who can suppose this is true of all the dead?

Great liberties are taken with the name of God; men on opposite sides talk as though they were familiar with him, as though he was enlisted for them, and was speaking to them, forgetting that it is three thousand years since he spoke to

Joshua. For more than two thousand years he has not spoken to any king or president, to any sanhedrin, or senate, to any general, in regard to war; yet all, on opposite sides, talk as though he spoke to them daily, as he spoke to Joshua. Great liberties are taken with the word providence. "See what God is doing" is a common expression, when men, with no divine authority, are engaged in the destruction of life and property, and violating almost every moral precept of the Bible. All nations and all parties engaged in war throw the responsibility of all their deeds upon God, under the plea of providence.

In this way every sin in the catalogue of sins is excused, nay, even charged on God in his providence. In this way every crime in the catalogue of legal felonies which would be crime in private life is excused, and passed to that account of Divine Providence because practiced in war. In this state of society no clear distinction between virtue and vice can be impressed on the public mind; hence disbanded armies fill the land with crime.

Solemn is the thought of that day when God shall judge a world in righteousness, when somebody will be called to account for the death of every man slain, from righteous Abel to the last war which shall be waged.

CRITICISM.

Public speakers of equal caliber differ much in influence. One, from a sixty pounder, throws out a thousand little bullets, scattering and lightly hitting in a thousand places; another throws a hundred larger shot, but no one can fix his attention on a hundred objects hit in one discourse; another shoots ten heavy slugs, and attentive hearers can hold their attention to ten points hit; another sends forth one sixty pound ball, which makes such a tremendous smashing where it hits, that not one of a thousand hearers ever forgets its effect; while the wounds of a thousand small shot are forgotten in one hour.

PROFANE SPEAKERS.

I lately heard a preacher say "God bless you" as a mere by-word, seven or eight times in one sermon. It was said in so light and playful a manner as to almost spoil his otherwise excellent discourse.

PRONOUNCING OUR CREATOR'S NAME.

Some ministers say "Gawd" and "Gaw-awd" in their exhortations; and in prayer we often hear, "O Law-ord." If there is no want of reverence in these persons, their language is grating on many ears and tends to degrade public worship.

A pious young lady commenced teaching in a very wicked neighborhood, and praying, perhaps not in prudent language. A boy of a very heathenish family said to his mother on returning from school, "The school-marm kneeled down and swore worse than dad or grandad ever did in their lifetime."

LONG SERMONS.

The great error of my life has been the length of my sermons; not that I have said too much, but that I have used too many words in saying what I have said. All apologies, all talk of self-abasement, all unessential comparisons and illustrations, all language of all mere display of oratory, and a great part of my adjectives and adverbs have been lost; nay, worse than lost, they have clouded the minds of my hearers, causing them to forget what truth I uttered, wearied them, inclined them to stay away from the house of God.

Some speeches of five minutes' length make lasting impressions, and some of two hours' length are forgotten in a day.

SIMPLICITY.

Let us be plain and direct, coming quickly to the judgment, conscience, and heart.   We have known speakers to rise above the clouds, if using high sounding words is rising, and string these words in long dark sentences, with no clear meaning, convincing nobody, instructing nobody. Some call these great sermons, but say they cannot understand them.   They who utter them do not understand them. There is no understanding to them.   They are harangues of great sound, and little or no sense.   It would profit a congregation more to hear a man who has not the use of a hundred words, provided he puts them together so as to be clearly understood.   While time is short, and death is at hand, it is shocking to fill the pulpit with sounding brass.

MODE OF ARGUMENT.

Let him whose infant has taken a razor not snatch it away, but present a more attractive toy; so let him who would win a man from mortal error, not attempt to tear his error violently away, but present truth more lovely and attractive, and let him feel self-convinced.

MANNER OF PREACHING.

Preaching from texts was unknown to the apostles and early fathers.   They were not trammeled by confinement to single passages of Scripture, nor to the rigid order and arrangement now required by all fashionable congregations. They expounded a whole chapter, and sometimes several chapters of Scripture in one discourse, instructing the audience in doctrine, experience, or religious history, as they seemed to need.   In the third century Christians began to take the lead in all useful learning and oratory; and in spite of ten terrible persecutions, Christianity commanded the confidence, respect and veneration of all men.   Each of these persecutions had aimed to exterminate Christianity entirely.

The last, under Diocletian, was the most terrible. This emperor fixed his seat at Nicomedia, where, on Christmas day, he caused six hundred Christians, worshiping in their cathedral, to be locked in and the temple set on fire, consuming them all. This was near the close of the third century. This great persecution, like all that preceded it, being borne with passive submission and forbearance, wrought mightily on the hearts of the heathen, bringing them to see the divinity of Christianity, and millions were converted; so that early in the next century that shrewd politician, Constantine, saw that the time had come to proclaim Christianity the national religion, from motives of policy. Through these bloody persecutions, and during the reign of forty-one pagan emperors, from Tiberias to Constantine, Christianity stood in the power of God, on its own merits. No worldly agency had been brought to its aid; the idea of fighting for religious liberty had never been entertained. "Father, forgive them for they know not what they do" arose from every martyr, and he who had said "Lo, I am with you," walked in beauty and majesty among the patient sufferers whose blood was the seed of the church. The professed conversion of Constantine was a melancholy epoch in the history of the church; when Christ was exchanged for a half barbarian emperor, or head of the church. His savage sons, Constantius and Constans, while Christians were marshaled under their banners, and fighting their battles, and acknowledging them the heads of the church, were monsters of wickedness. They murdered in cold blood all the kindred of the Constantine family. Julian alone escaped and succeeded them on the throne. Their savage deeds drove him from Christianity, and though bearing the hated name "apostate," he was better than his predecessors. From this fall Christianity has never recovered. Oh, when shall it return to its primitive spirit.

SACREDNESS OF THE HOUSE OF DEVOTION.

It would be well to have even the place of secret prayer sanctified, or set apart from all secular business; but yet more the house of worship, where we regularly meet for devotion. In the raging tempests of Utopian reforms, we have heard railings against brick and mortar; and as those tempests move on, we next have railings against ministers, sermons, sacraments and prayer. When we feel no more solemnity in the meeting-house than in the town house or bar-room, we may soon feel no devotion to God. When the meeting-houses of Paris were turned into horse stables, the legislature was ready to vote, "Resolved, there is no God," and eminent statesmen went with the rabble to place a harlot on a throne, and a bishop burned incense to her as the goddess of reason.

Antiochus Epiphanes entered the "Holy of holies," sacrificed a sow on the altar, boiled the flesh and sprinkled the broth through the temple, dedicated the temple to Jupiter, and then succeeded in turning away many Jews to idolatry.

The temple was scarcely more desecrated by swine's broth than our temples by tobacco spittle; indeed swine's broth would be less filthy, disgusting, and nauseating.

Forty years ago all Methodists knelt in prayer. Tobacco making the floors abominable, has fixed Methodists in their seats, and overturned a custom almost essential to Methodism. Let those who must chew and spit remain in the outer court, that is, out of doors, and hear through a chink in the window. If this outer court is too cold, let them stay at home; and if they would know the sermon let them ask their wives.

For thirty years a sense of the sacredness of the house of worship has been diminishing under the influence of lectures, so comic, droll, and vulgarly witty, as to keep congregations in roars of laughter, clapping, stamping and shouting.

If the power of habit is such that a young man cannot go through a ball-room without dancing as he goes, what can we expect of youth who, at the lecture, are expected to clap their hands, stamp, laugh and shout with all their might? They will come into the house of worship scuffling, pushing, tripping, laughing and jesting. They will be disorderly during service, and will go out more like a riot than a religious assembly.

Mr. G. made little impression on the Sabbath, because on Saturday evening he had given a lecture in the same pulpit, at the close of which was sung,

> "Old Tip's the boy that swings the flail,
> And makes the locos all turn pale,
> Hurra, hurra, hurra."

Again, the solemn " Let us pray" on Sabbath morning made little impression, because the last thing the lecturer did on Friday evening before saying " Let us pray" was to sing,

> " Do sign the pledge, and I'll marry your daughter,
> Then said the deacon I'll drink nothing but water,
> Oh, that will be joyful, joyful, joyful,
> When I marry the deacon's daughter."

Will it be said that public taste demands such comic lectures and songs? Then taste is vitiated, and we are tending to a state like that of the tenth century, when buffoonery was the popularity of the pulpit.

Will it be said that fun was the life of the Washingtonian movement? It may in truth be said that excessive fun and laughter, provoking drollery, and vulgar wit ruined that cause, and nearly brought down the whole temperance cause with its ruin. The Washingtonians deserve great praise for their sympathy for the degraded ; but in excessive mirth their enterprise evaporated.

You will point me to some erratic revivalist as comic as a Drury Lane stage, who carries a congregation along in whirlwinds of excitement, laughing, weeping and laughing again. I have seen him, heard him, and know him. I would rather read Shakespeare; for there is genius, while your revivalist has only low wit.   He might act on the degenerate stage of this day, but Shakespeare would be ashamed of him.   Do you tell of his glorious revivals? I have in mind one of them, where he counted one hundred converts, and in two years ninety-nine backslid, and the one who endured was rooted and grounded in the new life by some one, only known to God as a revivalist.

How did Christ preach? It would almost be blasphemous to even suppose him using the language of some popular preachers of our time. We almost turn pale to think of Jesus coming into a lecture, when a learned D. D. or professor has wrought his audience to uproarious laughter.

"No room for mirth or trifling here."

Sin, death and hell are grave themes.   The judgment is grave, eternity is grave.   Treating these themes playfully is the parent of infidelity.   Men often say that the minister does not believe, cannot believe, the doctrines he preaches of endless punishment, while it takes no hold on him.   He does not consider the awful meaning of the word eternity, or he cares little for the souls that perish, while he plays with the people at their homes, and plays in the pulpit, "Courting a smile, when he should win a soul."   "So did not Paul."   Mark his deep seriousness.   "For I have not shunned to declare unto you all the counsel of God."   And this was done "publicly and from house to house," and with "many tears."   He had great heaviness and sorrow, wishing himself accursed from Christ (crucified) for the salvation of his countrymen.   Read the Lamentations of Jeremiah, the fasting, mourning and weeping of Daniel, for their brethren, when they saw the awful consequences of sin. Let the house of devotion be sanctified; the pulpit, the minister, the sermon, the lecture, all be sanctified.   Let us open the doors of the sanctuary with devotion, and walk the aisles as on hallowed ground and silently take our seats, not with salutations and gossip, but with silent prayer.

> " How pleased and blest was I,
> To hear the people cry,
> Come, let us seek our God to-day!
> Yes, with a cheerful zeal,
> We haste to Zion's hill,
> And there our vows and honors pay."

THE MODEL CHRISTIAN.

" I am to start for Liverpool in five days" said Thomas Mason.

"What will you need for outfit, and expenses," inquired neighbor Jones.

" Five hundred dollars," was the reply.

" You have it in hand, I suppose?"

" No, not ten dollars; but I shall have it to-morrow."

" Going to the bank for it then, are you?"

" No, John Johnson owes it, and will bring it."

" Where does John Johnson reside?"

" About a hundred miles from here, at Philadelphia."

" When have you seen him, or heard from him?"

" Not in twelve months; but the money will be here."

Jones laughed aloud, but soon sobered. saying,

" Mason, you are insane, or you are trifling."

" Neither," said Mason; "the money is due to-morrow."

" Due!" said Jones; "is that evidence that it will be paid?"

" It is; Johnson has not failed in thirty years of paying a debt the day it is due."

"Some unforeseen ill-luck may have befallen him; so that he cannot command the money. This is possible, even probable."

"No ill-luck has ever prevented his punctual payment; and if ill-luck has made it impossible to pay me to-morrow, I should have been informed."

"He may be dead; then you know you may fail."

"No, I shall not fail even then, for John Johnson has kept himself prepared for death in this respect for thirty years; somebody will bring the money."

"What sort of unearthly being must this John Johnson be?" said Jones.

"Just such as every earthly being ought to be," replied Mason; "then nearly all the troubles of life would cease. Earth would be a paradise, compared to what it is now. His benevolence and generosity equals his punctuality. All of his income, above the plain support of his family, is given in charity and benevolence."

"I presume," said Jones, "he is cold and rigid in manners, stern and unsocial."

"The farthest from it possible," Mason replied; "he has a smile for everybody, a kind word for everybody; he visits all the sick, and finds the cottages of the poor. He is eyes to the blind, and feet to the lame, he has a word of encouragement for all who are cast down and discouraged, a word of cheer to the despondent. Children take pains to meet him on the street for the blessing of kind words and kind looks, and for the little books and tracts which he sometimes bestows."

"I should expect," said Jones, "that he would be hard with creditors who are not punctual with him to pay as they agree."

"He is prompt," said Mason, "to remind them of their faults; but it is done in so kind a manner that they condemn themselves and usually reform; and he has never found it necessary to sue."

"He must," said Jones, "be seeking a great name, to be esteemed a saint."

"No, sir, you are mistaken; he values reputation only as a means of doing good. He has a low esteem of his sancti-ty. When told of some who slandered him, he only replied, 'I fear they buffet me for my faults; I will try to live so as to be above their reproach.' When others are spoken ill of, he is most scrupulously careful of the truth."

A rap is now heard, and John Johnson enters with the money.

THE BLESSINGS OF A REFINED TASTE.

I would not encourage nor countenance extravagant ex-pense arising from pride. Simplicity and frugality becomes us in this world of want. Millions pine in poverty, the gospel and every benevolent enterprise asks for aid.

We ought, however, to bestow some attention on our-selves, for health of body and mind. Many suppose that this attention is confined to food and clothing, and houses to dwell in, or at most to that mechanical instruction which they call education. Taste with them is a matter of indif-ference, or even of sin. A devout man, passing with his wife the garden of a neighbor, saw a simple and cheap bower of flowering vines. "Why," said the wife, "do you not have such a bower?" "Because," answered the hus-band, "I suppose I am not so proud as my neighbor." An uncultivated preacher, describing the fruits of conversion, said his convert took his ax and cut down the ornamental trees in his yard.

The traveler, passing a house connected with a beautiful grove, often says, "I would cut it down and plant the ground to potatoes." These people are to be pitied rather than blamed. They are destitute of the principal enjoyments of life. But when they make their low taste a standard of morals, and condemn all whose taste is more refined, they become unpleasant and irksome; but they must be borne with patiently, and if they cannot be cured, must be left to such enjoyments as they have.

We are thankful to the Creator that we were not formed wholly for the rather low and vulgar exercise of eating and drinking; but for seeing and hearing, for the enjoyment of refined variety, and for beholding the works of God. The world is the Creator's great garden, in which mountains and plains, hills and dales, rocks and forests, spicy groves and eternal snows, from the grand variety. We cannot, however, see the whole at once, and few can travel.

What a blessing to have a miniature world of our own, a small forest, or grove, and a garden where we have green foliage, cooling breezes, a variety of edible plants, and of flowering herbs and shrubbery, and the songs of birds. What though the cottage be low and homely, it is beautiful; yea, charming, if covered with eglantine and Michigan roses, far superior in its attractions to the princely palace standing on the naked field. The poor have no occasion to mourn their poverty, if they have choice books to read, and time to cultivate a few flowers, and hearts to admire nature. To them the birds sing their sweetest notes, to them the sun rises, spreading its golden hair on the morning mist, and o'er them the fleecy clouds come skirted with vermilion when the sun is sinking to rest.

ESSAY ON THE POLITICAL DUTIES OF CHRISTIANS.

Governments are not of divine right, nor, in a particular

sense, of divine appointment. They are of divine appointment only as they are the effects of existing causes, in the
operation of those natural laws under which God has placed
men as social beings. Men have lived without organized
governments in early times, when they were few and scattered, dwelling far apart, without incurring any guilt in so
doing. They were at liberty so to do. But as they increased, and the land became filled with people, the possessions of different families came into contiguity, and the selfishness of man developed itself in innumerable collisions.
The weak were the prey of the strong, and property and life
were never secure. Under these circumstances the necessity of government became self-evident; and government
arose by the spontaneous choice of the people.

Governments arose under different forms. No form was
of divine right. As the people of different countries were
surrounded by different circumstances, in the operation of
the laws of man's social being, different causes producing
different effects, in one country arose an absolute despotism,
in another limited monarchy, and yet in another a republic.
In a country where men were ignorant and savage, having
little idea of the influence of mind, and paying the highest
reverence to physical force, some gigantic man, possessed of
great animal strength, would attract a multitude around
him, who would delight to do him homage. Thus arose
military despotism. As men advanced in knowledge and
came to have more correct views of their rights, they
checked the prerogatives of their kings, and enlarged their
own privileges. Hence despotisms gave place to limited
monarchies, and these gave place to republics. No one of
these forms could be claimed as of divine right; yet each of
these might be of divine appointment, in the sense above
named, *i. e.*, all may have arisen naturally, as consequences
following peculiar causes, causes peculiar to time and place,

and to the intellectual and moral condition of men. We are aware that these views give great latitude to human volition in the organization of government. In this wide field man is only restrained by his knowledge and conscience. We cannot agree with philosophers, who make conscience to be wholly the creature of education; it must be allowed that education wields a mighty influence over conscience. There must be a wide difference between the conscience of the enlightened Christian, and the savage pagan. It is to the enlightened Christian's conscience that we now appeal. There are among Christians four theories in regard to human governments.

1st, The divine right of kings.

2d, That human governments are usurpations on the divine government, and necessarily of the devil; and that all good men should leave them or cease from their allegiance to them.

3d, That human governments are not usurpations on the divine government; that Christians ought not to withhold allegiance, yet that politics are of the devil, ever have been, and ever will be, until the millennium; and that the millennium will come without the aid of Christians, and in spite of their opposition.

4th, That there are eternal and immutable right principles; that these principles may be dimly read in the volume of nature, and clearly in the volume of revelation, and that Christians ought to understand these principles, and apply them to government.

The divine right of kings is defended by so few in these United States, that it is not important to raise a weapon of opposition. The second theory which requires all good men to withdraw allegiance from human governments, is defended by a large party; but as the writer recently gave his views on the subject in the columns of the *True Wesley-*

an, in essays of reform, it is not necessary to repeat them now. We will at once meet those who tell us that human governments are not usurpation on the divine government; that Christians ought not to withhold allegiance ; yet that politics are of the devil, ever have been, and ever will be until the millennium, and that the millennium will come without the aid of Christians, and in spite of their opposition. To charge such a theory upon men may be said to be ironical and unjust ; but surely such is the vague theory of many, perhaps a majority of the people of this land ; indeed a majority of Christians. They attribute our government to God, and in the next breath cry out with horror against mingling any question of morals or righteousness and politics, on account of the diabolical nature of all governmental affairs, and yet in the next breath, they call on a Christian brother to aid them in carrying out some favorite political measure.

We appeal to them as Christians, and ask them if politics are of the devil, to abandon all political action at once, but if politics are not of the devil necessarily, but have unfortunately fallen into his hands, we call on them to arise and come to the rescue, and take politics from the devil.

On which horn of the dilemma will they hang ? If their theory is so vague that they have no definite idea it is time they were put to the necessity of thinking. We would press home the appeal. Christians, if politics are of God, enter upon political action as servants of God; if politics are of the devil necessarily, and ought not to be rescued, abandon politics at once and forever—hold office no more, nor ever again appear at the ballot box. But if politics are not from their inherent nature of the devil, but have unfortunately fallen into his hands, and ought to be rescued therefrom, arise at once in the name of God and aid in rescuing politics from the devil. How absurd for Christians, all immersed in politics, to boast that they keep politics out of religion! Have they learned to serve God, and mammon? They keep politics out of religion truly, like the gigantic Scotch divine, who, when insulted at table, arose, took off his coat, and saying, "Priest, lie there," cast it under the table, and having now for this emergency entered the service of the devil, took the gentleman who insulted him and cast him through the window carrying sash and glass with him into the street. He kept fighting out of religion by taking off his coat, and when the fighting was over he put on his coat and became a sacred priest. So they keep politics out of religion by taking off their Christian coat on election day, and unblushingly entering the service of the devil. Where have they received liberty to leave their allegiance to God, as often as they act the politican? Recognizing no eternal and immutable right principles, feeling no obligation to search for or abide by such principles, they feel at liberty to range the vast fields of expediency and self-interest, doing as they please. They meet in caucuses and stand at the ballot box, not as the servants of God, not to mingle politics with religion; no, for they have left their religion at home; nay, we feel it is not even there. When men have thus divorced political duty and Christian conscience, they feel at liberty to join a party from self-interest, and however corrupt their candidates may be, however immoral and profane, they will vote for them if they please; conscience is not to be heard, and finally have gone with their party through all their profaneness, till they have elected a profane infidel, they pray that God will grant that he may rule in righteousness.

At the close of this prayer they arise in the pulpit and warn their hearers against all who mingle with politics and religion; yes, they warn the people against men who, with eye single to the glory of God, labor to elect righteous men to office. Is not this atheism? and, alas! this atheism is in the church, and in the pulpit! This atheism has not come at once to pervade our country. It has been here from the days when Thomas Paine was the idol of many of our people in the origin of our government. Happy would it be if this atheism would marshal itself under its own banner; but, alas! it long ago shook hands with the church and compromised with her, and since then atheism has marshaled her strength under the banner of the church.

The fourth theory is this;

1st, There are eternal and immutable right principles, which may be dimly read in the book of Nature, and in the natural conscience, but clearly in the book of Revelations.

2d, The operation of the natural laws, under which God has placed men as social beings, governments arose.

3d, In consequence of man's ignorance and perverseness human governments have been in general very corrupt and imperfect, and have fallen far short of being that blessing to man that God designed them to be.

4th, It is the duty of Christians to labor with untiring zeal and faith to restore governments to righteousness, learning from revelation eternal and immutable right principles, and applying them to governments.

The advocates of this theory are confident that it presents the only consistent ground of Christian action in relation to government.

We are aware that the stereotyped cry of Church and State will be raised against this theory. The cry of Church and State has been loudly sounded as an alarm ever since Thomas Paine ran his brilliant career in this country. But his cry is fraudulently made, for this theory has no tendency to a union of Church and State, as developed in the church establishment on the Eastern continent, and no men are more opposed to such a union then the advocates of this

theory.   Such establishments are the offspring of Popery;
they had their origin amidst the ruins of righteousness and
gospel simplicity.   These establishments, arose not by applying righteousness to human governments, but rather by
adorning the forms of a fallen church with the pompous
robes of state.

Thus Popery arose, and from Popery have sprung the establishments of Europe.   Perhape no being was more instrumental in founding the Church of England than Sir
Thomas Boleyn's dog.   Sir Thomas, father of the celebrated
Anne Boleyn, being sent to Rome by Henry VIII., of
England, to negotiate the divorce of Catherine of Arragon,
was required by the Pope to kiss his toe before business
was entered upon.   This the independent Englishman
would not do.   The Pope, sitting cross-legged, still demanded this mark of humble submission, and pushed his
foot forward, when Sir Thomas's little dog, which had followed his master to Rome and into the palace, mistaking
the push of the Pope's foot for a kick at his master, sprang
forward and bit the sacred toe, on which the Pope broke off
the negotiation and abruptly dismissed Sir Thomas from his
presence.   On his return, Henry, still determined on the
divorce, resolved no longer to wait for the Pope's sanction,
and therefore declared himself head of the Church of England.   Thus arose this establishment, which has been so
often referred to, when the cry of Church and State has
been raised in this country.   But how irrelevant! How
widely different from the union of righteousness with government, which the advocates of this theory aim at!

The advocates of this theory above all men have seen and
exposed clerical and ecclesiastical usurpation and tyranny.
They are maintainers of the largest civil and ecclesiastical
liberty.   They are enemies of Church and State, as it exists in our country, and from this arises the severe opposi-

tion of their enemies.   For there is an unholy union of
Church and State in our country; leading divines courting
the favor of leading statesmen and vice versa, each moved
by self-interest, divines drawing the patronage of the state
and of individual statesmen by unholy compromises, by con-
formity to the world, and statesmen, by hypocritical smiles
of professed friendship, seeking to draw the votes of the
church to their support.   If a voice is raised against voting
for an infidel, some vicious statesman, in the midst of pro·
faneness and debauch, cries out Church and State, and his
favorite clergyman echoes the cry.   Oh, tell it not in Con·
stantinople, publish it not in the cities of China, that in
Christian America no effort can be made to render our
government righteous without raising the malice of our countrymen, and calling up the cry of Church and State.   They
might, with more propriety cry Popery! popery! when an
attempt is made to organize a Christian church.

Do men mean to say that an effort cannot be made to
render human governments righteous without bringing on
us the abominations of the establishments of the old world?
This would be making all the concession that the infidel
asks.   It would be putting the palm into his hand, and
voting like a triumph.   The infidel has long declared that
Christianity tends to corrupt itself.   Shall we concede this?
Never! No, never let this concession be made.   Let us
arise in the name of Israel's God and contend with atheism,
not in a crusade of unholy ambition with carnal weapons,
but with zeal for God and an eye single to his glory, with
spiritual weapons, which shall be mighty to the pulling down
of the strongholds of Satan.   With moral suasion let us
bear men to the ballot-box and to prayer.   Let us push the
battle to the gates of the enemy, and drive him from his
last stronghold, until election days shall be as the solemn
festivals when Israel walked with God, until the ballot-box,

instead of being a filthy hole, filled with every abomination, shall become a sacred ark in which to deposit the honest suffrages of a righteous people.   On our side is benevolence, humanity, philanthropy and truth; shall we be ashamed or dismayed? Shall national pride, clothed in covetousness, and luxuriating voluptuously in the praise of men, make us afraid? Shall the hissing of the profane dismay us? Shall the few who act with an eye single to the glory of God be discouraged, because the wicked are successful, and a pro- fane man, the despot of a plantation, is floated on the blood of men to the chief magistracy of our nation? No we will not be dismayed.   The God in whom we trust is eternal, and everywhere present, and his power and wisdom know no bounds.   " He giveth grace to the humble, but knoweth the proud afar off."   The millennium will come by the in- strumentality of Christians.   God calls all Christians to act at once, and will hold none guiltless that 'disobey.   Chris- tians of America can no longer be sinless going with a mul- titude to do evil.

1849.

CAPRICE OF THE MUSES.

The Muses came when I was born and were about to impose their hands on my head, but when it was almost done, the fickle jades flew away on some other errand.   I have therefore only mingled with the *literati*, sitting behind the door.   I have a thousand times climbed Parnassus al- most, when my feet have slipped, and I have come down. I have never reached the seat of Apollo or his dancing maids.

The poets are not my brothers, only cousins of the third degree, and not proud of that relationship.   I was fortunate in being born since Pope wrote his " Dunciad."   Oh, his cruel pen.

The Muses come, and I feel inspired; my fancy glows; ambition rises, and I hope to equal Milton; when just a little too soon they are gone, and all is spoiled.

Yet I am thankful for the inspiration I have; thankful to be cousin to the poets in the third degree.   It is a blessing to possess some fancy; some imagination; to go on ideal wings to all that is beautiful and sublime over all the earth, even beyond where our feet have trod; beyond what we have heard or seen.   It is a blessing, a precious gift of the Creator, these wings of fancy, on which we go down to the coral gardens in the depths of ocean, to the palace of Neptune; to seat us in his car, and drive for him his steeds along that nether plain, or drive upwards through the weight of waters amid a tempest, till the coursers' hoofs clatter along the summit of the mountain wave, and their flowing manes glow in the lightning's flash.

We stand on Teneriffe and talk with the spirit of the tempest of all the storms which have howled around since the world began.   We ride on a sunbeam, on the graven head of Mont Blanc, and look on a world below; mountain top after mountain top receding, far down glaciers, and cascades, and cataracts, till finally, in the almost infinite distance, lie nestled so cozy the sparkling lakes.

When we measure the heavens, the dimensions and distances of the planets, this is science; but poetry allows us to view the great oceans and long rivers of Jupiter; her high mountains, and deep valleys; the color, stature, and character of her people; her farms, her cities, and her merchandise; her commerce and modes of conveyance by land and by sea.

Thanks to the Creator, not only for manifold blessings in the facts of this world, but also for the wings of fancy on which to fly when our feet are torn and bleeding with the thorns and flints of our earthly path, for pastime in ideal worlds to heal the bruises of adversity and the terrible wounds of bereavement.

The divine inspiration of the Bible is to a large extent poetry, as we cannot comprehend things spiritual but by comparison. Nearly all that is said of heaven is poetry, presenting to our view the most beautiful things of earth, to give us pleasant impressions of a state of being which we cannot comprehend. So also the language of men of earthly inspiration, "fields dressed in green," rocks, hills, brooks, and vales "flowing with milk and honey," is all poetry.

REFLECTIONS BY THE WAY, No. 22.

THE OFFICE SEEKER.

Human nature is the same in all ages, and all lands. Ambition has, everywhere and at all times, been the bane of our social state. Ambition is selfishness; sordid, earthly selfishness. Man loves power and wealth; these mutually command each other. In this man is sordidly selfish; his own pride and passions are to be gratified.

He seeks office—studies law to accomplish his end; studies bar-room oratory, learns the art of disguise, deception, fraud, intrigue, duplicity and sycophancy. He learns to feel the public pulse; carefully watches the popular current; cultivates the power of observation, studies man, and learns human nature. Let Fowler give him what head he may, suavity oils his tongue, his conscience, his spine, and the muscles of his face.

He rents the best pew, listens to the popular preacher, looks grave in church, and sheds a tear, with the same motive that prompts him to laugh on hearing the obscene song, and to mingle with the profane. He spends an hour at church and another at the theater with the same motives. At times he is exceedingly polite and democratic, ready to smile on every face and grasp every hand that can lift a vote. He feeds the hungry, clothes the naked, and visits the sick with the same motive that leads him to the bar-room. He wants votes, wants office. To gain office he will sacrifice his sleep, his peace, his conscience, and his moral self-respect. Truth, righteousness and humanity are all borne down and carried away by the current of his ambition.

He is ever conservative, even when he sees by great discernment coming changes of public sentiment, and shaping his course to these changes seems to be radical; he is even yet conservative; self is still to be gratified.

Policy with him is the Juggernaut, beneath whose wheels Truth and Right are crushed. He is ready to join any society, secret or open, which will help him to the objects of his ambition. He loves revolutions, when they promise an opportunity to build his fortune on the ruin of something; but shuns as he shuns serpents all unpopular reforms. He cares not, though these reforms are faught with humanity, and the honor and glory of God; it is enough for him to know they are unpopular; he then pronounces them fanaticism. He takes not his cigar from his mouth. or his hand from his bosom, when the Press, which is the voice of Truth and Righteousness, is being destroyed; when the fire-brand is thrown into the hall of free discussion.

He is always a hypocrite, a whited sepulchre, with an outward show of the patriot, the philanthropist and friend of freedom. At what he deems the prudent and politic time, he professes conversion to a reform movement, when he judges it will pay.

When Constantine saw that the politic time had come to strike, he professed conversion to Christianity. This was shrewd policy. He aimed to lower the standard of Christianity and reconcile it with declining paganism for political

ends, and thus to strengthen a declining empire.   This was
shrewdly done.   Paganized Christianity rapidly spread and
absorbed the paganism of Europe.   Paganized Christianity
continues to our day.

Christianity stood on its own merits until the death of
Tertullian, pure and uncompromising, yet spreading with a
rapidity that gave promise of the speedy conversion of the
world.   But Christianity lost its integrity and its power in
the compromise with paganism under Constantine.

The office-seeker's conversion to reform is like that of
Constantine to Christianity.   He comes prompted by policy,
by ambition, by selfishness, to corrupt reform, to lower the
standard of reform.

He wants our votes, wants office, wants salary and honor.
Who is this office-seeker?   Who is so ready to lead us, to
pledge us to exhaust our anti-slavery zeal on slavery North
of 36–30, slavery in new territories, or on Lecompton con-
stitutions?   Where was he when Lovejoy fell?   When
Birney's press was cast into the Ohio river?   When Garrison
was dragged through Boston?   When Thompson escaped
through a window the death that awaited him at the door
of a church in New York?   Where would he now be, if this
was the age of martyrs?

How infinitely mean is selfishness! how contemptible the
office-seeker! how wicked is policy, that is regardless of the
glory of God, regardless of humanity!   On the morning before the crucifixion of Christ, Pilate went in and out in
mental agony.   He feared that his prisoner was divine.
Conscience was busy making this an awful hour; but ambition, love of office, prevailed.   Pilate was afraid to offend
the Jews; they might ask the emperor to remove him.   He
vacillated between conscience and ambition, like one between two raging fires.   He tried in vain to persuade the
Jews to suffer him to release his prisoner.   Like the ocean-

tide coming through inlet and bay, the people filled every avenue, every street and lane; crowding like the weight of waters upon him. Their murmurings were like the distant din of war, or the beginning of ocean's storm.

When to his last question the answer, "Crucify him, crucify him," came, like the tempest in its awful strength, conscience gave way, ambition prevailed, and the poor wretch had the consolation to reflect that though he had crucified the Son of God he had followed " *Vox Populi*," and secured the favor of the emperor. We find him next in exile, beyond the Alps, reflecting in that awful morning, when for office he bartered conscience and the Divine power. There he closed his life in the blackness of horror.

In our age, some in seeking office have violated conscience and disputed its authority, trampled the law of God and repudiated its claims; trampled justice and humanity, prostituted talent and genius; in old age tarnished all the honor of their lives by base compromises, and finally died without the office for which all was bartered which was noble and sacred, self-respect, an approving conscience, the divine favor. In spite of " whited sepulchres," infamy records their names. They lived for self, not for the honor of God or the welfare of man.

THE WAR MANIA.

If there is anything in which man in all lands and all ages is a monomaniac, it is his admiration, approval and love of war. This is a prominent feature in man's fallen nature. He gazes with unwearied pleasure on the strong; admires the stiff neck, the hard heart, the defiant look, the haughty mien, and the voice of thunder. His fancy, walking in the light of history, views in the past with indescribable emotions scenes, more sublime from their distance of time, mighty armies moving with vigorous tread, shining epaulettes, brandishing swords and spears, officers on mighty steeds grandly caparisoned, riding to and fro under tossing plumes, giving orders in stentorian tones, forming into line of battle, clarion trumpets sounding; then the shout, the rush, the clang of arms, the victory, the " Te Deum."

Depraved man admires all this and approves because he admires it.   Here in this universal bad taste lies the war mania.   The muses, having no moral scruples, have taken advantage of this bad taste; have inflamed it nearly to madness, and wrought men into devils, by inspiring their earth-born sons to clothe with the highest glory heroes and battle scenes.

If this ungodly work had been left to heathen literature, it would be well; hero worship would have perished with the expiration of the worship of Mars and Woden.   Christianity is to convert swords into plowshares, to cause men to learn war no more ; but after eighteen centuries our literature is, in this respect, but little better than that of the worshipers of Venus and Minerva.   Objections have been raised to reading Homer; but I have stronger objections to reading Headly and Abbott.   The former I read as a heathen, whose ideas of martial glory sink in the same tomb with pagan worship, while the latter are accounted Christians, divines, expounders of the doctrines of the Prince of Peace.

These living writers corrupt our youth. They have "stolen the livery of heaven" in which to inflate their vanity in wreathing the brow of murderers; not murderers of one, or three, of their fellowmen ; such they leave to the gallows ; but murderers of hundreds, thousands, millions; these they wreathe and worship, and would fain bring the millions of our ardent boys to their own heathen spirit.   This is the heathen literature that lies in the way of Christian progress.

Our sons are taught, or should be, while they in fancy tread the decks of Agamemnon's fleet, or follow Hector's bloody corse, dragged by Achilles around the walls of Troy, or witness the strife of gods, or a scene of bacchanalia, that all this belonged to a heathenism now obsolete.

Alas for Christianity! for truth! the war mania is in the brains of doctors of divinity.

We leave Macaulay to his opium and his fame, in his labor to prove George Fox a fool, and Penn a hypocrite, while we keep our attention to an eminent divine of our own republic, of our Protestant faith, who receives a gold medal from the Emperor of France, a usurper, a perjurer, a murderer, a despot, of no more Christianity than Nero. From his gracious condescension, our D. D. receives a medal for a halo of glory which he spreads over that sea of carnage, which rolled forth from Paris in 1793, and for twenty-two years rolled on with succeeding waves over Europe, and parts of Africa and Asia, until nine millions of human beings were swept away, with forty thousand millions of dollars of treasure.

Will our spiritual guides tell us in the light of this age that those wars blessed men? Yes, for men are very daring and audacious before heaven. Men in bar-rooms, when about to utter some great falsehood, preface it with an oath. We call it profaneness, and blasphemy. The author of the life of Napoleon tells us of his devout designs in his undertaking, as though he was acting with an eye single to the glory of God, the highest good of men. Away with this hypocrisy! It is no less profaneness and blasphemy because it is uttered in the sanctum of a historian divine. It is audacious to try to join one's self with the Almighty when about to sell one's self to do evil, to catch to the worst feature in our nature's depravity, to beat plowshares into swords, to encourage men to learn war no more. What has the war done to bless men? Where has it brought liberty? Look at France, Spain, Italy, Austria. Forty years have elapsed since the conflict closed, and Europe is still groaning under a debt of ten thousand million dollars. Shall we set no value on the lives of men? One million slain by the revolutionists at La Vendee, one million perishing in the Russian campaign, and nine millions in all? Their blood enriches many valleys; an extensive commerce has been carried on in their bones for manure; while their souls, most of them in as bad a moral state as could be, are gone to their account.

The tears of houseless mothers and their helpless children, who perished in countless numbers in the pelting storm and drifting snow, bore an appeal to heaven. The war mania must cease. It is the direct antagonism of the gospel. Love is the spirit, weapon, and power of Christ's kingdom. Infidels charge Christ with pusillanimity; and Christians fearing this reproach, hold in contempt the idea of "Returning blessing for cursing," "Turning the other cheek," and "Letting him have the cloak also." Alas! how few intend to pay any more attention to these precepts than infidels pay to them!

True courage is wanting—courage to bear reproach, courage to be called cowards. For want of this many deny Christ. Even Wesley failed on this point, and in an apology for Methodists to the crown, represents them as brave warriors, and refers to their conduct at Fontenay. Alas! that Wesley committed this error, and that the conduct of Methodists at Fontenay was emblazoned in the chronicles of Methodism. How many thousands, under its authority, have learned the trade of murder, and died in the act of killing their fellowmen!

That blending of religious and martial enthusiasm at Fontenay, a thing very convenient to our nature, has com-

mitted Methodism during a hundred years to patriotic war.
Men marching quickstep to the music of violin were expelled the church. This was called dancing. Men marching slow step to the music of French horn, bugle, drum and
fife, were guilty of no offense. This was called training.
The former, being in female society, heard no profane or
obscene language; the latter without this restraint, heard
from nearly all who trained, especially in my youth from
returned soldiers, the most loathsome profaneness and
obsceneness that ever shocked the human ear.

The strong objection to dancing was its associations.
Look at the associations of military training! Trifles in
dress kept many an humble female from the love-feast and
sacrament, while a soldier from the camp might pass the
church sentinel with tossing plume and epaulettes, and
kneel at the sacrament with his sword by his side.

The battle of Fontenay murdered one hundred thousand
men. How shocking to see Methodists engaged in such
work; and still more shocking to hear them talking of their
Christian joys while doing their utmost to tear out the hearts
and bowels of their fellowmen; not in self-defense, for they
were far from England, in a distant land.

"THE POWERS THAT BE ARE ORDAINED OF GOD."

Few passages of Scripture are quoted more loosely than
this at this time. Diverse and contradictory doctrines have
been built on this text, and which of these do our present
speakers and writers intend to endorse?

1. The "divine right of kings."

According to this doctrine, James was called to the British throne, because he was third cousin to Elizabeth, and
when Anna died, parliament looked through all Europe for

the blood of the Stuarts; and found, at length, an old Dutch soldier, who had a few drops of Scotch blood; having descended from the Stuarts through a sister of James I.   This was George I. first of the Guelphs.   In like manner the ancient Egyptians searched all their coasts to find the calf in which dwelt the spirit of their god.

2. The divine right of government.

The Non-resistants in British revolutionary times held this doctrine.   They were non-resistants in the Yankee sense; they were ready to fight to the hilt for their government, but never to fight against it, let it do what it would, for "whosoever resisteth the power, resisteth the ordinance of God; and they that resist shall receive to themselves damnation."

3. The freeman right of revolutions.

The believers in this doctrine appeared in the reign of Charles I., and again in the reign of James II., saying, " Resistance to tyrants is obedience to God."

This was the doctrine of the Puritans, and has ever been the popular doctrine in these States, North and South. Nearly all have approved of Cromwell, and the Prince of Orange, and of our former revolution.   Nearly all have approved of the revolutions, secessions and rebellions which in eighty years have resulted in many new governments.

They have found no difficulty in distinguishing between riots that aim at anarchy, and secessions that aim at the organization of fragmentary governments.   The former they condemn, but the latter they approve.   Our government has all along acknowledged the independence of these fragmentary governments, and made treaties with them, provided they were white.

We have educated four generations in the doctrine of the right of revolutions; hence we, that is, Americans generally, have not believed that secession is sin in itself.   Hence the

·sincerity of many in the South, and an extensive defection in the North.

The doctrine that " Resistance to tyrants is obedience to God," taught loosely, encourages any people to attempt revolution or secession, when in their caprice they judge their government tyrannical.   There is a world-wide differ-ence between passively or peacefully disobeying a wicked enactment, such as commanding Daniel not to pray, or to aid in the arrest of a fugitive slave, and taking up arms for revolutionary violence.

Some writers were filled with horror at the disobedience to the Fugitive Slave Act, but have shown themselves hypo-crites by conniving at the wicked rebellion.   Most writers against secession quote our text with great zeal, like be-lievers in the divine right of government, but they show their inconsistency in the praise of revolutionary heroes. They still believe in revolutions, rebellions and secessions.

FRAUD TO PRODUCE PREJUDICE.

I was in my fourteenth year, when, in March, 1819, I was one of a load of young ones who went out on a sleigh-riding excursion.

We had two objects in view, seeing Carthage Bridge, and visiting a museum which was stopping for a few days in the village of Rochester, N. Y.   We indulged our wonder for an hour at the bridge, astonished to see it resting on an arch nearly two hundred feet above the water.   It was my last sight of the wonderful bridge, for it fell the next sum-mer.

We now hastened to the museum, where wonder on wonder rose before me ; but what interested me most was the wax figures of distinguished men whose history I had begun to read.   In contrast with these noble forms and

faces was a caricature of Henry Christophe and wife, labeled
King and Queen of Hayti.   Their forms were almost too
ill to be human, and their looks so silly that they seemed
hardly fit to govern a herd of goats.   I thought the figures
true to nature like the others, and formed the most contemptible opinion of the new black government, of the king
and subjects.   I know not how far this fraud was practiced.
Let us hear Thomas Clarkson in regard to the same Christophe and family:

   "What shall I say of the talents of Henry Christophe,
formerly king of a part of Hayti, the son of a slave, and of
complexion as black as jet?   I corresponded with him for
three years, and therefore know him well.   He devised,
when king, a noble plan for the education of every child
that was born in his own dominions, and he carried it into
execution.   He founded a university, and introduced into
it the professors of Latin and Greek, and of mathematics,
as well as of sculpture and painting, and of some of the
other arts and sciences.   He had devised also a liberal and
well-digested plan of government for his people, but his premature death hindered it from being brought forward.
When I was at the Congress of Sovereigns at Aix-la-Chap-
elle, in 1817, I happened to have one of his letters in my
pocket, and I showed it to the Emperor Alexander of
Russia.   He was so struck with it as to have it shown, by
my permission, to the emperor of Austria and the king of
Prussia, who attended the congress; and the opinion of all
the three upon the letter was, that none of them had in their
respective cabinets a minister who could write on the same
subject a better political letter or one better suited to the
case.

   " May I be permitted to say, without giving you the least
offence, that you never had among all your American presi-
dents a man of greater genius and talents, or of a more

acute, penetrating, and capacious mind than the black man now mentioned, though undoubtedly these must have had a better knowledge of the world.

"After the death of Henry Christophe, his widow and two grown up daughters were at my house for five months, during which time I had an opportunity of judging of [their capacity and acquirements. Their acquaintance with history, literature and the fine arts, and their powers of conversation qualified them for mixing with the highest circles of English society, and they did afterwards mix with them in London, and were accounted as amiable and as intellectual as others in whose company they were."—*Clarkson's Letter to American Clergymen.*

LAND MONOPOLY.

BRO CROOKS: Permit me to answer J. Schenck, not in opposition, but in sympathy. I may not afford him much light, for he must be better acquainted with the working of the Homestad Law than I am, as he is in the Far West, or is the West always moving? I was born in the Far West, in 1805, in Madison Co., N. Y. In 1811 I moved to the Far West, to Genesee River; in 1835 I came to the Far West, to Michigan; but found the West moving, not stopping for a night. Onward it went over Lake Michigan, over the Mississippi, and if it stops not at Cedar Falls, it will not stop this side of the Sandwich Islands. It can get no farther, for beyond the Sandwich Islands is not West, but East.

Brother Schenck at his standpoint must see the working of the Homestead Law much better than most of your readers, and would confer a favor on many by giving "Light." That "Man's worst enemy is man" is written on every page of the world's history. Sordid selfishness makes man a

monopolist.   He becomes wakeful to his own interest, taxing all his shrewdness to gain the power of wealth over his
fellowmen.

It is not easy to determine at what time legal titles to land
began.   It is evident that few if any such titles existed in
the world's earliest history.   The immense tribes that
thronged the north of Europe had no such titles for two
thousand years after the flood; but they were mostly herdsmen.   Large tracts of land in the most civilized countries
continued common to herdsmen, while in grain producing
districts, occupants were protected by law in their possessions.   In Sparta cruel monopolies arose when Lycurgus,
over seven hundred years before Christ, took all the land
and divided it among thirty-nine thousand families, near as
possible of equal value.   Two hundred years later Solon,
finding cruel monopolists in the Athenian state had involved
a large part of the people in ruinous debts, declared the
debtors all free from liability to their creditors.   Rome,
under the kings, had large districts of government land taken
by conquest, which the plebeians worked as tenants, and
the rent paid the expenses of the government.   When the
Tarquins were expelled and Rome became a republic, the
patricians took the public lands to themselves, and taxed the
landless plebeians for the support of government.   The
taxation ruined them.   They were trampled beneath the
feet of the rich patricians, who held every office.   The
plebeians, being the rank and file of the army, revolted, and
Rome would have been ruined in a day if the patricians had
not conceded and compromised.   The strife however between the rich and the poor, the landlords and the landless,
the patricians and the plebeians, was often renewed, and
finally ruined Rome.   In the fall of Rome barbarian military chiefs monopolized the lands nearly everywhere.   Many
of these feudal or baronial lords where bishops, and all were

tyrants over the people who occupied their lands as tenants.

In the Norman conquest of England, in the eleventh century, William divided all England among his officers. From
these robbers have descended the great landed estates to
this day. How silly to boast of Norman blood. In Ireland
Cromwell began the work of confiscation, and forty years
later William, Prince of Orange, finished it, stripping the
Catholic Irish of their lands, and turning them into the
streets; and their descendants without lands, without hope,
for two hundred years, have come to be the low, vicious
Irish ¡which I often meet, with more pity than contempt.
My heart yearns for the most degraded, when I think of the
cruel oppression of their ancestors.

I cannot now express my views of the wrongs in disin-
heriting the American Indians. My attention must be confined to land monopoly.

I begin with the absurd idea of the " Right of discovery."
Spain claimed the New World because Columbus, a
Genoese, had discovered it under her auspices. England
claimed North America because Cabot, a Venetian, had
discovered it in 1497 under her auspices France claimed
the same because Verazzano, a Florentine, had coasted it
under her patronage. Holland claimed the same because
Hudson, an Englishman, had coasted it under her favor.
In 1583 Elizabeth gave Sir Humphery Gilbert all of the
heathen world which he might discover and possess; and
he, sword in hand, proudly took possession of North America, although the French had been fishing here for eighty
years. In 1603 the French kings deeded by charter most
of the same country to De Montz. In 1606 the English
under James I. deeded the whole by charter to the London
and Plymouth Companies, calling it North and South Virginia, divided by the mouth of the Hudson. In 1621 Holland deeded by charter a large part of the same country to

her West India Company, calling it New Netherlands. These nations were soon at war, setting the Indians, like hounds, on each other.

These charters, and other charters to individuals, started the land monopolies in this country. They have been sub-divided to various companies and individuals, often for one millionth of their present value, their titles thrown about at first like footballs. Sometimes when honest, industrious men have pressed into the forest, and began to clear away the timber, then half-forgotten, mildewed titles have been brushed up, and lands, which cost not a penny per acre, sometimes not a mill, or perhaps one-tenth of a mill, have been sold for two, three, six, or eight dollars per acre, often on articles so drawn that the toil-worn settler forfeited all by the failure of one payment of principal or interest. The great Holland Purchase in New York traced back to an original title so dim that some able jurists, thirty years ago, doubted whether a settler could be legally ejected. Some were driven off without a dollar, who had extensive im-provements with valuable buildings, because a payment was due at the Land Office. Commissioners canvassed the whole land, warning every one in arrears to be ready to go into the street at any day when the Land Office should sell his place to another man. I with others received this warning, for one payment had been due a few weeks. I could not meet the payment at once, and while the people were pre-paring to defend their homes by arms, I sold my farm for one hundred dollars and came to Michigan. I hope the Homestead Law is a great blessing to the poor.

WOE UNTO YOU, LAWYERS!

All must acknowledge the necessity of human govern-ment, with laws, civil and criminal; with proper penalties,

designed to protect the weak against the strong, the innocent against the guilty.   The legal profession therefore
ought to be one of the most honorable ; a lawyer one of the
most useful of men, explaining the relation of government
and citizen to each other, and the relation of citizen to citizen, their mutual rights and obligations, aiming in his counsels and his pleadings at right and justice.

Is this the character of lawyers?   It is doubtless of some,
but of the majority it is not.   Many openly declare that
they will take as client the party which will pay them most
regardless of where justice evidently lies ; and when thus
engaged they do not scruple to use their utmost ingenuity,
wit and eloquence, to deceive and mislead a jury, hiding
facts far as possible, aiming only for victory, caring nothing
for right or justice, if right and justice are against them.
They then have the impudence to tell us that their oath requires them to do all this ; as though they, like Ahab, had
" Sold themselves to do evil."   The lawyer who has the
greatest skill to change light to darkness, and darkness to
light, to entangle and darken, disentangle and enlighten,
gets the highest reputation with quarrelsome men who delight in lawsuits, bad men who desire to obtain the hard-
earned property of other men by unjust decisions.   Such
men will employ him at any price.   He rises in reputation
and wealth, while he is the dread of honest poor men.
Laws are made, or should be made, to protect the honest
poor, but such use is made of law that honest poor men
tremble and turn pale on hearing the word law, when a
threatened lawsuit hangs like a sword over them.   The
honest poor man hails with joy the counsel of Christ, " If
any man sue thee at the law and take away thy coat, let
him have thy cloak also."   Doubtless lawsuits were conducted then much as they are now, with so much unfairness
that Christ's counsel was to keep out of them, and if forced

into them, to get out of them at any sacrifice.   Truly peace
and serenity are better than warm garments.

I began life with a deep sense of the importance of government, laws and honest lawyers ; and early looked around
for a model.   A fine boy grew to manhood under excellent
tuition and studied law in my town.   My hopes were high
of an honest lawyer, a blessing to mankind.   My hopes
were shortlived.   He had scarce begun to plead when I
heard him say, " There is no doubt that John is innocent.'
" And yet," said a bystander, "you did your best to prove
him guilty."   " Yes," he replied, "my oath requires me
to."   Horrible oath, surely, if he was sworn to serve the
devil after this sort ; to do his best to send a worthy citizen
to state's prison, whom he knew to be innocent ! He knew
beforehand the very bottom of this malicious prosecution.
I gave him up, stood aloof, but others did not; he was flattered, encouraged and employed; settled in one of the
largest cities, and long ago was colleague in an important
suit with the present secretary of state of our nation.   So
little regard is had to this crying evil by the public.

My next choice for a model was converted in a glorious
revival.   I thought for a time his heart was so warm with
love to God and man that he would preach the gospel.
When he decided to go on with law I looked upon him as a
model, one who should exalt the legal professson.   Soon a
temptation arose and he fell.   A boy was guilty of arson.
When he looked on the glowing coals of a house which had
kindly sheltered him and saw the sorrowing family, he re-
lented, confessed his crime, and told in what manner he set
the fire.   My model lawyer was called, told the culprit to
stop confessing and deny the crime to every one.   He now
took his fee in advance, the only horse of his father, a poor
man, and tried to clear the boy by turning light to darkness,
but failed; the criminal went to prison.

My third and last candidate for a model was educated, intelligent and moral; my acquaintance with him was interesting, and I hoped to have it long continued, but finally gave up all desire for this. I was well acquainted in a town so infested with thieves that all property was in jeopardy; where gardens, orchards, bee houses and graineries were robbed; fat sheep and cattle stolen and slaughtered, and horses run off to other States. Thieves grew bold, threatened all who should dare to accuse them, carried out their threats by burning stacks of grain; honest men were driven to the wall, and thieves triumphed. Many dared not speak in regard to their losses, fearing the firebrand would next be thrown into their barns, houses and mills. A pretty large arrest of thieves was finally made, and my model lawyer managed to turn all but one loose on the people again. Years after I passed through that town and found the people in terror of these same men, thus cleared, and offering to sell their farms for three-fourths of their value; but men feared to buy where nothing was safe. I shall be allowed to express my surprise at public sentiment on this subject, when I state that the second lawyer described in this article has been United State's Senator from one of these States, and the third has been governor of another State.

Skill in clearing rogues has exalted them. My last surprise arose in conversation with one who had arisen high in my esteem, for his talents and principles, when I heard him say: "No prosecution for rum selling in his county would be carried to final conviction, because rum-sellers could afford to pay more money than temperance men were willing to pay. Lawyers," he said, "would work for the party who would pay most;" and then added, that he had offered for a stipulated sum to keep rum or alcoholic drink out of his village, and temperance men not paying it, he went over and defended the traffic, and got more than twice as much defending men who he allowed violated law.   This man told me his oath required him to do this.   He professed to be a temperance man.   I wish such lawyers were with rum-sellers in person.

———

The following, is the closing paragraph of a brief communication to the *Wesleyan* of Jan. 18, 1865, headed "Church Union," and shows the author's mind in reference to the union of Christians.—COMPILER.

CHURCH UNION.

My health failed, and I was brought near death in the commencement of his civil war, and I felt that the sun of my life was going down in dark clouds, but the prospect of the union of several denominations into one harmonious body, renews the sunlight on the horizon of my days, and I hope to say in view of ultimate success, " Now lettest thou thy servant depart in peace."

———

MY VISIT TO ADRIAN.

I had never seen Adrian College, and had remained silent in regard to its condition or prospects.   I found the grounds and buildings all that my most enthusiastic fancy had pictured.   I felt to award the highest praise to the men who projected this enterprise, and to pray for the blessing of God to rest on their vigorous efforts to enlarge the noble work in their hands.   Their names deserve to be imperishably inscribed on these noble structures.   The donors to the college were never surpassed in liberality.   May every blessing attend them ! I went back in reflection to the time when Oxford was no greater than Adrian now is.

The cabinet of geology, when arranged, will be one of the most interesting exhibitions in our country.   This is the generous gift of Dr. Kost, the learned professor of geology and natural history, whose urbanity and kindness are equal to his scientific eminence. I most highly value my acquaintance with him, and rejoice that he is permanently connected with the college.

The visit of the messengers from the Methodist Protestant convention, Dr. Brown and Rev. Mr. White, to our conference, gave me great pleasure, and I shall ever reflect with pleasing emotions on my acquaintance with them, and I most earnestly pray for union between our denomination and theirs. It gave me also great pleasure to meet the model chaplain, Brother Lyle, whose noble self-sacrifice had filled me with admiration, as I had seen him in the hardest and roughest paths, drenched with rain, and encased with snow and sleet, sleeping on the frozen ground, and eating the coarsest food, and often starving for want of that. I had seen him in the midst of shot and shell, on the battlefield, to cheer the dying with the name of Christ, to carry water, bandages and blankets; to lift the wounded to an easier place to die. I had seen him in hospitals the livelong night with the sick and dying.

When I had read his communications, I had thought of La Baum, who cut a raven's quill for his pen with the knife which had just cut the last morsel of horse-flesh, then bending one knee to the frozen ground, he mixed snow and powder in his hand for ink, and wrote his history. I was happy to meet this model chaplain, resting a few days from compaign life.

I shall ever cherish the most grateful remembrance of the hospitality of the kind families of Brethren Rice and McKeever, and the friendly greeting of many others, and shall ever pray for the prosperity of Adrian College.

WHAT SHALL BE DONE WITH THE BAD BOYS?

While so many of our young men are in the army, hundreds of young women are employed in teaching, who possess every qualification for teaching, but are left to the necessity of resorting to physical strength to maintain government. This would be unnecessary if children were properly trained at home. Then the wishes of a kind, gentle teacher would be met and order and harmony would prevail. Public sentiment is very bad on this subject. Parents in advance say, "That teacher will fail in government." This to the children is a license to begin the war. Next we hear it said, "She has no government; the school will be broken up." Now the children feel licensed to do their worst. Soon the officers in grave dignity inform the teacher that as she fails to govern the school it must be closed. The reputation of the teacher is ruined, the children are spoiled for obedience to parents, to teachers, or to magistrates. All blame falls on the unfortunate and ruined teacher, while the rebellious children feel proud of their success. It is a relic of barbarism to require teachers, male or female, to maintain school government by physical force and still worse to hold them liable to prosecution and penalty for physical injury inflicted on the pupil in punishing him. If children are not prepared at home to be orderly and obedient at school, let the district officers forbid their attendance, and for flagrant acts of rebellion let the penalty be imprisonment in the county jail, and all these evils will be cured.

PROPOSED DONATION TO GEN. SAERMAN.

General Sherman's services are doubtless appreciated by all, and his name is sure to be surrounded by a halo of glory on the pages of our country's history, in all coming time ; but raising by donation a hundred thousand dollars for him, and building a palace in Cincinnati for Mrs. Sherman, will not add to his glory in the estimation of the present or future generations. Does not our government pay its officers properly for their services ? Is this move in accordance with republican institutions ? Washington refused to receive even any pay for his long and arduous labors in the war which gave our country birth.

How would this movement look to the ancient Spartans, in their republican simplicity, or to the republican Romans, when, while Regulus was at the head of their armies in a foreign land, his family, dependent on the produce of a small farm for sustenance, or when Cato the Censor lived down to old age in a very small house, with simply one room below and above.

We are departing from republican simplicity, and aristocracy founded on wealth is arising in our country. The path of luxury led all the ancient nations to ruin. We as a people are beginning to tread the same.

MY TEMPERANCE VOW.

Among the pleasing recollections of early childhood is the beautiful, smiling face of my uncle C——. The happiest morning I had knoAn was when I, about five years old, met him and my aunt at my mother's door in 1810. The whole scene rises now before me. I see the horse and sleigh turning in at the gate, and here the bells coming up the hill, and see the morning sunlight on the snow, and see myself, a white-headed urchin without a hat, laughing, crying with joy, leaping, bounding, rolling in the snow; and failing in all this to find vent for my enthusiasm, I seized a cauldron and tugged away to lift it. This was three miles east of Cazeno-

via, N. Y., in which rising village my young uncle was a
flourishing merchant, entrusted with important military and
civil offices, and having an honorable membership.

Thirteen years later, 1823, I stood by a grave in a lone
spot where strangers and paupers were buried who died in
Rochester.   We had come out from the village, a small
group of the poor, mourning without hope, bearing the body
of a loathsome drunkard to this rough opening in the old
wildwood.   It was the body of my uncle C——.   My aunt,
my mother's younger sister, appropriately named "Ruby,"
who had always seemed an angel, so beautiful, so amiable,
stood there with her four little daughters, scantily clad in
black.   Oh, what an hour to me! It was one of the sultriest
days of August, the silence was oppressive.   As I looked
with horror on the face in the open coffin, the tall branches
of the wilderness cast shadows in streaks, interspersed with
sunlight, then a zephyr moved, and the light and shade
passed, slowly, mournfully up and down over the coffin and
grave.   The body was let down, a foot touched a large
lump of clay, hardened by the heat of the sunbeams, and it
rolled in, falling on the naked board.   The sound to me
was awful, echoing from the woods around.   In that sound
was a volume of history and ethics.   The causes of my
uncle's ruin fired my soul with indignation.   I thought of
young Hannibal, coming to the altar in the temple at
Carthage, and swearing eternal enmity to Rome ; and felt
that I was in the temple of Mercy, Humanity, Truth, and
Justice, solemnly swearing eternal enmity to *rum*.   I had
embraced the Quaker doctrine of non-resistance, and even
heard "Avenge not, I will repay saith the Lord," sounding
in my ears, or I would have joined an army to seize every
rumseller as a felon, and burn every distillery in the land.
The wrongs done by England to our fathers were insignificant, compared to the wrongs inflicted by makers and

sellers of drink who turn noble men to brutes and maniacs, moral men to devils, and pleasant homes to hell. These makers and venders of drink now make sixty thousand funerals without hope, like the above, every year, and recruit the drunkard army with sixty thousand more, seizing our dearest kindred, our most promising sons.

When my uncle had fallen and lost all, wealth, office, church-membership and public esteem, self-respect struggled nobly for life; 'struggled against appetite, habits and temptation, but fell, again and again. He broke away from his cronies and followed our family to our western home, determined to reform. There I saw his noble form, in 1818, as he arose in a religious meeting and confessed his fall, and asked for help to reform so feelingly that my young heart melted. Alas! the church all drank, every human house had its whisky, nicely stained. I have seen our aged Welsh minister drink a tumbler full at a draught, when on a paternal visit at my mother's house. A beautiful meadow, often trampled by my young feet, around its sparkling spring and brook, was now the seat of a distillery, where the leader of our church made whisky by day and night, amid the stench of putrid fermentation, in tubs, cow-yards, pigsties and mud sloughs; where devils in the full glow of the fire, held their dance. Amongst the whole, men often mingled and passed a winter's evening, or a mid-day summer's hour, talking religion, politics, obscene anecdotes and songs. The church was divided and in angry strife. All agreed in unconditional election, but one party maintained that Christ died in some sense for reprobates, not to save them, but to mock them with the offer of salvation; which the other party denied. Gloom and moroseness passed for religion, while cheerfulness was condemned.

Our eloquent young minister fell, became a drunkard, a blasphemer, and frightened his young wife, the gentle

Sophia from her home. She died of grief under the roof of her aged parents. My uncle strove against appetite, habit, example and temptation, like a brave man on the current of Niagara, plying the oar, yet going down, while I, as a lad on shore, ran along, out of breath with anxiety. There, he is coming to land—there—there, oh, he is whirling back into the current, but he springs for life; how he plies the oar! Pull hard, my uncle, pull, pull, catch the rock if you can; he's caught it—hold on, my uncle, hold, hold, I'll throw a rope.   I coil and throw, and try again, but my young arm is too weak, it does not quite reach him.   Oh, there he's stepped from the rock, turns to me a despairing look, crying, "Is there no man to help?" No man, my uncle; the minister has gone over the falls, the clerk is in the distillery, and the deacon is carrying whisky to market.   "My uncle is lost!" his last oar breaks, his boat whirls, plunges on, darts to the verge, there, he's gone! So my uncle strove with appetite, habit, example, and temptation, till all hope was gone.

I renewed my vow at the grave of Sophia. She had been my playfellow from the cradle, schoolmate and social friend. Our English is tame; it lacks the thunder and lightning words fit for this theme.   Pulpit eloquence is often bombast, over mint and anise, over fleabites of human ills, leaving the murderers of my kindred to go unrebuked, while political hypocrites prate of causes of war in threepenny tax on tea, and the impressment of a few seamen, then get down from the stump to defend a traffic which robs millions and kills sixty thousand a year.

ISAAC T. HOPPER.

How few of all who have lived are known to the present age! Oblivion covers the dead.   They slumber in silence everywhere, on the mountain, in the vale, and below the ocean.

Fame has seized the name of one in a million and given it to posterity. But fame is fickle and unjust. The good, who gently move, like the grateful zephyr or the distilling dew, live and die unknown, while the evil, who move like the tempest, commend themselves to fame. Vice gains no· toriety sooner than virtue from the vitiated taste of men. As the waiter at table brings any dish in his bill of fare named by the guest, so the historian brings any dish which the public taste demands. Yet there are a few exceptions, and historians of a higher and more noble purpose come,

" Like angels' visits, few and far between."

While Headley follows Napoleon, and re-echoes the thun· ders of Austerlitz and Borodino, Mrs. Child gently dips her pen to embalm the memory of a philanthropist.

Headley wakes martial ambition in the breast of every boy who reads; the eyes of his young reader are delighted with plumes and epaulettes; but Mrs. Child wakes divine philanthropy, and hushes the tempest of depraved passion. She leaves her reader in that beautiful serenity often witnessed in the devotions of Friends.

Nature formed Hopper and Bonaparte so much alike that the veteran of the Russian campaign, had he met Hopper in Philadelphia, would only have been restrained by his Quaker costume from exclaiming, " Vive la Napoleon."

True, phrenologists would have found the difference in the superior benevolence and conscientiousness of Hopper. Joseph Bonaparte used to say that Isaac T. Hopper resembled Napoleon the most of any man he had seen in Europe or America; that, in his brother's uniform, he would hardly be distinguished from him by his own household.

The Corsicans had been from all ages lawless bandits, with little or no reverence for the sacredness of human life.

Napoleon's father was a distinguished warrior, and his mother, a few months before his birth, rode with her husband through his wars. His education was military example and precept; the school task, and the song, and even his maternal nursing, all tended to fan to a flame the ferocious ambition born in him.

Hopper's ancestry were Puritans and Friends, and his education checked the stubbornness of an iron will. It was not however the education of despotism or rigor. It consisted of mild counsel and proper example.

In energy Hopper fell but little short of Napoleon or Cromwell; but in him energy was guided by the highest moral principle. From the former he differed in conscientiousness, from the latter he differed in disinterestedness and philanthropy.

Without conscience he could under favorable circumstances have usurped dominion over a nation; and without philanthropy he could have led the storming of Worcester.

Of all men on the pages of history perhaps he most resembled William Penn. He had not Penn's princely ancestry, education or fortune. If in this he failed of that perfect and courtly refinement, which gave Penn such great influence at court, he gained by it a more perfect democracy of spirit and manners, a more universal exercise of philanthropy.

Penn's noble arms were extended to take in all mankind, but he never found his way along the paths of the lowly like Hopper.

No man ever repeated that sublime sentiment of Garrison's, "The world is my country and all mankind are my countrymen," more heartily than Hopper. Political boundaries, though wide as oceans, were nothing to him; they could never diminish his brotherhood to man.

Patriotism, as the term was commonly used, sounded

hateful in his ear. "My country right or wrong," which gave Decatur immortality, was to Hopper as abominable as the sentiments of banditti. He loved the government of our country for its approximation to true democracy, to equal rights and privileges. But no sham could be palmed upon him; every departure from true democracy, in constitution, laws, or practice, was by him seen in spite of the dazzle of stripes and stars.

His moral sense and his perception of right and wrong was of the highest order. He saw the guilt of robbery and murder in our government in bringing on the Mexican war, as plainly as in a band of desperadoes, who in a bar-room plan to waylay, murder and rob a traveler. He saw the striking resemblance between the bombardment of Vera Cruz and the burning of a house by an incendiary over the heads of a family.

The shrewd speculator, who took fifty dollars in a sharp bargain from his honest and confiding neighbor, was to him on the same moral footing with the man who took fifty dollars from the pocket of a sleeping man. No man came nearer doing as he would be done by, or loving his neighbor as himself.

He is characterized by disinterested benevolence, and the generous acts that filled his long life arose spontaneous from his heart. Though he possessed great business talent he was generally poor. The wealth he gained was the happiness of mankind. It generally takes selfishness to accumulate wealth, and hence that awful declaration of Christ, "It is easier for a camel to go through the eye of a needle than for a rich man to enter into the kingdom of heaven."

Anti-slavery was spontaneous with Hopper. His keen perception went through the gauze of Bible arguments and pretended political necessities, and comprehended slavery in all its naked deformity.

While Napoleon was demolishing thrones and wading in blood, mingled with the ashes of villas and cities, rejoicing that his name was the terror of the world, his fac simile, in Quaker costume and simplicity of manners, walked the streets of Philadelphia, his ear ever open to the cry of the poor, the friendless and the oppressed.   To them he was a genial sun, whose warming beams chased away cold despair and inspired the despondent with hope.

As Teneriffe stands in mid-ocean unmoved by the tempest, ever holding its head above the storm, so Hopper, the friend of the slave, stood alone amid the storming ocean of prejudice.   How many poor colored men he rescued from the kidnapper will be known when "the judgment sits, and the books are opened."

To the superficial observer Hopper is scarcely seen on the page of history compared to Napoleon.   When, however, we cease to be dazzled by epaulettes and sword and plumes, when we cease to hear the huzzas of fame, the case will be reversed.   Napoleon moved over the surface of life's sea and made his mark like the keel that parts the waters, and as the waters close behind and all is smooth again, so Europe has resumed her former state.   France is no better governed than in the reign of Louis Sixteenth.

Austria and Naples have grown worse.   Spain and Italy are no better.   The unpretending Quaker, who might have been seen carrying bread to the cottage of the poor, or releasing the innocent from false imprisonment, or giving encouragement to the despairing vagabond, or rescuing immortal man from the grasp of the petty tyrant, while Napoleon was at his coronation, was the harbinger of millennial day to the oppressed, the pioneer of liberty.   When the last chain falls from the limbs of the slave, let him who wore it come and lay it at the grave of Hopper, and there feel that he who there so quietly sleeps laid the foundation in America to the great moral revolution which brought universal freedom.

Some poet has said, "An honest man is the noblest work of God." This will not be incredible when we consider the disinterestedness and moral courage of an honest man. No cowardly dissembling, no duplicity or prevarication tarnished the name of Hopper. His honesty commended itself to all men. It shone in his countenance and was heard in his voice. His benignant look overcome his enemies.

When we see the slaveholder with his blood-clothed whip over the quivering back of his slave, the rumseller rejoicing in his gains over ruined and despairing families, or the libertine, base wretch, worse than a common murderer, decoying his victim from the path of virtue, not caring how soon she dies in her shame, our indignation rises, and we sometimes feel that it would be well to seize these monsters of iniquity and hang them all, and rid the earth of men who live to curse mankind.

This is wrong. Christ has taught us to pursue these terrible sinners with untiring efforts to reclaim them. In this Hopper was eminently a follower of Christ. When he has rescued the victim from the slaveholder or the libertine, he is ready at once to assist the guilty in distress; and while he binds up his wound, he rebukes with so much kindness, and yet so faithfully shows the enormity of his deeds, that he breaks the stubborn heart and leads him to repentance.

Jesus came to seek and save that which was lost.

How well Hopper deserves the name of Christian for his imitation of Christ in his efforts to save the degraded, can only be known by hearing a record of his benevolence read from the books that shall be opened when "the dead, small and great, stand before God." While the drunkard was hissed, and men praised their boys for pushing him into goose ponds or setting dogs on him, Hopper kindly helped him to a shelter, warmed and fed him, and pointed him to the Lamb of God that taketh away the sin of the world.

Still more cruel was the treatment of the seduced. The matron who first learned her fall, went to church and whispered it in the ears of the sisterhood; and when asked, What did you do? she raised her sanctimonious face, and said, I turned her out of doors. Where is she? I do not know, she replied. I am not her keeper; she will know better than to darken my door again. Thus abandoned, every family warned against giving her employment or shelter, in her despair she plunged into the gulf of pollution.

Hopper saw that this course was shockingly at variance with the spirit of the gospel. His benevolent soul mourned over the wreck of woman. He had learned by happy experience what woman was when she accomplished her mission. This as well as the benevolence of his heart prompted him to make every exertion to save the lost. He saw in the degraded the wreck of some of the finest minds in the world. The poor lost Magdalene whom he could persuade to reform was welcome at his house. His kind words gave hope to many who had long felt that they had no friend on earth. His labors for the prisoners deserve the commendation of all mankind. His estimate of human nature was higher than that of most men. None was so degraded as to destroy his hope of his recovery.

Christ bade his disciples love their enemies, resist not evil, turn the other cheek; because, by a general law of human nature, forbearance and love will restrain, subdue and reform the wicked.

There are exceptions: some are not thus subdued; and for them we must have laws with penalty, and criminal courts, and jails, and prisons. These exceptions would be few if every child was brought up under the counsel of a Hopper.

But alas! many are surrounded by circumstances most pernicious, almost necessarily leading them into crime. Seducers go unpunished, though often more guilty than men who expiate their crimes on the gallows.

Speculators in every town in Christendom may use their shrewd perception to rob the dull and confiding, and break no civil law and incur no penalty. Women, whose honest and artless love has been made the occasion of their seduction, and who are then "cast, abandoned on the world's wide stage," friendless and abhorred, and hard working men, who have been repeatedly outwitted and robbed according to law, make war on society. The contest is unequal—soon with manacled limbs they pass the huge gate of the prison, and then their wild rolling eyes may be seen piercing through the iron grates. They feel now that the die is cast, nothing is left them but despair and shame. An indefinable sense of wrong done them makes them wish to gnaw off the grates, and to go forth and wreak their vengeance in mischief. The loss of self-respect and of all hope of being respected drives them mad. No one cares for them. They may speak to no one, and no one may speak to them. When their term expires they are turned out upon the world, which has been taught to abhor them; the world which they have learned to hate, with no purpose but to sin and die. Poor creatures! while Hopper lived they had a friend whose warm heart, kind look and encouraging words were like the light of the morning to them after a long night of despair. He inspired hope and repentance and abhorrence of their past lives and a resolution to reform. This resolution he nourished, bearing with patience their frequent relapses until he succeeded in establishing in them permanent habits of virtue. His influence over the inmates of prisons was such that scores were so permanently reformed as to be released before their terms expired. The discharged convicts were watched over by him as though they were his children—were aided with money—recommended to employers, and followed to haunts of vice if they fell for a time; and at last he saw nearly all honest and honorable citizens.

Alas for the lowly! Hopper is dead! Who will ever fill his place? Prison chaplains too often, like chaplains to kings and nobles, and chaplains of armies and legislatures, are mere machines of form, ever looking to the popular current and to the gold that pays them, or rather buys them. As this noble philanthropist quietly lived and peacefully made his exit, so he quietly went to his grave—no pomp attended his burial.

1855.

EVILS OF WAR.

War originates in selfishness, which prompts man to trample on the rights of his fellowman, and avail himself of his fortune. War has destroyed the lives of 10,000,000,000 of the human family. The wealth that has been destroyed and wasted on war cannot be counted in dollars, but it would be sufficient to feed and clothe the whole human family for five hundred years; or it would meet all the expenses of every benevolent society for a thousand years to come. The influence of war upon morals has been evil, and only evil, in every age and country, destroying fine sensibility, humanity and benevolence, and engendering malice and ill-will. It has destroyed all sense of the sacredness of property and life, and has been the parent of theft, robbery and murder. The severest penalty, even capital punishment, will never secure the safety of life and property while war, the school of theft and murder, continues.

Intemperance in this country had its origin mostly in the

Revolutionary War, and each succeeding war has poured a flood of intemperance over this nation. Licentiousness is the universal evil of the camp. From Nimrod to this day, wherever the army has moved, chastity has ceased to be revered, and the soldier, from the high rank of Aaron Burr down to the unlettered boy, has studied the art of seduction, and spread the path of the army with ruin more shocking than the ashes of fallen cities.

The war with England in 1812 cost the United States two hundred millions of dollars; and the probable damage to private property, including the fisheries, was two hundred millions more. The Seminole or Florida War cost our nation forty-one millions of dollars, and the Mexican War at least one hundred and fifty millions.

Sometime subsequent to the peace of 1815 the question arose, "What have we gained by war?" Mr. Clay in a speech of great eloquence answered, "We have gained national honor." This honor cost too much when we pay the debt ; the average tax to each man, woman and child was twenty-five dollars; or to each family of eight persons two hundred dollars. This only paid the direct expenses of war, while in addition to this the people on the seaboard, particularly in New England and those on the northern and northwestern frontier, bore the enormous burden of two hundred millions more.

The average tax on each man, woman and child for the Florida War was two dollars, or for each family of eight persons, sixteen dollars. The Mexican War, at one hundred and fifty millions, will cost every person six dollars and fifty cents ; every family of eight persons, fifty-two dollars. All of this will be paid by an indirect tax, which is far worse for the poor than a direct tax. The poor man not worth a foot of land will pay more of this tax than a banker worth $5,000,000, if his family consume more imported goods.

To the question, "What have we gained by the last war?" there is no voice of Clay to answer, "We have gained national honor."

The history of the Florida and Mexican Wars will stand on the pages of our country's history a record of sin and shame, to be read with abhorrence by coming generations. Posterity shall know that all of this taxation on twenty-three millions of people came upon them for the interest and benefit of two hundred and fifty thousand petty tyrants, whose tyranny exposes them to so much danger, that enormous expenditures are made on the army and navy for their protection, bringing on the honest poor an intolerable burden.   But we lose sight of taxation in viewing myriads of our sons sacrificed on the altars of the American Moloch, and beholding the blood and tears of a countless multitude of slaves driven upon territory previously free.

We deem ourselves insulted when called upon for our suffrages for the highest offices in the nation, to be treated almost wholly with arguments founded upon military reputation.   If the practice of filling the highest places of honor and trust with military men be persisted in, it will be likely to involve us in frequent wars, to increase the already enormous expenses of the army and navy, and finally to end in military despotism.   False notions of national honor lead to many wars, and false notions of glory have been the seeds of war in every age   On these subjects the literature of the world is corrupt and anti-Christian.   History, oratory and poetry teem with eulogy and panegyric on war scenes and heroes.   The fine arts are generally in fault; painting and sculpture pay obsequious devotion to Mars and Woden.

Wars began in the earliest age after the fall.   A signal victory was gained by Cain, and he spoke, in the spirit of Achilles, of Alexander, and of Napoleon, when he tauntingly said to the Almighty "Am I my brother's keeper?"

There is no reason why Cain should not have his fame, unless it is because he was so unfortunate as to live at too
early a day, before the ingenuity of man had invented pal-
liating circumstances.   He bore no general's commission;
he had no government order; but he was a government
himself and received his orders from his own will; this was
the executive of his government.   He wore no regimentals;
but in those times his bear-skin robe gave him all needful
martial appearance.   He wore no epaulette; but then there
were no gaping admirers to behold him.   Cain carried no
sword and practiced no fencing; but Abel was killed as
quickly with a club, though not so handsomely; the great
object of the battle was gained; the man, or to use a more
military term, the enemy was routed and slain.   He had no
formal commencement of battle, no sounding of trumpets,
no snorting of steeds, no chaplain's prayer; but in those
days strict orthodoxy was not important; perhaps the strong
desire of his heart that Abel's brains might be knocked out
was as good as a chaplain's prayer and as fully answered.
There was no formal sequel, no dinner, balls, or sublime
proclamations; but these things can be dispensed with;
they never make the victory more sure.   Cain had no contemporary bard to sing his fame, to give to other bards the
song, and hand it down to other times.   Ah! there he
failed, and for that reason only he has never been enrolled
on the list of heroes, the list of glory.   Instead of such a
bard as Homer, or Ossian, or Headley, there came the
truth telling Spirit of Inspiration and called Cain a murderer,
and that is the name he will bear through all time, while
millions who have murdered in the spirit of Cain have been
feasted and huzzaed.   They have borne laurels; music and
dancing have followed them, and when in death's cold arms
they have slept, pilgrimages have been made to their tombs.
Oratory, poetry and music have vied with each other in ef-

forts to make them immortal. They live in equestrian bronze statues, while good men are forgotten. The city built by Cain is barely mentioned. He probably founded an empire, but having no historian after the fashion of the world, his dynasty is unknown. From Revelation we learn, that in the ages which followed him violence filled the earth. They probably did as the Greeks, Romans, Carthaginians, French, English and Americans have done—coveted dominion, invaded territory, destroyed property, killed and enslaved men, committed rape and burned cities. But their college of bards closed by the flood, and their heroes are forgotten; there is none to tell how gloriously they drenched the earth with the blood of men, how sublimely their clarions called to battle and their shouts of victory sounded along the mountain and o'er the plain, or how music drowned the groans of the dying, when the smoke and flames of fallen cities arose to the sky. We have no catalogue of their giant chiefs, or their mighty generals, their Agamemnons, their Cæsars, and their Charlemagnes sleep in oblivion. The only record the world has, or ever will have of them, is that of the Revelation, and that is a record of infamy. They filled the earth with violence, and therefore God destroyed them with a deluge, and buried their fame with that of beasts of prey. Had not the promise of God secured the world against another flood, perhaps the fame of all the warriors of the world would likewise perish.

Nimrod, who did service to mankind as a hunter of wild beasts, became himself a beast of violence. Semiramis, although esteemed so highly by historians, so eulogized by Plutarch, was not so much to be esteemed as a she wolf, for a she wolf is prompted by maternal instinct in her greatest depredations; but Semiramis was prompted by love of personal aggrandizement and love of murder. She seems an enormous Amazon lewd as Venus but rough as Pluto;

masculinely mounted on a furious steed, with a voice of
harsh thunder, uttering oaths with her commands, wading,
by day in human blood, and spending the night in debauchery.   Sardanapalus has been universally despised for
inactivity; but if he was inactive, he did little harm; he
filled no land with wailing by his wars.   Historians admire
the fall of Sardanapalus by the Medes and Babylonians, but
this was an event more important to vultures and jackals
than to men.   It started a new dynasty, led to the fall of
Nineveh, to the transfer of power and magnificence to
Babylon; but who was benefited?   Surely not the hundred
thousand men called from their peaceful homes to become
soldiers, nor two score thousand made widows by the war,
nor a hundred thousand orphans, mourning the loss of
fathers slain in battle.   These were not benefited, nor the
millions impoverished in the wars.   Who then was benefited? The few who got into power by the fall of one government and the establishment of another.   These were benefited, if the gratification of selfishness can be a benefit to
anybody.   Yes, these were benefited, and historians admire
them in aggrandizing themselves at the expense of millions
of subjects.   Historians admire in them their pride, their
haughtiness, and their selfishness.   But historians are fond
of changes; nothing can please them long.   They are as
much pleased with the overthrow of this race of kings as
with its establishment.   They are in ecstacies in beholding
another grand drama.   By the aid of the romantic Xeno-
phon they beheld an illustrious youth in the little barren
province of Persia rising into power until Babylon and all
Asia owns his sway.   But we again ask, who is benefited?

From first to last during the protracted wars of Cyrus at
least two millions were called from the peace and quiet of
life to the army, and of these one million never returned.
Were they benefited? Were their widows and orphans?

These widows and orphans were scattered over nearly half of the world. Their wails were heard on every hill and in every valley, from the Indus to the Bosphorous, and from the frozen North to Upper Egypt; the historians have not told us how many of these starved to death. Who was benefited? Were citizens of a hundred provinces through which the armies from time to time passed and where they were quartered, when all of their substance was devoured? Will it be answered Persia was benefited? No; Persia was not benefited. She lost to some extent her simplicity of manners, and in one sense she lost her identity; and while she remained the same barren province, the name Persia was applied to almost all Asia, and Babylon was her metropolis; and when Shushan became the seat of government, Cyrus and all his virtues were buried.

The same historian that rejoices in the overthrow of Sardanapalus and Belshazzar; that sees with sublime emotion Arbaces and Cyrus slaughtering myriads and overthrowing empires, being blind to right and justice, capricious and changing, ever greedy as the tiger to glut himself with blood, now dips his pen for the coming of Alexander. Like Cleopatra, he embraces each successful chief and lends his music to each universal victor. Whenever the Macedonian moved, mourning and lamentation was heard; the winds that swept the plain bore along the putrid odor from masses of the dead; famine and pestilence stalked by day and night; while over field and glen the ashes of fallen cities were trod by wild beasts, and ravens darkened the air. Houseless mothers grouped their starving and dying children among rocks and hedges, and woe followed the march of Alexander over the world. How absurd to bestow praise on this great human tiger! Rome has been revered, not so much for being at first a band of robbers, for at first she was small, and a small band of robbers is rarely respected;

but that Rome is revered for continuing to be a band of
robbers, 'for robbing one after another every country on
earth of its freedom and its wealth, for drenching the whole
earth in the blood of men, for becoming the terror of the
world.

Roman statesmen and generals have been most extravagantly eulogized by Christian writers. They have quarreled
with Plutarch for his parallels, not satisfied with his extravagant praises bestowed on Romans, while he compares them
with the Greeks. Our Christian writers admire the Greek
heroes much, but they admire the Roman heroes far more,
because they were more cool, deliberate and systematic in
robbing and murdering men; more adroit in escaping punishment, more persevering, and in the end more successful.
While Rome devastated the earth, destroying and carrying
away the wealth of nations, making houseless wanderers of
millions, and slaves of millions more, keeping half the human family from age to age from all useful occupations she
is most unjustly credited with all the blessings of civilization.

We are allowed to weep over the fall of Rome, over the
ebb-tide of the universal empire. But why should we not
rejoice as much in the conquests of Marie, Atilla and Gen-
seric, as in the conquests of Scipio, Pompey and Cæsar.
The barbarian conquerers were moved by no worse motives
than the graceful Romans.

For nearly two centuries the civilized world was kept in
terror, beholding the dark North from which the tempest
of war was often pouring down with lightnings and thunder-
ings, devastating the land. The rural homes of millions
disappeared. The tenants, including the mother and her
babes, slept in their blood and mouldered away. The forest
grew up again, the wilderness spread around, and the wild
beasts slept amidst the ruins of king's palaces. Age after
age the raging tornado of battle rolled from the awful North,

mingling the clarion's blast, the shouts of savage victors, and the shrieks of despair.   The rivers ran blood, and the shrieks of man ceased, and from the awful North, the land of eternal snow, came wolves following on the track of deso-lation, to tread the ashes of burned hamlets and to howl within the walls of desolate cities.   If the fall of Rome had been the end of ambitious and murderous chiefs, we might rejoice in her fall ; but human nature is the same in all na-tions and all ages, and the world was still to be cursed by heroes.

From the ruins of the vast empire spread over an impor-tant part of Europe, Asia, and Africa, numerous small pow-ers arose, ever envious and jealous, and often moved by malice and murderous hate, waging war on each other. Italy, Gaul and Germany were each for many centuries the seat of the most bloody wars, while war's putrid flood was sweeping the last of literature from Africa and most of Asia.

When the Gauls had suffered the most dreadful calamities for centuries, when they had been wasted age after age and spoiled of their possessions, the Franks became firmly estab-lished in their land, and the independence of the Gauls was lost forever, with their language, and their very being as a nation.   Eastern Rome long continued to drag along a dy-ing life, until the Turks, originally one of the most bloody and ferocious tribes of Central Asia, having become potent by plunder, rapine and murder, took Constantinople, and waded in the blood of the last of her Christian princes.

Historians who delight to see murderers in uniform and regimentals, marshaled in brigades, who are charmed with epaulettes and plumes, with snorting steeds and war clarions, are never weary of the praise of these distinguished tribes—the Turks, the Franks, and the Saxons.   These three bands of murderers have gained the admiration of the world be-cause they escaped punishment for their sins, and went on

murdering and plundering men, grew rich by theft, and
climbed into power over millions of the dead, while other
bands of robbers, who have been guilty in the sight of
heaven, but who have not been so fortunate, and who have
been hanged for their crimes, or who have repented and
forsaken their sins, are by our historians ever held in contempt and treated with disdain.   The unholy doctrine that
might makes right guides the historian.   Murder and robbery on a large scale become grand and sublime.   Successful revolutions are nearly always pronounced noble and
even righteous, while unsuccessful revolutions or attempts
at revolution are called rebellion, and men hanged for rebellion and regarded as murderers in all ages, would have
ranked with Bolivar and Hancock had they succeeded.

The Turks were at first a small band of robbers, and
finally the robbers of all Western Asia and a considerable
part of Europe and Africa.   The Franks were a clan of
Goths, or Germans, and from small beginnings they came
at last with impunity to rob and murder through every province of Gaul, and thereby to found the French empire.
The Saxons were also a clan of Germans.   Historians say
they were one of the most warlike tribes of Northern Germany.   By which we are to understand that they were one
of the most thieving or murderous tribes or clans of that
country.   They were sufficiently strong in body to plunder
and murder with impunity; no other tribe was strong enough
to overcome and punish them.   These are our ancestors, of
whom we have so proudly boasted.   How came our English
and Saxon blood united?   By an act of base treachery.
The Saxons being hired to protect and defend the English
against robbers, chose to rob them themselves, and did rob
them in such a manner as they had never been robbed before; taking the whole country to themselves, murdering
innumerable multitudes and driving the residue of the

strength of the English into the western part of the island and shutting them up with a wall. While we think of this, our English blood and Saxon blood get at strife in our veins. The child of fornication is at a loss to know which parent to blame most, but the child of rape will doubtless cast the blame on the father for his origin. When our Saxon ancestors had killed and banished the strong men of England, they amalgamated with those who tremblingly prostrated themselves before them, and hence our Anglo Saxon origin. Probably our Saxon blood predominates. But to make us the more sure descendants of bloody men, we have received at another time a larger addition of North German blood.

During the time of the horrid slaughter of the Saxons by Charlemagne, when he to make them Christians marched from city to city, and striking his sword into the ground made the citizens march around it and cut off every head which was above its hilt, many strong men fled into Jutland, and mingling with the Danes, and perhaps with some Swedes, they built numerous ships and became a maritime nation, or rather a nation on the seas, under the name of Northmen, or Normans. Subsequently these Normans gained possession of the north shore of France, where their dukes grew so potent that they held the kings of France in subjection.

William, Duke of Normandy, conquered England and divided it among his principal officers in large land-estates, and brought in so many Normans that for a time the English language seemed in danger of being lost. Such is the Normo-Anglo-Saxon origin of the English nation, which has covered the seas with war fleets and crimsoned them with the blood of men. The sound of her cannon and her clarion has arisen on almost every shore. She has audaciously invaded all Southern Asia, Southern and to some extent Eastern and Western Africa, the East and West Indian

Islands, Australia, half of the American continent, and the islands of the Pacific. Proud of her conquests and her powers, she swells her sails with all the winds, in all climes and zones, and haughtily hoists her colors in the sight of all nations. Her wars have been murderous; the blood of many millions has cried to heaven against her, and the increasing cost of her military affairs, increasing her enormous national debt, must soon sink her.

Her army in 1835 was 145,846. It had arisen in 1851 to 272,481; in 1852 to 352,481. The increase of expense in army and navy from 1851 to 1852 was $556,635. The whole cost of war in 1852 £16,000,000—more than $70,-000,000, and this in time of peace.

Should England be engaged in such a war as Kossuth wished to see in Europe, it might increase her expense of war tenfold. How long can England continue at this rate to increase her already enormous national debt without ruin?

The Normo-Anglo-Saxons this side of the Atlantic have shown their pedigree. They have nearly annihilated the aborigines of North America, and possessed themselves of their lands. Some of these Indians have been slaughtered by our ancestors while defending their homes and the graves of their fathers, by as savage and yet as noble a bravery as that which has given immortality to the Greeks; some of them have been burned in their camps without the least regard to age or sex, with a heartless cruelty that would have graced Tamerlane, while others have been murdered in cold blood. A whole community of civilized and Christianized Indians, Moravian converts in Ohio, were murdered in a manner too barbarous to be compared with the deeds of savages themselves. These Moravian converts were non-resistants, and their religion taught them to resist not evil, to do violence to no man, and accordingly they used no

weapon of defense.   Such pacific attitude in Penn and his
followers subdued and disarmed the savages of the Delaware; but such pacific attitude in these poor Indians did
not subdue these white men.   They had started out to kill
and plunder the Indians.*   They wished for the booty and
the fame; and here was booty, as these Indians had cattle
and corn.   These unoffending Moravians gave themselves
up without resistance.   They were grouped together, and
when told that they must die, they asked the privilege of a
prayer-meeting, and knelt down, but were driven from their
knees and ranged in rows, and sturdy white men took
wooden mallets and knocked them in the head, and then
they took such plunder as they could carry and returned to
Pennsylvania.

Such were some of our fathers of the Revolution.   The
removal of the Cherokees under a spurious treaty made
with subordinate chiefs, and repudiated by the whole nation,
was most wicked oppression.

Any individual doing to his neighbor as our government
did to the Cherokees would be arrested for swindling and
punished in any law abiding community.   We have denounced the Seminole War because it was waged solely for
the benefit of slaveholders, and cost this nation $41,000,-
000.   We have denounced it, because at the dictation of a
few men who wished to recover their slaves this war was
waged, taxing twenty millions of people $2,00 each or tax-
ing each family of eight persons sixteen dollars.   We have
denounced it, because our government withheld an enormous sum due the Cherokees, the reputed value of fugitive
slaves with the Seminoles.   We have thought it enough to
compel the most enterprising tribe of Indians, at a price of
our own fixing, to leave the graves of their fathers, their

* The original reads, "plunder and kill Indians."   Take
which you prefer.

homes, orchards, fields of grass and grain, their mills, shop s
school-houses and churches, without attempting to rob them
in this dastardly manner, under the plea that they were
kindred to the Seminoles.   But let us waive all of these
considerations for the present and place ourselves in the
stead of the Seminoles.   Let us remember them as suffering with them.   For two hundred years their kindred had
been wasting away.   Tribe after tribe had forever disappeared.   Their former neighbors, the Cherokees, had been
compelled to follow the doom of their race and go toward
the setting sun.   But the Seminoles were permitted to remain in Florida.   Their country, or much of it, white men
did not covet, for white men could not live in it; but slaves
sometimes fled from intolerable tyranny to the everglades,
and threw themselves upon the generosity of the Indians.
Slaveholders were at liberty to go and take their slaves, if
they could.   In an excursion of this kind, the sacred home
of a noble chief was invaded, and an attempt was made to
tear from his bosom what was dearer to him than his life.
At length these dastardly men became weary in endeavor-
ing to take their slaves.   A much readier way was to get
government to pay them for their slaves, out of what was
due the Cherokees.   This would turn the "bird in the
bush" to cash, and enable them to bring in a claim with interest for slaves of past generations.   This abominable
scheme succeeded and brought on the horrors of the Florida
War, in which Cherokees were induced to fight rather than
lose their money, and to help white men kill the Seminoles.
How desperately the Seminoles fought and how nobly, if
war is noble! They were defending their wives and children,
and the poor Africo-American who had put himself under
their protection.

The hope of the Indian had failed.   He saw the policy
of the white man, and saw his nation's sun going down.

His mind was in the graves with his fathers.   He courted
the gloom of the wilderness, and loved the sound of the
moaning wind.   He had left the graves of his fathers, and
had his orchard and field and wigwan in the beginning of
the war, and now the plow of barbarous civilization was
turning out the bones of his fathers.   The white man had
murdered his wife and burned his wigwam and cut down his
orchard, and his children were starving in the wilderness or
were eaten by ravens.   Despair made him sullen and he sat
down in the dark woods, hungry, and cold, and meditated
revenge.   The scream of the raven over his head was to him
an omen of death.   He longed for the time when the sword
of the foe should send him to the spirit land.   He saw the
doom of his nation, the doom of his race.   He had no hope
in submission, no hope of victory, and yet he had nothing
to lose but his life, and that was not dear to him, since home
and friends and liberty were gone.   Despair made him terrible.   The wrongs of two hundred years rolled upon his un-
taught savage mind, lands gone, race almost extinct.   He
arose, the thunder of his shout broke the silence of night
and echoed along the hills.   He called his men around him
and aroused them to desperation.   As the wounded lion
rushes from his lair, or the tigress springs from her dying
cubs upon the hunter, so the Indian came down on the
camp of his foe.   Terrible was the slaughter around where
the Indian died.   And yet the Indian might have been
made a friend, a Christian, and a man of civilization, by
kindness and justice.   Covetousness has swept him away.
There is no spot on earth for the Indian, but what the
white man wants.   He has been promised the undisturbed
possession of place after place, but soon has been coerced
to sell it for a paltry sum and go.   The waning tribes, ascending the great western mountains, seeking an asylum

where the sun sinks to rest, are doomed to disappointment, and the white man is there by

"Christian's thirst for gold."

Oh, that there might be one faithful experiment of Christianity on this most injured race before their last waning shadow falls on the Pacific Ocean's shore!

THE RIGHT OF SELF-DEFENCE.

MR. EDITOR: I am requested by a highly respected friend to answer the following question through the *True Wesleyan:*

"Is it consistent with the spirit of Christianity to use physical force in the endangering of limb or life to man?"

This question is not intended to include the question of capital punishment. Many writers on the question of capital punishment have brought confusion over the subject by confounding capital punishment with defence, and with the arrest of criminals. The question of capital punishment ought to be kept distinct and stated thus: When a criminal has been arrested and chained in his cell, shall he not be put to death, or punished in some other manner?

The question of my friend refers to defence, and in the arrest of criminals, and may be stated thus: Is it consistent with the spirit of the Christian religion, for defence, or for the arrest of criminals, to use physical force to the endangering of life or limb to man?

God designed that man should be a social being. His destiny to be a social being is seen in variety of state, from infancy through childhood, youth and manhood to helpless age; in variety of intellect, from the dependent idiot to the philosopher and statesman; in variety of temperament, from the dependent son of melancholy to the man of buoyant spirit, able to meet adversity's darkest storms unmoved;

and in variety of aptness for all the various callings, trades and professions.

Secondly. In his contiguity to his fellow-man, his destiny to be a social being is seen. Ten hundred millions of people inhabiting this little globe, renders it difficult for man to isolate himself if he would. Man is born and reared amidst society; he is like a slender stem of grass in the meadow, propped on all sides, and is under almost incomprehensible obligations to society, yet he often forfeits his obligations and in his peevishness curses and anathematizes society. The question now arises, are humanity and justice spontaneous and universal, so that man is safe in his character, property and life, without organized government.

If humanity and justice are spontaneous, they are far from being universal. It is not necessary here, as a technical theologian, to enter the lists for discussion on total or partial depravity. The disciples of Calvin and Channing are left to the enjoyment of their respective opinions. It is not necessary for the present object to show that man is totally depraved; it is sufficient to show that he is not totally good. All history shows that man is not totally and universally good, and that selfishness is so extensive that character, property and life are not secure without government. By government, I mean rules or laws for the protection of character, property and life. Necessity has driven all men to resort to government in all ages and all countries, from the largest nations to the patriarch's family or the clan of Arabs. Laws must have penalties. If men were universally and totally good, and also highly intelligent, it might be sufficient to teach them these laws; they would approve and obey; but there have been men in every age who were not influenced by any laws merely advisory; they know the rights of men, but they regard them not. It will be said that if more was done to improve men in morals and intelligence, crime would be lessened.   This is true, and this work has been going on for many ages—crime has been diminishing, and yet there are bad men enough to destroy the world, to exterminate all property and life, if they were not restrained by penalty.

The power of love is great; it has disarmed many a ruffian and tamed many a violent man; it should be the common instrumentality for restraining and governing men. This is plainly taught in the gospel; but some men are beyond the influence of love.   Infidels read the volume of Nature, shutting their eyes to the volume of Revelation, and fanatics read the volume of Revelation, shutting their eyes to the volume of Nature, while the intelligent Christian reads both, knowing both are the gift of God.

Infidels follow Reason, discarding the Spirit, and fanatics follow the Spirit, discarding Reason, not knowing that when Reason is discarded a false Spirit leads them; but the intelligent Christian follows the Spirit in the exercise of Reason, which is the gift of God.   In order to determine our duty we must take the world as it is, and men as they are, not as they should be.   There are men who cannot be subdued by forbearance and love.   Before the rage of their avarice, or even their bigotry, the most forbearing Christian will fall; and before the rage of their lust the most meek and lovely innocence will become a prey.

There must be with law, penalty, to restrain such men. Penalty as far as possible should be reformatory and preventive.   Penalties are generally inflicted after process of law, but some indefinite penalties are allowed by law to be inflicted without process of law, by men in defence such as of property or life.   It is here important to make a distinction as between defence and arrest.

The war question is principally concerned with the subject of defence, while the subject of arrest belongs to police regulations.   As far as possible these questions should be kept distinct.   I shall first consider the question of arrest and police regulations.

Men who are too deeply depraved to be influenced by forbearance and love will steal, commit rape, robbery and murder to accomplish these ends.   Some are so extremely depraved that they murder for pastime or wanton pleasure, and if not restrained would make a bonfire of every city and village in their way.   They must be arrested.   They are fearfully armed and will resist; yet they must be arrested— the very existence of society depends upon it.   How much physical force may be used? So much as is necessary to arrest and secure them, be it more or less.   Policemen must have the aid of armed men, some times of hundreds, under proper officers and martial discipline.   Felons in resisting the police will be liable to be wounded and even killed; this is unavoidable, unless we let them go at large until the earth is destroyed and man exterminated.

Secondly. Defence. This is a subject very complex and difficult; under the plea of defence fourteen thousand millions of men have been slain; under the plea of defence probably an amount of property has been destroyed equal to ten times the whole property now on earth, and under this plea crimes the most shocking have been committed that have ever disgraced human nature.   Some honest and good men have doubted whether so much crime and so much destruction of life and property would have happened if no government had ever existed.   But the cause of war is not the existence of government; it is the selfishness of man's depraved nature.   Men would congregate in armies, large and small, where there was no government, rallying under every ambitious man; and some would never be satisfied until they had destroyed the last family from the earth.

Governments must exist that such men may be arrested and secured.

It is said self-defence is the first law of nature.   Let those who are fond of this maxim remember that human nature is corrupt and deeply depraved, and that the first law of nature is to depart from God and commit sin.   Dr. Edwards uttered a great truth when he said, "Selfishness is the foundation of all vice."

See, says Man, how every animal but the sheep arises in self-defence when he is pursued, or his rights are invaded ; and Buffon calls the sheep the most contemptible of all animals, because he will not fight.   Another writer tries to rescue the sheep from contempt, by declaring that he will fight in his wild state, very manlike.

How low human nature must be when such men as Buffon and Lord Kames are eager to take their example from the swine, the dog and the tiger.   If we would know our duty we must consider ourselves and our fellow-men not brutes left to brute force, but beings of moral intelligence. Paley somewhere remarks in substance, There are always two classes of men, the one yielding and forbearing, the other determined, unyielding and overbearing.   He then adds, the latter class always commands respect, but the earth could not contain one generation of them, *i. e.*, if there should be one generation of them they would destroy each other, until there would be but one man upon the earth.   They should not command respect, for they are the bane of society.   Says one, Without them what should we do for generals?   In answer it may be said, if earth was rid of them there should be no wars, and we should need no generals.

Paley's second class of men is the minority, and most of these may be subdued by forbearance and love, perseveringly exercised toward them.   A few of them, the most selfish and ferocious, cannot be subdued by forbearance and love, and these must be arrested and confined, or, few as they are, they would destroy the human family. If there was an entire nation of these desperate men, national war would be justifiable, for such whole nation would need to be arrested; but the number of these desperate men is small in the most savage nations, hence Penn subdued the savage tribes of the dark forests of the Delaware by appearing with his followers with benignant countenances, unarmed and bearing in their hands valuable articles for the Indians. What a shame that two hundred years have elapsed since that event, and Christian nations have profited so little by Penn's example! Forbearance and love, persevered in by any nation toward any other nation, even the most savage, will bring it to reasonable terms and subdue it in the end. Then how unjustifiable and wicked to go to war with an intelligent Christian nation ; Christians opposing brute force to Christians, and deluging the earth with each other's blood !

Christ has commanded us to love our enemies, to return good for evil, to resist not evil, and when smote on the one cheek to turn the other. Probably in ninety-nine cases out of a hundred this will subdue them, but if one in a hundred cannot be subdued by the above course, and is extremely dangerous, we must arrest him in a legal manner and confine him. If he attempt to murder my family by night, and expostulation fail to check him, I must arrest him if I can, though I am liable to take his life in attempting to arrest him. In this case my family would be a nation by themselves for the time being, and I must defend them by a police of my own. If he attempt to murder me when alone, it is only one life against one ; I do not think I could intentionally kill him barely to save my own life.

———

SPIRITUALISM.

"With the talent of an angel a man may be a fool."

YOUNG.

"Who wickedly is wise, or madly brave,
Is but the more a fool, the more a knave."—POPE.

The Hon. Mr. ——, once a leading mind in this country, says he has just heard from Paul, that Paul, having lately been released from prison, where he has been shut in with Judas ever since he was beheaded for offering licentious insult to Nero's concubine, has confessed it through some medium. That this silly and blasphemous tale should be greedily embraced by a class of our fellow-men, is a new development of the tendency of the human mind to sink to· dirt under diabolical influence. Spiritualism has now sunk so low that a crisis must soon come, reaction must take place. Such extreme degradation cannot long endure the light of this country and this age. Yet many are past cure, and will perish in their folly. How low their views of God, of angels, of human spirits, and of the spirit land! Heaven in their view falls below the elysian fields of the ancient heathen, and is rarely above a ball-room, or a drunkard's saloon.

How degraded the pretended spirits of the dead, in language and action, as they appear in the circles! Many rush into Spiritualism to escape their fears of hell, being unwilling to submit to God through Christ! They pretend to conjure up Wesley, to recant all the terrors of his alarming exhortation, and to cap the climax, Paul is represented as· creeping from prison, a mean culprit, confessing that he was a debauched hypocrite, died for crime and went to purgatory. To a mind elevated by truth, how sublime the contrast between Nero and Paul!

The imbecile Claudius had brought infamous women to

the palace; one of whom brought Nero, the child of her debaucheries, with her, and ruling the mind of her beastly husband, got him appointed heir to the throne. With small mental capacity and groveling animal nature, he mingled with the low and mean, and in spite of the influence of his noble tutor, Seneca, he never rose above the chief brawler of a tavern in ability, yet chance and vice made him emperor of the world. It would be impossible to find any one placed in authority more destitute of any virtue. Neither gratitude, humanity, benevolence, or philanthropy are ever exhibited. He soon murdered all his kindred, not sparing his mother, with a host of noble Romans. Seneca fell a victim to the diabolical passions of this biped tiger. In comparison with his pleasures, he saw no value in the peace, property, or lives of his subjects. He had a song on the burning of Troy, and caused Rome to be set on fire to gratify his eyes in seeing a great flame, and witnessing the consternation of a million of citizens as they fled from the ashes of their homes. He was now becoming intolerable to his subjects and in danger of assassination, but escaped a short time by charging the burning of Rome to the Christians and joining in a terrible persecution, when one of many modes of torture was to dip sheets into pitch and wind them around Christians, to be burned for lamps at night in the emperor's garden.

It was then, when thousands were tortured and dying, that we beheld one of the most noble characters that have appeared on the stage of human action. This was Paul, then in Crete. He was born in Tarsus, in the province of Cilicia. His superior mind received all the advantages of the highest education, both in the Greek and Hebrew schools. He had by nature all the qualifications for a leader, and while a Pharisee, every eye was on him as the leader in exterminating Christianity. He was on this errand, when proudly approaching Damascus, God met him; divine light flashed across his mind, the divinity and Messiahship of Christ was revealed beyond all doubt, and "immediately he conferred not with flesh and blood." For more than thirty years he is seen in untiring labor for the glory of God and welfare of men, a noble specimen of disinterestedness, not accounting any self-interest, wealth, friends, ease, peace, or even his life, dear, when by sacrificing all he could the more to honor God and do good to men.

When we consider this noble career of toil, self-denial and suffering, his courage and energy, his spotless purity, his exalted love to God and men, language lacks power to express our contempt of the meanness of this silly tale; but when we consider his divine call and inspiration, this story of Paul's confession is daring blasphemy, and we shrink from the company of men of such foul language. Alas! to what shifts men resort to get around the fear of hell, without repentance, faith and holiness of life! "Wait the great teacher death, and God adore."

CREATION.

To me the study of Geology throws a beautiful light on Mosaic history. "In the beginning God created the [substance of] heaven and earth." Such is the translation of Dr. Adam Clarke.

How far back the word (beginning) should carry our minds none can tell, when the substance or matter was created which now forms our earth, our sun, and all this solar system, and thousands of suns with their systems of worlds around them, constituting our universe. I say our universe, for there may be others.

What if astronomers with the most improved telescope should tell us that beyond the bounds of ten thousand suns, nothing can be seen? This only shows that finite vision can go no farther, while the eye of Infinite may see outside of the vast vacuum which encircles our universe, each having its ten thousand suns and solar systems, and all these united may not be a ten thousandth part of the material creation.

With this view, our whole universe is a speck in creation; our solar system is a speck compared to our universe; and our earth is a speck in our solar system, not a millionth as large as our sun.

Let me go down in this descending scale to the spot I call my home; and yet farther down to the little fly, made visible by the sunbeams on which it rides, and down yet farther to creatures so small that one hundred thousand embodied into one would not make a body half as large as the dot of my pen over the letter i, and though animal life may go below, I cannot follow any farther down. " From infinite to Thee, from Thee to nothing." He who governs all worlds, all systems, all universes, cares for creatures so small, that three hundred may play at once on the point of a sharp needle, and march three hundred abreast on the edge of a razor.

There is no infidelity in supposing that matter was created in the state of igneous gas, in most intense heat, and brought into form by cooling into liquid, and then to solid matter. The distance of the stars, and the speed of light being determined, we know that the light which this night shows us the most distant star must have left that star countless ages before the time of Adam.

I asked a friend how the trunks of trees came to be charred, and lie in coal beds one thousand feet below the surface of the ground in England; and how shells and bones of animals came to be in rock more than twenty thousand feet below the surface of the earth. He replied,

"God made them there, six thousand years ago."   "What!"
said I, "made coal in the form of the trunks of trees, lying
horizontal, with bark and limbs, and stumps of equal size,
standing there just as though the trees had broken off?"
"Yes," he replied, "God made these trees lying horizontal-
ly just as they are, and made the stumps.   They were never
living trees and never stood erect, the stumps were there
from the beginning, the trees were never on them, and all
were created coal."   "And how," said I, "about shells
and bones, so far below the surface of the earth—how came
they there imbedded in rock?"   He replied, "God made
the rock with bones and shells in it, twenty thousand feet
below the surface, but they were never living creatures."
The same answer is given to all that may be said of sea-
washed gravel on all high lands, of fishes in rocks on the
mountain tops, and everything that would indicate progress
in the earth's formation.

The answer to all is, "It was made as it now is, the same
week that Adam was created."

If I may be allowed a little irony, I will give a new theory
of Pompeii.   For ages no one knew where Pompeii had
been.   I will assume that it has not been found.   A peasant digging a well found the appearance of a house, and
foolishly thought that it had been a house, when it was only
a part of the original creation.   Excavations began and
still continue with the foolish idea that they are digging up
an ancient city.   They find striking appearances of public
and private buildings, with windows and doors, gardens,
gates, alleys and streets; but all these might have been
created just as they are, the same week that Adam was
created.   Do you ask, For what were these created, so like
human dwellings. gardens, alleys and streets?   I answer, for
the same reason that prostrate coal trees were made, that
is, because trees were to fall in coming ages, and lie by their

stumps, in like manner; for the same reason that bones and shells were created in the rock; because marine animals were to be created having bones and shells some like them.

Here we walk along the exact resemblance of a street, pass what seems a gate, enter through a seeming door into a spacious room, like a dining-hall, with a table and its furniture and food, and human skeletons seated around, as in the act of eating. What a wonder of creation? Here is the appearance of a school, and there is the master just punishing a culprit. Here again is the baker with his loaves, and here is a wine cellar with barrels and human skeletons. How strange that these apparant streets were never traveled, these houses never occupied by human beings; and these skeletons were never human living men! How strange that all these, with their Latin and Greek inscriptions, were created just as we now find them? Who knows but thousands of such appearances lie all through the earth, created when the earth was spoken into being, fac similes before-hand, within the earth, of what should appear on its surface? If this view is sufficiently ridiculous, I will drop the tone of irony and say that equally ridiculous is the pretence that the fossil remains of plants and animals, found in the secondary and tertiary rocks, were never alive. These rocks could not have been formed since the creation of man. The convulsions which formed them were almost infinitely more terrible than Noah's flood, sweeping into rocky tombs millions of animals and vegetables, of which thousands of species have since been unknown.

DIVERSITY OF TASTE.

Every admirer of Ossian is astonished to see Montgomery's severe criticism appended to what he considers his improved version of "Morna." How different his taste from that of Blair! Every Christian lover of poetry admires Montgomery, the pious, delicate and meek Montgomery; but we would rather he would let Ossian alone. If he had transposed all of these poems as he did " Morna," the original Ossian would have been preferred.   How any poet could have such an extreme dislike to the style of this work, is to me incomprehensible.   Take away what he calls its " Baby-lonish style," "broken sentences," "Prose run mad," and the work is modernized and spoiled.   It is no longer the " Voice of Cona."   Let us have it as it is from the hands of Macpherson, and we walk with the bards of Selma, seven-teen hundred years ago, through the woods of Morven, be-neath the autumn cloud.   We see his footprints on the heath; stand with him on "The rocks of roaring winds," and sit beside him in his airy hall.   We become acquainted with the manners, customs and the whole wild life of the ancient Highlander in his wild savage state.   To the lover of antiquity, here is one of the most grand and interesting fields that the mind can roam.   I would not exchange its wild granduer for all the smoothness of measure of the deli-cate Montgomery.

Who would think of employing an actor from the London stage to give a new and polished version of the North American Indian's war-whoop and war dance?   Let us keep them to all coming ages as they are; and as we cannot have these songs in Gaelic, let us have Macpherson's trans-lations, doubtless the best ever made.

Napoleon was a great admirer of Ossian, usually carrying it with him in all his campaigns.   If it had been in the smooth rhyme of Addison, or the imposing verse of Milton, he probably would not have read it a second time.   How different his constitution from that of Montgomery, whose delicate taste was as the sense of touch; of that French queen, who was told by Richelieu, that hell to her would be lying eternally in Holland sheets.

There is no book except the Bible which I have read as often as Ossian.   From my youth I have delighted to walk with the Highlander of yore; often out on the hill by night, seated on the heath by the blazing oak, listening to the harp and song, "Tale of the Times of Old," till the king struck the boss of his shield, and called his hosts from a thousand fires.

There is a melancholy pleasure, now in old age, sitting in the hall of Ossian, aged and blind, and hearing of the past. Ossian, the last of his race; his Oscar is dead, and Malvina, the betrothed of his departed son, sits by him, and often leads his aged form into the genial sunlight.   How much like my own case.   My sons have likewise fallen; my family name is to be blotted out!

How touching the last song of Ossian, composed in part when he was dying! May my last hour be as serene, and may I be cheered by a better hope, the Christian's hope!

INFLUENCE OF THE PRESS.

In my travels, which have been somewhat extensive, I have observed the influence of certain secular and even religious journals, spoiling the conscience and the heart of some of the best of men and women.

Boys from the army, who left their homes generous and humane, tell me that their principal reading in camp was the *New York Herald*, because it contained the latest news. A great change had come over them ; they had abandoned their anti-slavery integrity.

A journal, published in the City of the Straits for more than a quarter of a century, always makes its mark, corrupting every family where it is read.   Some of these readers are intelligent, refined, moral and amiable; yet all have barbarbous views of the rights of man and human equality, from the corrupting influence of their newspaper. From my youth, I have occasionally found in the families of my friends that embodiment of conservatism, published in our national metropolis; always somber and grave in its religious department; and I expected to find the readers always behind the times in all measures of reform.

Some allowance should certainly be made for error in judgment; men may have an honest motive in a bad cause; yet it is palpable that many editors and publishers intend to encourage vice. When they, or their friends, are candidates for office, we see multitudes pouring forth from the vilest haunts to vote for them.

They always receive the votes of Sabbath-breakers, debauchees, blasphemers, drunkards and gamblers; and their journals have the patronage of these men.

Some of these publishers make a show of refinement, morality and religion, while they furnish fuel for the fires of hell. How much this pampering of sin has had to do with the late elections in the Empire State I cannot say, but I have seen the day when more than half of the press in this Peninsula was "Sold to do iniquity."

INCONVENIENCE OF ASSUMING THE PLURAL.

Old men remember with what awkwardness some ministers of the plainer denominations forty years ago said, "We have chosen our text," etc. How every child and some old men and women, stretched their necks to see if there were two in the pulpit. Little urchins, being put to the study of grammar, get puzzled when the editor writes, "We fell out and hurt ourself." Or when a minister writes in his journal, "We started with our wife for the convention."

Salt Lake refinement has rendered polygamy a common idea; but who ever heard of two or more men having one wife? Some would attempt to avoid this dilemma, by writing, "We started with our better half." But who can avow the idea of subdivision? The idea that each of the two constituting the plural has a quarter of the divided substance!

The great argument for this is the plea of humility. "We use the plural," says some one, "to avoid the too frequent reference to ourself. Who can endure to see the long I in almost every sentence?"

Any man of sense can endure it much easier than to see the plural, We, Our, and Us, occurring fifty times in one short communication!

It is folly to charge men with egotism for applying the singular to themselves, when they who use the plural refer to themselves the most frequently of all speakers and writers.

Many centuries ago English princes and nobles required the people to address them in the plural, to distinguish them from the masses; and this custom finally wrought corruption of language; a violation of grammer became universal. At first this custom served the purpose of distinction of rank; hence the Friends refused to say "you" to an individual; but when the custom became universal, it could no longer distinguish rank. Now that every peasant says "you," instead of "thou" to his fellow; now when it is you king, and you beggar, the Friends need have no scruples of conscience; though we may all wish that the purity of our language had been preserved.

The We, individual, is now supposed to belong to a higher class, an editor, a professional, or a literary man; but if the custom becomes universal, and everywhere we hear,

" We handle our mop and our broom; we put on our coat and went to ditching." When every child shall say, " Where is our bonnet ?" " we took our hat and and satchel, and went to school," the folly will have destroyed itself.

In the mean time the custom is not democratic, and it makes an awkward appearance amidst the improvements of the nineteenth century.

NIGHT ON THE LAKES, NOV. 23, 1860.

Nothing could be more dreadful than the storm on the lakes on the night of Nov. 23, 1860. Not volcanic eruptions, burning cities, nor earthquakes sinking cities beneath the ocean, nor the frightful pestilence, nor the awful scourge of war.

In all these man suddenly meets death, or struggles with disease, or with a foe, with hope of final victory.

But when at midnight all the power of the wind comes unlooked for in a moment, plowing the deep to waves, surge and spray, and driving rain, and sleet, and snow, blinding every man; such horror seizes the soul as nowhere else is felt. Soon canvas, ropes and spars all rattle with ice; every foot treads ice ; every hand grasps ice ; and the strong-hearted sailor grows stiff with ice; his hair is frozen, his clothes are frozen ; still he struggles with the elements; struggles mightily, hoping to outlive the storm, to come once more to land, to meet his Mary again, and his little cherubs.

The rudder has failed, the cable has parted, they are driven at the mercy of the wind. Oh, such a wind, such waves, such surges ! Some are gone, swept off by the billows. Every living heart palpitates ; for every sailor knows that rocks are near. There ! she strikes—strikes again— and again ! She is going down ! Oh, what a time to die !

The tempest is deafening, the driving snow makes the darkness felt.

Every brave fellow is at his post, fixed by frost. Messmates cannot greet each other with the grasp of warm hands; hands are ice-covered, eyes are closed with ice. They are dreamy now, dreaming of home, warm home, dreaming of mothers, sisters, of wife and children.

God alone hears the last gurgle of their breathing, and all are dead. Some sleep between the rocks, while others toss awhile on the waves then freeze to the shore.

The storm howls along, and when every fragment of the wreck is gone the darkness frowns and the waves break over the rocks as before.

This is but a dim picture of the wrecked sailor who is prepared to meet his God; but it is not in the power of language to describe a sailor dying in his sins on that dreadful night.

How many on that terrible night left their beds and walked their rooms with tears, sighs, and wringing their hands; for husbands were on the lake, sons were there, brothers were there.

One class of mourners stifled their sighs and hid their tears, being under pledges of holy wedlock with brave young sailors, who were off on the bosom of the deep in the awful storm.

Oh, how every howl of the tempest goes to the soul; how they look out on the darkness; how they listen to the roar of the waves; to the crash of forest trees, fancying they hear the last low wail of the dying sailor, mournfully calling for aid!

———

REFLECTIONS BY THE WAY.

VISIT TO INDIANA.

I left home at Leoni, Nov. 28, 1866, called on Dr. Curtis at Wayne, Mich., for medicine for chronic diarrhea of long standing and seemingly incurable, and proceeded on a journey for my health to South Indiana, invited by friends who knew me only by reading the *Wesleyan*. I left Wayne at evening of the above date, proceeded to the Junction, thence to Toledo, and thence to Troy, Ohio, 80 miles north of Cincinnati. Here late in the night I stepped from the cars, a stranger, in the rain storm, at a railroad building which would disgrace a station in any swamp on our Michigan roads. Every door of this miserable ruin was bolted— no ingress but for small bodies through broken windows, and no one could tell whether the dismal darkness inside was inhabited by ghosts or living animals. No awning, not even a cornice covered my head from the storm. Not a voice of man or beast gave any sign of a present living generation. My destiny seemed to be to stand in the storm till morning, then write "Troy was," and go on ; when lo ! a lantern approached, and a human voice directed me to Rev. S. B. Smith's, where I obtained shelter and kind greeting, though Bro. S. was absent. It was Thanksgiving Day, and I went out through a very beautiful city to the Baptist Church, where I found the city clergy, six or seven, on the platform, a venerable body, and a large intelligent audience ready to hear the sermon by Rev. Mr. Miller, pastor of the Christian Church. It was able and eloquent, out-spoken and fearless on human rights, loyal and patriotic. Not having slept since leaving home, I fell asleep at Bro. Brandriff's by 6 o'clock, arose at 1, had a short but pleasant visit with Mr. Sellers, son-in-law of Bro. B., who kindly conducted me to the depot, where I took the night train for Cincinnati. Arriving about sunrise, I hurried to the Indianapolis depot, but was too late—the morning train had gone. I was sick and lame, and the atmosphere being dark and humid, I remained at the depot until 2 P. M., and then left, having scarcely seen the city.   I had never seen the Ohio. I had my eyes on it most of the way to Lawrenceburg, Indiana.   I was surprised.   It looked like cream rather than water, and seemed much narrower than I expected.   The color being so near like that of the soil, made it seem incredible that there was nearly forty feet depth of water.

The Kentucky shore is much of the way a solitary wild, which must have given fine opportunities for slaves to escape, if all had been their friends on the free shore.   I had designed to go into Kentucky and form some acquaintance, but learning that the rebel spirit was rampant all along the line, Kentucky looked uninviting, and I never crossed over. There are thousands of rebel sympathizers in Southern Indiana, including the German Catholics, but the true Union men are among the most earnest in our country.

I arrived late in the day, Nov. 30, at John Hawkswell's, at Guilford, Indiana.   The kind hospitality of this dear family will rest soothingly in my memory while life lasts. Their quiet home, just out of a rural village, in a romantic dale or valley, through which Tanner's Creek comes dancing and smiling along; meadows and pasture grounds, interspersed with groves, rising gradually on each hand far away up to the clouds, is one of the best places to call my muse that I have found.   Every acre of his extensive fields is in view from his door, where he can count all his animals to the summit of the hills.   Brother and Sister Hawkswell are both natives of Yorkshire, England.   They are very intelligent and model patterns of Christian temper and life.

Bro. H. has been a subscriber of the *Wesleyan* since its commencement, and of its predecessor, *Zion's Watchman*. Their ancestors were friends of Wesley in his day; and judging from letters and notices published in a religious magazine, their kindred in England are among the most excellent of the earth.

Saturday, Dec. 8, I went, accompanied by Sister Hawkswell, to the city of Lawrenceburg, where we met at the cars her kindred, John T. Parker, a worthy specimen of the well-educated independent middle class of English, often more intelligent than the aristocracy. Here I met the warmest greeting, and most true hospitality. They have for several years been subscribers of the *Wesleyan*. They worship with the Methodist Episcopal Church, whose pastor, Rev. Mr. Hester, I visited; heard him in the morning, Sabbath, Dec. 9, and preached for him in the evening. He is a true anti-slavery man, true from childhood. I retired from meeting weary, passed a restless night, followed by a day of sickness, and went early on Monday evening to the church to lecture on Temperance. It was a very cold night, but the distress of my stomach and head caused a cold sweat. Seating myself in a cold corner, far from the fire, I prayed for relief to speak once more for temperance. I prayed in agony. It was a gloomy winter night—the wind howled along the Ohio and around the church, as I mentally cried, O Lord may I be relieved to just deliver this one lecture, though it be the last, and this the last night of my life! See! the people are coming! shall they be disappointed? I arose and my sickness almost left me through the time of lecturing, and returned soon again with great severity, so that I was scarce able to undress and retire to my lodging; yet I was to arise at four o'clock, and take the cars at five for Cincinnati; and through the mercy of God and the kindness of Bro. Parker's family, this was accomplished, and I arrived in Cincinnati at the dawn of day.

Standing at Bro. Parker's door and looking eastward, I had the Ohio on my right; one vast sea of cornfield east to the mouth of the Miami, and northeast to a boundless extent.   "Where," said I, "is the mouth of the Miami ?" "To the east, where you see those large sycamores." "Where is the State line ?"   "Six miles east."   "Beyond that high ridge ?" said I.   "Oh, no ; that ridge is two miles beyond the State line in Ohio, and between the State line and ridge is the course of the Miami."   That rocky mountain ridge turns the Ohio south, forming North Bend ; and the Indianapolis Railroad passes through a long tunnel. Just as you enter the tunnel, going west, you have passed Harrison's house on your right, and his grave on your left.

Sometimes these corn lands are covered with a sea, over a million of acres.   Brother Parker has seen the day, when a steamboat could have sailed around his house and moored at either door ; and last September, within a stone's throw of his door, water was four feet deep in his corn, and yet it was little damaged.   The Miami bottoms are here six miles wide.   In so broad a sea there is not much current to break the corn down, and the water soon falls.   These bottoms continue up the Miami more than a hundred miles, forming one of the gardens of America.

My return was by daylight from Cincinnati to Troy, through one of the richest agricultural districts.   My visits at Troy were very pleasant.   At Rev. S. B. Smith's I met Reverends Lee, Brandriff, and Professor Tuckerman, late president of Farmer's College, now general agent of the Sabbath School Union for Ohio.   I also visited several interesting families, and met in the evening at a temperance meeting all the clergy of the city with but one exception.*

* In a letter the compiler received from Elder Crane, shortly after the foregoing appeared in the *Wesleyan,* he said :

"I there" [Troy, O.] "met Brethren Lee, Smith and Brandriff, and learned with astonishment that they and many others were going to give up the non-episcopal Methodist Union and seek a union with the Episcopal Methodist, and transfer the col-

Traveling gives a good opportunity to study human nature. At the Indianapolis depot, having to wait six hours for the cars to leave Cincinnati, a man of fine address and fascinating manners entered into conversation with me, and said he was from Michigan—a merchant in Ann Arbor—lately purchased lots in the very heart of Jackson—was going into business there—going to erect his dwelling on Main Street on the hill. Learning that I was going to take the next train west, he was going to take the same; and learning that I was going to stop at Guilford, he also was going to stop there. He invited me to walk with him, saying he was going to get his baggage down; but I had no occasion to walk, especially into the underground terminus of the Indianapolis road. As I expected, I saw no more of him. He did not take the cars. Waiting at Guilford for the cars on my return, I was annoyed by the shocking profanity of two Irishmen, mixed with religious talk, as though they esteemed themselves pious men. They were doubtless Catholics. They were boasting that they were the "workers and voters," and said they were appreciated as such. I thought I here saw whisky and popery holding the balance of power, and electing a congressman, who on the stump said he was "For whisky without duty, and its free sale to all, and at all times. He would repeal the law which forbids its sale on the Sabbath, and its sale to minors."

EXTRAVAGANCE.

This subject is attracting some attention, and it is curious to see how different writers fix the standard of Christian

lege to them. I cannot go with them. The episcopal government, in my view, is unscriptural, and anti-republican. The independence of local churches is a sacred right; also the independence of each individual minister."

economy.   One says, "A common dwelling house need not cost over five thousand dollars, that to lay out twenty-five thousand is extravagant."   A late writer says, "A family can be as happy in a house that cost twenty thousand dollars, as in one that cost one hundred and fifty thousand."   Astonishing discovery! In like manner Seneca, on a gold table, wrote an essay on moderate desires.   I have seen as happy families as I have ever found, in houses which did not cost one hundred dollars each, and some who did not complain whose houses did not cost twenty dollars; and such was the house in which I lived, when riding my first circuit thirty-five years ago.

The same is true of clothing, furniture, and carriages. In these our real wants are few, and beyond these, all is comparative.   Bennett is a prince in New York, because his house cost two hundred thousand dollars, and the Indian chief is a prince in his village, because his wigwam cost ten dollars.   Bennett's house is the best in his neighborhood, so is the Indian's the best in his neighborhood.   They feel equally rich, though the Indian is the most happy, the most contented.

MEERSCHAUM AND CAVENDISH.

[In a letter received from the author of this poem soon after it appeared in print, was the following: "My poem on tobacco came to me like lightning—a flash of inspiration. I thought it rough but truthful, and and gave it to the people."—COMPILER.]

Meerschaum, meerschaum, was the loud, shrill cry,
    As the loafers sat along the hall,
And the curling smoke ascending high
    Hid all above and around the wall,

Blurring the windows, hiding the door,
   Making invisible each smoker's self,
Obscuring the horrible slimy floor—
   Meerschaum, again shouted the unseen elf.

A breath of wind through a sliding door
   Swept the whole cloud of smoke away;
Meerschaum again, like the tempest roar,
   Then a low chuckle—aha! aha!
There sat the devil, with horrid leer,
   His meerschaum filled with best Virginia weed,
Perched on his haunches, with majestic rear,
   Gloating on sin with infernal greed;
He held the long stem with both iron claws,
   While the great bowl between his hoofs was seen;
His black lips parted, revealed his jaws
   Beneath his rolling eyes of deadly green.

The background lay, to their astonished sight,
   Over a bottomless region of woe—
Region of darkness, eternal night,
   Where the doomed, the damned, the lost, all go!
The smoke of their torment thence ascends,
   Not from the glorious meerschaum bowl,
But from the pit where all hope ends—
   Pit of eternal loss of the soul!
From the fatal slope—the verge, the brink—
   Thousands were sliding to the pit below;
Downward through smoke and darkness they sink,
   Where the dread fires unquenchable glow!

Deep horrible slime hastened their fall—
   Slime from the mouths of cavendish chewers—
Fetid, putrid, stenchy and foul—
   Foul as intolerable London sewers;
Such as often covers the floors

Of cars, saloons, bar rooms and coaches,
Where custom does not turn out of doors
    These unmannerly biped roaches.
Oh, the nauseous, horrible slime
    Along the church-aisle, pulpit and pews!
Yes, the nauseous, horrible slime,
    Fouling a lady's dress, smearing her shoes.

Think of a wife inhaling the breath
    From such a filthy slavering man!
Compound of vile weed, foul stomach, and death—
    Oh, woman, what bondage! bear it, who can?
A stove made the butt for the spitting
    By her lord, leaning back in his chair;
There it fries; and wife, cooking or knitting,
    Sickens while breathing the nauseous air.
Again, her lord, leaning back in his chair,
    Poured volumes of smoke from his black meerschaum.
The poor wife bears it all in despair,
    Coughs and retches and vomits with qualm.

Is there no law for woman's protection—
    None to be found in church or state?
Wives never to vote at an election,
    Doomed to bear (tame and passive) their fate?
Let young maidens hold firmly the power
    That nature has given their virgin charms,
Never, no, never, surrender their dower,
    Never be clasped in a foul tyrant's arms;
Till pledged against cavendish and meerschaum,
    Let him sue for your hand in vain;
Till pledged for temperance in every form,
    Stand aloof from wedlock's fatal chain.

———

THE BEAUTIES OF TOBACCO.

"Let me alone till I swallow down my spittle." Job vii. 19.
"Forbearance ceases to be a virtue."

I do not know, Mr. Editor, who first used the above sentence. It may have been some morose misanthrope or cynic who ought to have had a better temper.

When for long years I have thought of writing a rebuke to tobacco chewers and smokers, a host of unfortunate and suffering humanity has stalked before me: A man, with hips nearly dislocated with rheumatism, in my vision hobbled along, with old torn and greasy clothes, with toes projecting from his boots, and coming into a smoky house, steadied the chair on a broken hearth, and drew from his pocket a rickety jack-knife and the precious pigtail, and enjoyed an hour's—amelioration of his woes, spitting at the chimney back. Poor old man! The woman who had spent the day in petulance, scolding the urchins, bringing their scanty meal to a bare table, drawn out on the warped and loose floor, racking under every step; poor woman, when the toils of day are over, draws her chair up to the fire over against her spouse, and drawing her pipe from its shelf in the jamb, sends up from the point of her sharp nose a curling cloud of smoke, and sighing, says, "Another day of toil and sorrow is over; dear me! what a world!"

Again I have thought of young men, too ill-formed and awkward to ever expect to be loved by the fair; who, in their despair, poor fellows! think they might as well just give up to it, and have their breath as disgusting as the odor of the pole-cat; and old maids, who, despairing of ever coming well into market, give up to smoke their faces brown as the board over a Dutch fire-place.

I have refrained from writing a word on the subject of tobacco for fear of wounding these woe-burdened souls; but my pent-up feelings have at last broke their barrier, and what the end will be I cannot tell. Memory seems now determined to keep me busy with visions of the past.

Old Elder Brown, who was the first minister under whose instruction I sat in childhood, breathed on me, when I was six years old, the horrid odor of his tobacco-case throat. He used to commence every sermon with his cheek distended, chewing and spitting, endangering the clean pants of tow and linen worn by the deacons around him.

Before he got to thirdly, he couched down, dropping one side of his face in his hand, as though he had the toothache, took from his mouth a huge quid, threw it under the chair which served as a pulpit, and with the other hand replenished his yellow mouth with a long cut of lady's-twist, or pigtail.

Fortunately there was no kneeling in those days in time of prayer. The deacons stood in tobacco spittle forty-five minutes by the clock, while the strength of one quid lasted, then the prayer ended.

Now, Mr. Editor, I must pass over the subjects of spitting on men and women in meeting and elsewhere, spitting on stoves, floors and ceilings; spitting over pudding-kettles and frying-pans while dinner is cooking; I must pass over burnt sleeves, aprons, shawls, and worse yet, burnt brains. I must pass over these and a multitude of other ills, to man and woman, and come to spitting in the church.

Association of ideas is a property and law of our nature. Decorum, propriety and neatness are naturally associated with the ideas of the worship of God. Even private prayer can hardly be practiced profitably in a filthy place.

Again, our ideas of worship are naturally associated with ideas of separation and setting apart from all that is secular. Such is the idea of dedication. We, in a manner, dedicate our places of secret prayer, selecting them, if possible, where no secular business is done; where we never go except to pray.   Our Puritan fathers were wise in forbidding all men the wearing of hats or talking in church, before and after service.

The sacredness of churches is almost lost in this age; men and boys stalk in and talk and laugh with hats on; boys sometimes tripping, pushing and scuffling; women talking, and girls giggling.

Again, shocking to all sense of propriety, when the discourse is called a lecture, the stampings, clappings and boisterous roars of laughter are enough to make one think himself in Pandemonium.   But yet the most shocking of all the desecration is the spitting.   Wherein were the Augean stables worse than some places of worship ? Do you ask men, and even women, to kneel in such horrid places ? Do you ask mourners to go to the anxious seat and kneel in tobacco spittle at the risk of vomiting in the church? You are almost as bad as the prophet Isaac, who compelled a young lady, one of his disciples, to roll in a state of nudity in a mud-puddle in the street.

I recently attended a meeting where a protracted effort was being made.   Mourners were called forward to be prayed for by mouths which ought never to open, or when open ought never to shut, but stand ajar, ventilated by the north wind.   On Sabbath morning I came in for love feast rather early ; the congregation had not assembled.   I saw behind the seat, extending nearly across one end of the house, what seemed to be a rivulet of blackened blood.   I turned and was still more alarmed to see another stream nearly across the side of the house.   As these streams were from twelve to eighteen inches wide, I had reason to fear that two full-grown men had been murdered there during the night; but I was hardly relieved when I found it to be tobacco-spittle, which had been accumulating during the

progress of this meeting. I left in doubt whether such efforts would really promote godliness.

Some years since I was requested to assist brethren of
another denomination at the table of the Lord. It was in
an unfinished meeting-house, with movable benches. I
looked for some time in despair for a place for the table of
the Lord. Far as I could see puddles joined puddles, and
in agony I said in my heart, Where are men and women to
kneel? I looked around for the murderers of decorum.
Lo! there they sat! honorable officials, who had seated
themselves near the pulpit, and showed their deep interest
in the sermon in a zealous spitting match. I seriously think
it would have been better for the presiding minister to have
called on the stewards to take the elements away, as there
was no place for the table of the Lord. What could we
remember or commemorate at such a place? To kneel in
tobacco-spittle and inhale such an odor would be likely to
keep the Augean stables constantly in mind.

Oh, where is a pure sanctuary to be found? Give me the
open field, the wildwood for a church, rather than these
filthy holes!

Do not talk of getting off by spittoons, horrid hiding
places of filth, sending forth the most loathsome of all odors.
No! There is no remedy but to stop manufacturing this
abominable stuff, or to swallow down your spittle; one or the
other you ought to do, or never again enter church.

TOBACCO—OH, THE SPITTING!

Once the horrid liquid, which seems made up of the
essence of the weed mixed with all that is sour, dead, fetid,
putrid, rotten, in the human body, fried on the red-hot feet
of the andirons, when much of the fumes went up the
broad chimney; but in later times, as polite habits improve,

this liquid is fried on the hearths and doors of the stoves, when the fumes, unable to get out of the room, go round and round, seeking and lodging in every gentleman's and every lady's nostrils and mouth.   Then, as change in nature's law, next comes the smoke from the corner yonder, curling up like incense from an altar of Dagon.   Does it come from the old black pipe? Yes, but it comes by way of that belching, nauseous stomach, and putrid lungs, before it is blown out of that sepulchral throat for our benefit.   The particles of human death come in the smoke, and in spite of shutting our mouth and eyes, go into our lungs and blood. Smokers on the railroad have their special car, rent free, but spitters are not required to move an inch, but may drench the floor and bespatter every lady and gentleman near them, drench the aisle, and every trailing silk carries off its portion of the abominable slaver.   In the church we fain would have our thoughts on things pure and holy, but often the sight and stench around forces upon us unwelcome memories of the most loathsome and disgusting sights, and scenes, and fumes, we have ever witnessed, and as fashion sweeps the floors with silk, our female hearers are often too much anxious about their apparel to listen to any instruction.

DEATH IN THE FOREST.

The following lines were suggested by reflecting on the death of old Mr. Hayden, which occurred more than thirty years ago. He had been a soldier in the Revolutionary War, and had contracted a habit of drinking. After the war his drinking habits increased, until his family fled from him. I first saw him in 1813, and often saw him until his death.

His life was that which is common to a drunkard—a life of blasphemy and sottishness. His blasphemy surpassed all

that I ever heard.   For forty years his words of blasphemy
have been locked up in my mind.   I have never dared to
repeat them.   He left a tavern in East Rush about midnight late in the fall of the year, and crossing a forest near
the Honeoye, he attempted to climb over some fallen trees,
when his foot slipped through and he fell back with so much
force that he was never able to rise, and nearly a week after
was found dead upon his back, his feet still fast between the
logs, and his bottle between his knees.   How long he lived
in his cold wet bed, and listened to the winds and water-
falls, no one knows.

Long years have passed since that night, and the name
"Webster's Mills" may be unknown to the present generation; the village of East Rush may cover the spot where
the old man died; the railroad track may cross his cold bed;
but the Honeoye is still the same, and roars now as it did
when the dying man cried:

> "Dark is the night and the tempest is loud,
>   As here I die, here I die;
> North winds are bringing the snow for my shroud,
>   As here I die, here I die.
> Dreary my bed; oh, so cold is the ground,
> Freezing the rills that encircle me round;
> Loud roars the tempest—how dreadful the sound,
>   As here I die—here I die.
>
> "Once I had all the endearments of home;
>   Then I was blest, I was blest;
> Cursed be the day that I tasted of rum—
>   Now I am lost, I am lost.
> Fond wife and children I drove from their bed,
> Sadly they mourned when grouped in a shed,
> Loud were my ravings, and frightened they fled;
>   Oh! I am cursed—I am cursed!

"Hark! do I here the voice of a friend?
    Oh ! is there help, is there help ?
No! no! I hear but the wail of the wind ;
    There is no help—no ! no help !
Never again a friend shall I see ;
Never again shall the fire blaze for me ;
Soon in the cold arms of death shall I be ;
    Here I must die—I must die !"

THE COUNTRY, OR RURAL LIFE.

The solstice of Summer is come,
    The heat of the most lengthened day;
Leave the pantings and deafening hum,
    And come from the city away.

Oh, come where the winds gently move
    The green robe of nature's sweet shade,
The mighty Creator's in love
    With the noble fair creature he's made.

See the sheep on the green grassy hills,
    And the cows in the valley below ;
There the cool and the bright sparkling rills
    Meander where wild lilies grow.

See the mother-bird feeding her young, .
    As they swing on the branch in the shade,
Their tiny house skillfully hung
    And wisely and artfully made.

The winds bring sweet odors along
    From nature's wild gardens of flowers,
The woodlands are vocal with song,
    Oh, come to the wild forest bowers.

Hear the happy children shout,
From the school room just let out,
Swiftly hieing o'er the hill,
All are hastening to the rill,
Where the grateful waters flow
To the verdant vale below ;
Merry lads with tiny hook,
On the green bank by the brook,
Angling for the wily trout ;
Hear them, hear them, how they shout !
Hear the plowman's cheerly song,
As he slowly moves along,
While behind him, shy and coy,
Runs his little laughing boy.
There the larger boys now go,
Each with bright and shining hoe ;
Soon the merry group is seen,
In the cornfield richly green.
To the meadow whistling blithe,
Goes the mower with his scythe.
For an hour at mid day,
Old and young may join in play ;
On the charming silver lake,
Let them sweet excursion take.
Hie away ! ply the oar
Where the waters kiss the shore ;
Wake the waters sleeping laid
In the stately forest shade.
Hear that saucy screaming loon ;
There, there, down she's gone !
Guess we'll never see her more ;
There, she rose on t'other shore.

Oh, come where the winds gently move
The green robe of nature's sweet shade ;

The mighty Creator's in love
With the noble fair creature he's made.

———

THE OLD PLOW.

AN EMBLEM.

Oft I've seen the brave old plow
By the fence where the wild weeds grow,
All neglected, black and old,
Drenched in rain and clad in mould.

Once along the verdant lawn
By seven yoke of oxen drawn;
Huge rocks breaking with a crash,
Echoed with the sounding lash.

Every obstacle is spurned,
Turf and rocks and trees o'erturned,
Till the rough burr-oak plain
Smiled with waving fields of grain.

Now the toilsome breaking's done,
Number Three, and Two, and One,
Join to push the Number Ten
Aside, to rot within the glen.

Poor old plow ! it is thy lot
Here to lie and thus to rot.
Now the small plow has the field—
To thy fate in patience yield.

Often from life's busy stage
Thus we see that toil-worn age
Is rudely, rashly pushed aside
By headlong zeal and youthful pride.

In a happier golden age
Youth revered the reverend sage ;

Grave old Nestor's every word
All the Greeks in silence heard.

Strong Achilles, Ajax brave,
And Agamemnon audience gave;
All along the martial field
Every hero dropped his shield.

Now, alas! for Nestor's day,
That golden age has passed away;
Later in degenerate times
Stained with parricidal crimes.

Tullius' mangled, reverend corse
Is trampled by young Tarquin's horse;
'Neath the wheels the reverend sage—
His blood is in his locks of age.

Socrates in prison lies,
There he bows his head and dies;
Colon, carried o'er the main,
Wears the cruel galling chain.

Erasmus from the age of night
Brought the glorious morning light;
Ungrateful sons, in zeal and strife,
Sought the reverend patriarch's life.

Reverend sire, thy work is done,
Thy deeds unwritten and unknown.
Thou art jostled from the stage,
Uncared for in thy weary age.

Let oblivion's sober pall
Spread around and cover all.
Sire, let it be thy lot
Thus to die and be forgot.

In the bosom of thy God
Let thy name and life be laid ;
Soon thy dark and dreary night
Will be lost in endless light.

THE HERMIT OF MOUNT GARGARUS.

I found in the depths of the wilderness wide,
  The cabin of Jonathan Low ;
Where dark gloomy mists and tempest clouds glide,
  O'er Gargarus covered with snow.

By moss-covered rocks, never warmed by the sun,
  The cabin of Jonathan lay;
I found him at rest, his task being done,
  At rest at the close of the day.

He had gathered his food from lakelet and glen,
  His food for the evening and morn ;
And come to his cabin as cheerful as when
  One comes at the call of the horn.

He sat on the moss at the low cottage door ;
  Scamander, of old Homer's song,
Flowed fearfully by, with horrible roar,
  From cascade to cascade along.

Lo ! over his head, on the dark brown rocks,
  The evergreens moving on high,
Seemed the head of old Jove, with ambrosial locks,
  Giving his nod in the sky.

It was twenty long years that Jonathan Low
  Had dwelt in the wilderness wide;
In the deep mountain gorge where wild tempests blow,
  And darkly the storm-clouds glide.

Poor Jonathan Low, in the days of his youth
    Had tried fickle friendship to woo ;
Had trusted frail man, for his honor and truth,
    But, alas! poor Jonathan Low !

He trusted in man, but he trusted to rue
    His faith in deep sorrow and pain;
He leaned on man, and it pierced his hand through,.
    Like a reed that is broken in twain.

Cold selfishness, greedily grasping for wealth,
    Supplanted the toil-worn and poor ;
Cold selfishness, everywhere creeping with stealth,
    Drove hope from poor Jonathan's door.

The shrewd caught the simple each day in his gin ;.
    He lived by his wits, as he said ;
His priest ever taught him he practiced no sin,
    And promised him heaven when dead.

The shrewd the avails of the honest man's toil
    Bore away to the heaps of his gain ;
The priest always came, and divided the spoil,
    And doctored his conscience again.

'Twas money divided the little and great,
    And money, they said, was power;
It was power to crush, at the rich man's gate,
    The helpless, dependent, and poor.

Oh, is there no land of benevolence ? cried
    Poor sorrowing Jonathan Low ;
To the deep dark shade of the wilderness wide,
    The gorge of the mountain I'll go.

Peace to the soul of poor Jonathan Low,
    As he dwells in the wilderness wide,

In the valley beneath old Gargarus' brow,
  Where the mists and the storm-clouds glide.

May he gather his food from lakelet and glen,
  His food for the evening and morn;
And come to his cabin, as cheerful as when
  One comes at the call of the horn.

May his meek, his gentle, and innocent soul
  In evening devotion be blest;
And Scamander's roar, and the wild tempest's howl,
  Be music to lull him to rest.

Note.—Mount Gargarus, in Asia Minor, lifts its bald head of rocky snow to the clouds. Here neither tree nor herb is found; but in a milder zone below the snows melt, and there the Scamander, of Homer's song, has its source, and rushing down through awful gorges of incredible depth, foaming, and thundering, from cascade to cascade, it becomes tamed in the plains of Troas, and moves serenely to the sea. Near its mouth stood the city of Troy, which was destroyed by the Greeks three thousand years ago.

Hermits once resorted to the valleys in those deep gorges. Their bones were found in their cabins or caverns many ages after.—See "Clark's Travels."

GOOD OLD TIMES.

In the merry morn of life,
Free, free from ever sordid strife,
Happy, gleeful, jocund, gay,
Simple, innocent at play.

Now a labyrinth we wind,
Through a swamp of sighing pines,
How we chase each other round,
O'er the mossy carpet bound!

As we shouted, Lo! the hare,
Springing from her little lair,
Galloping off with all her might,
In a moment out of sight.

Then the coy partridge springs
On her nimble whirring wings.
Hurra, boys! away we go,
Where the luscious chestnuts grow.

Where the pretty sparkling rills
Wind and murmur from the hills;
Happy streamlets, soon you'll be
Mingled with the Genesee.

Cattle low and cow-bells ring,
Pigeons fly and squirrels sing;
Let us cheerly shout and play,
Hurra, playmates! what a day!

Night's approaching; comrades, come,
Shoulder bags, and hasten home;
Boys! the cottage fire is bright,
See the windows glow with light.

Reader, those were happy days,
Only known in ballad lays.
'Twas before the wrath of Jove
Cursed us with the gloomy stove.

Nuts from every forest tree,
With a genuine hearty glee,
From our well-filled bags we pour,
Making up our ample store.

Good old-fashioned chimney back!
Reader, sure it had no lack;

Square, erect as temple wall,
Firm, and thick, and wide, and tall.

The noble hearth, our family pride,
Was made of stones and ten feet wide.
Hickory wood by maple logs
Piled on strong old-fashioned dogs.

Oh, the glorious blazing fire!
Nothing had such power to cheer,
Before the wrath of angry Jove
Cursed us with a gloomy stove.

See the whitened table-spread!
Mother made it, every thread.
Pewter plates and pewter bowls,
Pumpkin pies and smoking rolls.

Grandpa tells us what was done
In the days of Washington,
How they fought by land and sea,
Paul Jones, Schuyler, Green and Lee.

Sisters with the singing wheels,
Keeping time with hands and heels,
Turned the woolen rolls to yarn,
Cloth to make, and stockings darn.

Mother at the distaff head
Drew off in each hand a thread
From the flax, our wants to meet,
Frocks and trousers, bags and sheets.

We and father shelled the corn,
Ready for the early morn;
Soon as light dispels the dark,
Away to mill, blithe as a lark.

Where the Irondequoit flows,
Through the oakland hills it goes,
'Long the beauteous valley low,
Where the whortleberries grow.

Sometimes to the Honeoye,
Whistling all the day with joy;
In the plum groves how we ran,
Crowding plums in with the bran.

Sometimes to the mighty falls,
Where the Genesee from her walls
Dashes down with awful sound,
Spreading clouds of spray around.

Then the stealthy rattlesnakes,
Alder swamps, and bogs, and brakes,
Covered all in wild repose,
Where Rochester has since arose.

BAD ECONOMY IN AGRICULTURAL LIFE.

I would not join hands with those rich men who, having robbed the poor by their oppressive money power, taking advantage of their necessities, selling to them at high prices, and paying them low wages, then turn upon them and taunt them with "bad economy." Humanity forbids that I should endorse them in saying that all poverty is in consequence of shiftlessness; that the poor do not deserve sympathy. I claim no higher rank, no higher honor, than to be counted with the industrious poor. I ask no higher brotherhood. If I had all that I have earned by hard labor, I should be far above want. I have seen the palace of the rich, his carriage, and the costly clothing and furniture of his family, and felt that a part of this came from my half-requited toil, while my children were most poorly clothed. After this

preface, let me say, there is much bad economy. In my
extensive travels I have seen costly frames rotting for want
of roofs; hay thrown to cattle in the mud, half of it trodden
under foot; cattle unsheltered from winter rains; again in
the coldest winds, shivering in open fields, unsheltered except by a coat of snow and ice. I have seen sheep drooping in winter rains, carrying all the cold water that their
wool would absorb; and hogs in unsheltered pens, standing
deep in the mud, out of which they were rooting the corn
fed to them, then lying down to sleep in the mire; and
other half starved hogs running all day in the snow, seeking
to break through and steal. Hens and other domestic
fowls often have no house, and scanty food, and are frequently seen with frozen heads and feet.

How melancholy have been my travels in the spring of
the year, to see men lifting cows and oxen, too weak to rise
alone, and to see the carcases of the dead animals about
the yards and fields, and to reflect on their long continued
sufferings from starvation and cold. "A merciful man is
merciful to his beast." Oxen and horses are sometimes
wintered so poorly that they have not strength to plow in
the spring. A little is done in a day of shallow plowing; on
this half-prepared soil planting is done, three or four weeks
too late, exposing the corn to frost in the fall. Sometimes
this poor crop is picked out of the weeds, and badly shocked
and greatly injured by late fall rains. In October or November the same ground is sown to wheat, with foul seed,
and harrowed in with the millions of foul seeds raised with
the corn. In the winter the fence is down, and cattle and
sheep run over the field at their leisure, and they often
break in during spring and summer. Five or six bushels of
foul wheat to the acre is gathered; after which this worn
out and yet foul ground is lightly plowed and sown again.
Plows are used fit only to be sold for old iron. These bad

farmers are not all tavern-haunters, nor lazy hunters with
starved yelping hounds at their heels.   Some of them are
honest, hard-working men.   Why do they waste their
strength?   Partly from ignorance, and partly from poverty.
I have rarely seen a badly managed Quaker farm.   They
advise one another and help one another, so that they plant
on well-fitted ground in season, with good seed.   Should
not Wesleyans do the same?

AGRICULTURAL.

TERRA CULTURE.—When Professor Comstock was lecturing on Terra Culture, professing to have made discoveries
which would enrich the world, and farmers were flocking to
hear him, and paying one dollar admittance, they simply
learned to plant shallow.   This was the sum of Terra Culture.   Trees planted shallow were never to sprout, and were
to thrive wonderfully.   I planted an orchard shallow.   It
was sickly and drooping, several trees dying.

Where the earth was turned to the trees by the plow, I
hoed it away.   After three years trial my orchard seemed
nearly worthless, what life it had going to sprouts.   I then
plowed, turning the furrows to the trees on both sides, and
did the same in cross-plowing, so that each tree stood in a
kind of knoll, since which time, my trees have revived, and
are now doing finely.

GRAPES.—Why should any family be without grapes?   If
you own a cottage, and one foot of ground outside of it,
plant a grape vine.

A family in this town has one vine, an Isabella, which
covers two sides of their house, and produces twelve bushels
in a year, and sometimes more.

NECESSITY THE MOTHER OF INVENTION.—The Yankee
who gathers his stinted harvest from among the rocks of

New England astonishes the world by his inventions; while in the valley of the Mississippi, the farmer grovels in stupidity amid his thousand acres of corn.

FENCES.—When, in my travels, I see all fences high and strong, I say, there people live in peace. Here I should look for religious prosperity.

WEEDS.—Weeds, like sins, are easily destroyed when starting; but a little delay will give them the mastery over you.

TEAMS.—Do not drive them when suffering from hunger, thirst, weariness or soreness.

BALKING.—Govern your temper, and you will govern your horse.

PLEASURE OF GARDENING.—Diocletian said he had more pleasure in cultivating his garden, than he enjoyed in ruling an empire.

June, 1863.

THE ENLARGEMENT OF JAPHETH.

"God shall enlarge Japheth." Gen. ix. 27.

These words were spoken by Noah more than four thousand years ago. His prophetic vision came down over the past forty centuries, nor stops at the present, but passes on over the vast length of the future.

Noah says nothing of Ham's three oldest sons. The genius of history, perched on the fane of Belus, beheld Cush Mizraim and Phut wending their way to the southwest, passing the Gulf of Suez and spreading up the Nile and beyond the Libyan desert; and beheld the families of Shem spreading eastward beyond the Indus and over the plains of Tartary, while Japheth was lost in the dark forests of Europe. But the spirit of Noah's prophecy seems principally confined to Canaan's subjugation, and Japheth's enlargement.

Canaan's subjugation occurred when the Hebrews under Joshua subdued all of the Southern tribes of Canaan.

Japheth's enlargement did not immediately take place. His families were but dimly seen by the genius of history after they crossed the Dardanelles and Bosphorus, and journeyed around the Euxine. As they spread up the Volga and Danube and down the Mediterranean, they sank into ignorance and barbarism the most profound. For long ages they inhabited the shores of the Baltic and the British Islands in a cloud of mental and religious darkness so dense that no historian's eye beheld them, and all that is known of them in those early times the modern historian learns by tracing back the monumental proofs of their early existence.

Although Noah lived five hundred years after the flood, yet during this long time not a ray of light fell on all the regions of Europe, and Noah saw nothing, except by faith, of Japheth's enlargement. Although he saw among the children of Ham the empire of Mizraim arising in the south, and the lamps of science lighted in the ancient city of the Pharaohs, and saw the children of Shem rally under Nimrod, a grandson of Ham, and found an empire on the Tigris and Euphrates; saw that empire under Semiramis, the most illustrious heroine of antiquity, spread until it held dominion over the most important part of Asia; saw Babylon and Nineveh arise with walls and public works surpassing all that has ever since appeared on earth, and saw science as the morning light over the plains of Shinah; yet to the time of Noah's death, darkness unbroken was over all the regions of Europe, and the Pelasgi roamed the islands of Greece so savage that they ate the flesh of men raw from their bones, as wild beasts devour each other.

This darkness continued five hundred years after the death of Noah, or one thousand after the flood. Then a few scattering rays of light from Chaldea and Egypt fell on the Greeks inhabiting the shores of the Archipelago or Ægean sea. This was the first dawn of Japheth's enlargement. The early Greek historians were poets, and often indulged in all the latitude of poetic fancy. Hence Grecian history can be but little depended upon before the days of Theseus. This was about one thousand and two hundred years before Christ. Shortly after Theseus, flourished the great Homer, father of poetry. His poetry was historical, and from the vast fields of his fancy we have to cull the facts historical of Agamemnon and Hector, of Grecian enlargement and the fall of Troy. From the Trojan war, or the days of Agamemnon, the Greeks arose in the arts and sciences with great rapidity, and arrived at the zenith of their glory in the age of Socrates. In this age flourished a great number of eminent men, artists, poets, orators and historians.

Long after Chaldean and Egyptian light fell on the shores of the Ægean sea all the rest of Europe was in profound darkness.

About 750 years before Christ the eastern light began to illumine the banks of the Tiber. A band of robbers under Romulus stopped their wanderings and built a city. Science arose with the rising strength of Rome, until Italy, and finally all Europe, was illuminated.

The zenith of Roman greatness was the Augustan age, the time of the Christian era, when the God of heaven set up a kingdom that should never be destroyed. Rome had now been advancing in strength seven hundred and fifty years, and had made the conquest of the world. She had not only brought home the trophies of history, but she had brought home the arts and sciences of all nations. The school and the masters of Greece were transplanted in Rome, and this great city, containing more than four millions of people, became the seat of all improvements, except in morals and religion. When the light of Egyptian and

Chaldean science fell on the sons of Japheth it brought no
religious improvement.   The Greeks and Romans were no
better in religion for all of their science.   " The world by
wisdom knew not God."   At the time of the Augustan age
more than two thousand years had passed since the uttering
of the language of the text; yet but a few comparatively of
the sons of Japheth were enlightened, for Roman and Grecian literature covered but a small portion of Europe.   The
barbarian Goths inhabited Germany, and the equally barbarian Gauls inhabited France.   Into these countries
Roman conquests had carried the elements of improvement,
and the Goths and the Gauls began to experience the dawn
of civilization.   But scarce a ray of light had yet fallen on
the British Islands, and the Scandinavians and Scythians
were in the midnight of a savage light.

Norway, Sweden, Denmark and the vast region of Russia
were sunk in superstition and barbarism, that no poet's imagination can paint.   Scarce any of the soil of Great Britain
was cultivated; most of the inhabitants roamed naked in
summer and slept at night without houses, on the ground,
unsheltered, and in winter dwelt in caves or in huts constructed of brush and turf.

The Augustan age is the second great epoch in time.   It
was the time of the end of the Mosaic dispensation, and of
the Jewish nation; the time of the setting up of Messiah's
kingdom.

Shem and Ham had both arrived at their zenith and both
were henceforth to wane.   This was the meridian time of
heathen science; it was to rise no higher, but to wane away
through coming ages.   Japheth's enlargement thus far, as
seen in the Greeks and Romans, was in the light of pagan
science, first received from Chaldea and Egypt.   This was
not Japheth's true enlargement.   Rome and Greece were
to wane in the general wane of pagan wisdom.   The lamps

of Grecian and Roman literature were to decline to their
last flickering, and then to be seized by barbarian hands and
borne away to be trimmed and replenished on the banks of
the Rhine, the Seine and Thames, under the influence of
the gospel.

The land of the Goths, covered with its dark forests,
where barbarian darkness was as midnight, was to become
our modern Germany, the seat of conscience, where Luther
was to move as the bolts of thunder, or as the rumbling
earthquake, upheaving and overturning the foundations of
society, religious and civil; while Erasmus (may heaven forgive D'Aubigne for the injury he has done to his name),
Reuchlin and Melancthon were to polish the materials for
rebuilding.   Gothland was to become the land of universities, and give to the world during the sixteenth, seventeenth,
eighteenth and nineteenth centuries a host of giant sons of
science.

The land of the Gauls, spreading from the eternal snows
of the Alps to the western ocean, and where the Seine in
olden time flowed darkly through the forest-covered plain,
when the wandering savage Gaul sat on its banks only with
his warrior harness—this land, too, was to become the seat
of science, and give to the world orators and philosophers
of the highest order, and here was to arise the great Rol-
lin, the prince of historians, the man of all ages.

Under the genial influence of the gospel, the furious
Scandinavian from the shores of the Baltic was to leave the
altars of Woden, gory with the blood of men, and arise to
humanity and intelligence.   But there is one portion of the
inheritance of Japheth that above all others arises to my
view.   'Tis an island which on the south had its albion
banks washed by an expansive channel; to the east lay the
German Ocean; while the tempests that swept o'er the
Atlantic howled along its western shore and roared among

the highlands of Morven.   Probably the sons of Japheth
came to this island shortly after they spread through Europe,
but how or when no one can tell; oblivion holds her pall
tightly over their names and deeds for nearly two thousand
years.   We find the country at the time of the first Roman
invasion nearly all a wilderness, and the people naked wanderers, living by the chase.   The inhabitants of the south
of the island were called Britons, and those of the north
Scots.

From the time of the invasion these islanders steadily improved, gradually changing their habits and learning the
arts of civilized life.   For some ages after this their history
is but little known, as they were wholly unlettered and had
no historians of their own.   In the highlands of the north
they had an excellent mode of tradition.   They had always
a class of historical poets, who composed and sung the
names and deeds of great men.   These historical poets always had successors, and their historical songs probably
varied but little in a thousand years.   These poets, like all
other poets, embellished and exaggerated much.   From this
source we learn that the highlanders were strangers to agriculture and all the arts of civilized life.   They are represented as sleeping, even in that cold climate, in the open
air, around fires kindled by the trunks of fallen oaks.   The
palace hills of the great Trenmor, Trathal, and Fingal, kings
of Morven, were so rudely built that when the chiefs were
assembled at the feast of shells and seated in the halls
around a fire rudely built on the ground, the poet who sang
the tale of other times is represented as with hair waving in
the breeze, and the leaves of overhanging oaks were swept
by the wind through the halls.

The Saxons, a tribe or nation of northern Goths, many
centuries after the Roman conquest, conquered the ancient

Britons, and drove all the strength of their nation into the west of the island, or land of Wales.

They mingled with the remainder of the Britons and this amalgamation is the origin of English nationality. From this time there were only slight changes by a small mingling of Scots, Danes, Normans and Germans. For many ages their nationality has been finally and permanently fixed. From this commingling of nations has arisen a new language, *i. e.*, the English, the most copious on earth. This language is now spoken over half the globe, and will probably yet become the language of the world.

The English lack the sprightliness and pleasant gayety of the French, and the confiding generosity of the Germans, yet they have a striking national character. With profound intelligence they have great firmness, often amounting to the fault of stubbornness. They are remarkable for planning great schemes, and slowly, but generally surely, accomplishing them.

In viewing Japheth's enlargement no nation deserves more particular attention than our own. Nearly two and a half centuries ago some of the most devout families of English Protestants, who had formed the most exalted ideas of civil and religious liberty, left their native land and resided some years in Holland. But, not finding the liberty that they deemed the right of all men, and reflecting that this liberty was not enjoyed by any people on earth, they looked to the new, or western world, for an asylum. South and Central America and Mexico had then for one hundred years been receiving a population of Spanish and Portuguese Catholics. To those countries they looked in vain for freedom. For one hundred years attempts had been made to plant colonies on the eastern shores of North America, but all had failed. In the estimation of the Old World these inhospitable regions were never to be peopled

by civilized men.   Our Puritan fathers had long been
trained to walk by faith and not by sight.   They believed
in God and in his providence.   They formed the great idea
of unfurling the banner of the gospel among the wilds of
North America.   They spread their sails to the cold winds
of autumn on the great western ocean, and at the end of a
long and dreary voyage, they hauled their boat to Plymouth
Rock, amidst a snow-storm in the beginning of winter.
There they planted their standard, and there it has stood in
spite of pestilence and war.   Friends of freedom from the
Old World have been joining their number for many ages.
Many of the noblest sons of earth, after failing in a struggle
against tyrants, have made this land their home.

Here a new nation has arisen, mostly of Saxon blood,
yet mingled with friends of freedom from nearly all the nations of Europe.   I may be charged with not giving sufficient consequence to the Jamestown colony; but the Jamestown colony was not the germ of our nation.   It consisted
of a gay, worldly, pleasure-taking people, disposed to aristocracy, neither Puritan nor democratic.   Their character
and disposition has descended to the present generation of
slaveholders.   The Plymouth colony was the germ of our
nation.   The noble character of the passengers of the Mayflower, their devotion to God and their exalted views of the
rights of man, and their noble dignity of manners, descended to after generations, and spread through New England.

In Northern, especially New England, schools nearly all
the great men of our nation have been educated.   Education has a power vastly superior to the boasted power of
moneyed aristocracy, and it is to be hoped that by the blessings of Providence the Puritan leaven will spread over the
South, inspiring men with a noble sense of the rights of
man, rusting to dust the chains of the slave, bringing down

the effulgent light of liberty, intelligence, and to all the dignity of citizens and servants of God.

Emigrants to this country flee from the opressive laws
and customs of the Old World.   They are coming in great
numbers, probably one thousand in a day.   Let them come
and remove the forests and plow the vast prairies of this.
western world; there is ample room.

Let them come, even the Catholic, for we could not cure
him of his error by driving him back or drowning him in.
the sea.   Let the Catholic come where the Puritan leaven.
is destined to make all evangelical.

Let them come, peasant and serf, for here serfdom ceases,
and here the peasant may become the man of wealth, science
and power.   The sons of Japheth seem destined to bring to
perfection every useful science.   He has learned the true
philosophy of our solar system.   See his ships of a size that
would astonish a Phœnician, crossing in a few days oceans
deemed by ancients impassable.   Lo! on the land his rail-
ways so near that the earth between is nearly all shaken
every hour, as the enormous iron horse comes proud of his
might, hauling with the tornado's speed a load equal to the
annual exports of an ancient kingdom.   And see, or let an
angel's vision see, news by telegraph going on the lightning's
wing.   What is yet to come? Perhaps this generation may
see ships traversing our seas with amazing swiftness, with no
wind or fuel, and the telegraph and printing so improved
that Americans may sit by their own fires, reading the
speech of some Pitt or Brougham in the British House of
Peers, before the noble lord has concluded.   And yet if
Father Japheth should revisit the earth, he would be more
absorbed in viewing our future Howards, and Burrits,
preaching peace ; and our future Hebers and Judsons bearing the gospel light, scattering Mohametan and Pagan

darkness from the sons of Shem and Ham, and bringing in the glorious day of Messiah's reign.

HISTORY—CHAPTER III.

GENERAL VIEW OF ANCIENT ASIA.

After the confounding of language and dispersing of mankind, one of the first foreign people seen in the dim light of early history is the nation of Bactrians, whose metropolis was Bactriana, a great city, east of the Caspian Sea, twelve hundred miles northeast from Babylon.

Ninus, son of Nimrod, invaded Bactria, more than four thousand years ago, with four hundred thousand warriors, and took Bactriana by siege.

Osmandyas, one of the early kings of Egypt, built a temple, on the immense wall of which he was represented at the head of four hundred thousand Egyptain soldiers, marching against Bactria. This temple was standing when Herodotus visited Egypt, and this wonderful engraved record was seen by him. Each of these expeditions was as great as Napoleon's Russian campaign, and shows the importance of one great nation in the center of Asia in the earliest times. At a day, equally as ancient, the Indians were a great nation, from the "coral strand" of the Indian Ocean to the sources of the Indus and Ganges, the charming plain of Cashmere, supposed to be the original Eden.

From these two great nations doubtless emigration was setting eastward to Burma, Thibet and China; but no light of history falls on their path so early, except their own uncertain records. We see them at this great distance of time as we see men by starlight, moving in the distant part of a woodland. The early inhabitants of the north of Asia bore many names, most prominent of which were Scythians in the northwest, and Hans in the northeast. The Armenians dwelt in the mountainous region where the Tigris and Euphrates rise. Media was south of the Caspian, and Persia farther south, toward the Persian Gulf.

Asia Minor was peopled by numerous small nations. Canaan inhabited the east shore of the Mediterranean, while the families of Arphaxad, Assur and Nimrod were blending together in the great plain of Shinar, and on the oases of the great desert along the Red Sea, a wild roving people were arising, who subsequently took the name of Arabians, and blended with Ishmael and Esau. Of all these nations the Chaldeans, a small tribe on the Euphrates, were the school of science and morals. Everywhere else pagan superstition and idolatry prevailed, and generally great ignorance and most savage customs. The Chaldeans themselves became idolaters, and Abraham was called to leave them, and finally to separate from all his kindred; when his family alone retained the knowledge of God, and from them, all religious light has come.

The science of Ethnology, or of races of men, has been carried to such extremes as to confuse and disgust every reader, often supported by the most whimsical arguments. Whether we make three races, five, or nine, we must trace all to one origin. From one family all have sprung, and changes have been always arising; men have been dividing and subdividing into thousands of tribes; changing in stature, form and color, by the influence of climate, food and occupation. They have mingled again, nationality has been a hundred times lost, and new nationalities have arisen. Whether Shem, Ham and Japheth differed in color is uncertain.

It appears from Genesis X, which is the only reliable account of early tribes and families, that Asia was principally peopled by Shem. As the children of Japheth moved westward toward Europe, they lingered in Asia, about the shores of the Euxine, Mediterranean and Ægean Seas, and passing over the Bosphorus and the Hellespont, left many of their kindred in Western Asia.   The Chaldean arts, literature and civilization, after they existed a thousand years on the Euphrates, were carried westward by these tribes to the Grecian states.

The literature of India seems to have arisen indigenous on her own soil.   It came on the gold tinged waves of her tropic seas, in the soft winds that fanned her mild and gentle sons with odors from her spice forests and orange groves.

Their literature was beautifully sentimental, but not remarkably profound.   It has not progressed.   It does not perhaps stand higher to-day than it did three thousand years ago.   China and Japan surpass all nations for standing still eternally.   They have long had a dull practical civilization of art and practical science, which may be the same to-day as when Cadmus carried letters to Greece, but they never were literary.   Poetry cannot stand still.   They, however, deserve credit for standing still, while Chaldea and Egypt are lost in the wreck of nations, and even Greece and Rome have been lost in the dark ages.   Bactrian, Mongol and Tartar signify about the same people, the inhabitants of Central Asia, though they have gone through numerous divisions, and re-unions, migrations, conquests and amalgamations.   They have conquered and mingled with the Chinese.   Twice an empire has arisen from this great Tartar hive, one under Ghengis Khan, another under Tamerlane, each fixing his throne in Upper India, and nearly conquering the world.   The former extended his conquests to the Baltic, and the latter came near the walls of Constantinople.   As the great "ice slide" of geologists carried fragments of Arctic rocks, strewing them over the United States to the Gulf of Mexico, so these great conquests strewed fragments of Mongol´blood over all Asia and half of Europe.

The Hans, subsequently called Huns, and now called Hungarians, in the earliest times lay on the northern borders of China, always at war, sometimes reducing the Chinese to subjection, mocking the wall built to shut them out. They were at last expelled by Mongol Chinese, when they sullenly moved west and lingered for ages on the north of the Caspian and then on the Euxine, and finally, under Attila, over-ran and conquered Rome perhaps a thousand years after they were first known in history. They were, in ancient times, the most beastlike of human beings, hardly having the features of men.

The Arabs were a scattered, small, but independent people, until the time of Mohammed. From this time they arose, with uncommon and astonishing rapidity, until their empire embraced all Africa, and all Western Asia with a very small exception. When Roman and Grecian literature was buried under the tread of barbarians, the Muses fled to Bagdad, where Arab Mohammedans became poets, orators, and men of eminent science and polished manners, till the Turks, a barbarous clan of Tartars, over-ran the whole Saracen empire, and though they embraced the faith of the vanquished, they made an end of all refinement, and blackened half the world with barbarism.

HISTORY—CHAPTER XXVI.

ATHENS.

When Cecrops landed with his Egyptian colony on the wild shores of Greece, fifteen hundred and fifty-six years before the time of Christ, the savage people were still roaming the forests, strangers to marriage and all of the domestic customs of civilization. Cecrops built a fort for the protection of his colony, and around this gradually arose the city of Athens, destined to become the queen city of the literary world.   The barbarian tribes had been there five hundred years, with very little improvement, and we may date the earliest dawn of Athenian civilization in the advent of the Egyptian colony of Cecrops.   He came not to conquer and expel the inhabitants, but to win them by kindness; to mingle with and improve them, to introduce all the arts of Egypt.   Marriage was instituted, agriculture introduced, permanent dwellings erected, and the family relation began to appear.   These changes were slow; while a few were thus civilized the masses lingered long in their rudeness; and five hundred years more passed before there was anything like general civilization, more properly half-civilization, for the time of Athenian literature had not arrived.   It was yet the heroic age, in which the intellectual man was little cultivated.   Strength and activity of body received the highest praise, and here and there a hero stalked with giant tread, while the ignorant masses beheld him with wonder, exaggerated his deeds, and thought him a demigod.

Cecrops was a wise prince, and was succeeded by kings who deserve the name of fathers of the Athenian people. The court entitled Areopagus acquired in the earliest times a reputation through the world.   The wisdom of this court gave Athens the ascendancy in Greece.   Two kings in Thessaly brought an important trial there for decision. One had killed the son of the other for seducing and violating his daughter.   The court acquitted the homicide, judging seduction worthy of death; and in like manner, more than three thousand years afterward, an American court acquitted Sickles for shooting Key, who had seduced and violated his wife.   Amphictyon, one of the early kings of Athens, took the lead in uniting many of the Grecian states in a league of confederation, already described.   Ægeus is

famous for giving name to the Sea of Islands, the Ægean,
or Archipelago. His son Theseus was one of the most famous of Grecian heroes; famous for great deeds of courage
and strength, not always virtuous. He generously laid aside
the most of kingly prerogative and power, and gave the
Athenians a republican government. He flourished about
three hundred years after the foundation of Athens by
Cecrops, and more than twelve hundred before Christ. His
successors bore the title of king more than a hundred years,
to the time of Codrus, who abolished it, and left the title of
archon to his son, who held it for life. At a later day the
archon held his office for ten years, and still later for one
year. The kings from Theseus, and especially the archons
from Codrus, possessed power and occupied a position much
like the president of a modern republic.

The Athenian republic degenerated into an oligarchy.
The common evil of our social state—great diversity of property, became the bane of the Athenians, as in Sparta before Lycurgus. The Athenian government had been maintained without written laws. In the idea of written laws
some hope arose in the minds of the poor, and Draco was
chosen to frame a code. He fixed alike the penalty of
death to every crime, killing a man or stealing a chicken.
They shocked the common sense of men, and were not executed. They were written about six hundred and twenty
years before Christ. The evils still increased for fifty years
more, when arose the most illustrious law-giver the world
has ever known.

Solon was born about six hundred years before Christ.
Prompted by a most generous philanthropy, he sought from
every source the wisdom to give laws to his countrymen.
For this purpose he spent many years in traveling, and
learning of the wisest law-givers of the most enlightened
nations. Returning to Athens, he gained the confidence

of the citizens to such an extent that they submitted to most extensive innovations and changes in the government.   As the poor were oppressed by debts, Solon began by decreeing repudiation.   He did not, like Lycurgus, sieze upon all of the property and divide it equally.   He left every one what wealth he had gained; but seeing the poor crushed by the money power, he took from the creditor the rod which he held over him.   He then provided for the punishment of idleness, making it the duty of the magistrates to arrest and punish all who were not engaged in some proper business.   All parents were obliged to train their children to labor.   The citizens were divided into four tribes, or classes, according to property.   Each class elected one hundred senators.   The senate of four hundred proposed laws, the twenty thousand citizens passed laws, and the Areopagus confirmed or vetoed them; and what is strange, the twenty thousand citizens were the final judiciary, to determine the meaning, or intent of law.   The citizens dwelt in the city of Athens and in one hundred and seventy-four incorporated villages.   There must have been a large part of the people in the condition of aliens and slaves.   These, though not allowed to take part in the government, were not overlooked by Solon, who aimed at the happiness and elevation of all mankind.

More than any other man, he opened and prepared the way for that glorious literary age in Greece, which will be the admiration of scholars to the end of time.   Greece shares largest in ancient civilization, and in this view, Athens sits as queen.   Her Attic tongue was the nucleus of Greek language, the Muses were partial to her Attic hills and dales, and she has written on the scroll of literary fame more illustrious names than any ancient state, or indeed any modern, till the seventeenth century.   Rome was never literary, till from her conquests she brought home the Grecian schools, language and masters. Like New England, the Attic shores were rugged and her hills were sterile, yet like the Puritan, the Athenian reared a giant mind amidst honest toil and frugal fare. Boston is New Athens, and her John Adams was Demosthenes again.

In the later days of Solon, Pisistratus usurped kingly power, but ruled with much wisdom and left his authority to his sons, Hippias and Hipparchus. The latter was slain by Harmodias and Aristogiton; the former was banished for tyranny, when he fled to the court of Artaphernes, satrap of Sardis, then a province of the Medo-Persian empire. He there laid the foundation of war between Persia and Greece, which continued at intervals till the conquests of Alexander.

HISTORY—CHAPTER XXVIII.

GRECIAN LITERATURE.

When we consider the influence of the Greek language and literature on the world, every believer in providence will see that the Creator had a great design, and accomplished an important purpose in the Greek nation; yet we are still at a loss to see the second cause by which his purpose was accomplished.

The first inhabitants of Greece were among the most brutish ever named in history. They appear to have descended from Japheth, through Javan, or Ion, which word is the same in Hebrew, and his sons Elisha, Tarshish, Chittim and Dodanim, all of which have fixed their names as monuments in Greece. For three hundred years they were below the beaver in the arts. Then Inachus, eighteen hundred and fifty-six years before Christ, came from Phenicia to Argos, and introduced the most simple arts of savage life. For three hundred years more they were wild wandering barbarians, without the institution of marriage.   Then fifteen hundred and fifty-six years before Christ Cecrops came from Egypt to Attica, and brought the arts of building and agriculture, and instituted marriage, built the city, and established the kingdom of Athens.   About the same time Danaus from Egypt made similar improvements in the country of the Argives.   A hundred years later Cadmus came from Phenicia, some say from Egypt, and some from Phrygia, bringing letters and the art of writing.   This was the dawn of Grecian literature.

We can never be certain where the art of writing with alphabet arose, or when the invention was made.   The art must have been practiced in Egypt.   It was practiced by Moses, and brought by him from Egpyt, forty years before the advent of Cadmus in Beotia, and brought by the Hebrews to Phenicia or Canaan about the age of this migration of Cadmus to Greece.   As the Hebrew and Canaanite spoke the same language, Cadmus may have obtained this art from the Hebrews, and hastened with it to Greece, where many colonies of his countrymen had gone.   The progress of the art must have been slow, for seven hundred years passed before writing became general or common in Greece.

Poetry was long kept by tradition, unwritten.   To the memory of the bards was committed the care and preservation of literature.   Not one in a hundred during these long ages took the pains to help his memory by writing.   Written compositions were seldom transcribed and circulated; hence for some centuries after Homer not one in a hundred had heard of him; and when the "Iliad" and "Odyssey" began to be transcribed and circulated, no one knew when or where the author was born.   His time is fixed from eight hundred to a thousand years before Christ, and no less than ten cities claim to be the place of his birth.   From Homer and Hesiod few great geniuses appear, till Sappho, a most brilliant poetess, born six hundred years before Christ, contemporary with Solon, whose wise regulations form an era in ancient literature. Anaximander was also contemporary with Solon. Thales, the great mathematician and astronomer, born at Miletus, accounted one of the seven wise men, was but little older than Solon. Aristophanes, the father of comedy, was born five hundred and fifty years B. C. From this time schools were everywhere established in the Grecian states, islands and colonies. Although long harassed by Persian invasions, the Greek mind was everywhere being developed, and from the time the last of the invaders left the shores of Greece, there was rising on the stage a countless host of the most eminent poets, statesmen, historians, philosophers, tragedians, comedians, sculptors, painters, orators, architects and mathematicians, that ever did honor to any age of the world.

Of statesmen, some of whom were military leaders, Athens had her Themistocles, born five hundred and thirty-five years before Christ, the great Aristides, contemporary with him, followed by Cimon, Pericles, and Alcibiades. Thebes produced Epaminondas, and Pelopidas, and Sparta Agesilias. Philosophers flourished everywhere; Pythagoras in the preceding century, born five hundred and eighty-six years before Christ; Anaxagoras, five hundred years, Socrates, four hundred and seventy-one, followed by his great disciple Plato. Bias, Chilo, Cleombulus, Pittacus and Periander were reckoned with Solon and Thebes the seven wise men of Greece. Every state swarmed with poets. Alemon had flourished in a preceding century, born six hundred seventy years B. C. Anacreon, born five hundred thirty, Pindar five hundred thirty-two Euripides four hundred eighty, Æschylus four hundred fifty-six, Aristophanes, dramatic poet, five hundred fifty, and a countless number for

which we have no space.   Among the great painters are
Apelles, and Apollodorus, born four hundred and eighty
years before Christ.

Of sculptors Praxiteles stands foremost, born four hundred years B. C.; next Apollonius, three hundred years, and
Aristarchus two hundred and eighty.   Of orators, Demosthenes and Æschines were most distinguished.   Of physicians, Hippocrates and Galen were eminent.   Of musicians,
Orpheus and Timotheus, the latter born three hundred and
eight.

More than any other, the Greek historians demand our
attention; for without them we could have no knowledge of
ancient Greece, and very little of any part of the ancient
world.   Herodotus, the father of history, was born at Halicarnassus, in Caria, four hundred eighty-four years B. C.,
four years before the invasion of Greece by Xerxes.   The
Carian government had submitted to Persia.   Its home
government was oppressive, and Herodotus fled in early life
to Samos, where he acquired the Ionian language, and in
that wrote his history in so attractive style as to win the
most overwhelming applause, when he read it at the Olympic
games.   Thucydides, then a boy, on hearing it wept with
enthusiastic joy.   Herodotus predicted the future greatness
of this youth, and truly his mantle fell on the young disciple.
Thucydides, born at Athens, four hundred and seventy
years B. C., became an eminent historian, more reliable
than Herodotus, less imaginative, and so excellent in his
style that Demosthenes took it for his pattern.   Polybias,
born in Arcadia, the highland center of the Peloponnesus,
was one of the most eminent Greek historians.   Of his great
work of forty volumes, only five and some fragments of
others remain.   Dionysias, of Halicarnassus, was a celebrated Greek writer of Roman history.   Dion Cassius, born
at Nice, was also a Greek writer of Roman history.   He

wrote the history of Rome in eighty volumes, most of which were lost.

Of all the Greek historians perhaps Plutarch is best known, as his works are preserved. He was born at Chæronea, in the apostolic age, fifty years after the birth of Christ. He was a priest of Apollo. After traveling extensively, he became a teacher in Rome; was contemporary with Josephus, and probably conversant with him. Later in life he retired with the materials which he had gathered to Chæronea, and wrote his biographical history or lives of eminent men. He is amiable in spirit, and more correct in moral sentiment than almost any other heathen writer. We can however nowhere find in all heathen literature correct moral sentiment. With the deep penetration of Socrates, the honesty of Plato, and Aristotle's rules of truth-finding, and Plutarch's piety, all leave us in comparative moral darkness.

HISTORY—CHAPTER XXV.

SPARTA.

In the dark and gloomy period which followed the Trojan war, when most of the Grecian States were at war with each other, and civilization was put back two hundred years, the Heraclidæ, descendants of Hercules, joined by the Dorians, conquered the Pelopiæ and other nations in the south and west of Peloponnesus, as has been related, making Sparta the seat of a new nation, which took the name of Lacedemon, Laconia, and Sparta, generally bearing the latter name.

Two brothers, Euristhenes and Procles, led the conquerors and established the Spartan kingdom, reigning jointly, claiming to have descended through Hercules from Jupiter. The two families continued to reign jointly through long continued dynasties.   They reduced the conquered people to tribute, and when they made a laudable attempt to gain their freedom, they were reconquered and reduced, under the name of Helots, from Elis, Helis, or Helas, to the most abject slavery.   About forty thousand families bore the name of citizens; ten thousand of whom lived in Sparta, and thirty thousand in the rural or country districts of Lacedemon.   These citizens held in this abject bondage hundreds of thousands, compelling the first conquered province to aid in conquering the next, until the slaves were more than five times as numerous as their masters.   This oppression fixes lasting disgrace on the Spartan name.

Nearly nine hundred years before the time of Christ, Lycurgus, one of the Spartan kings, descendants of Hercules, reduced the Spartan government to a most peculiar system.

There were under his government two kings as before, who had executive power.   To a senate of twenty-eight the two kings were added, making thirty.   In this legislative body the kings were simply senators, each having one vote as others.   From the senate there was a final appeal to the people: so that the highest legislative body consisted of forty thousand citizens.   Above all, however, was the Ephori, a supreme court of five judges, to whom all, even the kings, were subject.

Under the system of Lucurgus every man surrendered to the government his real estate, and all was divided into thirty-nine thousand farms, as nearly equal in value as possible.   Though a farm was allotted to each family, yet the whole land belonged to the state, for all was cultivated by the Helot slaves, and the product was carried to the public tables, where all the people ate in companies or divisions. No one was allowed to erect a splendid house, or wear a costly garment.   Money was not allowed to be used or possessed, except iron coin, and that was of so low a price that a half ton would only buy a cow. This was soon laid aside, and for many centuries trade was only carried on by exchanging one useful article for another. All delicacy and refinement were forbidden, literature was condemned, and even the refinements of gardening and agriculture were not allowed. Every effort was made to beget strong children, and for this purpose some men invited neighboring men to their beds. Feeble infants were destroyed, and such as were allowed to live were taken from their parents at an early age, as the property of the state, and brought up by public authority. Children were put to severe hardship often, and daily exercised in the open air, in the chase, in running, leaping, lifting, pitching stones and heavy bars of iron. Both sexes were thus employed entirely naked, not only in childhood, but in adult years, in the gaze of assembled multitudes.

No people surpassed the Spartans in strength, courage and patriotism; and few could compete with them in military prowess. Their name was a terror in all lands. They were ambitious to die in battle, despising natural death. Spartan women rejoiced to hear of the death of their sons in battle, walked over the field, and shouted with joy when they turned up the cold faces of their sons.

The Spartans were only famous for these qualities, which they held in common with the tiger, yet tigers were more noble than Spartans in affection for their young. They were always semi-barbarian; public sentiment and law required them to be so. Gymnastics and military arts were all their improvements. Their manners were rough and harsh towards each other and toward all men, and every one was trained from childhood to the most vigorous tyranny toward the Helots. These poor degraded creatures had descended from noble ancestors, more worthy than the Spartans. They had been robbed of manhood, trampled down and imbruted, until hope, ambition and every noble aspiration ceased, and they felt, and lived, and moved as beasts. Patriotism becomes diabolical when it extinguishes all generous feeling towards the people of other states or nations, and we cannot respect the patriotism of the Spartan, who, while ready to die for Spartan freedom, could rob the Helot of all liberty, manhood and hope.

The glory of Greece was her high civilization and literature, but Sparta shared little in this. She is worthy of praise for the part she acted in resisting the Persian invasions. In this she seems to have felt some generous emotions of brotherhood towards the other Grecian states. This invasion was made on the northern border, far from Sparta, yet she was prompt to send her armies far from home to defend the common interests of the confederation. Sparta was one of the states confederated in the Amphictyon League, formed in the heoric age under Amphictyon, king of Athens, nearly fifteen hundred years before Christ. Delegates from the several states met twice a year at Thermopylæ, Athela, or Delhi, camping in early times on the open field, when they planned the defence and improvement of their common country, formed acquaintance with each other, and engaged in athletic exercises.

The Olympic Games, practiced in the Peloponnesus, was the strongest tie of brotherhood between the Grecian states, binding all the states, whether in the Amphictyon, Beotian, Ionian, or Achean League, into one Grecian family; and in a manner drawing into this family the Greek colonies, which were hundreds in number, all along the west shore of Asia from the Ægean Sea north, along the south, the west, and even north coasts of the Euxine, on every island of the Mediterranean, the south shore of Europe and north of Africa. After the close of the war with Persia, Sparta and Athens were almost constantly engaged in war with each other, until both thus weakened fell a prey to the ambition. of Philip and Alexander.

HISTORY—CHAPTER XXIV.

HEROIC AGE OF GREECE.

While Egypt and the east were under absolute monarchs, often despots, the Greeks were, as individuals, self-reliant and independent. Their kings were simply chiefs of small clans of proud men, who would submit to no proud ruler, but simply allowed a strong wise man to rule, or rather lead them. These chiefs were far less ambitious to rule their fellowmen, for such they deemed the men of their own tribes, than to perform great deeds of valor in their defence..

No condition could be more favorable for the full development of mind and body than that in which every Greek was placed. He had the advantage of social intercourse with men, and yet was nearly as independent and self-governing as though he was monarch of all Greece. This individual independence would in other countries have led to anarchy, but every Greek felt an interest in the common welfare, a noble feeling of pure patriotism, and was ever seeking opportunities to do some public act worthy of praise, worthy of immortal song. To prepare himself for such great deeds he cultivated both his mental and physical nature for strength and activity, and exercised himself in various feats of wit and gymnastics. Thus arose the public games, which gradually settled into system. These games—Nemean, Ismian and Olympic—became the great instrumentality for forming Grecian character. The praise bestowed upon Olympia, for the best song, oration, historical essay, or the greatest strength or activity of body, was the highest ever bestowed. These games originated in the heroic age, but were reduced to system at later times. The

Olympic were the most important. They were celebrated in the province of Ellis, in the Peloponnesus, near the village of Olympia, once in four years, when from every Grecian state and every distant Grecian colony came competitors for the prize of success, in the foot race, the chariot race, and a great variety of bodily exercises, exibhitions of art, science and literature.

The ostensible prize was only a crown of laurel leaves, but when the successful competitor, crowned with laurel, stood forth in view of a million spectators, their shouts of praise rolled down from the surrounding mountain slopes, nature's amphitheater, like the voice of a tempest; the poet composed his eulogy, the song of his praise arose; the historian recorded his fame, which was handed down to all succeeding ages.

All during the heroic age is mixed with fable. Menelaus, having married Helen, daughter of Tyndarus, king of Sparta, succeeded to the Spartan throne. Paris, son of Priam, king of Troy, visiting Menelaus, carried away Helen. Every Grecian prince felt the insult, and all united under the lead of the great Agamemnon, the brother of Menelaus, in war against Troy. This war lasted ten years when Troy fell; eleven hundred and thirty years before Christ the city was burned, and the nation blotted out. The Greeks had become tired of this long continued war, which, by withdrawing all the strong men, had nearly ruined Greece. The Trojans knew the Greek soldiers desired to return home, and the Grecian generals feigning the same desire, lulled the Trojans into security, affected preparation for retreat, and treacherously joining in a religious festival, introduced through the gates of the city an enormous wooden horse as a religious offering, from which issued a band of men who seized the gates and let in the whole army, and Troy was immediately in flames. Thus ended three thousand years ago a nation which, but for the fortune of war, might have vied with Greece or Rome.

The last few weeks of the Trojan war forms the basis of Homer's "Iliad." We know much more of this wonderful poem than we know of its author. He is supposed to have composed these songs about three hundred years after the fall of Troy. The story had been kept by tradition, and was probably often told in song for three centuries, when a bard of most towering genius told it in the lofty strains of the "Iliad," taking the largest liberty to exaggerate, to make his heroes giants and demigods, and to bring the gods themselves into action. For grandeur and sublimity it has rarely ever been equaled; but very little in it can be relied on as history. There is no certainty when or where he was born, nor where he lived. The story of his blindness is very uncertain. Indeed the "Iliad" and other songs are the only certain proof that Homer ever lived. It is doubtful whether he ever wrote a word, or whether his songs were written by any one for ages after. If they were kept for ages unwritten, the bards who kept them must have been extraordinary men. When these songs began to appear in written form and obtain general notice, the author had been so long dead that his time was uncertain, and even his name, and at least ten cities claimed to be his birth-place. Solon's wise laws opened the door for literature, and soon after Homer was everywhere known.

It was in the heroic age, in the reign of Eyeus, king of Athens, nearly thirteen centuries before Christ, that the Argonautic expedition occurred. A band of adventurers left the shores of Greece and sailed away after a famed golden fleece, at the eastern extremity of the Euxine or Black Sea. At Cholchis gold was collected by straining through a compact fleece of wool, and from this circumstance a wonderful account, full of exaggeration, went forth of a golden fleece, and far away on the shores of Greece it became the romantic talk of rude, wild, and yet heroic adventurers. They returned after several years, and their voyage, the most wonderful ever performed, was full of strange discovery, and was related in song and handed down through succeeding ages, second only in interest to the "Iliad." These songs had an important literary influence, arousing the Grecian mind to energy. These songs had been sung for one hundred and fifty years when the war with Troy occurred, and more than four hundred years before the "Iliad" was composed, and must have been kept by the bards unwritten for five or six centuries. Rough and unpolished as the general manners were in the heroic age, there was a noble ambition for great deeds for the public welfare. These deeds were performed with such disinterested patriotism that they were adored. They seemed divine, and their grateful countrymen placed them among the gods; the poets taking boundless license to enlarge their wondrous deeds.

When the Greeks had spent ten years in destroying an interesting nation, they returned from the ashes of Troy to find their own country nearly destroyed by their absence; barbarian manners returned, wars between the states, and the overthrow and ruin of many of them

---

HISTORY—CHAPTER XIX.

THE RELIGION OF THE GREEKS AND ROMANS.

The religion of Greece and Rome is so mixed with their government and religious myth or fable is so blended with their early history, that the historian must be under the necessity of frequently explaining, unless Grecian and Roman history is preceded or introduced by Mythology. This subject is manifold. The lively fancy of the Greeks gave sentient being to everything, to every law of nature, to every element, and these beings were, by the fancy of the poets; but with others these allegorical beings became gods; and thus arose the religion of the Greeks, and afterwards of the Romans. Sometimes the names of men were given to these gods, as Neptune and Mars, who were literal earth-born kings, and reigned in Thessaly. Again, Io, the personification of agriculture, seems to have been the earth-born daughter of a Grecian king, and mother of a dynasty of Egyptian kings. Ionia probably has its name from her. However, the names of the gods generally are arbitrary, or are derived from circumstances unknown, and have no reference to any mortals.

Jupiter signifies electricity, or life principle in nature; Iano signifies the moist atmosphere; Ceres vegetable life; Vesta fire, or caloric; Inferno the growing season; Pluto mineral wealth, and also burial and the control of the future destinies of the dead; Vulcan mechanical skill in metals; Venus beauty in general, especially as the wife of Vulcan, beauty in polished metals. Minerva signifies genius, or intellectual power; while nine merry sisters, the Muses, signify intellectual inspiration and creations of fancy. Apollo signifies the sun's heat and light; Neptune the ocean's power; Mars the rage of war; Diana the moonlight, also chastity, and the woodland solitude; Mercury human speech; Esculapius the healing power; the Cyclops and Titans the greater and less powers of nature. Chaos signifies unorganized matter; Saturn or Kronos, time; and Eros or Love signifies attraction, by which all organization commences. These illustrations are endless, as Hesiod counts thirty thousand gods; and subordinate gods, Manes, Lares, Penates, Genii, Silenos, Satyrs, Fauns and Nymphs numbered millions. Every man had his genius. Sea nymphs danced on the smooth surface of every sea, wood nymphs thronged every shade, and domestic or household gods thronged every hearth, and flew, unseen, smiling merrily, around every table; and besides this every tree, plant, river, brook and fountain had its living and sensible spirit.

The poets who invented this religious system may have been atheists, believing in no god; and this may have been true of many who admired its ingenuity and beauty. Some grave senators, who enacted laws for the worship of the gods, may not have had any other than political motives, knowing the influence of religious faith on the masses of the people, while they themselves had no faith. It is however certain that Greeks and Romans in general were sincere worshipers of their gods through all their early ages. In view of gross and flagrant immoralities and childish follies in their worship, an intelligent skepticism arose in the age of Socrates, and continued to the apostolic age, five hundred years. This skepticism had then become quite general among the wisest and best of men, whose minds were open to the arguments of Christian teachers. About the beginning of the fourth century Constantine, a shrewd politician, saw that a majority of the intelligence and wisdom of the Roman people had abandoned paganism, and embraced Christianity, and therefore declared it the religion of his empire. One hundred years later, Theodosius the Great made an end of pagan worship, prohibiting it by law. Thus ended this remarkable religious system, after existing more than two thousand years. With all that was disgusting in the immoralities and follies of their system, it was far above the pagan systems in general, and almost infinitely above the groveling worship of Egypt, where snakes and loathsome vermin were worshiped as gods.

Under the Grecian religious system men advanced to a very high civilization, refined manners and great intelligence, and while despots cursed nearly all the world, republican

freedom in the Grecian states made every man a ruler and
participator in the government. The Grecian state was his,
with its privileges and its responsibilities, and hence his independent soul developed all its energies. The Roman,
during the republic, stood up in the same independent
spirit and noble manhood. Yet this pagan system of religion, of civilization and government, contained in itself
the seed of its own dissolution. This was their martial
spirit fanned to an all-consuming flame by the Homeric literature. The praise bestowed on martial heroes led all to,
take the sword; and the words of Christ, "All they that
take the sword shall perish with the sword," had proved
terribly true in the destruction of every Grecian state; and
Rome, when Christ spake these words, though so great, sat
over a thousand magazines of destruction which she had
planted in seven centuries of conquests. These eventually
all exploded and laid in one vast ruin the great empire of
the world; and with it ancient civilization ended, and barbarian feet trod all the fair portions of the earth. The battle-ax fell on statuary and the finest works of art, and the
firebrand was thrown into the library and the gallery of
painting.

The ancient or pagan literature educated the physical
and intellectual man, but left the moral man unimproved.
In the zenith of Grecian civilization, the temple of Minerva
at Athens was the seat of most shocking debauchery, and
Plato says he has seen all Athens drunk in a day. This
was probably on the feast of Bacchus. Modern civilization,
under Christian influence, is destined to advance to the
world's entire reformation, though it is yet encumbered
with a great degree of heathenism.

BROTHER CRANE'S LETTERS.

Bro. Crane's valuable series of historical letters will be continued, the XIX of which will appear in our next week's issue. These letters, as well they may be, are highly appreciated by the readers of the *Wesleyan.* Of themselves, they are worth more than three times the subscription price of the paper. The Lord bless our venerable Father Crane. And as in liquid lines he narrates the history of the past, may his soul's vision, cleared and strengthened, from the mount of a long and rich Christian experience, sweep the not distant but glorious heavens.— *Copied from editorial column of Wes. of Sep.* 13 1865. *Adam Crooks, A. M., Editor.*

HISTORY—CHAPTER XIII.

THE HEBREWS.

The history of this most remarkable of all people is largely given in the Bible, and in hundreds of volumes of religious works. I shall therefore give but a brief account of them ; mostly confined to the fulfillment of prophecy, in the connection of their history with that of other nations.

The descendants of Arphaxad, who took the name of Chaldeans, and dwelt near the junction of the rivers Tigris and Euphrates, were the most intelligent of the early nations of the world. They were enlightened, cultivated the arts, and versed in science, especially philosophy and astronomy, when the earliest inhabitants of Greece were cannibals, living without the use of fire.

Nearly two thousand years before the time of Christ, Abram, afterwards called Abraham, was born, the son of Terah, the tenth from Shem, and seventh from Eber, from whom Hebrew is derived. He was the most eminent of the Chaldeans in wisdom, standing nearly alone in the true knowledge of God. As this knowledge was dying out, and nearly extinct with the Chaldeans, Abraham was called of God to go out from among them, and finally to separate from his kindred and sojourn in a land of strangers.

There was little system of government in that age and country. Patriarchal kings reigned over their own families, and such as resorted to them. Abraham, from physical and mental superiority, became a powerful prince; many resorted to him for protection, whose necessities he met, and by a careless transalation, this is made to read, " Bought with his money." He sold nobody, and owned no slave. The history of Isaac, Jacob, and Joseph, is before every reader of the Bible, so beautifully written that it would be presumption and folly to attempt to rewrite it. Rhamesis, king of Egypt, decreed the destruction of all the male children of the Hebrews; when his daughter, Thermuthis, found on the waters of the Nile a cradle, woven of rushes and cement, in which lay a beautiful and promising child, which she adopted and named Moses (saved from the water), and presented it to her father, as heir to the throne of Egypt. When he was come to years he declined this honor, and chose to identify himself with his oppressed brethren, and led them through the sea and the wilderness to the borders of the land long promised to the seed of Abraham, when his work was done. Joshua succeeded, and led them over Jordan and into their full inheritance.

The whole world had turned to idolatry. The Hebrews alone held the truth, and they held it so loosely that they could not mingle with any nation or people without becoming idolaters. The Egyptians had greatly corrupted them. The Canaanites were among the worst idolaters in the world. God saw fit to exterminate them, and plant his chosen people in his place; and to indelibly fix in the minds

of his people the sin of idolatry, he made them instruments
of the destruction of the idolatrous Canaanites.

Because whole tribes were slain by divine command, and
Agag was hewed by a holy prophet, as the only means to
clear a single spot for the truth, men have taken the liberty,
for three thousand years, to go to war without any divine
command, under entirely different circumstances, when
truth needs no extermination to make it room, and while
God has said "Thou shalt not kill." Because Agag was
hewed, thousands have been slain by self-constituted Sam-
uels, who have been heroes in the sight of men, but murderers in the sight of God. Self-constituted Israels have
waged terrible wars against those they pleased to call Canaanites; sometimes wars nearly of extermination, as of the
American Indians. The cry, "Resistance to tyrants is
obedience to God," has long been loosely made. It has
undermined a sense of the sacredness of human life, and led
to revolutions, rebellions and assassinations.

For several centuries after the time of Joshua and Caleb,
Othniel, Ehud, Shamger, Deborah, Barak, Gideon, Tola,
Jair, Jephtha, Ibzan. Elon, Abdon, Samson, Eli, and Samuel
governed, or judged Israel; with frequent intervals of anarchy between, when they fell under their enemies.

Kingly power began with Saul; under David the kingdom
became strong; and under Solomon arose to the highest
glory; but at his death ten tribes revolted under Jeroboam,
whose wife, a daughter of Pharaoh, was sister to a wife of
Solomon. Being offended, that Jeroboam was preferred
to the son of Pharaoh's daughter, and placed on the throne,
the tribe of Judah and the small remnant of Benjamin were
all that adhered to Rehoboam, who remained at Jerusalem,
while Jeroboam fixed his seat northward, where he and his
successors, a very wicked race of kings, ruled Israel first at
Tirza, and afterwards at Samaria, for more than two hun-

dred years, when Shalmanezer bound their last king, Hoshea, and carried him and his people captives to Nineveh, and thence to Halah and Habor by the river Gozan, and the cities of the Medes, and planted in Samaria colonies from Babylon, and Cuthah, Aoa, and Hamath, and Sepharvaim.

Israel was carried away about seven hundred and twenty years before Christ. The several nations which were planted in Samaria brought each its national gods, and their worship became greatly confused. The wilderness having increased in the absence of the people, wild beasts had become numerous and bold, and some of these new-comers were devoured by lions. They thought Samaria had its gods, as every country had, and feared that unless they could learn how to worship the gods of Samaria, they might all be slain by lions; they therefore sent to the king at Nineveh, requesting him to send one of the priests, whom he had carried away, "To teach them the manner of the God of the land." A priest was accordingly sent, who dwelt at Bethel, and taught them about the God of Israel. They paid a sort of worship to him, still worshiping their former national gods.

After the Jews returned from Babylon, the disaffected, especially such as refused to put away their heathen wives, fled into Samaria, and finally a temple was built by Sanballat, on Mount Gerrizim, where there was at least the pretence of worshiping the God of Israel.

This strange people underwent another great revolution. Alexander conquered them and drove them in part out of their land, and planted Macedonian colonies in Samaria. This was about four hundred years after the strange nations were planted there, and about three hundred and fifty years before the time of Christ's preaching. No nation could be more mixed. Such were the Samaritans when Christ passed through that country.

HISTORY—CHAPTER XXXI.
CHRISTIANITY.

The origin of Christianity is the great epoch in the world's history. Wherever we fix the date of the deluge, it is certain that man had time to vastly increase, and shockingly degenerate, before he is first seen in history forty centuries ago. The grossest ignorance and most degrading vice everywhere prevailed, with slight exceptions on the Euphrates, and on the Nile. As civilization radiated from these two points over the east, there was no improvement in morals, as pagan civilization only educated the physical and intellectual man. The gods of the most polite nations were patterns of malice, falsehood, and debauchery. The more they were imitated, the more every vice prevailed. There was much in the tales of their gods, and in their ceremonies, childish in itself, which commenced in early and extremely barbarous times, and which, though woven into civil jurisprudence, and the framework of government, became insipid and disgusting. From the days of Socrates and Plato skepticism had been rising in the best minds.

The Jews were less than a hundredth part of the human family. "To them were committed the oracles of God." They had been set apart as a religious and moral lamp, to shine on all nations. This light had become dim. They had come to "hold the truth in uurighteousness," even more than the heathen. They were looking for a Messiah, and many of the heathen seized with eagerness their oracles, and looked for a Messiah with more spiritual ideas. While the Jews looked for a secular prince, the heathen looked for a divine teacher. The former looked for one who should "restore the kingdom to Israel," the latter looked for one whose "kingdom was not of this world." While the former despised the Babe of Bethlehem, the latter, as "Wise men from the east," came and worshiped him. When the miraculous star which guided them stood over the place where the young child lay, silence prevailed, the temple of Janus was shut, the clang of war was hushed, the "stone was cut from the mountains without hands," no human pride, pretence, or boasting, no pageantry, or pomp, no clangs of arms or din of war attends, when "the God of heaven sets up a kingdom." How simple yet how grand !

This was the Augustan age. Rome had made the world one in empire, in commerce, in literature, and in language, and then furled her banner, hushed the clarion of war, and sat in silence at the incarnation ! The same simplicity marked all the career of Jesus on earth. Though he was from eternity, filled immensity, was infinite in power, had created all things, and governed all things, yet in his human nature he had no where to lay his head, while the foxes had holes, and the birds of the air had nests. He chose simple, unlearned men to teach his doctrines; unpretending obscure men; yet doubtless men of sound judgment and clear perception, men of stern integrity. Thus arose the kingdom of Christ, the stone from the mountain, which was to fill the whole earth, the grain of mustard seed which was to become a tree. Every thing was calculated to inspire confidence. Christ healed unnumbered multitudes of sick, he cast out devils, and raised the dead. His disciples, after his resurrection and ascension, accompanied their preaching with like miracles. As they told the story of his crucifixion, resurrection and ascension, their honesty was proved by their sacrifice of friends, fortune and life ; and circumstances showed that they could not be mistaken. Christ came to his own, to the Jews, though they received him not; and after he had ascended, his disciples continued to preach to the Jews only, supposing the gospel was confined to that small nation. Nothing short of a marked and striking mira-

cle was able to arouse them from this limited idea. When
the door was clearly opened to the Gentiles, and the apostles and other teachers went forth through Arabia, Syria
and Greece, they still clung with tenacity to the Mosaic
ceremonies.   They themselves had all been circumcised, so
also had been the Jews, whom they found in every city;
but when they came to the conversion of Greeks, as the
Gentiles were called, they were staggered.   A religious man
offering no sacrifices, practicing no ceremonies, uncircumcised, seemed so nude, that nothing short of miracle and
inspiration could induce even an apostle to take him into
his fellowship.   So strong was the prejudice of education,
that a Jewish convert to Christianity slept more soundly,
and thought of death with more serenity, in the idea that he
had been circumcised; and often to more fully quiet his
fears, he returned to the practice of other rites.   It was a
hard struggle and more than some could bear to risk their
children dying uncircumcised; and many, no longer allowed
to circumcise their children, were quieted by being persuaded that baptism was a substitute for circumcision.

Nazarenes was the name given to the disciples at first;
and after they began to be called Christians in many places,
many of the converted Jews still bore the name of Nazarenes for several ages.   Practicing Jewish ceremonies so
distinguished them from other Christians, that they became
a separate sect, under this name.   Some of them, under the
name of Ebionites, fell in great errors, regarding Jesus as a
natural born prophet like Moses.   Some of these Ebionites
went yet farther into error, rejecting some of the Scriptures,
all, except the books of Moses, and gospel of Matthew.

It cannot be wondered that this prejudice of education
so long influenced the converted Jews, when the apostles
themselves were sometimes overcome.   Peter was sternly
rebuked by Paul for dissembling to please the prejudices

of the Jews; and Paul himself was carried away by the same desire to suit himself in these prejudices; which act of human prudence involved him in most serious trouble. In such acts the apostles were left to their own strength, and were weak like other men. The inspiration which gave them supernatural power and wisdom rarely left them. In this they were almighty for the work they had to do. Their miracles proved the divine presence with them, and their writings, which constitute the New Testament, doubtless inspired of God, formed a standard around which the whirling elements of confused opinions finally rallied and settled.

While error was getting abroad, the same inspired apostles, who have given us the Scriptures, were teaching the same unerring word in their extensive travels, so that truth was wide spread. Those inspired teachers taught personally in most of the cities of Western Asia, Northern Africa, and Eastern and Southern Europe; and when they sealed their testimony with their blood, they left many wise and holy successors, among which was Ignatius of Antioch, Polycarp of Smyrna, and Clemens of Rome. Under these, inspiration was subsiding, and miracles were rare. The written word became the only standard of faith and practice, and in proportion as they rallied to this they prospered.

HISTORY—CHAPTER XXXI.

ROME.

Rome stands in the center of the historical chart of the world. Around Rome all history clusters; all before Rome prepared the materials of which this empire was built; all contemporary was appendage to it; and all which has followed is built of its ruins. The zenith of this empire was the zenith of ancient civilization; and in the decline and fall of Rome ancient civilization failed.

It was at the zenith of this empire that a new civilization commenced—the Gospel, the kingdom which "The God of heaven set up, which should never end." The ancient civilization, which educated only the physical and intellectual man, and left the moral man unimproved, contained in its martial spirit the elements of its own destruction; but Christian civilization, educating the whole man, physical, intellectual and moral, contains in its unmartial spirit, its spirit of forbearance, patience and human brotherhood, the elements of perpetual existence and improvement. Though it suffered by the fall of ancient civilization and ancient empire, yet it arose again in the fifteenth and sixteenth centuries, among Scandinavians, Teutons and Celts, and will forever advance. Rome carried her Latin tongue to all lands; and, as in conquest of Greece, she brought home the Greek masters and language, she made the Greek the language of the world.

Seven hundred and fifty-five years before the birth of Christ about three thousand men, who lived by plunder, stopped on the banks of the Tiber in Italy and commenced a rude city, which was finished in two years, with a coarse wall, when Romulus was chosen king. His early history is so mixed with fable that little that is reliable can be gathered from it. He and his twin brother Remus were accounted the sons of Mars. Their mother, a priestess of Vesta, was buried alive for violating her chastity. A shaft, or pit, was sunk, from the bottom of which a lateral cell was excavated, in which was placed a table and some food, beside which on a stool the unfortunate vestal was seated, when the earth was thrown in, filling the pit and leaving her in that awful place to die. In this manner all seduced vestals perished, a doom more fitting the seducer than the seduced. Fable represents the babes thrown into the Tiber, by the jealousy of their royal uncle, and rescued and nursed by a she wolf. Remus was slain for leaping over the wall, in contempt of its weakness as protection for a city, either by Romulus or by one of his guards. The innocent act for which he died shows his great strength and noble sentiment.

At an earlier period there were more than three hundred small kingdoms in Italy; each of which was as important as Rome in its beginning. At first it no more than equaled an American township. During the reign of Romulus it was enlarged by a union with the Sabines, which doubled its territory. The Romans were all bachelors until their city was built. They then proclaimed an exhibition of games, like an Indian war dance, to which the Sabines came with their wives and daughters. At a signal every Roman rushed among the spectators, and seizing a woman carried her to his hut as his wife. The Sabines made war on the Romans, but the captive women went between the armies, declared they were reconciled to their Roman husbands, and persuaded their Sabine fathers and brothers to unite with the Romans. Their influence over their husbands was equally great; from bandits they were changed to civilized men, and to the influence of Roman women we are to credit most that was noble in Roman character.

Romulus died after a long reign, and Numa Pompilius, a Sabine, was chosen king. He was a generous and wise prince, of peaceful temper, and during his reign of thirty-nine years great improvement was made in civilization. During the reign of his successor, Tullus Hostilius, the Abans were conquered and annexed to Rome; but it was not until in the reign of his son, Ancus Marcus, one hundred and forty years after the foundation of Rome, that the Roman territory extended to the mouth of the Tiber, making the whole kingdom about as large as an American county.

The fifth king of Rome was Tarquinius Priscus, who

adopted a son of a bondwoman, whose father was never known, who was next elected king. This was Servius Tullius, the noble and generous friend of the people. He, in his old age, married his two daughters to the two grandsons of Tarquinius. One daughter was of a proud and violent temper. She was married to Tarquin's mild and generous grandson, while her mild and generous sister was wedded to Tarquin's proud and violent grandson. The good king thought to mould and equalize their tempers by these unequal marriages, but nothing could have been more unfortunate. The violent ones murdered their companions and came together, then caused the murder of the aged king. As they were hastening to the royal palace, the body of the king lay in the road. Tarquin would rein the horses aside, but the infamous daughter seized the reins and drove over her father's body.

The change from a generous friend, a friend and father of his people, to a proud and haughty tyrant, was borne as a galling yoke by the Romans, until Lucretia, a noble Roman matron, planted a dagger in her heart, having been violated by Sextus, the king's son. This caused the end of monarchy, and the banishment of the Tarquins.

HISTORY—CHAPTER XL.

SUFFERINGS OF THE EARLY CHRISTIANS.—UNFAIRNESS OF GIBBON'S HISTORY.

We are mostly dependent on the Acts of the Apostles by Luke, and the Epistles of the other inspired writers, for a knowledge of the spirit and temper of the early Christians, of their sufferings, and the spirit of their persecuting enemies. Later and uninspired writers, some of them were learned, candid and reliable; but others were ignorant, superstitious and careless. They have been thoroughly sifted by men of most profound erudition, during the last three centuries; men who have spent long lives in laborious research; who have been able to determine what is reliable, and what is not. While they have rejected much which during the dark ages was called history, they have left us much that cannot be doubted, which is deeply and often painfully interesting. While they were piously employed, the learned Gibbon, having vacillated from a Protestant to a Papist, and from that to a Freethinker, bent his vast energies to destroy our confidence in all the Fathers and in the Apostles themselves. A cordial dislike, not to say hatred, of Christianity seems ever lurking in him, strangely blinding him to evidence.

Through the thin gauze of his affected complaisance to Christians, we see him walking in sympathy with pagan emperors and magistrates, and framing apologies for the persecution, torture and murder of Christians. He is incapable of appreciating the noble disinterestedness, the holy devotion and true benevolence which prompted their self-denial, their crucifixion to the world, their patience in suffering, and firmness in dying. The mass of the early Christians he holds in contempt; such as bore their sufferings with noble manly fortitude and calm serenity, he regards as merely obstinate and stubborn; and such as were eminent in learning, genius and talent, he insinuates may have been influenced by ambition, by a carnal desire for the exercise of power, and for the praise of men.

No man ever occupied a better position to honor Christianity by the pen of a historian than the author of "The Decline and Fall of the Roman Empire." He compassed all lands and all languages for his materials, and labored with an assiduity worthy of all praise during an important part of a lifetime, to connect ancient and modern history, to draw from obscurity the manners, customs, temper and spirit of men who walked in the darkness of the declining and falling empire of the world. Unfortunately for truth and for his own reputation, he was in all this great work possessed of a strong and blinding prejudice, and even a spite which, though covered for decency with many compliments, is seen beneath in a sneer designed to give his reader a contempt for Christianity. While Gibbon is justly regarded as one of the world's greatest historians, and while no work in existence could supply the place of the "Decline and Fall," it is to be desired that there will yet rise a historian who will travel over the same ground with equal ability, and with an honest Christian heart; who, while he sees the fanaticism and superstition of some, the carnal spirit of others, will see the great majority of the early Christians pure and holy in life, law-abiding in all things not contravening the laws of God, honest towards all men, patient in suffering, returning good for evil, blessing for cursing, loving their enemies, doing good to them who hated them, and praying for their persecutors and murderers.

It was not the low-minded, groveling and spiritless who became Christians in the early ages. Such tamely trod the beaten paths of their ancestors, believed all the silly tales of their gods, and cheerfully worshiped gods and goddesses, whose adulteries, fornications and all manner of crimes would be intolerable in mortal men and women. Men of active and capacious minds and independent spirit turned from such abominable deities and senseless and often shockingly licentious ceremonies of their worship, and embraced the rational doctrines of Christianity. Such men and women, having come to the truth, stood firm in its defence, where feeble minds would have quailed and recanted; stood firm under torture, and firm in death. A candid historian would not fail to see in them exalted minds, noble integrity, consistence and benevolence. They lived, suffered and died for the glory of God and the welfare of man. Why

·should such men be hated? A Persian philosopher said, "A gentle hand leadeth the elephant itself by a single hair." Solomen said, "A soft answer turneth away wrath," and Jesus said "Love your enemies." It is evident that love and forbearance constitute the only power to overcome ·wicked men, to subdue their hearts and bring them to terms. Wrath only awakens wrath, and violence arouses violence; kindness can only subdue. Why then were the Christians, the most kind of all men, hated, tortured and put to death? This question has troubled many. It may be answered in the following manner.

Christ makes Love and Forbearance our general rule of conduct. Hence it is evident that the general law of human nature is, that men, even bad, malicious and violent men, may be melted, subdued and brought to terms by Love and Forbearance. If there were no exceptions to this general law of human nature, there could be no continued hatred to a Christian who fully practiced Love and Forbearance, unless through ignorance of his character. There are exceptions—a few men have been so deeply depraved, that the most persevering efforts of Love and Forbearance have failed to melt and subdue them, and these few men have controlled the ignorant masses, misrepresenting the Christians to them, and stirring them up to violence against men whom they would respect and love if they were acquainted with them.

When Christ was about to be nailed to the cross, he looked upon the same multitude who had been crying "Crucify him" and prayed, "Father, forgive them for they know not what they do." They who had come from distant parts to attend the annual feast knew nothing of him but by misrepresentation. From this they joined the cry against him, but toward them he felt compassion. Paternus, proconsul of Africa, about the middle of the third cen-

tury, banished Cyprian, bishop of Carthage ; a succeeding
proconsul recalled him; but when Galerius came to that
office, the aged pious and noble Cyprian was beheaded, because one infamous man desired it.

The first general persecution by Roman authority was
under Nero, after the burning of Rome.   In this persecution, terrible for its cruelties, Paul suffered martyrdom about
the year sixty-five.   The second was under Domitian, in
ninety-five, when forty thousand are supposed to have perished.   The third began under Trajan, in the year one
hundred. The fourth, under Antoninus, drove the Christians
from their homes, plundered them, stoned them like vile
beasts and drove them to the deserts.   The fifth, under
Severus, in one hundred twenty-seven, was terrible.   The
sixth, under Maximinus, in two hundred thirty-five.   The
seventh, under Decius, in two hundred fifty, was most terrible of all.   The eighth, in two hundred fifty-seven, under
Valerian, followed with like terror.   The ninth, under
Aurelian, in two hundred seventy-four, less severe.   The
tenth, under Diocletian, in three hundred three, was long
continued, and seemed a war of extermination, destroying
the lives, directly and indirectly, of nearly a million.   This
emperor shut six hundred christians in their meeting-house,.
at Nicomedia, on a Christmas day, and burned down the
house over their heads.

CAUSES OF THE DECLINE AND FALL OF
ANCIENT EMPIRES.

Historians, falling into the wake of their predecessors, all
endorse the doctrine that empires necessarily have youth,
middle age and old age, and then expire.   The argument is
this: all the empires of antiquity—Egypt, Assyria, Carthage,

Lydia, Persia, Greece and Rome—have declined and ceased.

This argument may be sufficient for mere human reason, when going from modern Rome to view the still greater desolations of Tyre, Ephesus, Sardis, Nineveh and Babylon.

The awful change which has swept away wealth and men, talent and genius, impresses the traveler, who quails amidst the horrid sights and sounds in the ruins of Babylon, or faints in searching for the foundations of Troy, with the perishing nature of all earthly things.

He has searched in vain in Italy for a Virgil, a Cicero, or a Cæsar; no Herodotus meets him in Greece; no Solon, no Pericles, no Plato. In Carthage, Numidia, Egypt and Asia, the barbarian pitches his tent with brute like indifference on the ruins of the most renowned cities of his ancestors, or breaks, cuts and mars the marble slabs which contain a record of their deeds, to build a temporary cabin.

Alas! it is true, the ancient empires have gone to decay; the ancient civilization has failed; the ancient literature is blotted out. But must, therefore, modern empires go to decay? Must modern civilization fail, and modern literature be blotted out? I deny the correctness of the logic which would assert this. To assert this is to dogmatize, not to reason. Who had candidly searched for the causes of the decay of ancient empire, civilization and literature, in the light of Christianity?

The ancient world was heathen. In its civilization, in its literature, it aimed only at the cultivation of the intellectual man, leaving the moral man entirely unimproved. Plato flourished in the zenith of ancient civilization, yet he tells us that he has seen all Athens drunk at once, during the Bacchanalian festival. The licentiousness practiced in the name of religion, in the temple of Minerva, at Corinth, would shock a modern libertine. If the degrading debauchery of drunkenness and fornication was not enough to demolish ancient empire, there was one element, peculiarly heathen, though dignified with the name of virtue, which must necessarily overthrow the ancient world.   This was the martial spirit.   Homer took the lead in exalting the martial spirit, surrounding every act of violence with glory, from the war of the gods, to Ajax crushing with a stone the breast and vitals of a fellowman.   Homer's mighty genius makes even the flow of blood from the nose, mouth and ears of the dying man, a glorious sight.   Historians, poets, orators and artists, all inflamed by Homer to great enthusiasm, vied with each other in efforts to arouse the whole ancient world to the same mighty enthusiasm, for the glory of war. They succeeded too well.

Heathen literature killed the ancient world—killed itself —arousing the martial spirit so high that the sword finally fell on the neck of historian, poet, orator and artist; and the enthusiastic warrior threw the firebrand into the library of the ancient literature and the gallery of fine arts, and the battle-ax fell on statuary, and then wild beasts roamed in forests which grew again in the ashes of a thousand cities. Thus the light of civilization was extinguished in blood, and the olden empire died of a million sword-wounds.

Christ came to sheath the sword, to teach men that they who take the sword perish with the sword; that wrath arouses wrath, violence wakes violence, taking the sword invites the sword.   Christ came to teach the true power to overcome evil—the power of patience, forgiveness and kindness.   This is the true spirit, and the very essence of Christianity, and is not only the salvation of individuals, but also the salvation of nations.   Shall this Christian spirit prevail? If it prevail, it is the preserving element of modern nations. They need not decay, but may grow in knowledge, in enterprise, in benevolence, and in every virtue, until the great image seen by Nebuchadnezzar, which represents their errors and vices, not their existence, shall be demolished, and the stone from the mountain shall fill the earth.

This Christian spirit was pure in all the early churches. They all deemed the martial spirit essentially heathen, necessarily associated with the worship of local national gods, entirely inconsistent with the kingdom of Christ. Tertullian, bishop of Carthage, found by diligent search, in the third century, that not one Christian bore arms—not one was in the army. He examined two-thirds of all of the Roman armies in the world. Constantine, a rough Dacian barbarian, held the sceptre of the world in the beginning of the fourth century. Though a devout worshiper of Mars, he, through political policy, professed the Christian faith, desiring to unite the worship of Jesus and of Mars. From that day the Christian Church has been largely heathen; and, most astonishing of all, the martial spirit—the worst element in heathenism—is fairly incorporated into the Church. It is no wonder that the march of the Church is slow—the march of civilization slow. Faint must be the heart which offers the heathen a religion which contains the worst element of his own heathenism. The War of the Reformation, or Thirty Years' War, where every tongue was Christian, and every hand was heathen, reduced the population of Germany from fourteen millions to four millions.

But "The gates of hell shall not prevail." The spirit of Peace, increasing in the masses through the world, will yet prevail, in spite of kings, of admirals, and marshals; in spite of priests, Catholic or Protestant, who profane the pulpit by advocating war.

PARTIALITY OF HISTORIANS, AND PHIL-
OSOPHY OF RELIGIOUS BIGOTRY.

History is partially written. Without impeaching the integrity of historians, and without questioning the facts recorded, we yet see great defects in history. Many important facts are ignored. Important, because in them could be found the springs of action and the motives of men in the drama of human life. The historian is often a zealous partisan, having a favorite theory to support, and making the partial facts recorded throw a false light on his theory. Macaulay has been pronounced by a friend, "A writer of essays on man; using historical facts to illustrate his theories." This has been done so much in party zeal as greatly to impair the integrity of history. This is more especially true of ecclesiastical historians; almost every one has had a creed to honor, and a sect to defend.

> "Pride often guides the author's pen,
> Books as affected are as men."

If an able and impartial pen should ever write the history of the Church, it might check our veneration for our adored saints, and diminish our abhorrence of those whom we have ever been taught to execrate. Perhaps we should often find the foundation of bigotry in an honest zeal for God, for his truth, for his Church, for the salvation of men. If we can find the proper bounds of this zeal, find where it ceases to be a virtue and becomes a vice, we shall see the origin of bigotry. If we can learn how much of lenity, forbearance and concession are consistent with integrity; and on the other hand, how much stern and intolerant inflexibility is consistent with human frailty, we shall have gained important knowledge. It is proper that we should inflexibly adhere to our opinions, while all the evidence in our reach is for them; but not proper for us to be intolerant towards them who differ in opinion from us.

It is absurd for fallible man to claim the right to be intolerant because he is right and his neighbor wrong.   He
does not know but evidence exists, at present beyond his
reach, which would sweep his opinions away, should he
reach it.   Papists have seen this, and to avoid an awkward
dilemma, have claimed infallibility; and now with three
sources of infallibility, the pope, the assembled cardinals,
and the ecumenical council, they proceed to the awful work
of intolerance, with a sort of consistency.   They have a
cloak for their sin, which cannot cover the murderers of
Servetus, and Barnedelt, and the Quakers hanged in Boston.
Candor will award to that gloomy monster, in the form of
woman—that embodiment of bigotry, the bloody Mary,—
the exercise of conscience.   She was devout and conscientious.   Firmly relying on the infallibility of the church, she
exerted the great power which Providence had clothed her
with for defence, terribly destroying its enemies ; probably
often taking the platform in her mind for her acts from the
destruction of the prophets of Baal at Mount Carmel.   She
finally wrapped herself in the smile and approval of an infallible church, in its absolutions, and the virtue of its sacraments, to pass the valley of death.

My education has been Protestant to partiality.   I was
fully instructed in the bloody history of Mary, but left in
comfortable ignorance of the murders in the reign of Elizabeth.   No less partial was my education as Puritan.   My
early reading more than reconciled me to the tragic death
of Charles I., and brought me to bow in adoration before
the image of Cromwell.   It was not until I broke away from
leading-strings, that I learned that the tyranny of Charles
was not new; he was but moderately following the example
of Elizabeth; he claimed no preogative that was not allowed
in a greater degree in Elizabeth and by her Protestant subjects.   Yet the same pen which makes her a saint, makes

Charles a tyrant worthy of death.   The true character of Cromwell will never be seen without becoming independent of the one-sided literature handed to us by our Puritan fathers.

But who can have a heart to find a fault in that noble band who came to "A stern rock-bound coast," for "Freedom to worship God?"   Our veneration, I might almost say our adoration, for our noble Pilgrim Fathers, shuts our mouths on their faults; nay, makes all their faults virtues. "For shame," cries one; "let alone the honor of the Puritans, in the old or new world.   What harm can arise, though posterity never see their faults?"   He would gladly let them alone if their faults were not made the pattern of men's lives in our day.   In one branch of reform, the one in our estimation which embodies all others, our most inflexible opposition arises from men who make the vices of the Puritans virtues to be imitated.   We are compelled to make an effort to remove this opposition.   It will be a thankless task to throw off the mask and reveal the fact, that grave and long-faced bigotry, cruel as death and relentless as fate, has often had the character of the most exalted piety.   It might tarnish the glory of the holy wars.

Hon. Gerrit Smith delivered the address before the American Peace Society at its last anniversary.   In this excellent speech, which the venerable secretary intends to publish so largely as to put it into the hands of a million readers, Mr. Smith makes some wise remarks on superseding war by a strong and well regulated police.   He speaks in a lucid manner of the importance of virtue, probity, and gentlemanly-bearing policemen.   He finally proceeds to speak of killing men for the public good, in a Christian manner, giving dignity to the work, and here spoils the whole by pointing to Cromwell's armies as our pattern to follow.   Give me to the jaws of the tiger, to the coils of the anaconda, rather than to the hands of a religious bigot, who thinks he does God service in killing me. It would be a strange police movement, to commence in every land to pattern after Cromwell's wars; and to call this a "Peace movement," would be passing strange. Catholic bigotry has had conscience and sincerity in murdering heretics in every age. We concede that in hunting heretics, a multitude of the most unprincipled men were let loose like dogs, tigers and hyenas; but the judges were conscientious, though their judgment was darkened and their conscience misguided.

No one can doubt the sincerity and conscientiousness of the emperor, Charles V., when his debauched armies returned from the most horrid scenes of rape and murder in Germany. We are chilled with horror to see his bishops offering in his cathedrals thanksgiving for the success of these armies, but we do not doubt the emperor's conscientiousness; he felt that heresy was checked, and God was honored. Neither the psalms and prayers of Cromwell's camp after the victory, nor the Te Deums and thanksgivings after the victories of the emperor's army can prove the Divine approbation. Dr. Duffield, in a very interesting centenary lecture, at Carlisle, says the early settlers there were Scoth-Irish; the descendants of those who, from the North of England and South of Scotland, came with Cromwell to Ireland and settled there, to evangelize Ireland. Intending no reproach to the good people of Carlisle, our veneration is somewhat abated for their ancestors, when we reflect that the Genius of History has recorded the fact that Cromwell robbed a great part of the Irish of their farms, and put his favorites from England and Scotland in possession of them, into the very dwellings of those who were driven into exile. Many were slain, enriching with their blood the very soil which was now to be taken from their children and given to the stranger. Thousands of these conquered and disinherited Irish people were transported to the Western World, and sold by Cromwell's command. Cromwell and his host at the taking of one fortress slew every man, woman and child in cold blood after they had surrendered, doubtless conscientiously. It shocks humanity and common sense to call this evangelizing Ireland.

After the Revolution a small part of the disinherited Irish were called back and put in possession of their homes, in the reign of Charles II. James II., who succeeded his brother, undertook to bring back as far as possible the disinherited Irish and their heirs, and put them in possession of their homes. This he did not accomplish, as he was soon deposed and succeeded by his daughter and her husband, William the Prince of Orange. For this design James has received unmitigated censure. Macaulay finds no language too strong to express his indignation and contempt, when contemplating a design which, he tells us, would overturn the state of society as it had existed for forty years. We would ask the historian, of how long standing was that state of society overturned by his favorite Cromwell forty years before, when he drove from their lands their owners, whose ancestors had held them from time immemorial? After the battle of Boyne Waters, when William gained a final victory over the fallen king, poor Ireland was scourged again in a manner that should make the heart of humanity bleed. Three hundred thousand were disinherited, drove from their homes, and vast numbers again where shipped to the Western World and sold. Oh, tell me not that Englishmen, and Scotchmen, favorites of their sovereigns, who could take the homes of a crushed and down-trodden people, came there to evangelize Ireland! Do not insult one's common sense. Since the battle of Boyne Waters there is no heart in the Irishman. In the sight of the mansion where his ancestors lived he toils at the mercy of a haughty descendant of some favorite of Noll or the Dutch Prince, taxed to starvation to pay his rent, and to pay a priest of the English church for sitting idle in his parish, for no one will hear him preach.

> "O give me three grains of corn, mother,
> O, what has poor Ireland done?"

TRUTH IN HISTORY.

The historian should feel while writing that the truth stands with the sword of justice over him.

Truth in history is of so much importance, that wrath of God must rest on him who writes falsehoods for the annals of men's deeds; and it is proper that he should be watched with scrutiny and criticised with severity. Historical criticism is so vigilant, that falsehood of facts can hardly get into history; yet by publishing some facts and omitting others, the reader is deceived—is led to a false view of men and of nations—a false view of human action, of motives and responsibilities. Political and religious party zeal leads to these falsifications of history.

The violent divisions between Catholic and Protestant, between Churchman and Puritan, between Calvinist and Armenian, between Unitarian and Trinitarian, have biased historians for three hundred years. The political zeal of Monarchists and Republicans has biased them little less. I have now arrived in this brief biographical history to a point which requires these remarks.

The age of Elizabeth, of Calvin and Knox, was the age of Protestant triumph in England and Scotland and French Switzerland. Catholic bigotry had reeked in the blood of fifty thousand Protestants in the Low Countries, and an un-numbered multitude in other kingdoms; and now, as the tables were turned, the Reformed showed less violence.

Human nature was universally sour; men were everywhere morose, and, most unfortunately for the honor of Christianity, the most devout were often the most morose and cruel. Calvin's "Decretum Horribile" was born of the dark, gloomy spirit of that age, when men's religious blood was acid. That terrible being, whose glory depends not only on the damnation of men, but also on their ungodly lives, and who, to this end, made them for damnation, decreed their every act of sin and instigated them to perform it, was created by the gloomy fancies of men when their spirit was most unamiable. The horrid Woden had appeared again in the being set up by the Reformers as the object of worship; and if he was not worshiped as Woden was, through an image with flaming eyes and streams of blood from each corner of his devouring mouth, yet the character of Calvin's god inspired the devout with great ferocity.

The Scandinavian chief who yelled the name of Woden amidst the clang of arms and howls of tempests, wading in blood, felt the same inspiration of Cromwell yelling, "The sword of the Lord and of Gideon," at Marston Moor.

It was the fault of the Puritans that they interpreted the New Testament by the Old Testament. Jesus gave place to Moses. Joshua was the model man for all ages. "Resist not evil" was interpreted by "Eye for eye, tooth for tooth." "Love your enemies" must be consistent with exterminating Canaanites. "Pray for them that dispitefully use you" must be consistent with the prayer, "Persecute and destroy them." There were Canaanites to be exterminated, and Agags to be hewed. Moses had appeared again in John Knox. Cromwell was Joshua, the Irish Catholics were Canaanites, the Irish fortress was Jericho; and if the walls would not fall at the sound of trumpets, yet they fell before the assaults of the Round-heads; and "the sword of the Lord and of Gideon" not only cut down every man, but every boy was killed; every maiden who clung to her dead father, or ran for life, or shrieked, or prayed, or begged for life, was thrust through with the sword. Why should these holy soldiers turn chevaliers, and have tender, worldly, humane hearts at the sight of youthful beauty and inno- cence? Mothers stood with frightened children clinging to them, when "the sword of the Lord and of Gideon" was thrust through their hearts; the children were thrust through or knocked in the head; the babe, still nestling at the mother's breast, and drowning in her heart's blood, was either pierced through or its brains were dashed out. This spirit came with the Pilgrims over the ocean. They too bore "the sword of the Lord and of Gideon" against the Canaanitish Indians; took their lands, made slaves of In- dians and killed them as they killed wild beasts, burned their dwellings, destroyed their corn, and cut down their orchards, assuming that God would help them exterminate these Canaanites, and give this promised land to them. The translation of the Bible gives strong marks of the spirit of that age. Slavery and war receive an encouragement which the original Scriptures will not justify.

In an age, when almost every Puritan deemed himself elected from all eternity to the divine favor, and his neigh- bor doomed from eternity to damnation; when he loved to meditate on infants in hell, tossed forever on the lake of fire, we do not wonder that his temper should bias his pen, and that he should write a partial and garbled history. At that great day, when God shall review all history, American his- torians will be found guilty of suppressing a multitude of facts, of wrong committed on the Indians.

Macaulay, one of the most literary man of our age, has made the great effort—which will never be surpassed—to grace the Puritan side of the Puritan age. He is dead; his historical works survive; but his is the last great effort to make a sage, a patriot and a saint of Oliver Cromwell. Sure as human progress, Cromwell's fame shall fade.

D'Aubigne, one of the most able and beautiful writers who ever dipped a pen, has, in his "History of the Great Reformation," made the last effort to resuscitate and immortalize Calvinism.   It is in vain to attempt to drag this relic of barbarism into the light of this age.   The eminently Christian temper and noble bearing of the great scholar of Geneva may revive it for a time, it will then fall, to rise no more.

SIR THOMAS MOORE.

One of the most remarkable men of any age was Sir Thomas Moore, who, on the fall of Wolsey, was promoted to the chancellorship of England.

In literature he was second to no man except the great Erasmus, the morning star of modern civilization.

Moore was to the British Islands what the great scholar of Rotterdam was to Europe.   He was a model man in beauty of countenance and features, and symmetry of form, in graceful motions and refined manners, in sweetness of temper and voice.

This prince of courtiers had the highest fame in the court of Henry VII., amidst the literati whom the patronage of the king's mother had attracted.   Here Erasmus met him, and without introduction called him by name, by the agreement between his fame and himself.   Prince Henry was then a child, and in the estimation of the learned was one of the most lovely and most brilliant children in the world. All eyes were upon him for the promotion of religion and science, and the welfare of his subjects, when ten years later he succeeded his father on the throne of England.

Moore was in ecstasies at the coronation of the young

king.   In his views the golden age had come, darkness was to flee away, light and truth were to abound.

Mercy and truth were to meet together, righteousness and peace were to kiss each other, and barbarism and oppression cease.   These were the hopes of Moore, Erasmus, and all the great scholars of that age.

The history of Henry VIII. shows how greatly they were disappointed.   His great learning was used against the truth, his silver tongue became foul with blasphemy, and his beauty and graceful manners lost their power in the filthy pools of licentious debauch.   All of this could be accounted for.   There are many similar characters in history.   Great men have been vacillating, and one part of their lives has been inconsistent with another.   But Sir Thomas Moore differs from all of these; unexplained by them, and unexplainable.   The amiable character, or rather spirit, which I have given him, seems to have continued through life.   The historian would almost be justified in saying that his love of learning continued, while he put to death the best scholars of that age, and while he labored to extinguish the great fountain of knowledge, the Bible; that his love of virtue continued, while he put to death the best men in the kingdom; that his mercy continued, when he practiced the most terrible cruelties, and that he was the most amiable and lovely of men, when his name was a terror to the most holy men and women, the most devout Christians.   Yet he was no hypocrite.

He was open, frank, honest and sincere, conscientious in every movement, generous and humane, kind to the unfortunate and poor.   This noble man, towering above common temptation, rising sublimely above all that was sordid, earthly and sensual, is led by superstition to become a most relentless persecutor.

How blind is religious zeal!   Sir Thomas Moore goes in

person to search the libraries of worthy citizens to find a
Bible or a New Testament, as an occasion for imprisonment
and death. Other books were deemed equally wicked, and
to have them was a crime worthy of death; the writings of
Tyndale, Luther, Melancthon, Zwingle, Ecolampadius,
Pomeranus, Brentius, Bucer, Jones, Lambert, Fryth and
Fish were all condemned.

These books contained much of the choice literature of
that day; and yet we see the great patrons of learning, the
king, and his chancellor, not only burning these books, but also burning meek and innocent men and women in whose
hands they were found. How strong is religious bigotry,
when the most independent monarch on earth, and his
highly enlightened minister, become the willing tools of a
sensual, sordidly selfish, and malicious priesthood!

Hilton, for bringing Testaments from Antwerp, was burnt
February 20, 1530. Bayfield, for doing the same, was cast
into the Tower, and finally confined in a coal-house, lashed
to the wall, in a standing posture, tied about the legs, the
waist and neck to the cold stone, and there stood night and
day, because he brought the New Testament into England.

A brother of the great Tyndale, and a fellow tradesman,
for a slight offense no more than sending a little money to
Tyndale, and saying the truth of Scripture was reviving,
were fined by Moore one hundred pounds, about five hundred dollars each, and then this learned and accomplished
judge, debauched by bigotry, condescended to fasten scraps
of the Testament on their garments, and place them on
horse-back, their backs to their horses' heads, and then
paraded them through the streets of London, amidst the
jeers and shouts of a base rabble.

An innocent musician was cast into prison for singing a
Lutheran hymn. A painter, by the name of Freese, wrote
some passages of Scripture under his work, for which he was

cast into prison.   His wife came and asked for admission, when she was kicked by the bishop's porter so that she died soon after.

This poor man, suffering every hardship before, after hearing of his wife's death, became deranged; his hair grew long and hung over his eyes, which glared most wildly through it.

To extend this catalogue would give increasing pain to the reader, and would increase the difficulty of comprehending this mysterious man.   During all of this bloody persecution, Moore remained the same polished gentleman, the kind husband and father, unblemished in his morals, kind and humane.   Misled by zeal for holy mother church, he degraded, tortured and murdered God's servants, and yet was so conscientious in it, that no remorse seems ever to have disturbed his peace.

Moore fell under the displeasure of the king, and was beheaded.   He had rather expected this tragic end of life, from the fickle character of his sovereign.   His buoyant spirit did not forsake him at death.   Being fat and heavy, he found it difficult to climb the scaffold, and said with a smile to a friend, "Help me up, and I will shirk for myself in coming down."   Thus ended the life of Sir Thomas Moore, a man of no disguise, and yet incomprehensible.

MODERN HISTORY—CHAPTER L.

CONSEQUENCES OF THE THIRTY-YEARS' WAR.

The "Peace of Westphalia," begun in 1648, and completed in 1655, closed the "Thirty years' war." When this war began Germany had fourteen millions of people. Without war she might have increased to eighteen or twenty millions. When the war ended Germany had four million left, amidst graves and bleaching bones of ten millions, and

the ashes of nearly all German cities.   When it began religious bigotry and party hate existed, and when it closed this
hatred was for greater ; and after all that has been said of
this as a war for religious liberty, the Westphalia treaty of
peace fell back upon the Augsburg treaty, made one hundred years before, with a slight amendment in relation to
the Reformed.   They who had drowned Germany in blood
agreed at last to accept of the same small liberty which they
had before the war, and during the first eleven years after
the war began.   So long and murderous wars end ; sur-
rendering all that was contended for, after both parties are
impoverished and ruined.

The poor liberty allowed was liberty of princes to believe
and worship as they please, while their faith and their mode
of worship must be fastened on all their subjects.   Freedom,
conscience, thought, expression and worship for individual
men and women of the masses was yet unknown ; and as
this war had put back the civilization of Germany two hundred years, the half savage Germans were almost willing
slaves of this religious tyranny.   Cultivation of mind, manners and morals had been suspended for a whole generation.
Most of this small remnant of a great people had been born
during the war, in families flying from the ashes of thirty
thousand villages, before the yells and spears of savage warriors ; often houseless, on the fields, and in the woods.
During this terrible war, church was against church, state
against state, and clan against clan.   Hatred was cultivated
as a virtue, wrath provoked wrath, violence aroused violence,
and taking the sword brought the sword.

"All they that take the sword shall perish with the sword."
"Whoso sheddeth man's blood by man shall his blood be
shed."   These kindred passages show that as human nature
is, retaliation and vengeance will commonly follow the taking
of human life, either in individual murder or wholesale mur-

der, called war. Sometimes this goes on till whole families
are exterminated. A. killed B. ; C., a brother to B., kills
A. ; D., brother to A., kills C. Sometimes this extends to
sons, cousins and more distant kindred. See for instance
the entire destruction of the family of Alexander the Great.

The laws of Moses regulated this vengeance and put a
check on it by "Cities of Refuge." Nations take up the
quarrel of individuals, and plunder and kill in their behalf.
Each act of depredation arouses deeper hatred in the spoiled
nation. She retaliates, destroys a ship, in turn has a harbor
spoiled. Then she burns a city, and in turn has a province
laid waste. Thus France and England have for eight centuries been kindling deeper and deeper malice, till Admiral
Nelson said to his men, "You are to hate the French as
you hate the devil." What advice to a professedly Christian navy, from a professing Christian leader.

Such is the proud, unbending spirit of nations. Wars
end by exhaustion, when one or both parties are worn out
and nearly ruined. Otherwise this proud spirit would continue war till the human race was extinct; and yet the literature of Christendom, history, oratory, poetry, music and
painting praises this proud, unbending spirit, and contemns
the forbearance, patience and kindness which alone can
subdue and reform mankind. In addition to this, and calculated to increase the love of war, are toys in the form of
warlike weapons, put into the hands of millions of boys—
guns, swords, drums, flags, epaulettes, and plumes. These
are the foundations of the public sentiment which supports
war. These foundations must be removed, and this public
sentiment give place to true Christian sentiment, before the
mad work of human butchery will cease. Germany has not
yet recovered from the "War of the Reformation." Many
late wars have grown out of the barbarous spirit then en-
gendered; she is financially poorer; some dark barbarian

spots continue; and though she abounds in learned men
and noble universities, yet the fighting habits of the students
are a disgrace to Germany, in the judgment of all Christians.

Historians, who abound in praise of heroes, and laud so
much that proud, unbending spirit which engenders war, are
unfair in argument.   Instead of meeting us at that early
day, when forbearance and patience, meekness and kindness, would prevent war, they choose to meet us where
some emergency has come, when those proud ideas of
honor, and that haughty unyielding spirit which they love to
praise, have brought a crisis, when the enemy's at the gate.
They then cry out in amazement, "What is to be done?
Shall we not fight?"   They admire the unbending Luther,
and despise the mild and gentle Erasmus.   John Knox is
their model man, model reformer, while they count William
Penn pusillanimous.   "Forbearance," say they, "invites
aggression." This is opposed to the teaching of Christ; and
until his doctrine is acknowledged, and kindness and forbearance depended on, wars will continue.

Germany seemed destined to lead in modern improvement.   The first light of modern civilization glowed on her
hills and softly settled on her plains four hundred years ago.
Then were born and coming on to the stage those intellectual giants, under whose tuition Germany advanced more in
one generation than in five hundred years before.

Her situation in relation to other nations, her climate
and soil, her seaports and rivers, all tended to open her way
to glory and happiness, and to allow her to rank foremost
of all nations.   Alas! pride, self-conceit and stubborn will,
under the specious plea of contending "for the faith, once
delivered to the saints," darkened the sky of this fair morning; dark clouds appeared, one after another, on all the

horizon, and finally the black tempest came and laid Germany in ruin.

Will men tell us that war advances civilization? This falls little short of blasphemy. Is it not saying that Jesus casts out devils by Beelzebub the prince of devils? The two hundred years which follow the birth of Reuchlin and Erasmus should have made Germany glorious in the light of civilization; but alas! at the end of that time she was darker than in the beginning.

MODERN HISTORY.—CHAPTER VI.

RELIGIOUS PERSECUTION IN FRANCE.

All history shows that men under the influence of religious zeal can be more cruel than under any other influence. They are at first honest and sincere, and if unerring and infallible, their zeal would spend itself in the defence of truth, the glory of God, and the good of men. But man is fallible and erring, and, proud of his opinions once formed, he becomes anxious to force them on others. In this work his better feelings, the finer sensibilities of his soul, are lost; he becomes hardened, and deems sympathy and mercy weaknesses unbecoming a servant of the Most High. Such has been human nature in all persecutions; such was man in creating the Inquisition. Men naturally kind have, in laboring to force their opinions on others, come to that coldness and hardness of nerve that they could break a man on the wheel without pity; bending him on his back on the wheel until his heels nearly reach his head, when he is asked to believe the creed of the judge and executioner, and if he cannot do it, his ankle bones are crushed with the stroke of an iron club. He is asked again to believe, and failing, the club falls again and crushes his knees. So stroke after stroke falls after the question "Do you believe?" the last falling upon his breast.

The doctrines of the Reformation were introduced into France by Farel and Calvin, stern and severe men, not wholly free from the spirit just described; and we may fear that some of the persecution of the Huguenots, or French Protestants, was unnecessarily provoked by their stubbornness. Simultaneous with the Reformation arose the Order of Jesus, or Jesuits. Ignatius Loyola, a Spanish knight, being severely wounded in the siege of Pampelona, in 1521, was for some time cut off from active life, when his ever-active mind invented a new religious order, differing from every other order. They secluded men from the world, while the Order of Jesus called men to every activity, introducing them to every rank, to men of every occupation, placed them at the head of schools and universities, introduced them to the courts of nations, and made them the counsellors and confessors of kings. All these activities were to aim at the prosperity and enlargement of the Catholic Church.

The Jesuits, in fifty years from their origin, were at the head of the schools of Catholic Europe, were confessors to nearly every Catholic sovereign, and had under their influence the principal men of commerce and the leaders of armies. Their missionaries thronged the Indies, China and Japan, counting their converts by millions, and a little later they were looking after the spiritual welfare of the Indians of North America, along the great lakes, beyond Lake Superior, and along the great length of the Mississippi. Much of their action was secret, unknown to all but Jesuits, and even to the mass of their own members. They were leagued for the overthrow of Protestantism, and possibly for the extermination of Protestants from the earth.

The family of Medici in Florence arose to great power,

gave a pope to the Church, a queen to Scotland—Mary wife of James V., and a queen to France—Catherine, wife of Henry II. and mother of Francis II., Charles IX., and Henry III. Two brothers of these queens resided in France; one the famous, rather notorious, duke of Guise. This Medici family were in the interest of the Jesuits, and had a double hatred of Protestants, as the unfortunate Mary, Queen of Scots, was the daughter of Mary de Medicis, and niece of Catherine de Medicis, of France, and niece of the Guise, and had been the wife of Francis II.

The great armada, the largest fleet of modern times, blessed by the pope, and pronounced invincible, sailed from Spain to dethrone Elizabeth and crown Mary in her stead; to make an end of Protestanism in England, as some on board the armada said, not leaving one Protestant alive. The armada was carried by tempests to ruin.

A more stealthy move was made in France, worthy of Jesuits, planned by Catherine and the duke of Guise and agreed to by the king, Charles IX. A marriage was negotiated between the daughter of Catherine, the king's sister, and Henry, the Protestant prince of Navarre. It was to be connected with St. Bartholomew's day. The queen of Navarre came with her son to Paris, and many Protestant nobles from different parts of France, being assured of safety. All, everywhere, were lulled to carelessness, feeling that persecution must end with this union with the Protestant family of Navarre. The queen of Navarre was poisoned, and on the night of Bartholomew's, 1572, the most shocking work of butchery began. The houses of Protestants were broken into, and ten thousand murdered in Paris, in every horrid manner, and about seventy thousand in other parts of France. The good and great Coligni was slain, with numbers of the chief men of the nation. The head of Coligni, who was admiral of France, was sent by Guise to the king and his mother. In cold blood, men, in the spirit of demons, hewed down decrepit age, matrons with their infants, maidens and children. For three days and nights the cries and entreaties and groans of the dying went up from all France to heaven. When the news reached Rome, the cardinals assembled, the pope, Gregory XIII., in the midst, and resolved that he should lead them to the church of St. Mark, to offer thanks to God, that solemn mass should be celebrated in the Church of Minerva, and a jubilee be held throughout the world, to thank God that eighty thousand Protestants were dead. Could devils be worse than such men? Could heathen be worse than such a church?

In the long reign of Louis XIV. more murders and cruelties were perpetrated, surpassing the massacres of Bartholomew's day. Soldiers were let loose on the Protestants by this wicked monarch, inspired by the diabolical spirit of a church that had become an abomination on the earth. They broke into houses, robbed the inmates of all they wished, and broke and burned what remained; turned parlors and dining-rooms into horse stables, whipped the families about their desolated rooms until they were nearly dead, hung up men alive, and tore off their flesh with pincers, applied red hot irons to the hands and feet of men and breasts of women, hung up women naked by their feet, tied mothers to stakes and laid their infants just out of their reach to starve to death, burned some half to death and let them go, hung some by the hair, some by their feet, and smoked them to death in chimneys, stripped others naked and filled their bodies with needles, blew up men and women with bellows till they burst, and tied husbands and fathers to bed posts and violated their wives and daughters in their sight. This was done in the name of religion, encouraged by bishops and priests, who were gratified and laughed at the woes of the sufferers.

MODERN HISTORY.

FRANCE SINCE THE RESTORATION OF THE BOURBONS.

For one hundred and thirteen years the throne of France was filled by two kings, Louis XIV. and Louis XV., his great-grandson. This long period of political quiet ends in 1774, and from that time this unfortunate nation has been swept by a succession of storms: the execution of Louis XVI., a republic declared, then anarchy—the reign of terror; after this the Directory, than the Consular government, followed by the Empire.

Nepoleon swept away the last vestige of republicanism, and restored nearly all that the revolution had destroyed; and when his injuries to other nations brought them upon him, his oppressed subjects were ready to rejoice in his overthrow.

Some yet survive who witnessed the show of monarchs in Paris, when Napoleon was in exile in Elba. All eyes were fixed on the noble forms of Nicholas and Constantine, sons of Alexander of Russia. In the group was a heavy, corpulent old man, unable to mount a horse, or, without help, to mount a throne. This was Louis Stanislaus Xavier, brother of Louis XVI., now to be imposed on the nation by the congress of princes, as king Louis XVIII. With the people he could not be popular. They hated the name of Bourbon. He was in sympathy with the aristocrats, who fled during their struggle for freedom, was one of them, and was now brought back by the enemies of freedom and forced upon them. His reign was tyrannical and oppressive; the press was proscribed, and elections were so controlled as to keep a majority of men favorable to the king's measures in in the legislature; the aristocracy was favored, and the masses denied the privileges and rights for which they had struggled for thirty years. Louis XVIII. died in 1824. A young Bourbon, a brother of Louis XVIII., succeeded as Charles X., and followed the example of his predecessor in censorship of the press and ministerial interference with elections, securing thus the control of legislation. A majority of the Chamber of Deputies were emigrants, men who fled from their country in its sore trial, and had courted the favor of the enemies of freedom. The king recommended to these, his tools, a bill to indemnify these and other emigrants for losses which they had sustained in turning their backs on France. This, of course, passed, and increased the national debt 100,000,000 francs.

In 1828, in spite of coercion, the people elected a majority of true patriots, when the ministry, fawning tools of the king, resigned. A new and liberal ministry was appointed, the censorship of the press was abolished, ministerial influence of elections put down, and Jesuitism suppressed. The Jesuits, always opposed to freedom, had from their origin been the cause of the greatest calamities in France. They had been suppressed, but restored by Louis XVIII. In 1829 a new ministry was created, perfect tools of the king, who grew bold and menaced the legislature in his opening address. The king and his ministry were now preparing for a crisis, expecting to triumph. To divert attention, an expedition against Algiers was instituted. A war in Africa was begun, which has only added arguments to the folly of war.

The ministry in 1830 went the greatest length of intrigue on elections, with persuasion and threats, but failed. The people were awaking to a sense of oppression; the election was a triumph of liberty. On July 26, 1830, the king published the following ordinances: First, the liberty of the

press was denied.   Second, the newly elected Chamber of
Deputies, which had not yet met, was dissolved.   Third,
the mode of election was declared altered; cutting off the
people from the possibility of being represented by men of
their choice.   Fourth, a new election was ordered in this
mode.   This was beyond endurance, and discreet and prudent men began to meditate another revolution.

On the day that this infamous decree was published the
laboring people began to rise, and continued rising July
27th, 28th and 29th, meeting in doubtful contest the king's
forces, but with final success, and on the 30th, Charles X.
was declared dethroned, and Louis Philippe, duke of Orleans, was proclaimed Lieutenant, and soon after the king
of France.   He was the son of that duke of Orleans who,
forty years before, was so active and so unprincipled in the
great revolution and who was beheaded in 1793.   They
were Bourbons, of the younger line.

La Fayette led this revolution.   He was one of the
greatest and best men of any age or country, possessing
philanthropy and benevolence in the highest degree, joined
with profound judgment, prudence and discretion.   Fifty
years before this he was aiding in the American revolution,
and forty years before this was laboring to lead the king of
France in paths of safety to himself and his people; then
laboring to control the turbulent elements of the revolution.
Napolean dazzled the world, but La Fayette lives in the affections of all virtuous men.

The people were again disappointed, Louis Philippe was
no better than his predecessor.   The number of voters was
reduced to about one in a hundred of adult men, and these
were bribed to vote for deputies, who in turn were ready to
receive bribes from the ministry.   The king's oldest son, the
duke of Orleans, who was very popular, the hope of the nation, was killed by leaping from his carriage when he sup-

posed the horses were running beyond the control of the driver.   After this the king strengthened his family by marrying one son to a princess of Brazil, and another to a sister of the queen of Spain, but did nothing for his people.   They assembled in different places, and listened to orators who described their trampled rights.   A meeting of this kind was appointed in Paris, in February, 1848.   The king forbade the people assembling.   They disregarded the king's commandment, and a vast procession coming was met by the soldiers, when a collision ensued.

All Paris and the adjacent country was soon in arms.   No La Fayette was there to calm the tempest, but Lamartine, whose eloquence was like oil on troubled waters, harangued them for eight hours, till night approaching, the moral tempest subsided.   Nothing short of a republic would meet their demands.   This he promised.   A provisional government was formed at once, the members elected on the spot by acclamation, the mob voting with the deputies.   A republic followed, with Lamartine at its head, as the leading spirit of the executive commission.

In June, 1848, the laboring people out of employment arose in arms, and Paris again reeked in blood.   Lamartine fell under most unjust censure.   General Cavaignac, who put down this rebellion, was next the leading spirit a short time. A new constitution was formed, and this fickle people chose as president for four years Louis Napoleon Bonaparte, once made king of Holland by his brother Napoleon I.   He showed at once his favor to monarchy by sending an army to put down a republic in Italy; and shrewdly grasping the reins of power, threw into prison all who might hinder, December, 1851, and arose by election to the office of Emperor of France, Napoleon III.

ERASMUS.

Erasmus has been called the morning star of modern civilization.   When the glory of the Platonic age gilded the
shores of the Ægean sea; when Genius walked proudly to
the cities of Greece; and the Muses, then fair and young,
came with careless, independent smiles, to touch with the
wand of inspiration that host who filled with song the Achean
hills and dales, scarce one beam of light had penetrated the
dark forests of the Rhine and Danube.

When the tongue of Plato had been hushed in death for
nineteen centuries, Argyropoles, an illustrious Greek, met
Reuchlin in Rome, and finding in him the living model of
the ancient classics, Argyropoles exclaimed, "Alas! alas!
the fugitive and exiled Greece has gone to hide herself beyond the Alps!"   This pathetic exclamation should moisten
the eye of every scholar.   The Muses had left the Arcadian
groves; and barbarism had for long ages inhabited the land
of ancient art and song.

Who would have predicted, even so late as the Augustan age, that barbarism would cover the classical shores of
the Ægean and Adriatic?   That ten dark centuries would
succeed, in which time the fox would put his head through
windows in the walls of fallen temples!   Who in that age
would have thought, while looking upon the dull Teuton, so
gross and earthlike, that after fourteen hundred years he
would lift again the standard and unfurl the banner of
science?

Erasmus surpassed all others engaged in restoring the literature of the olden time.   Luther surpasses him in decision,
.energy and indomitable will; but Erasmus is the greater in
patience, forbearance and indefatigable application to study.
This great scholar, this Hercules of science, was raised by
Providence at the fit time, to dig from beneath the dust,.

which had been accumulating from the conquests of Attila, the ancient literature. Under the sway of the most super-human pen of Erasmus, the lamp, which had been extinguished in blood, was relighted. Timotheus sung again; the pathetic strains of Orpheus melted hearts on the shores of the German ocean; Demosthenes reappeared in the forum, and Cicero's voice guided the state.

If Erasmus had gone no farther than this, his name would have ever stood high in the temple of fame. He had a holier aim than the mere gildings of literature; his high aim was the moral improvement of the world. His keen eye penetrated all the walks of men, and reached their motives, the mainsprings of action. He saw with deepest pain that everywhere the most debasing superstition usurped the place of Christianity. His "Praise of Folly" went to the ends of the earth, everywhere bringing into contempt the heathenish superstitions of a fallen church, and the gross impostures of a sensual and earthly priesthood. His New Testament in Greek was a light from Heaven on all the paths of literary men. It shook the foundation of religious error and clerical tyranny in the universities, and in the courts of kings and nobles.

From Rome to London, from Paris to Vienna, Erasmus was esteemed the great scholar of his age. His authority was boundless, and his text, which was doubtless very correct, rivaled the Vulgate. Perhaps no publication did so much for the Reformation.

The character of Erasmus has come down to us much darkened through one class of historians. Prominent among these is D'Aubigne. The historian of the great Reformation charges him with rationalism, and pusillanimity.• Every reader of D'Aubigne knows that he uses the term rationalism in a very broad sense; including almost everything anti-Calvinistic. Not only Socinianism and Arianism, but Arminianism also, is Rationalism in his estimation.

Although Erasmus had preceded Luther nearly in the relation of father to son, and although he was superior to Luther in literary attainments, in the full relation of master to his pupil; yet Luther, walking in the light which Erasmus had spread over Europe, treats his father and master very roughly.

In the controversy between these great and good men, we can detect no doctrine of Pelagius or Socinus in Erasmus. The doctrines which were afterwards reduced to a system by Arminius, and which have ever been the standard doctrines of Methodists, were, in the mind of this prince of scholars, rather vague and indefinite. For this he incurred the violent opposition of Luther. For a treatise on "True Will," he was most unsparingly denounced, as an enemy of the Reformation. Luther's doctrine of Predestination, Irresistible Grace, and Unconditional Election identified the Reformers; and when Luther failed to bring the venerable sage to these views, he poured reproach and contumely upon him. There is great injustice in charging Erasmus with vacillating, and this charge comes with an ill-grace from Luther.

Our philosopher had condemned a corrupt church, and stood aloof, holding the standard of reform in his hand; but in his old age Luther snatched this standard from his hand, and pushed him back upon the Papists, because his generous nature could not embrace the doctrine of Unconditional Election.

The generous nature of Erasmus became the ground of the charge of pusillanimity. His noble heart panted for human welfare, and the warmest enthusiasm of philanthropy. He shrunk from inflicting a wound even by a word. No man was more in love with the gospel. Its precepts,

teaching forbearance and charity, most genially distilled upon his heart.   His well-instructed reason agreed with the
word of his Divine Master, that forbearance and kindness
constitute the only true power to overcome evil.

No man was more keenly pained by the alienation of
friends.   Friendship with him had a meaning of almost infinite magnitude.   " Give light, and darkness will disap-
pear," was his favorite saying.   In this spirit Erasmus was
moving the world in true human progress, his influence
reaching from the palaces of kings to the cottages of peas-
ants.   He recognized Luther as a true reformer and defended him against his foes; but when Luther, failing to
draw him into his own violent spirit, and to an endorse-
ment of his creed, treated him with most unbecoming contempt, the venerable philosopher saw that his own methed
of reform was ahead of his age.   He saw that storm arising
which, in spite of his pen or tongue, must rage on under
Luther's impetuous lead.   And this storm did rage on, long
after both Luther and Erasmus were dead, and finally
spreading itself in the terrible "Thirty Years War," which
carried ruin through all Europe, reducing the population of
Germany from fourteen millions to four millions.   The old
age of Erasmus was unhappy.   He could not embrace the
creed of the Reformers, and they were everywhere denouncing him as a Papist and Pelagian, a time server and coward.
When Basle was in a state of revolution, Protestants and
Papists under arms, churches broken open, and everything
obnoxious to the Reformers destroyed, the life of Erasmus
was in danger from both parties, though in most danger
from the Reformers.   He stepped into a boat and glided
down the Rhine, to seek some quiet place for thought, and
prayer, and death.

LUTHER.

If greatness is estimated by influence, Martin Luther must be pronounced one of the greatest men of all ages and all lands. We may charge him with presumption, rashness and temerity; with superstition, with pride, intolerance and tyranny; yet we concede that he made his mark on the face of the moral world as no other man has done since the apostles fell asleep.

We might criticise the extravagance of historians, their fawning and bombast; we may loath the pen so lavish of panegyric, ignoring every fault, yet Luther rises before us on the bosom of time's great ocean, looming up so giant-like that our attention is fixed and our veneration moved. From the opening of the fourth century, when Constantine wedded paganism to Christianity, with the decline of heathen persecution, corruption commenced and soon pervaded the Church through all Christendom, increasing with every age. The inward life of Christianity was lost in outward rites, many of which were pagan ceremonies.

False and pernicious doctrines undermined the very foundation of evangelical faith. Merit of works, especially voluntary penance, or self-torture, pampered pride, and left no place for faith in the Atonement. Purgatory encouraged sinners that the wealth of surviving friends would buy their ransom. Next came the Mass, and Transubstantiation. A priest repeating a written prayer over bread and wine, professed to remove every particle of it, and to bring in its stead, by transubstantiation, the real presence of the body and blood of Christ, thus offering up Christ again a ransom for sinners. The priest then professed to eat the flesh and drink the blood of Christ, or to use his strongest language, to eat God. Such was the mass. The mass was repeated to increase the merit, and sold to any sinner who wished its benefit, the priest agreeing to say mass so many times for so much money. Masses were bought for the living and the dead. Mass and purgatory bore a strong relationship. Kind men, whose friends were in purgatory, would buy masses for their relief by scores, or hundreds, or thousands, according to their wealth.

A *valet de chambre* at the court of Francis I. of France, who was contemporary with Luther, a merry sensualist, resorted to various tricks to replenish his pockets. Being a noted ventriloquist he feigned himself a priest, and called on a superstitious miser. "I am going," said he, "a missionary to the Indies." It was at the time of Loyola's great move in the East, when, under Xavier's untiring zeal, millions were bowing at the standard of the Order of Jesus. A voice from the earth beneath the house startled the miser; he turned pale and looked beseechingly at the priest. "I am your father, and in purgatory," cried the voice from Hades. "Oh, my terrible sufferings! and you, my son, have hoarded money and never bought one mass for my relief. Here is the servant of the Lord, with holy zeal, about to leave native land, home, friends, and all that is dear in life, and go to sacrifice himself on the missionary altar in a foreign land, but is hindered for want of money. He cannot go. Oh, give him the ample outfit, and in a moment I shall leave this flame and go to the mansions of the blessed." The poor miser was in agony. Two mighty powers had fastened iron teeth at once on his heart; love of father and love of gold. As he hesitated, the wailing from below became too awful. Half distracted, he most reluctantly poured the money into the lap of the missionary, who had sat a meek and astonished spectator of the scene. The miser killed himself when he heard how he had been mocked.

There were many priests who had became such with no

better motives than this courtier had in playing this fraud, and who spent their ill-gotten gains in a manner no more decent. The celibacy of the priests and monks only tended to fornication, and this scandal was almost universal.

The decisions of ecumenical councils claimed the authority of divine inspiration, and writings of the Fathers during four centuries were reckoned of the same authority as the Bible. They even superseded the Bible through the world, for the Bible, being confined to the Latin language, was not read by one in a thousand. The power of the pope formed a painfully interesting subject of contemplation for Luther's philosophic mind. How had he created that terrible instrument, the bull of excommunication, which fell as the anathema of heaven upon men, like the sentence of eternal damnation?

How had he been able to absolve subjects, to depose kings, to humble the greatest sovereigns, to bring them to bow at his feet, to literally kiss them, to stand for days in winter, clad in linsey-woolsey at his gate, waiting in the most suppliant manner for his pardon and benediction? Even with the Germans, a people proverbially incredulous and independent, the power of the pope, though less than in other lands, was yet very great. It was there like an overflowing stream, bearing along in its course nearly all things. Here and there a sturdy German lifted his head above the waters, planting his feet in the firm earth and resisting the current.

Highest of all arose the head of Luther. He traced the resemblance between the pope and those secular princes, who, in different in ages, practiced universal tyranny. But it was in tracing the resemblance between the pope and the terrestrial gods of the pagan world, that he learned to comprehend him. He found that superstition was the great secret of the papal power. Fear is man's strongest passion;

and it is strong beyond description when it reaches beyond this life. It has been the instrument of tyranny in every age ; and when it was universally believed that the pope held the keys of hell, his power became boundless. The subjects of any king would refuse obedience to him, or even would assassinate him, at the dictation of one who by a word could consign them to eternal death.

At the dictation of the pope, for his benediction, or the benediction of a bishop, or a priest who acted in the pope's stead, the bigoted people were everywhere ready to murder any one who questioned the pope's authority, or questioned the use or propriety of any ceremony or rite.

FRIENDSHIP.

MR. EDITOR:—Some years ago I saw in a popular religious journal the following,

"Be familiar with but few."

In a late number of my favorite paper I saw a line by itself, the substance of which was—

"Become intimate with none."

Such counsel I can no more forget than I could forget being buried by an avanlache in a ravine of the Alps. I feel a transient ague when I think that such counsel has been given to selfish men. The man who declares himself independent of friendship, should, if it were possible, be placed upon a planet of his own, and if he can endure to never see the face or hear the voice of man, let him have his solitude long as his planet whirls in its orbit, or let him have St. Helena all to himself.

There have always been some misanthropes upon the earth. Ancient monarchs on the thrones of oriental empires sacrificed friendship to ambition, and made the throne an awful solitude. I care not whether my subjects love me

or not, said an ancient monarch, if they fear me it is sufficient.

I sometimes meet a man who has received the above
named counsel.   I bow to him, but his neck never bends.
I smile, but he will not smile; it would spoil his dignity.
If I had patrician rank he might bow and smile, but he is
afraid of contamination if he approaches a plebeian.   If I
had great wealth he would sell me his smile for value received, but I have not the ability to buy his smile if I had
the disposition.   If I could control a hundred votes, and
bring them to bear on his prospect of political promotion, I
should have his smile.   I cannot have his smile; it is, however, a consolation to think that I am as well off without it.
His friendship would be like the apples of Sodom, beautiful without, but when tried only ashes and dust.

Some will say that "Friendship is but a name." This is
a rash conclusion.   Friendship is a reality, a fact.   There
are men who bow because they are humble, and smile from
the promptings of genuine friendship.   There are men who
feel that the welfare of mankind is their interest, their highest interest—dearer to them than their personal honor,
pleasure or wealth.   There are true philanthropists, men
whose philanthropy is not spoiled by the selfishness of an
unholy patriotism.   The world is their country, and all
mankind their countrymen.   Every Christian should be a
friend.   Christianity may have her sanctuaries and her
sacraments, and the eloquence of St. Jerome may grace her
pulpits, and yet if the votaries at her altars are not friends,
what is she more than Mahometanism or Paganism.   The
Christian is an angel of kindness.   The warrior chief says
in his heart, what is it to me who suffers, if I may but arise
to fame? The Christian walks in tears over the bloody field
bearing oil and wine for the wounded and words of consolation to the dying.   The worldling says in heart, What is

it to me who dwell in weary poverty, if I may but rise to wealth; if my house, and furniture, and apparel may be unsurpassed? The Christian goes over the world of ruin where the worldling has made wreck of human bliss, bearing alms to the poor and words of consolation to the broken-hearted and despairing; he enters the dilapidated cottage where the north wind brings the snow upon the pale cheek of a woman dying with grief, whose husband, the father of her helpless children, was ruined in fortune by the speculator, and then, poor man, he was sent to his grave by the merciless hand of the rumseller.   The libertine cares not what becomes of his victim; when by lying and false professions of love his object is gained, he inquires no more after her. She is disowned by relatives and all her former friends, and "cast abandoned on the world's wide stage."   Amidst the wintry tempest she wanders by night, despairing of shelter and bereft of reason, comes to the verge and is about to plunge into the river that flows beneath darkly mingled with the falling snow, whose Christian kindness rescues the poor Magdalene? When slander has brought its victim to feel that he has no friends, go, Christians, and meet him in the lonely path, and cheer his breaking heart.   Let them who hate him, hate you with him, do not save your own reputation by abandoning an innocent man.   Better often be deceived and imposed upon than to wound an innocent man. Christianity is not selfish.   Do not confine yourself to a select number—the beautiful, the wealthy and the intelligent.   This might gratify self, but this does not answer the end of our being.   The abject poor, the deformed and the ignorant have claims upon our friendship as fellow men.

———

MR. FRAZER'S CONGREGATION: OR FASHIONABLE RELIGION ILLUSTRATED.

Can you tell me, Johnny, what was the text yesterday? said Rev. Mr. Frazer to the son of Deacon Jones, a bright lad of eight summers.

John. Yes, sir, it was the first epistle of John, 2d chapter, and 15th verse, "Love not the world, neither the things that are in the world. If any man love the world, the love of the Father is not in him."

Mr. Frazer. Well done, my lad; you have done well to commit it to memory so soon.

John. My mother taught it to me a great while ago.

Mr. F. Deacon Jones, how do you like your home?

Deacon J. I am well pleased with it; I selected it with care.

Mr. F. It is a charming situation, only a mile from the city, and in the vicinity of so many privileges. You were at church yesterday, Deacon, for the first time since your removal to this place, Do you not think we have a respectable church and congregation?

Deacon J. The church is large; that is well. I suppose on extraordinary occasions it will be filled; but the unnecessary expense of ornament would build a comfortable meeting-house in the town from which I removed, where the congregation worship in a private dwelling house.

Mr. F. We must compete with the other denominations of the city in the ornaments and costly finishing of our church, or we cannot compete with them in respectability of an audience; and now, sir, there is not a more brilliant display of carriages about any church in the city, and the richly dressed congregation, and so many men of wealth, and eminent office and station; the mayor of the city always with his family in his pew, all confirms me in the proud assurance that we shall not be outdone.

Deacon J.   I saw no colored people in your congregation.

Mr. F.   We have a seat appropriated to them, but they now worship by themselves, and their seat is vacant.

Deacon J.   I saw an aged man, with poor and patched garments, in the negro seat, all alone.   Who was he?

Mr. F.   He is the only abject poor man belonging to my church.   His name is Bates.

Deacon J.   He is then a member of your church.   I thought he was a man of deep piety; he paid the strictest attention to the sermon, and was often in tears.

Mr. F.   Indeed; well I did not know that he was in the church until the audience were dismissed.

Deacon J.   He ¦stood near the door, meekly, waiting your approach, but, Mr. F., you turned so suddenly from him, when near enough to take his hand, that I thought you affected not to see him.   Just then you shook hands with a gentleman you called Mr. Maxwell, with gold spectacles, and gold-headed cane, and very costly apparel.   His wife and daughters were with him, surpassing almost any in jewelry and apparel.   Who was that?

Mr. F.   That was Judge Maxwell, the richest merchant in the city.   He is a constant hearer, and liberal supporter and patron of our church.

Deacon J.   What made me so particular in my inquiry was, that I heard him on Saturday challenging gentlemen to engage him in a horse-race, and swearing most profanely, and drinking brandy with very wicked company at the Eagle Hotel, as I called a moment on business; he was also most blasphemously ridiculing the Bible.   Did you know that he was an infidel?

Mr. F.   I did; I regret it, for he is in many respects a gentleman, and he pays one hundred dollars a year of my salary.

Deacon J. I saw a carriage containing a gentleman, his wife and daughters, drive directly from the church to take a pleasure excursion. Who were they?

Mr. F. The mayor's family. They generally do the same every Sabbath after they leave church. I am sorry to see it.

Deacon J. Shortly after you descended the pulpit stairs, you spoke with three gentlemen so much resembling each other, that I thought them to be brothers.

Mr. F. They were the firm of Anderson & Brothers wholesale dealers. They own most of the stock in our city bank, besides large investments in shipping. They are regular attendants at our church.

Deacon J. Are they not the sons of George Anderson, of B——?

Mr. F. They are.

Deacon J. They were school-fellows with me a short time in my childhood. My father has often spoken of George Anderson. But let us return to old Mr. Bates, who occupied the negro seat. I saw, when you passed him without speaking to him, a tear started in his eye, and he walked slowly away; when out of church he was soon alone. I kept my eye on him as he moved along, a solitary object, until he was nearly out of the city. Where does he reside?

Mr. F. He resides back of those hills, down the lake somewhere. In going to his home he leaves the road, and takes a foot-path winding among the hills towards the lake-shore. When I have taken an excursion on the lake, I have seen a cottage nearly covered with wild vines, which I supposed was his, with a little garden spot, surrounded with high rocks.

Deacon J. Have you never visited him?

Mr. F. I have not; he is a very obscure man, of a most

abject appearance, earning his living by sawing wood in the city.

Deacon J.   Is not this Thomas Bates of B —— ?

Mr. F.   It is.

Deacon J.   I have often heard my father, with tears, tell the history of Thomas Bates, of B——.   He was a young man of intelligence, of amiable deportment, and generous and disinterested to an extreme.   He possessed a small fortune, which he had accumulated by industry, when he went into partnership with George Anderson, father of the firm of Anderson & Brothers, of this city.   Anderson was unprincipled, selfish and shrewd; was always watching his opportunity, and when the property of the firm had arisen to thirty thousand dollars, succeeded in transferring all to himself.   Subsequently he foreclosed a mortgage on Bates's house and land, and stripped him of all.   And now, sir, the vast wealth of these brothers had its beginning in the hard labor of this poor old man that sits in the negro seat, for he owned nearly all, when he and Anderson became partners.

Mr. F.   Had Mr. Bates any children?

Deacon J.   He had one daughter.   While George Anderson, jun., now senior, of the Anderson firm was at college, she was residing with an aunt in the vicinity of the college.   Anderson was ten years older than Martha Bates. Having been acquainted with her from her infancy, he often visited her—succeeded in gaining her juvenile love and confidence, seduced her, and left her abandoned on the world's wide stage at the age of fifteen.   Overwhelmed with shame, before her aunt knew her guilt she left for home, but with worse dread of meeting her parents, she turned aside from her way and sojourned among strangers until concealment was impossible, and then many a matron with false notions of propriety refused her shelter under her roof. In the midst of a winter tempest she called in the evening

at Hon. John Morgan's for shelter.   Mrs. Morgan rudely
ordered her out.   George Anderson was there, in another
room in company with Mrs. M.'s daughters, one of whom
he subsequently married.   My father, who had called in on
business, interfered, but to no purpose; and seeing the
child pushed out into the pelting tempest, he took her to
his house, where she died in a few weeks.   The news of
her death was the first news her parents had of her disgrace
or her sufferings.

(Mr. Norris enters with Mr. Knowles, and is introduced
by Rev. Mr. F. as a member of his church.)

Deacon J.   I believe you are of the legal profession, sir.

Mr. Norris.   I am, sir.

Deacon J.   I have heard you plead in B——.

Mr. N.   Very probable, sir, I have attended several
terms of the court there.   I called in to see you, Mr. Frazer.   Mrs. Norris is in want of a maid servant.   Perhaps
you know one that we could employ.

Mr. F.   Deacon Jones, do you know anything of Mr.
Page's family, who have just come to this vicinity from
B——?

Deacon J.   I am well acquainted with them.   Mrs. Page
has several daughters.

Mr. N.   Is Mr. Page poor?

Deacon J.   He is.

Mr. N.   Have the daughters been accustomed to do
service?

Deacon J.   They have often assisted neighboring families,
especially in nursing the sick.

Mr. N.   Do you think that we could employ one of
them?

Deacon J.   I do not know, it will depend upon the treatment that servants receive in your family.

Mr. N.   You would not question that we treat our servants kindly, would you, Mr. Jones?

Deacon J.   If you make a distinction of rank or cast in
your family, Mrs. Page's daughters cannot be employed.

Mr. N.   No family of any distinction in our city, or in
the country, will have servants, male or female, rank with
their employers.   Servants must know and keep their place,
and that is not in the parlor with company, nor at the table
with their employers, and their guests.   No, Mr. Jones,
working men with us are not to come in without coats, and
seat themselves with gentlemen at table, and servant maids
are to learn that their empire is the kitchen.   I think you
understand me.

Deacon J.   I do, Mr. Norris.   You cannot employ one
of Mrs. Page's daughters.

Mr. N.   Then you think their foolish pride would make
them refuse a good situation, and ample wages.

Deacon J.   Sir, their pride is noble, it is the inheritance
of the daughters of America.   Mrs. Page's daughters will
never become your slaves; they will sooner braid hats, or
even range the wild swamps, and gather cranberries for
market.

Mr. N.   Well, Mr. Jones, you are very eccentric in your
views of propriety.

Deacon J.   That refinement must be fastidious that
looks with abhorrence upon a worthy young woman at table
with her employers and their guests, because she has
been seen in the kitchen; and how great the inconsistency
in that false refinement that is shocked to see a man in genteel company without a coat, and looks with complacency
on a lady in genteel company, or even in church, with her
arms naked, or only covered with gauze.

Mr. N.   There are hundreds of American girls of intelligence, in our city, engaged in braiding, cap-making, etc.,

for one-half or three-fourths of what we would pay them as servants, while we are obliged to employ the most ignorant Swiss or Irish emigrants.

Deacon J.   I hope you will find none less ignorant, willing to crouch into the condition of your servants; and I hope the Swiss and Irish emigrant will soon become too intelligent to be thus degraded.

Mr. N.   In every age there has been distinction of rank, and probably there always will be.

Deacon J.   Men and women are, and ever will be, distinguished by intelligence, but wealth should make no distinction.

Mr. N.   But will not the most intelligent in the very nature of things, become the men of wealth.

Deacon J.   No, sir; the unscrupulous, the selfish, and the man void of conscience, will more commonly become the man of wealth; while many of the best hearts in the world are found among the poor.

Mr. N.   You differ, Mr. Jones, from some of the wisest and greatest men of our age.   In the lectures of Dr. B., great respect is paid to head labor; hand labor of the most respectable kind, is placed far below head labor in the scale; common labor far below this; next the dregs of society, and next perdition.   Dr. B. allows the right to sell knowledge and talent as high as we can, and I think the man who has a superior talent to discern the value of property, and to foresee coming changes in the commercial world, may use his talent in accumulating wealth.

Deacon J.   He may, if he do not supplant or wrong anybody of less shrewdness, but he has no more right to take advantage of a man of less shrewdness, or slower perception, prostrate him, and travel over him to a fortune, than a man of superior physical strength has to knock down a man of feebler frame, and travel over him to a fortune.   Dr. B., if you rightly understand him, has tarnished his reputation.. If such are his views, I have little confidence in his anti-slavery, or in his republicanism.

Mr. N.   Mr. Page will find it impossible to rank with those whose quicker perception has placed them above him in wealth.

Deacon J.   This family, sir, can never be enslaved; I know their stern New England nature.   Fifteen years ago Mr. Page's prospects were flattering; at that time the gentleman who is now your partner, sold him fifteen thousand dollars worth, nominally, of stock, which he knew was rapidly depreciating, and would soon be worthless; he, how-ever, represented it to Mr. Page as good, and rising in value.. Page had at that time the utmost confidence in Jasper, your partner, and sold him in that bargain five thousand dollars worth, nominally, of city lots, which Jasper knew would be worth twenty thousand in one month, in consequence of an act just passed by the legislature, information of which Jasper had got that morning by express.   Stripped in one day of his fortune, by the head labor of a treacherous friend, Mr. Page rented a small farm, which he has cultivated ever since until he removed to this place.

Mr. Knowles.   I have listened with great attention, ex-pecting that Mr. Jones's strictures would fall on me.

Deacon J.   You were as poor as Mr. Page two years ago, although you now rank with the moneyed gentry of the city.

Mr. Knowles.   I think my speculations have been lawful and honorable.

Deacon J.   Your speculations in the mines may be law-ful, and by the decision of popular opinion honorable; but they will hardly stand the test of the rule of right contained in the gospel.   You sold your lots too high, taking advan-tage of a time of great excitement to sell, and taking ad--

vantage of the ignorance of men who had recently arrived, and were not capable of judging of the value of property in the mines.

Mr. Knowles. I never gave a false statement of the value of any property I sold in the mines.

Deacon J. Perhaps not, but you sold for more than you would have given, had you been a purchaser, possessing the knowledge of the facts, as you knew them in selling.

Three brothers left their families in B——, mortgaging their possessions for a few hundred dollars which they paid to you for lots, and after working the lots with hard toil for eighteen months with little success, they abandoned them, and returned to their families penniless. They are now reduced to abject poverty. How many others have suffered in like manner I do not know, but these I should suppose were enough to embitter all the joys of wealth. Your jobbing on the public works is likely to result in a similar manner on some honest hard-working men. The commissioners are to pay you fifty thousand for your job, and you have let it in small jobs for thirty-five thousand.

The public works should give a fair opportunity to the laboring poor. The money drawn from the state treasury for the public works should go to the honest poor, who perform the work, and what right you, or any other man, has to pocket fifteen thousand dollars, seizing it on the way from the treasury to the laborer, the day of judgment will determine.

Some of the men to whom you let jobs may do well, others will be made bankrupt, and a great number of men in their employ will return to their families without a dollar. So that your fifteen thousand dollars comes in the end from the miseries of the people. If the commissioners were honest men, they would let the work to you for what in their judgment it was worth; if they were not capable of judging of its worth, they should be removed from office and above all, if they connive at iniquity in the speculation they are unfit for the public confidence.

Mr. Frazer. Deacon Jones, you will not question that distinction in wealth is necessary. Some men must have capital, or how could mills and manufactories be established; and then men of wealth do much good in giving employment to laborers.

Deacon J. Mills and manufactories could be established by a union of men with small fortunes. It is true men of wealth give employment to laborers, but they usually appropriate to themselves from one-eighth to one-fourth of their earnings. They help the poor to money by purchasing their horses, cattle, or sheep at four-fifths of their value, or by loaning to them at an enormous interest. They furnish the poor with grain or meal, at from thirty to fifty per cent. more than it cost them.

Mr. F. Do you think all wealthy men wicked?

Deacon J. I do not; there are some men of wealth who are great benefactors of mankind, as Mr. Smith, and Mr. Harris, but you know, Mr. Frazer, that these are rare exceptions to a general rule. Wealth is generally earned by the laboring poor, by hard labor, and by innumerable speculations it is transferred to idle men, of head work, who despise the poor whom they have robbed, and whom they would make servants.

Mr. F. My only wealth is my education, and my professional standing; I came honestly by these.

Deacon J. I doubt not you came honestly by these, as far as you are personally concerned, yet I have heard your father say, that during the five years that you spent in college he employed four men, at ten dollars per month. He said he could have paid them twelve dollars per month, and

made a fair profit on his farming, but by paying only ten,
he saved just enough to meet your expenses at college.

(Mr. Norris, Mr. Knowles, and Rev. Mr. Frazer, having
dined with Mr. Jones, have walked out with him to view his
farm.

Mrs. Norris, Mrs. Anderson, and Mrs. Knowles, have
called to see Mrs. Jones.)

Mrs. Anderson.   Mr. Jones has selected a beautiful
situation here.

Mrs. Jones.   I think so, I am highly pleased with it.

Mrs. Norris.   I saw you at church, Mrs. Jones ; do you
not think Mr. Frazer has a very respectable congregation ?
there is not a more respectable congregation in the city; I
am glad you have selected Mr. Frazer's church as your
place of worship.

Mrs. Knowles.   What object of pity was that in the negro
seat, with coat and pants so patched ?   I was astonished to
see him in Mr. Frazer's church.

Mrs. Anderson.   That was old Mr. Bates.   He has always worshiped there since he came to his present home
more than twenty years ago.

Mrs. Jones.   Mr. Jones was deeply interested in that old
man.   He will soon visit him.

Mrs. Anderson.   Indeed !   I do not believe Mr. Anderson was ever in his cottage.   Such persons deserve no attention, unless it be in almsgiving, and I am sure Mr. Anderson would be as ready to give alms as any man although
he has no time to be running after the poor to see when
they are in want.

Mrs. Jones.   Mr. Bates is said to be a very pious member of the Church, and yet Mr. Frazer has never visited
him, and I do not know that anybody has visited him.
How do we know what sufferings his family may be enduring ?   Mrs. Bates may be sick.

Mrs. Anderson.   Possibly she is; I have not seen her at church in eighteen months.

Mrs. J.   I believe Mr. Bates has neither child nor grandchild?

Mrs. A.   He has neither.   He had a daughter; I have seen her at her aunt's, near my father's.

Mrs. J.   Are you the daughter of Judge Morgan, of A.?

Mrs. A.   I am.   I wonder what became of Martha Bates.

Mrs. J.   She died at Mr. Jones's father's.

Here Mrs. Anderson stept hastily to the window, and stood silent a long time, probably reflecting on that scene, when poor Martha, the victim of Mr. Anderson's treachery, was driven by her mother, Mrs. Morgan, into the pitiless tempest in the night.

Mrs. Knowles.   What family, Mrs. Jones, occupied the pew in front of yours?

Mrs. J.   The family of Mr. Page, lately from B——.

Mrs. K.   What a coarse looking group!   How ridiculous Mrs. Page and her daughters looked with their old-fashioned bonnets, and such shawls!   I wonder at their choosing our church as their place of worship.   I should think they would have gone to Mr. Norton's congregation on Lake Street, or to Mr. Parson's in the country.   But they will receive so little attention that I presume they will soon leave and go somewhere else;   for, as Mr. Knowles says, it will be too hot for them there.   They are a disgrace to Mr. Frazer's congregation.

Mrs. J.   Mr. Page's family do not go to church to receive or bestow attentions.   In intelligence and piety they are surpassed by no family.   I have passed some of the pleasantest hours of my life with this excellent family, in their humble cottage in B——.

Mrs. K.   I hope, Mrs. Jones, you do not intend to associate with them here!   Mr. Jones's standing in the legal profession will give your family the privilege of classing with those of the first rank in this city, but you cannot expect it if you associate with such coarse people. I hope, especially, Mrs. Jones, you will not allow your daughters to associate with that family. They are young, and strangers here, and should be introduced into the best families first.

Mrs. Norris. It would be their ruin to be seen with that low family now.

Mrs. Anderson. Have your daughters had an invitation to the ball, which is to be on the fourth of July?

Mrs. J. They have.

Mrs. Norris. They will go, by all means.

Mrs. J. They will not.

Mrs. Anderson. Will not! Why, Mrs. Jones, how can you deny them?

Mrs. J. They have no inclination to go.

Mrs. A. How strange! Have they never learned to dance?

Mrs. J. They have not; they never desired to learn.

Mrs. A. What a misfortune! How will they acquire grace and ease of manners?

Mrs. J. Dancing has more credit than it should have for grace and ease of manners; all the benefit to be derived from the art will fall far short of balancing against the evils arising from it.

Mrs. A. What evils can arise from dancing?

Mrs. J. With many who dance easily it becomes a passion, absorbing the whole mind, dissipating not only all religious sobriety and elevation, but even all taste for the acquisition of substantial and useful knowledge. It begets inordinate love of company and of dress. It also pampers selfishness; the votaries of the ball-chamber live not for the glory of God, nor for the happiness of mankind; they live for their own personal enjoyment, having a total distaste for all the self-denial enjoined by the gospel.

My daughters have engaged to visit Mrs. Page's daughters on the fourth of July.

At this announcement all were silent for some minutes, when Mrs. Jones proceeded.

Mrs. Page's daughters are intelligent, and amiable, and of most exemplary piety, and being several years older than mine they have been their instructors.　I am more indebted to their counsels than to any other human instrumentality for the early piety of my children.　My daughter Jane, whom we buried last February, said to me when dying, "O, mother, what a debt of gratitude I owe to those excellent young ladies, the Misses Page, for their pious councils."

PEACE.

MR. EDITOR :—The subject of peace is to me one of the most interesting subjects of reform, or of Christianity.　My own evil nature was early developed.　At eight years of age I shouted and leaped about for joy, during a cannonading at the mouth of the Genesee River, as each gun sounded along the wild forest where I was at play.　Weems and Goldsmith kindled a flame of martial ambition in my boyish bosom in my backwoods home, and Homer raised the flame to a tempest.　My green fancy busied itself with epaulettes and plumes, with brandishing swords and roaring guns.　In my dreams by day I was at Saratoga and Monmouth, on the hills of Monongahela, or the heights of Abraham.　I became entranced in contemplating Platia, Marathon and Pharsalia.　Hector and Agamemnon I saw in their might through the vista of the past, and "Troy is no more, sounded o'er the bosom of the Archipelago."

The war with England had just closed ; men met for

training almost every month ; their fathers came also, and when heated with rum, told of their own great deeds in the days of Washington. Everything was military ; the fireside, the school, the press, and the pulpit. Independence day roused all. Strong men bore guns, maidens danced, old men came with their staves, and boys came bounding along in groups through every lane. Martial music, war songs, and stories, oaths and rum. The chaplain's prayer and orator's declamation made us think that Englishmen, Tory, and Devil, were synonymous terms. While barefooted at the plow I often became a field-marshal in fancy, fought great battles, on which the fate of the empire depended ; and when the vision had fled my ambition was so inflamed that I sat down to consider how I might rise to fame, and seeing the poverty of my parents, and the great difficulty of obtaining a suitable education, and an introduction to the world, I arose from the plow-beam and smote my fists in desperation, bade defiance to difficulty, and resolved that I would arise to fame.

Thus it was with me when God brought me to feel the force of the Scripture, " What is a man profited if he shall gain the whole world and lose his own soul ?" and it was never, until broken by the tempest of conviction, and nearly brought to the grave, that I parted with my darling object. The struggle of my nature with the divine Spirit was mighty, and no demon in me was more tenacious of its possession than military ambition.

For twenty years I have preached the same doctrine as that held by the Friends, on the subject of war. I found little sympathy with my views in the M. E. Church, but when I perused the Wesleyan Methodist Discipline I found among its excellences the doctrine of peace. The follow-ing is Section XX of our Discipline : " We believe the gospel of Christ to be in every way opposed to the practice of war, in all its forms, and those customs which tend to foster and perpetuate the war spirit, to be inconsistent with the benevolent designs of the Christian religion."

This is all a Quaker could ask.   Here is no exception ; not of defensive war, nor of revolutions.   The gospel of Christ is opposed in every way to the practice of war, in all its forms, and those customs which tend to foster and per- petuate the war spirit are inconsistent with Christianity.

The Michigan Conference formerly corresponded with a Friends' Yearly Meeting in Indiana, and by vote, which I think was unanimous, adopted the entire Quaker doctrine of peace.   It has been said, " No people were ever better than their laws."   Perhaps no religious people were ever better than their Discipline.

The twentieth article of our Discipline is a nobly elevated mark, which I trust will never be brought down ; and if our brethren have not all come up to it we hope they will.

Many peace men in America make an exception of the American Revolution, and thus open a leak, through which all their peace principles leave them.   It is placing a low estimate upon human nature, and upon our English kindred in particular, to suppose that a majority of the English government would have continued incorrigibly oppressive against the patience and forbearance of the American colonists.

It will be claimed by my opponents that a majority of the noblest minds in England have long ago approved of American independence.   This proves that patience and forbearance would have given us all that we asked ; for my opponents will not say that their noble minds have been tamed into this approval by defeat, or that Pitt, and a host of noble Englishmen, espoused our cause from the first through fear.

If patience and forbearance would have brought us all we

asked, could we not have waited a few years, and bought stamped paper, and paid a trifling duty on tea, and saved the sea of bloodshed during eight years' war, and saved an immense amount of property, and yet, perhaps, dearest of all, saved the morals of our country ? A moral pestilence accompanies the military camp. Intemperance in America had its origin mostly in the Revolutionary War. Of all the Revolutionary soldiers that I knew in my early childhood, more than half were drunkards.

The illustrious Hungarian, whose unparalleled eloquence joined to the romance of his history, has aroused so much enthusiasm in this country, has turned the heads of many peace men, and for the time being they are bewildered. Some of them will become right when the excitement is over, but others may be spoiled for life. They may refrain from deadly weapons because they are committed to peace principles, but with strange inconsistency will urge their neighbors, not committed, to shoulder arms and march to the field of conflict.

If we enter into the exercise of the wisdom of the world, on the question of policy, we shall find difficulty in guessing what would be the result of war between Hungary, Great Britain, and the United States, on the one hand, and Austria, Russia, and France, on the other. What would be the attitude of the rest of Europe ? What part would remain neutral ? What join the Hungarian interest, and what the Austrian ? Some things would be certain. The earth would be smeared with the putrid blood of thousands, and the air would receive its horrid odor. The ashes of cities, hamlets, and country dwellings would bleach the hillsides and plains of Europe, while tenantless mothers, with starving children, were drenched and pelted by the cold storm ; beauty, innocence, and virtue would shrink in the grasp of human fiends ; licentiousness, profanity, and intemperance would increase one hundred per cent. per annum, and national debts would tax and distress the poor for one or two generations to come. Ah I more, a few men would get immortalized, and be remembered by the historian, and be named in orations and songs of posterity, while the names of common soldiers would be lost, as their flesh is lost in the mass of the dead.

But what would be the result on the liberties of men ? In human reason we have no data from which to judge, only the present state of Europe, and the world's past history.

I copy the following from the *Independent* of Nov. 27th. It is an extract from a speech of Kossuth, delivered to the workingmen of Copenhagen House, near Islington, England :

" Hungary can in no other way regain its freedom, but in that way in which it was deprived of it—by war—as every nation which is free and independent conquered its deliverance from its oppressors; like Switzerland, Belgium, Spain, Portugal, France, Sweden, Norway, Greece, the United States, and England itself; that is, by a revolution, as some would call it ; by a war of legitimate defence, as I would call it."

With nearly the same propriety he might have named every kingdom since the world began.

This losing and recovering freedom is something very equivocal. Did England lose or gain her freedom by the Saxon conflict ? The English boast of their Saxon origin. Was the Norman conquest the gain or loss of England's freedom ? The present lords and nobles of England are principally Norman, and they consider themselves England's heart. Was the freedom of England gained or lost, when the head of the second Stuart rolled on the scaffold ? or when the protectorate slipped from the hands of the imbe-

cile son of Cromwell ? or when James the Second was forced
to leave his throne and kingdom ?

Why did not the Hungarian orator put Scotland in his
list ? Probably he did not consider Scotland free, and yet
the throne of Britain has been filled by a Scotch family for
two and a half centuries. When did France gain her freedom? The country of France was conquered by the Romans, and subsequently, during the decline of Rome, by
each succeeding wave of Northern barbarians ; finally the
Franks conquered and possessed the land, and the Gauls
were lost in the Franks. The Carlovingian has displaced
the Merovingian race of sovereigns, and succeeded them ;
they have passed away ; the Bourbons have had their day,
and are no more. France has had her first and second
revolution, her first and second Bonaparte, but when she
gained her freedom, or whether she ever gained it, I cannot
tell. Was the freedom of France gained by the fall of Louis
Sixteenth ? or by the battle of Waterloo ? by the promotion
of Louis Philippe ? or by his fall and banishment ? It
would be equally difficult to show what good has arisen to
any nation from the shedding of blood of thousands of our
own sons, and thousands of the sons of other countries.
The ancient Greeks fought themselves out of being, and
the modern Greeks, after all the lauding of their glorious
revolution, are in a miserable condition. All the benefits
of their independence we should not dare to place in the
scale against the loss of blood and treasure during the war.
What good have revolutions done to South America ?
where are her republics ?

The nations of the peninsula, conquered by the ancient
Spartans, might probably have amalgamated with their conquerors, as the Gauls did with the Franks ; but in attempting to repel the invaders they failed, and, under the general

name of Helot, became the most abject slaves the world
has ever known, except Algerine and American.

The Jews, after Pompey's conquest, might have had all
the privileges of Roman provinces, but in attempting to
gain their independence they lost all, and became homeless
wanderers in all nations.

It will be said, If South America and Mexico had been
more improved, morally and intellectually, we should have
seen their prosperity resulting from their wars.   I answer,
If they had been morally and intellectually improved, we
should have seen their prosperity without their wars, and,
perhaps, in spite of their wars, but not in consequence of
their wars.   This is the great error, nay, the sin of historians, that they teach their readers of every rising generation
that war has brought all the blessings of nations, while war
has done its worst to prevent moral and intellectual improvement.   The historian again is guilty of a most wicked
felony, in stealing flowers from the providence of God, to
wreathe the brows of his deified heroes.   He might as well
steal flowers from the glories of redemption, to wreathe the
brows of Herod and Pilate, and seat them deified with
Bolivar and Napoleon.   God will make the wrath of man
to praise him.   In his providence he will bring good from
every possible source, but woe to him who shall make this
an apology for sin.   These doctrines will be called pusillanimous.   I have learned to bear the scoffs of the proud.
Christ has been called pusillanimous, and Christianity, while
its spirit has saved the world of men from exterminating
themselves by violence, has been called pusillanimity.   Unless Christians abandon the world's notion of national honor,
they may as well abandon all the vital principles of the gospel.   What Christian standing in the same relation to an
individual that Hungary stands to Russia, would be disposed to kill or mutilate him, or burn his barn or house?

Have we no faith in the power of the gospel in national relations? Austria, wicked as she is, and perhaps there is none more wicked, is not beyond the reach of Christian influence. We have millions of the oppressed in our country; oppressed almost infinitely more than Hungarians, and we depend on a Christian appeal to the oppressors and to our government.

1852.

THE POLITICAL DUTIES OF CHRISTIANS.

This was the title of an essay which I wrote for the *Wesleyan* about ten years ago, the substance of which I wrote again six years ago, for the Detroit *Free Democrat*, in a series of chapters entitled "Political Millennium." My old friends, who have read the *Wesleyan* and the *Free Democrat*, know my views on the political duties of Christians.

I was present at Jackson when the Republican party was born, and also present at Kalamazoo, two weeks before, at the Michigan State Convention of the Free Soil party, when that party made arrangements to merge itself into the great party about to be born. I then struggled, as a man for his life, to hold on to all we had left in free soilism, of integrity and righteousness. I need not tell the reader that I failed. Half of the anti-slavery of free soilism was thrown aside, the Maine law was torn out of our platform and thrown aside, and the popular current flowed on, carrying a most heterogeneous and motley multitude, men of all creeds, influenced by all motives.

Non-extension was the feeble attenuated cord that bound them. A stronger cord,—party spirit,—came spontaneously into being soon after organization, and this, every historian knows, is capable of holding a party strongly together without any regard to principle or doctrine. Anti-slavery men in Michigan are generally with this party.

There is no other field for us ; we must act with them, or
cease to act politically.

When we began twenty years ago to labor to bring into
being a righteous party which should act with a single eye
to the glory of God and human welfare, our mass meetings,
conventions and anniversaries were seasons of the Divine
presence, of prayer and hymns of praise.   Many of the
wisest and best men in Michigan graced those meetings
with able speeches, which would not have dishonored the
Earl of Chatham.   We then mingled politics with preaching, praying and singing.   Persecution was violent, friends
forsook us ; some of us, being forbidden to open our mouths
for the dumb, left the churches of our choice for

" Freedom to worship God."

We were threatened with rail-riding, tar and feathers,
and death.   On some the hand of violence fell.   From
experience we have learned the sweetness of Divine approval when toiling in the midst of violent persecution.

I do not ask what we have done, what important consequences have followed our former integrity, how much
present incumbents are indebted to us for the offices they
hold, or what our influence has been on the politics of our
State or our nation.

All these are grave questions, but I leave them to the
historian who shall dip his pen when I am dead.   The
great question is, What are we now to do ?   Already the
party rod is over our heads, and we are threatened with
terrible chastisement if we do not follow the leaders wherever they go.

The Republican State journal, published at Lansing,
shortly after the late election came out flourishing the whip
over the delinquents.   They are to be marked and remembered at all future caucuses and elections, and given up to
political perdition, no more to hope for the emoluments of

·any office. We have rarely seen anything so contemptible. Can the knowledge of human nature be gained in political life, when the renowned editor of this journal is so ignorant of his fellowmen ?

Does he need to be informed that the old grenadiers in the cause of reform have ever been influenced by noble emotions of philanthropy ? Can he think they have borne the persecutions, toils and sacrifices of reformers so long, for the meagre boon of office, and the huzzas of the people ? No, Mr. Journal, you know little of the men of whom you speak ; your whips fall harmlessly on the broad shoulders of men of conscience and integrity. They fear not your threats and ask not your favors. Go back with your baits to the lips of men who were never known as anti-slavery men or temperance men, but who launched their barks on the Republican current, when they judged it strong enough to float them to office.

They will quail at the sight of your whips, and greedily follow your bait of office anywhere, through any filth. Conscience, integrity, truth and righteousness, are cheap commodities with them, and will be given up at your bidding. Put their names on your ticket and you may put any other names on, no matter what the characters may be, and they ·will tamely vote the whole.

Be it known unto these self-constituted leaders, we will not worship the image which you have set up. Give us ·candidates which honest men can vote for, if you expect our votes. If you give us candidates who have nothing to recommend them but sordid selfishness, we will erase their names from your tickets, or we will abandon the polls, as your reckless course has sometimes compelled us to do. Bargaining at caucuses, and nominating for availability, esteeming success more than principle, spending great sums of money in indirect bribery in election campaigns, the little

regard to righteousness, to truth, to integrity, to disinterested
generosity and philanthropy in men nominated for office,
give painful omens that the Republican party is on its way
to the maelstrom of corruption into which the old political
parties have fallen.   Political preaching, to promote the
interests of such a party, is a disgrace to the sacred desk,
and clerical stump-speakers cannot fail to throw off their
ministerial character, and to degrade themselves in the esteem of all men.   There are many noble men in office in
this party whom we delight to honor, and a vast host of
good men, and true, among the voters; but virtue and
righteousness do not lead, and corruption increases.   To
answer the question, What shall we do? we will inquire of
reason, of conscience, and especially of the Infinite wise.

THE PAST, PRESENT, AND FUTURE OF AFRICA.

The world's history begins with Egypt.   In the dim light
of early history, we see three of the sons of Ham, Misraim,
Cush, and Phut, with their families, on the Nile.   Phut
turns away to the west, and peoples Lybia; Cush journeys
south to upper Egypt, and Abyssinia; while Misraim remains in lower Egypt.   The word of inspiration calls Egypt
the land of Ham; and every one should know, that Canaan,
on whom the curse of Noah especially rested, remained in
Asia; while Africa was peopled by his brethren, not by
himself.

Nimrod, a son of Cush, was the mighty builder of Babel,
of Babylon, Enech, Accad, and Calneh, in the land of
Shinah.   His brethren in upper Egypt were equally mighty
builders, as the ruins of their cities show; but while they
were building the most astonishing cities and temples ever
seen, the eye of no historian was upon them.   The names
of builders and kings are lost, and no one can tell when

these mighty works were built, or when forsaken. Herodotus, the father of history, found them in his day, in as desolate a condition as they are now in, and his voice was only
answered by echo, when he asked, "What has become of
this people?" Near that age, Cambyses wasted a great
army, trying to follow the Cushites to Abyssinia. Beyond
this last named country, they are lost to history.

North Africa is brought into notice by the planting of a
colony of Phenicians, under Queen Dido, and the founding
of the city and empire of Carthage, at the most northern
point of the continent. Carthage grew up with Rome, and
these two proud empires were soon engaged in wars, which,
after two hundred years, gave the Romans the mastery of
North Africa.

To them, however, the great desert was the southern
boundary of the world. Nothing was known beyond it. In
the decline of Rome, and the long dark ages which followed, Africa was more and more a mystery. How far it extended, and what beings inhabited it, no one knew. Where
did the Nile come from? What mighty fountain poured its
waters into the valley of Egypt? All was conjecture, often
the wildest conjecture.

In latter ages, the Portuguese sailed to the shores of
Gambia, Guinea, and finally the cape, showing that Africa
was not boundless in the south. The slave trade followed;
but little knowledge of Africa arose from all this coasting
for three, or even four hundred years.

Some to excuse the horrid slave trade tried to believe
that the Negro was the highest species of the ape; while
divines excused this great wickedness, by pouring the curse
of Canaan on the poor Negro, forgetting that Canaan remained in Asia; so that, if a curse pronounced by a man
just waking from drunkenness was spoken by inspiration, it
was fulfilled in Asia, not on the African.

Africa is now known.   The great outlines of its geography are determined by the labors of Livingstone, Barth, and
Speke ; and this strange country, differing from all others in
landscape, climate, people and animals, is no longer an im-
penetrable mystery.   Nearly all the world now condemn
the slave trade. It cannot long continue.   Africa is henceforth to be visited by friends of humanity, who will seek to
civilize and christianize her, developing her vast resources
of soil and climate, navigating her rivers, and connecting
them by railroads and canals   The ancestors of these tribes
took the lead in ancient art and science, and though hidden
and lost for three thousand years, the darkness is removing,
and light is penetrating those wilds along the track of ex-
plorers and missionaries, and the descendants of the Pharaohs will yet stand up in intellectual and moral dignity.

The deserts of Africa are her only waste lands, and these,
lying level, will yet be traversed by railroads from oasis to
oasis, connecting the north and south.   In this great country nearly five thousand miles in length, and the same in
breadth, centering on the equator, winter is scarcely named.
There are no glaciers, no mountains covered with snow,
and no extensive ranges of mountain rocks.   Why should
it not become the garden of the world ?

At Lake Nyanzi, the source of the Nile, on the equator,
one would suppose he was in an extensive low country, although he is six thousand feet above the sea.

What will Africa be at the end of this century ? England
seems determined to explore every district, and open trade
with every tribe, and to plant cotton wherever it will flourish ; while English and American Missionary Societies are
awaking to the importance of that great field of Christian
enterprise.   It only needs Christian civilization to make
Africa the most productive, most beautiful, and most happy
of all lands ; where orange and palm groves, and orchards

of all tropical fruits, pruned by the hand of industry, shall be a second Eden; where grain-fields shall flourish, grass-grounds shall be as Bashan, and vineyards as Eschol; where church and university spires shall reflect the golden light of the sun, and bells, from every hill-top and valley, shall call to study, and to prayer.

1863.

FIFTY YEARS AGO, OR, THE SORROWS OF SOPHIA.

(CONCLUDED.)

Our ministers were sturdy old men, who
> "Proved their doctrines orthodox,
> By evangelic blows and knocks;"

not by fist and heel, but by faithful hard words against any departure from the creed of Calvin. They had never seen a college, nor passed the threshold of an academy; had not meddled with the writings of old heathen philosophers, poets, orators and historians, whom Samuel would have hewed down had he found them; nor had they wasted precious time with grammar, the art of smooth deceptive speech. They knew the sun moved, for Joshua commanded it to stand still; and knew the stars would yet fall to the earth, and therefore they would not be very large. They read the Bible much, especially the Old Testament, and more especially all that related to the extermination of the Canaanites, and the planting of the Lord's chosen people in their land. They saw the same in modern times. The Puritans were the Lord's chosen people, England was Egypt, Cromwell was Moses, Carver was Joshua, America was the promised land, and the Indians were Canaanites doomed to extermination.

Our sturdy old ministers grew infirm with years. Elder

Brown, when I first trembled before him at six years of age, was an old man with long white hair.   He had come out of the Revolutionary War in middle age.   He had long been our minister.   When others failed he filled our school-house pulpit; always at secondly, and again at thirdly, bending in the most comical manner, one cheek in his hand. Oh! has he the toothache? said I.   No, he was only chang-ing his quid of tobacco for a new one, when he revived and spoke with more power.

A young man, fresh from the school of Hamilton, came when our school was vacant, and was employed.   He was a model man in stature, symmetry, feature and countenance; noble, dignified and beautiful.   The prejudice of our good people began to give away before the fascinations of our young orator; and I think they were a little proud to see such multitudes come to "our meetings."   They had been prejudiced against ministers manufactured by men at Ham-ilton.   They wanted them fresh from the plow, by divine call.   They could not fail of feeling disgust at his fastidious pronunciation.   "Natshure," for nator; but they bore it, inasmuch as a deep interest was rising, and "our denomi-nation was taking the lead."

There were some things in our young minister which seemed much more censurable than his new-fashioned pro-nunciation.   I thought the attention he paid to Sophia en-tirely inconsistent with the dignity of a minister, I could not reconcile courtship with my ideas of the sacred office of a minister, especially courtship with a child of sixteen, with one, although highly intellectual, yet gay, mirthful, as full of innocent glee as myself.   It seemed to me quite summary. The day came when there stood at the altar a pair, so beau-tiful, so dignified, of so intellectual expression, that nearly all were charmed into reconciliation.   Hymen must have smiled with pleasure that day.   How odd to see old Elder

Brown—his thin white locks straying over his broad shoulders, his gray eyes peering from beneath long lashes, his head, on the short neck, dropping with quick jerks forward, then on one shoulder, his busy tongue rolling his huge quid from one cheek to the other. There he stood, on his stogas far apart, bracing for the great task before him ; and with many a-hems he joined them in wedlock in less than one hour. I cannot be expected to tell, at this distant day, how many times during that orthodox marriage his weary hands went to rest in the pockets of his butternut coat, or gray trousers. As the nicely-sweetened sling went around, and many an old-fashioned joke, Sophia's father, an aged deacon, who had fought Baume at Bennington, sat by the aged elder, who had come from the fields of many battles. They were venerable men of olden times, remembering the French War of seventeen hundred and fifty-five, very grave men. I revered old age almost to adoration, and the solemn countenances of the deacon and elder are indelible on my memory. I did not so much revere the young minister. I was never fully reconciled to his marriage ; yet I said, with others, "Sophia has married well." I could have hoped her husband would equal Whitefield. Alas! he had brought with him some strong, though concealed, habits of early life. He had been a sportsman, understood the rifle, and also the social glass. He was often at the distillery, visiting the clerk of the church, drinking with him. All of the church members drank with him at weddings and all parties. He met the social glass on his pastoral visits. Our religious distiller paid his minister's salary, in part, with whisky. Saturday became a day of sport. Our minister went with the boys, with his bottle in his pocket. This custom was long continued, when finally a note was sent in on Sabbath morning, informing us that the minister was sick, when the religious service was conducted by the distiller. This notice came too often, when investigation showed that our young minister came home drunk from hunting on Saturday nights.

Oh, what a day! when Sophia wrapped her boy in his cloak, mournfully climbed into a wagon, and moved with a drunken husband down to Rochester. These were rough winds on this tender plant, the cherished pet of her aged parents; one who had never known want or grief. It was terrible the first storm should be so overwhelming, so long continued, for wave after wave came over this frail bark, until it was all broken and crushed. The career of the wretched husband was rapidly downward. Sophia's fine poetic mind became the riot of devouring sensibility. Slowly the night hours passed—the fire was out—the light extinguished—the winds of winter roared—and the waters of the swollen river ever plunging from the rocks. Closer she pressed her infant to her aching bosom, thought of the past, her innocent, happy childhood and foreboded the future. The clock had struck twelve, when, mingling with the sound of waters and winds, the maniac yell of her drunken husband as he burst in so frightened her that she lay speechless, while he stood cursing her with awful oaths. Deeming her life in danger, she went home to the arms of her parents, to waste with grief and die. I last saw her when on her pale cheeks sat the smile of trust in God. Forty years ago she was buried a half mile south of the home of her childhood.

THE END

www.ingramcontent.com/pod-product-compliance
Lightning Source LLC
Chambersburg PA
CBHW032013110726
47901CB00004B/1069